NEZAMI
AND THE
NONPROLIFERATION

also by
POONEH SADEGHI

RUMI & THE RETRIBUTION

A GABRIEL MCKNIGHT THRILLER

NEZAMI
AND THE
NONPROLIFERATION

RUN WHILE YOU STILL CAN

POONEH SADEGHI

ROGUE
RIVER

An imprint of Roan & Weatherford Publishing Associates, LLC
Bentonville, Arkansas
www.roanweatherford.com

Library of Congress Cataloging-in-Publication Data
Names: Sadeghi, Pooneh, author.
Title: Nezami and the Nonproliferation | Gabriel McKnight Series #2
Description: First Edition | Bentonville: Rogue River, 2025.
Identifiers: LCCN: 2025937553 | ISBN: 979-8-89299-038-7 (hardcover) |
ISBN: 979-8-89299-039-4 (trade paperback) |
ISBN: 979-8-89299-040-0 (eBook)
Subjects: BISAC: FIC055000 FICTION/Thrillers/Suspense |
FIC028110 FICTION/Thrillers/Historical |
FIC028010 FICTION/Thrillers/Espionage
LC record available at: https://lccn.loc.gov/2025937553

Rogue River trade paperback edition January, 2026

Cover Design by Casey W. Cowan
Interior Design by John Bredesen
Editing by Staci Troilo

To Mom, whose captivating bedtime stories shaped my childhood. Thank you for your unwavering belief in me! I love you.

AUTHOR'S NOTE

Khosrow and Shirin is a tragic love story written by Nezami Ganjavi, one of Persia's greatest romantic poets. It is the story of the Persian Sasanian Prince, Khosrow II, and an Armenian princess by the name of Shirin.

Nezami's poetry includes the romantic elements of human relations as well as adventure. Spirituality and spiritual consciousness are embedded in Nezami's poems, yet unlike Rumi, they aren't the central theme of his work.

Often referred to as "Hakim" or "the Sage," Nezami was a learned poet and master of multiple subjects, which include Arab and Persian literature.

Poignant, melodic, and captivating, *Khosrow and Shirin* inspired the events in this novel.

I'd also like to clarify that while Neuschwanstein Castle in Bavaria features a grotto and is rumored to have hidden passages, the tunnel and secret rooms in this story are purely a creation of my imagination, designed solely to enrich the story.

CHAPTER ONE

Long ago, in the land of Persia, a powerful king yearned for a son. His wish was granted when his wife gave birth to a boy. The king named the prince Khosrow after his grandfather. The prince grew into a powerful and handsome warrior who excelled in all the learned disciplines.

One night, young Prince Khosrow and his companions went hunting. At sunset, they arrived at the home of a farmer who served them food and wine. Amidst loud revelry, and unbeknown to Khosrow, his servant wandered into the farmer's vineyard. The servant frightened Khosrow's steed, who trampled all the grapes and ruined the farmer's vineyard. The next day, word of the prince's wild evening reached the king. Furious at his son's reckless behavior, the king imposed harsh punishment for Khosrow and his companions. Regretting his actions, Khosrow humbly begged his father for forgiveness. Moved by Khosrow's genuine remorse, the king forgave him.

That night, Khosrow dreamed of his grandfather, who foretold the following. "You will receive four blessings because of your willing repentance. First, you will ride Shabdiz, the world's fastest steed. Second, you will sit on Taqdis, the throne of thrones. Third, the world's greatest musician will play for you. Finally, you will have Shirin, your destined love, to fill your life with light."

The next day, Khosrow woke, determined to meet his destiny.

—Nezami, Khosrow and Shirin

TEHRAN, MARBLE PALACE, 1965

SOMETHING BAD HAS happened! That's what five-year-old Mina von Mayer thought perched on the edge of the velvet couch, sucking her thumb. Mama was late. Why was she late? Mina lowered her hand. She was a big girl now, one with a secret.

Sunlight poured through the large windows, throwing golden beams across the rooms. Everything in Tehran was bright, from the shiny stone statues to the bright flowers, and large mountains smiling up at big blue skies.

Mina choked back a sob. None of it could settle the butterflies in her stomach.

The trip to Iran had been fun. She went to the bazaar with her parents and jumped on colorful rugs. She liked the pretty parks, saffron ice cream, and jasmine flowers. She'd even seen the ruins of an ancient city. It had been great until that horrible moment before the ball—until Papa's words scared her. It wasn't what he'd said but how he'd said it.

On the night of the Shah's—or king's—ball, Mama and Papa said they would check on her at bedtime. Mina couldn't attend the event because she was a child. To cheer her up, Papa promised a private dance with her in her room. Mina waited and waited, but he didn't come. Tired of being alone, she sneaked down the hall to their rooms. Giggling, she ran across the sitting room to surprise them.

Mama looked beautiful in her gown, and Papa looked grand in his military uniform. He was a general back home in Germany. Mina didn't know what generals did but knew it was important work.

"The map proves everything," Papa said.

Mina blinked. Cheerful Papa who laughed and teased her sounded... worried.

Mama wrung her hands. "The map is dangerous, Karl. Let me talk to Cousin Farah. She'll help us."

"I have a plan, Kiana," Papa said. "I'll return to Berlin and talk to the authorities. You and Mina stay here while I settle everything."

"No!" Mama cried. "The courts will blame you. Having the map makes you look guilty." Tears streamed down Mama's cheeks. "I hate that map! It will break us."

Oh! Mina's stomach dropped. She inched closer and gripped the doorknob.

"There's no reason to worry, love." Papa put his arms around Mama.

"Richter's dangerous."

Papa stroked Mama's back. "The council knows me. It will be over soon."

"What do I tell Mina?" Mama asked.

"Tell her I had to leave for business, and you'll both join me in a few days." Papa kissed her. "The ball is in our honor. The queen will look for you if we don't hurry."

"You promised Mina a dance."

"We'll make an appearance at the ball, then check on Mina."

"Give me a moment to freshen up." Mama hurried into the bathroom.

After Mama's cousin Farah married the Iranian king, she became the queen. Iranians called their king the "Shah." Mina had no idea why. Cousin Farah had invited them for a visit, and here they were in the big marble palace.

Papa retrieved his briefcase from the closet, then pulled out a sheet of paper. His brows made a deep *V*, and his mouth flattened into a thin line.

Mama returned, patting her hair. "I'm ready."

Papa put the page in his briefcase, locked it, then buried the key at the bottom of a drawer. "You look stunning."

"Thank you." She smiled and clasped her hands. "Will the map be safe in there?"

"Yes." He escorted Mama to the door. "As long as no one knows where it is, we are safe."

Mina scurried to hide behind a cabinet. She sank to the floor and hugged her knees. Her parents were sad because of the map. *How can I help them?*

Papa said they were safe if no one knew where the map was. Her mouth curved into a smile. "I'll hide it and fix everything."

Once they were gone, she rooted through the drawer where Papa hid his key, then padded to the closet. Just before unlocking the briefcase, she paused. It was wrong to touch her parents' things.

"No! I won't let them be sad."

Mina took out the map. Why was such a pretty drawing bad?

She shrugged. It didn't matter. Clutching the paper, she fled to the corridor.

The entire second floor was a long hallway covered in red carpet. White marble columns surrounded large doors. Mina ducked behind a pillar when two guards passed by. She waited for them to leave, then opened the first door. No one was inside.

She wrinkled her nose. The smell of stinky cigarettes, like the ones Papa smoked, lingered in the room. A wooden desk with gold designs sat in one corner, and across the room stood a fireplace and bookshelves. It reminded her of Papa's study, only bigger. "This is a good hiding room."

Pictures of the Shah and Cousin Farah decorated shelves. She noticed a tray on the Shah's desk. On it lay two small gold cases. The first one was full of cigarettes. She reached for the second. Oh! It was heavy. She held it with both hands. A beautiful bird with brightly colored stones decorated the lid. This one was empty.

"This is the best hiding place. The Shah will use the full one." She folded the paper, then placed it in the second case.

Satisfied she'd accomplished her goal, Mina scampered back to her room, then snuggled under the covers. *Everything will be okay.*

The next morning, Mama's soothing voice woke her. "Happy birthday, my angel."

Mina rubbed the sleep from her eyes and sat up. Sunlight flooded the room, and the mountains outside looked like giant chunks of chocolate. A bird hopped onto the windowpane. She smiled. "I'm a big girl now."

Mama smiled. "Yes, you are."

"Where's Papa?"

Mama's smile faltered. "He went back to Germany for business. We'll join him in a few days. I planned a special breakfast for you. Cousin Farah and the children will be there."

Mina wanted to tell Mama everything would be okay because she hid the map, but she didn't want to get in trouble for interfering. Instead, she scrambled out of bed. "Do I have any presents?"

Mama hugged her. "Wash your face, and we'll go see."

Several days passed. No news came from Papa. Mama's smile dimmed each day, and she jumped whenever someone called her.

As Mama grew sadder, Mina grew more worried.

"Don't you want to go outside and play?" Nanny asked one morning.

"I want to stay with Mama." Mina grabbed her teddy, then ran down the hall.

Mama was in her chambers reading a book on a couch. Her eyes were shadowed, her skin pale.

Mina climbed up beside her. "Why hasn't Papa called us?"

Mama set the book aside and pulled her closer. "He's very busy."

"He always calls us when he's away."

"He'll call soon." Mama stroked her hair. "Do you want to go for a walk?"

"I want to stay here and wait for Papa."

A knock sounded on the door. A guard entered their rooms.

Mama's cheeks turned even whiter.

"The Shah and queen would like to see you, ma'am."

"Very well." She started to follow the guard.

Mina rose.

"You must stay here." The guard blocked the exit.

Mina's chin jutted out. "I want to go with Mama."

The guard shook his head.

"Stay here, love. I'll be back soon." Mama kissed her. "Nanny will come to sit with you."

Mina's stomach did a little jump, like when she was on a plane.

She knew how to count to twenty and did that while waiting for Mama with Nanny. She'd just finished counting to twenty for the fourth time when the door burst open. A guard carried Mama inside.

Cousin Farah rushed in behind him. "The doctor is on his way."

"W-what's wrong with Mama?"

Cousin Farah's eyes filled with tears. "She's had a shock." She hurried to the bathroom. A moment later, she returned with a wet towel, then dabbed it on Mama's forehead.

Mama's eyes fluttered open. She sat up and wept. Cousin Farah held her while she cried.

Mina sidled up to Mama's side. "Are you sick?"

"My poor darling!" She pulled Mina into her arms. "Your father--he's gone!"

Mina swallowed the lump in her throat. "Yes, Papa went on a trip. We're going to join him."

Mama sobbed. "Gone forever!"

"No. H-he's home. In Germany."

"Your father had an accident," Mama wailed "He's with God now."

"No!" *I hid the map. I hid the map!* Sobbing, Mina ran to her room and flung herself on the bed.

TIME PASSED. PEOPLE came to visit them. Mina didn't care. Her heart and stomach were cold. Nanny brought her soup and sweet cakes. She didn't want them. Cousin Farah and the Shah visited. And Papa stayed with God while Mama was ill.

Mina spent her waking hours sitting on her bed with Teddy. At night, she cried herself to sleep. As each day passed, the cold inside her belly spread.

She missed Papa and his laughter, missed his whiskers tickling her cheeks with every cuddle, and missed snuggling in his strong arms.

One night, Mina woke to find Mama sitting at her bedside, stroking her hair. She scrambled to hug her. "Are you better, Mama?"

Mama held her close. "I've been so distraught over your father's death, I haven't cared for you. I'm sorry, sweetheart."

"I miss Papa."

"Oh, baby. I miss him too." Mama kissed her cheek. "I want to tell you something important about your Papa."

"Did Papa go to heaven because of the map?"

Mama stiffened. "How do you know about that?"

"I heard you and Papa talk about it. I hid the map to keep Papa safe." Tears filled her eyes. "Did someone find it? Is that why he went to heaven? W-was it my fault?"

"Oh, darling, no. It wasn't your fault at all." Mama rocked her. "Where did you hide the map, love?"

"In one of the Shah's rooms."

"It's for the best." Mama sighed. "A bad man did terrible things, then tried to hide his actions. When Papa found out, that man hurt him and made it look like an accident." Mama paused. "You're going to hear things...."

"What things?"

"Terrible lies about your papa. He was honest and brave, but the wicked man made it look like Papa did bad things. It's all lies." Tears filled Mama's eyes. "We won't go back to Germany."

Mina's head bumped Mama's chin. "But our home is in Germany."

"I'll buy a house in Tehran." Mama held her close. "You'll start school here."

The cold in Mina's stomach turned into ice. Tears streamed down her cheeks. "Why must we leave Germany when it's the bad man's fault?"

"Because it's our destiny to be here for now."

"W-what's destiny?"

"It's magic that makes things happen in your life." She sighed. "Richter is dangerous, and he's grooming his son, Farid, to follow in his footsteps. We're going to stay away from them. We'll be safe in Tehran. Meanwhile, you will grow into an intelligent lady."

"What's an intelligent?" Mina hiccupped.

Mama looked into her eyes. "Intelligent means smart. I foretell you'll become an intelligent and powerful lady. One day, you'll find true love like I found with your Papa. You'll have a beautiful family and will make the Richters sorry."

She searched Mama's face. "How do you know this?"

"Moms have magic powers." She lay down beside Mina. "Go to sleep, love. Tomorrow, we'll go house hunting."

That night, Mina dreamed she went to school and became an intelligent. She dreamed of Papa. And she dreamed of making the very bad Richters sorry.

CHAPTER TWO

Like the moon you're detached from your stars,
You're not the sun, why live solitary and far?
—Nezami, *Khosrow and Shirin*

THE FRENCH RIVIERA, 2018

ZITA SAT AT a table outside of a quaint café facing the azure coastline. A liquid gold sun blended into clear skies, and the ocean stretched out like an endless turquoise blanket. Jewel-toned parasols littered the coastline, where thousands of onlookers were eager to capture the grand opening of the annual regatta—Les Voiles de St. Tropez.

Hundreds of sailing yachts gathered annually for this unique combination of competitive racing and lively social events. For most, it was the highlight of the season. For Zita, it was the perfect opportunity to escape.

She scanned the crowd. Three men her guardian, Farid Richter, had assigned to her surrounded the café. Two stood at the front, wearing colorful T-shirts and bright ball caps, a poor attempt at blending in. The third—whom Zita privately referred to as Snakey because of the impressive blue-and-green cobra tattoo circling his forearm—stood to her far right.

Richter insisted the guards were necessary protection for her, claiming he had her best interest at heart. He'd recently increased her restrictions, then lectured her on safety and his plans for her future. Sick to her stomach, Zita had thanked him with a smile. She'd learned deception from the best. Richter was evil and a liar.

Feigning ignorance had been her salvation. But even her carefully crafted facade couldn't last forever. The time had come to put her plan in motion.

Sweat trickled down her back. If Richter knew what she was up to.... No, she'd been careful. Zita patted her tote bag. *Freedom.* The mere thought of it brought a lump to her throat. She took a compact mirror from her bag and pretended to check her reflection.

Snakey moved farther to the right, where he had a full view of the corner where she sat. He occasionally glanced toward the coastline.

Zita tilted the mirror. The café's back entrance was clear. *A few more feet to freedom.*

"Excuse-moi," a young woman huffed, cutting through the aisle, high-heeled sandals clicking on the floor.

Did her feet hurt? Zita's did.

The willowy twenty-something scooted by, chatting on her phone, her bright summer dress fluttering in the breeze. She took her seat at the next table, tossing perfectly styled tresses over one shoulder.

Zita wondered if the woman's hair color, so similar to her own, also came from a bottle. The name of her shade was Baby Blonde. She almost sympathized with Baby Blonde. *Almost* being the key word. Everything Zita did and wore was carefully designed armor adopted for survival.

The announcer called out to the boats. Onlookers faced the shoreline like a monster with a thousand heads. Baby Blonde disconnected her call. A server wound through the crowd carrying Zita's latte and a carafe of fruit juice on a wooden tray.

The countdown started. *"Three... two...."*

The server stopped and turned toward the shore. Baby Blonde cursed and leaned to the side, focused on the coastline.

Boats with various flags and forms stood in lines along the St. Tropez shoreline. Energy vibrated in the air as everyone held their breaths. The foghorns blasted, announcing the start of the race. The crowd came to life, cheering on the racers.

Baby Blonde reached for a pair of binoculars. The server placed the latte in front of Zita. Snakey shifted, focusing his attention on them.

One yacht gained momentum and pulled forward. The crowd roared. The server's gaze slid toward the coastline.

Heart hammering, Zita drew in a shaky breath and began her own countdown.

Three....

The server turned. Zita extended her foot out from under the table.

Two....

The server tripped. His tray flew into the air, toppling the carafe and its contents onto Baby Blonde's lap.

One....

Baby Blonde shrieked and jumped out of her chair, cursing in multiple languages. The server apologized and offered a towel, while other wait staff rushed to help. The chaos blocked Zita from Snakey's view.

Go!

She dashed to the café's restroom, then changed into a pair of dark shorts, a white T-shirt, and running shoes. She shoved her old clothes into her bag, covered her hair with a dark wig, then shimmied through a small window to the alley. Zita sprinted to the train station, clutching her tote.

Two hours later, she studied her reflection in the train's bathroom mirror. The young woman staring back didn't look like Richter's ward. Her mouth turned up. "Hello."

CHAPTER THREE

Shahpour spoke of Mihan-Banou, the powerful queen of Armenia.
—Nezami, *Khosro and Shirin*

PARIS, FRANCE

JURGEN MULLIGAN WAS mulling over accounts in the back office of his antique store when someone pounded on the door. "Damned tourists!" He shuffled toward the door to scold the persistent shopper and froze when he saw the young woman standing outside. The woman—or girl, for she was young—looked familiar. He scrubbed a shaky hand over his face. Who was she?

When she glanced at the locked door, Jurgen shook himself out of his stupor and let her in.

She glided past him, slim and beautiful in a pair of jeans that accentuated her long legs. She'd topped the denim with a white shirt and ivory raincoat. Dark hair fell in waves below a firm chin, emphasizing high cheekbones, creamy skin, and a heart-shaped face. Fringed with thick lashes, her eyes, so mournful, gleamed like rich whiskey.

It hit him then. *Dear God!* Jurgen cleared his throat. "You resemble your grandmother."

The girl appraised him with eyes too old for someone her age. "I need paperwork."

He tugged at his collar. "You don't understand. Richter—"

She raised a hand to silence him. "Whom do you fear most, Farid Richter or Mina von Mayer?"

Jurgen wiped the sweat off his forehead. "I had no idea Richter would kill the girl."

Her voice held no emotion. "You must decide fast."

He rubbed clammy palms against his jeans. "Come upstairs." In his office, he pointed to the corner and grabbed his camera. "Please stand in front of the white screen."

She moved with unnerving self-assurance.

"What name would you like on your documents?"

Her eyes glinted under the lights. "My true name."

Jurgen set to work, biting back a smile as she watched him with furrowed brows. His work was art. Finally, he set the last document aside. "The ink will dry in a few minutes. Would you like something to drink while you wait?"

"No, thank you." The girl retrieved a stack of bills from her travel bag. "How much do I owe you?"

"You owe me nothing." He wanted to tell her how sorry he was, but no words could change the past.

"Nothing is free." She placed a wad of cash on his desk. A piece of paper fell from her satchel.

He picked up the flyer, an advertisement for the Frankfurt Book Fair, where author Gabriel McKnight was a keynote speaker. She'd underlined his name. Jurgen cocked his head. "Aren't you going to your grandmother?"

Silence.

"Go to your grandmother. She'll protect you. You must—"

"I can take care of myself."

Jurgen massaged his neck. "Why are you searching for Gabriel McKnight?"

. She picked up her documents, then headed to the exit. "It's in

your best interest to disappear for a while. You have a day at most."
The door clicked shut behind her.

Jurgen raked a hand through his hair. Did Mina von Mayer know about the girl? *Why is she going to Frankfurt? What does Gabriel McKnight have to do with this?* Something niggled at the back of his mind. He searched the web and found the article he was looking for.

"Jesus!" He realized what the girl was up to.

Gabriel McKnight, on the other hand, was clueless.

Drawing a shaky hand over his face, he poured himself a drink. The girl was wrong about one thing. He didn't have time. He was already dead. Richter's henchman would arrive any minute. What to do?

Over the years, he'd kept meticulous files on his clients. Shifting through them, he found what he needed, copied the document onto a flash drive, then put it in an envelope, which he dropped in the mailbox.

This was going to upheave Gabriel McKnight's life. *So be it.*

As he reached for a bottle, the door chime sounded. Ready to meet his fate, Jurgen poured two fingers of whiskey.

Clunk, clunk. Footsteps announced his visitor. Funny, he hadn't noticed the old staircase moaned and creaked.

The flyer! Jurgen grabbed a pair of scissors, cut out Gabriel McKnight's name, then stuffed the scrap in his sock. "I'm making things right."

He downed the capsule he'd kept for emergencies with the whiskey. Seconds later, his muscles twitched and spasmed. Jurgen Mulligan took his last breath as the door to his office swung open.

CHAPTER FOUR

Nezami pray spin your tale,
for the songbird's song is a bitter wail.

—Nezami, *Khosrow and Shirin*

WASHINGTON D.C., USA

BRANDON ROHR PULLED Anna closer to the edge of the bed then thrust harder. Her breasts jiggled, her inner muscles spasmed, and her mouth formed a perfect *O*. She was close to release. He adjusted his hips and pushed deeper. "Now, baby!"

"Argh!" She keened and flew over the edge.

Thank fuck. He allowed himself to dive off that cliff and join her. His release began at the back of his knees, traveled up his thighs, then shot through his groin. The room blurred, and a kaleidoscopic of stars exploded behind his eyelids. A strangled cry escaped his throat while his body twitched and spasmed. He rode wave after wave of pleasure until his legs went numb. Panting, he toppled onto the bed beside her.

Sex with Anna Bloom was like being thrown into a volcano then catapulted into bliss. He closed his eyes and waited for his pounding heart to settle. He cherished these moments, where his mind and body lingered in limbo, free from the duplicity of government officials, stressful deadlines, and his overactive brain.

She stirred and opened one eye. "Are we alive?"

Grinning, he pulled her closer, enjoying the feel of her soft breasts against his skin "If we aren't, it was the perfect way to go."

Anna sighed. "What an end to a boring day. I had to search for musty old manuscripts all week."

He dipped his head to study her. "Why did you apply for the job if you don't enjoy working in the history department?"

She lifted a slim shoulder. "You like history, and you write about it."

Brandon caressed her back. "Sweetheart, I'm an investigative reporter. History is a hobby."

"You're interested in classic Persian poetry, and I wanted to learn about it. Great sex shouldn't be the sole basis of our relationship."

"Great sex"—Brandon kissed the hollow in her neck—"is a key factor in a relationship."

She grabbed a cigarette from the nightstand.

He caught the flash of hurt in her eyes and tipped up her chin. "We agreed to keep this light. You said you were okay with that."

Like him, Anna had grown up in a dysfunctional family. He'd been candid with her from the start. She'd claimed she wasn't looking for long-term either. It's why their relationship had lasted this long.

Anna blew the smoke out the open window. "I want there to be more than sex between us."

For as long as he lived, he wouldn't understand women. Still, he didn't want to hurt her. "You're beautiful inside and out. You're generous to a fault." He kissed her nose. "You have a beautiful laugh, great taste in movies, and you like football. That gives us more in common than sex."

Her eyes brightened. "Is that so?"

Relieved the mood had lightened, Brandon trailed his tongue down her ribcage.

Giggling, she pushed him away. "We're talking."

He grinned. "You have my undivided attention."

"Professor Bower told me to search for an old Persian trage-dy. The poet was the one you mentioned the other night. What was his name?"

Brandon stiffened. "You searched for Nezami's poems?"

"I spent the whole day in the archives."

It took effort to keep his expression neutral. "Did you find it?"

"Yes." She held up a hand before Brandon could comment. "I borrowed it so I could show you. I'll take it back tomorrow." She hopped out of the bed, then retrieved a small leather-bound journal from her purse. "Here you go."

Butterflies fluttered in his stomach. Could it be that easy? He held out his hand. The journal fit in his palm. "Incredible." He flicked through its pages. "I don't want to damage the paper. I have cotton gloves at home. Can I borrow it for a few days? I promise you'll get it back in prime condition."

Anna climbed back into bed, then dragged on the cigarette. "What's so important about this journal?"

"It's history." He marveled at the journal's excellent condition.

"You find the travels of a German engineer exciting?"

He leaned over and kissed her. "No. I find you exciting. The journal feeds my curiosity. Can I hold on to it for a couple of days?"

"Fine." She stretched. "We're out of ice. Do you mind getting some?"

"Sure." He pulled on his jeans, then tucked the journal under his sweater. There was no point in taking chances with it.

"What are you doing?" Anna demanded.

"The ice machine is on the ground floor. People don't want to see a naked man roaming the building."

Her lips curved. "It depends on the man."

Brandon swatted her backside. "Lock the door behind me." He waited for the click of the deadbolt before taking the stairs to the ground floor. Call him paranoid, but since publishing the article on Farid Richter and his business with Andersen Pharmaceuticals, he worried someone was watching him.

The ice machine was behind the lobby. He was filling the bucket when his cell phone vibrated. "Hello."

"It's me. I have the information you need."

Brandon leaned against the ice machine. "I'm all ears."

"Gabriel McKnight found the old artifacts."

"McKnight? The writer?"

"Yep. There's more to it."

Brandon listened to his source with interest. "Thanks, I owe you one." He disconnected the call and raked a hand through his hair. This was unexpected.

The corridor behind the lobby had floor-to-ceiling mirrors on both sides, offering a full view of the elevator and the western side of the lobby. Brandon stopped short and stared.

Erik Drussel, Richter's second in command, exited the elevator with two men. Erik checked his phone and nodded at the men. The trio left through the western exit.

Brandon ducked behind a stone pillar. What was Farid Richter's henchman doing in Washington? Was Richter after the journal? The reporter in him itched to follow Erik and find out.

Then, he remembered where he was.

Anna! God, please let her be safe. He circled the lobby to the emergency staircase, took the stairs two at a time, then burst onto the fourth-floor landing. Heart racing, he stopped outside her apartment.

The door was slightly ajar.

His chest tightened, making it hard to breathe. With a ragged inhale, he nudged it open. Sweat drenched his skin, and despair mounted with every step. The crunch of broken glass under his shoes stretched his raw nerves.

Anna's apartment was in shambles. The couch was turned over, magazines littered every surface, and the TV lay on the floor. Outside the bedroom, he paused, pulse pounding. The grandfather clock she loved announced the passing of each second with a loud *tick*. He eased into her room.

The mewling sound that came from his throat was more a whimper than a cry. Anna lay in the center of the bed, naked, legs spread open. One arm lay close to her body, the hand tightly clenched, while the other lay aside, palm up. Her eyes were open and unfocused, and bruises covered her neck and chest. Her mouth formed an O, a grotesque mockery of her earlier pleasure.

The half-empty bucket fell to the floor, scattering ice chips everywhere. Brandon's vision grew hazy. He inched closer to her to check for a pulse.

Anna was gone.

Shoving his fist into his mouth, Brandon backed out of the room, then dashed down the emergency staircase. In the alley, he vomited. Dizzy and sick, he pulled out his phone, then dialed 911.

He arrived home when the first rays of sunlight pierced the sky. After checking the locks, he peeled off his clothes, then climbed into the shower. The scent of Anna's perfume lingered on his skin. Her laughter rang in his ears. Tremors traveled up his spine, and the tears he'd held back spilled over. He slid down to the tile and sobbed. He sobbed until the water turned cold and his skin wrinkled.

Poor, innocent Anna. Richter's henchman had killed her. *Why?*

Brandon gritted his teeth and turned off the shower. "I'll find justice for you." An hour later, he booked a flight for Germany. "I look forward to meeting you, Gabriel McKnight."

CHAPTER FIVE

At dawn, Shirin rose for the hunt.

—Nezami, *Khosrow and Shirin*

SINGAPORE WATERFRONT, SINGAPORE

F AN BAU STARED up at the modern glass high-rise overlooking the ocean.

Her brother, Alex, straightened his tie. "What if Kousha's information is false?"

"We'll find another solution, young one."

"You're only six minutes older than I am," Alex grumbled.

"Six minutes is all I need for older sibling privileges." She linked her arm through his as they entered the building. Like many of Singapore's buildings, the modern décor transformed the lobby into an artistic display. She checked her reflection in a mirror, assessed Alex, then nodded her approval. "We should thank our parents for our good genes."

Alex raised an amused brow. "Should we? Have you forgotten daddy dear hasn't claimed us?"

Fan refrained from sighing. "He loves us, and you know it." The elevator pinged their arrival. "Bastards or not, we look good."

A stocky man with inky hair and a thick mustache greeted them at the penthouse. "Security check, please."

She bit back a smile as the man ran a metal tube over them. Security was overrated.

Mustache Man led them to a pair of ivory double doors and knocked.

"Come in," a squeaky voice called out.

They entered a rectangular space with grey marble floors and walls. Stone sculptures lined one side. In the center, two white couches flanked a red coffee table, and a large crystal chandelier hung above them. A massive burgundy desk sat in the far corner.

The man seated there rose to greet them. Pale and pudgy, with a shock of silver hair and a matching goatee, Ash Kousha held out his arms. "Welcome to my humble abode."

Humble indeed. His taste ran toward vulgar.

Fan shook his hand. "Thank you for meeting with us."

"The pleasure is all mine." Kousha motioned to the couch. "Please."

Fan chose the larger sofa. Alex declined and stood to her right. Mustache Man hovered by him. Three other men entered the room and took positions behind their boss—a pathetic intimidation attempt. The gleam in her twin's eyes betrayed his amusement.

"Can I offer you a drink?" Ash asked.

"Scotch, neat," Fan said.

Alex declined.

Kousha poured two drinks, then sat beside Fan. "Do you have the jewels, my dear?"

She took the necklace from her purse.

Snuffling like a greedy pig, Kousha pulled a small magnifying from his coat pocket. After appraising the gems, his head tilted up. "They are spectacular."

"It's your turn, Mister Kousha."

"Ah, yes. The information." He chuckled. "What you seek is in three priceless miniature paintings depicting *Khosro and Shirin*, a famous tragedy by the Persian poet, Nezami. Prior to the Islamic Revolution in Iran, Tehran's Central Bank housed a secret vault. A handful of people knew the king hid the miniatures there." Ash sipped his drink. "Hidden in the first painting is the longitude of the location, written in code. The second has the latitude. What's on the third is a mystery."

"Wouldn't it have the key to the codes?" Fan asked.

"That would be too easy." Ash smirked. "A cunning Iranian general hid the miniatures in secret locations during the chaos of the revolution. He died during the revolution, and the artwork disappeared. In recent months, information on the whereabouts of the miniatures surfaced." His mustache twitched. "Gabriel McKnight has the key to the map and location codes."

Fan's fingers tightened around her glass. "The writer? How is he connected to this?"

Kousha leaned close enough for her to smell the alcohol on his breath. "McKnight is romantically involved with the general's only daughter, Noor Rahman."

"Interesting." And unexpected. "I'd like to see the first miniature."

Ash trailed his finger along her thigh. "I want to renegotiate our agreement."

Fan's eyes hardened. "I don't renegotiate."

A corner of Ash's mouth rose. "Isn't that a shame?" He nodded to the men in the room, two of whom moved closer to Alex, while the other two positioned themselves behind the couch she was sitting on.

Fan placed her drink on the glass coffee table and rose. "It is a shame. Isn't it, Alex?"

Alex bared his teeth.

She leaped onto the sofa, cartwheeled off the back, then landed between two guards. With a vicious kick, she slit one's neck. *Thank goodness for stilettos.* She punched the second man's neck, compressing his carotid artery. He passed out.

Fan turned from her fight to find Alex had broken the other guards' necks and had restrained Kousha in a chokehold. The man's face turned an ugly shade of red as he struggled to breathe.

"I see parallels between killing and composing poetry. There are poets who go on and on with wordy narratives, then you have wordsmiths who wield the pen the way a sniper uses his weapon—efficient and effective. When it comes to killing, I'm in the second category." She waved a hand in his direction. "I can, however, make an exception and draw this out. What will it be, Mister Kousha? Will you hand the miniature over and continue to live your greedy life? Or will these moments be your last?"

Ash squeaked and flailed. "I-I'll g-give you the miniature."

She smiled. "Excellent choice."

Alex loosened his grip.

Ash stumbled to his laptop. After typing a code, the western wall slid aside, revealing a safe. He retrieved a folder with shaky hands.

Fan snatched it from him. "My brother will knock you out. When you regain consciousness, we will be gone. If you ever try to contact me or come after us, I will destroy you. Do you understand?"

Ash gulped and nodded. Alex pinched a spot between the man's neck and shoulder. He slumped to the floor.

In the elevator, Fan said, "Contact our connection in white-collar crimes. Drop a hint about a jewel heist and bring up Kousha's name."

Her twin grinned. "You carry a grudge, old one."

She checked her lipstick in the elevator mirror. "We must find Gabriel McKnight."

He did a quick Google search on his cell phone. "He's speaking at the Frankfurt Book Fair in two days."

"I believe a visit to Germany is in order."

CHAPTER SIX

Khosrow looked forward to his destiny....
—Nezami, *Khosrow and Shirin*

SIERRA-BLANCA, MARBELLA, SPAIN

SATISFACTION THRUMMED THROUGH Rafael Molina's entire being. His latest hotel was a grand success and would make tomorrow's headlines. From the balcony, he enjoyed the view. The Mediterranean Sea stretched like an azure blanket. Below him, elegant couples danced, while other guests mingled by his signature glass bar, Ice Heaven.

Not bad for an orphan boy.

One of the richest men in Spain, Rafael still recalled the never-ending spasms of hunger and the uncertainty that came with living in the streets. He crossed the suite with panther-like grace. *It's show time.*

Latin music greeted him once he arrived at the outer bar. He plucked a glass of sparkling water from a server's tray and worked the crowd, stopping by tables to flatter celebrities and strengthen business alliances.

A blonde with generous cleavage stepped into his path, then gyrated her hips. "Will you dance with me?"

Rafael set aside his drink, wrapped his arm around her waist, and led her across the floor. "What's your name?"

She leaned closer to him. "Christina."

He did a mental review of the people invited to his VIP party. She was the cousin of a business associate. She would end up in his bed, a fact he anticipated while her luscious body rubbed against his, the dance a tantalizing foreplay of what would come later. "Welcome to my opening, Christina."

His assistant signaled him from the bar area.

Rafael kissed the back of Christina's hand. "Please excuse me. There's something I must attend to."

Christina pouted. "Will you come back?"

"Count on it." He winked, then joined Manuel.

"Your guests are here, *señor*. I showed them to your private conference room." The man was nothing if not efficient.

"They'll wait."

The thug he was about to meet respected power. Rafael was an expert at power games. He spent some time in his study prior to heading to the conference room. Manuel held the door as Rafael strode in.

A stocky man with a pugnacious nose sat at the table. His blue silk shirt clung to his protruding stomach. He held a Cuban cigar in one hand and a drink in the other. His entourage—two beefy men, bodyguards no doubt, and three women in cheap scanty dresses—cluttered his office. The women lounged on the sofa behind the conference table.

"Rafael!" the man boomed, as if they were old friends.

"Lorenzo."

"Your new place is wonderful. I promised these ladies I'd bring them to your opening." He wagged a thick finger at them. "Lorenzo keeps his word, yes?"

The women giggled on cue.

Rafael glanced at his watch. "I trust Manuel has taken care of you?"

Lorenzo waived a hand. "*Sí*, we have the drinks, and the girls are eager to join the party."

Rafael allowed the corners of his mouth to tilt upward. "There are several parties tonight. You are welcome to attend the one at the club. It's on the house." He had drawn a line for Lorenzo by omitting him from the VIP gathering.

Lorenzo waved at the women. "You heard *Señor* Molina. Join the party at the club."

Manuel, who had been hovering outside, entered the room with a server. "Diego will escort your guests, *señor*."

The women followed the server out of the conference room.

Lorenzo puffed on his cigar and chuckled. "Gotta keep the flock happy." He placed his cigar on an ashtray. "I have the information you seek."

Rafael repressed a sigh. Every lead he'd found was false. Chances were this one was too. "If I'd known you were coming here for a mere curiosity of mine, I would have spared you the trip."

Lorenzo blinked, disappointed he hadn't impressed Rafael. "It was no trouble. I have the information if you will hear it."

"Make it quick," Rafael said.

Lorenzo nodded. "Gabriel McKnight has what you're looking for."

Rafael narrowed his eyes. "The writer? You're saying the writer has the coordinates?"

Lorenzo bobbed his head. "He found that diamond several months ago. It was in the news. One of Richter's guards told me McKnight's woman had a family member who hid the codes along with the list. McKnight has the entire list."

Interesting. Richter was already staking a claim. Rafael pulled cash from his pocket, then threw the wad on the table. "Manuel will show you to the club." He neither shook hands with Lorenzo nor bid him goodnight.

In his office, he fired up his laptop. Thirty minutes later, Rafael dialed a private number.

An older gentleman answered. *"Rafael. How is opening night?"*

"Better than expected."

Eduardo chuckled. *"I'm not surprised. Congratulations, my boy."*

"I found a lead."

"I don't want you to place yourself in danger."

"I'm going to the Frankfurt Book Fair, Eduardo. Would you care to join me?"

CHAPTER SEVEN

GRAND HOTEL, STOCKHOLM, SWEDEN

THE FRESH SCENT of death was an aphrodisiac unlike anything. Slayer glanced at the ceiling while Beethoven's first symphony played on the old radio.

Slayer moved with the music, graceful and euphoric. A twirl, a turn... a bow to an imaginary opponent. Death was an art, and Slayer wielded the blade like a master. "Ta da!"

Behind the leather couch, a man's motionless body lay on the bed, face purple, mouth twisted with horror. Blood trickled down his neck, seeping into the white duvet and spreading like a crimson blossom.

Richter's first gift was on its way. Slayer couldn't wait to see Richter's face. Above the bed, a clock chimed seven. *I can't be late. Such a shame the fun must end.*

"Tonight, I meet Richter. Tomorrow, I find Gabriel McKnight."

CHAPTER EIGHT

As twilight's perfume brushed the sky,
daylight was drowned by a raven dye.
Out from the curtain of fate did appear,
a sly moon which made the sun disappear.

—Nezami, *Khosrow and Shirin*

FRANKFURT BOOK FAIR, GERMANY

GABRIEL MCKNIGHT STUDIED the expanding crowd. The mass of humanity, dressed in everything from business-casual to grunge, became a living organism. Laughter filled the massive tent known as the Lesezelt stage. People chatted while the book fair's event team helped with crowd control.

Gabriel's mind and body fought an internal war. On one hand, he was flattered and grateful. Fans always showed up to see him, no matter the weather or wait. His body reacted differently. Muscles tightened, his senses heightened, and sweat ran down his back. He rolled his shoulders to ward off the unease. He wasn't fearful of crowds, but years of military training made him wary of stepping into the spotlight.

While attendees searched for their seats, he focused on a digital screen displaying world news.

Richter Holdings will merge with the San Francisco biopharma giant, Alum Pharmaceuticals. Farid Richter announced the company will introduce a revolutionary technology once they finalize the merger.

"Interesting," Gabriel murmured.

"Isn't it?" Harvey Cornwall, Gabriel's long-time literary agent and friend, munched on a strudel. "Who would've thought Richter Holdings would move into biopharma?"

From what Gabriel had observed, the more success business moguls had, the more they hungered for power.

Harvey beamed. "This is a great gathering. I'm glad we partnered with Noor's PR folks. Your gal has impressive connections."

Gabriel's gaze shifted to the other side of the tent, where Noor spoke with representatives from a Dubai publishing house. The forest green dress she wore clung to her generous curves and showed off her long legs. Her hair cascaded to her waist, a dark, silken waterfall. She was beautiful, inside and out.

She caught his eye and smiled.

His heart clenched and his body tightened. This time the response was different.

Harvey stepped into his line of vision. "You got it bad, kid."

Gabriel thought of the small velvet box in his suitcase. "If you mean I'm fond of Noor, I admit it."

"Fond?" Harvey chortled. "People are fond of kittens and fuzzy socks." He tilted his head. "You realize you love her, don't you?"

"This is why I don't write romance. I don't have what it takes." He held up his palms before Harvey could comment. "Yes, Harv, I love her."

Harvey's eyes gleamed with satisfaction. "She's a great gal."

Noor shook hands with the Dubai people, then turned to greet a woman and a boy. She laughed at something the kid said before steering them toward Gabriel. Her gaze locked with his. The mischievous glint in her emerald-colored eyes made him wary.

"Gentlemen, meet Marci Saleh. Marci is here to promote her latest book, *Chicken Kebabs and Murder*."

Gabriel extended his hand. "It's nice to meet you."

Harvey grinned. "I've read your books, Ms. Saleh. Are the recipes your own?"

Marci blushed. "My grandmother's. I learned to cook from her."

The curly-haired boy tugged on Noor's sleeve. "I know I gotta wait for the grown-ups to finish talking, but it's taking forever. Are you gonna introduce me?"

Noor patted the boy's shoulder. "Gabriel, meet one of your greatest fans, Saman Saleh."

The boy bounced closer to Gabriel. "Call me Sam. Most people do."

"Thanks. You can call me Gabriel."

"I wanted to meet you 'cause Jason Vann's the best." Sam wrinkled his nose. "Why does he keep kissing the girls, though? Mom reads the books first and whites out parts I'm not supposed to read."

Gabriel didn't know how to reply. Thankfully, Sam didn't notice.

"My friend Joey says it's a grown-up thing to kiss girls. All the bada—" he glanced warily at his mother. "I mean, all the grown-ups do it. You kissed Noor outside of the tent, didn't you?"

Noor blushed.

Gabriel grinned. "Yes, I did."

Sam scratched his head. "I mean, Noor's nice and all for a girl, but I don't get it." He raised solemn brown eyes to Gabriel's. "Is Jason Vann gonna punch that Stringer in the throat and teach him a lesson? 'Cause I hope he does it in your next book."

Gabriel's mouth twitched. "I think you'll be pleased with Jason's next adventure."

When Sam sidled up to Gabriel for another question, Marci pulled him away. "Mister McKnight is busy. Let's get some ice cream."

"Why can't I stay here?" Sam muttered.

Gabriel kneeled to get eye-level with the boy. "Get some ice cream. After I finish my talk and the signing, I'll bring you an autographed copy. You can ask as many questions as you like."

Sam's eyes widened. "Gosh, thanks." He lowered his voice. "Is it true you can fly a plane?"

"It's true," Gabriel answered.

"Cool!" Sam breathed. "'Cause you're Jason Vann."

"Wait, I'm not—"

"I swear I won't tell anyone." Sam drew a cross over his heart. "It'll be our secret."

"Let's go, honey." Marci steered her son out of the tent.

"You'll bring us the book, won't you?" Sam called over his shoulder.

Gabriel nodded and raked a hand through his hair. "Jesus."

Noor laughed. "You were very sweet, Mister McKnight."

He circled an arm around her waist. "Thank you, Ms. Rahman. I hope you'll remember that when I'm in the throes of writing."

"There's the event coordinator," Harvey murmured, heading toward a corner nook.

Noor laughed. "We embarrassed Harvey. If you don't need anything, I'll go chat with a business associate."

Gabriel grinned. She made it too easy. "What if I need something?"

"What can I get you?"

He lowered his voice. "For starters, there's a booth outside selling copies of the *Kama Sutra*. You can get a copy while I wrap this up and talk to the kid. We'll go back to the hotel and spend the afternoon trying out the positions you like."

Her laughter warmed him like a shot of fine whiskey. "While I love the idea of an afternoon in bed with you, I don't think Harvey would appreciate us abandoning the book fair." Her eyes softened. "I know you don't like crowds. Two more hours, and I will happily join you in bed." Her voice turned husky. "I'll purchase the *Kama Sutra*."

"I can sign books fast."

"Then get to work." She pecked him on the lips before joining Harvey.

A sallow man with hollow cheeks approached Gabriel. Two security guards trailed after him. "Mister McKnight, I'm Jan Henschel, the director of stage programming. Welcome to the Frankfurt

Book Fair." Henschel's handshake was sweaty. "We've set up the alcove on the left for your book signing. Security will also assist with traffic control."

"Thanks." Gabriel headed toward the stage. Halfway to the podium, a woman in a cream-colored raincoat collided with him. She grabbed his jacket to keep from falling.

"Careful."

"Thank you." She turned her face up to him. Not a woman. A teenager.

Gabriel eased her fingers from his coat. "Are you all right?"

"Yes, thanks." Her whiskey-colored eyes scanned the crowd as she shoved one of his older novels into his hands. "Will you please sign my book?"

"Sure, but I have to stick to the schedule. I'll do it after the talk." Gabriel held out the book. "Do you want to hold on to it until the signing begins?"

She leaned in and lowered her voice. "They're coming for you."

Did he hear her correctly? "I'm sorry, I didn't—"

"You have the key to the map," the girl interjected. "You must be careful."

Gabriel had encountered strange fans in the past. He studied her, looking for signs of drug use.

Though standing poised and calm, her gaze darted around the tent to each exit. "Be careful." She backed away, blending into the crowd.

Frowning at the book in his hands, Gabriel joined the conference host, who was waiting on the stage. He took a seat by the podium, unsettled by the warning. The girl's fear was genuine. Either she was crazy, or....

When the host tapped on the microphone, the buzz of conversation fizzled. A ripple of unease slid up Gabriel's spine. He studied the crowd. Rows of faces with expressions ranging from bored to excited and expectant, blended into one amorphous, undulating mass.

The host cleared his throat, then began his welcome.

Gabriel searched for anyone with unique body language signaling impending trouble.

Noor sat beside Harvey at the front of an alcove to his right. Two rows behind them, a man leaned against a pillar. He was tall with dark wavy hair and wore a Navy jacket like the one Gabriel had on. An Asian man stood by another pillar in the next alcove.

The host moved onto Gabriel's biography.

A heavy-set man wearing a beanie rose. He lumbered toward the drink stand. The Asian man followed, flicking a glance at Noor as he passed.

"Please welcome Gabriel McKnight!"

The audience broke into applause.

Gabriel approached the microphone. The air was thick with tension, and the pounding in his ears drowned everything out.

Beanie hat moved away from the drinks.

The Asian man shifted his stance. His gaze locked with Gabriel's for an instant.

A prickle of unease crept up Gabriel's spine, his shoulders tensing as he scanned the crowd once more.

The teenage girl stood by the exit. She mouthed one word, *"Run."*

Boom! A deafening roar erupted. Two more explosions sounded. Smoke rose from center stage, and pandemonium erupted. People ran in all directions. Chairs turned over. Cries of fear shook the tent.

Oomph! Something knocked Gabriel down.

Beanie hat landed on him. He held a knife.

Gabriel dodged the plunging blade and leaped to his feet.

Beanie rose and charged.

Gabriel punched him then knocked him off the stage. "Noor!" He sprinted to the other side of the tent.

Crack. A gunshot splintered the wooden post beside him. Gabriel ducked behind the drink stand.

A red dot grew on Beanie's mid-section.

Jesus! Someone was shooting people.

Gabriel crawled to the alcove and found Noor on her hands and knees, coughing. He took hold of her shoulders, trying to gauge if she was hurt. She nodded, indicating she was fine. Relieved, he found Harvey several feet away. Gabriel grabbed his arm, then led them out of the tent.

The main plaza resembled a war zone. People ran in all directions, while security guards rushed to the Lesezelt. Gabriel guided Noor and Harvey to a series of metal displays behind the outside stage. "Stay behind the metal displays till you reach the main entrance."

Noor gripped his arm. "Where are you going?"

"It wasn't a real explosion," Gabriel explained. "A real one would've killed me and many others. This was a scare tactic." He brushed his lips against hers. "Go with Harvey. It's important I find someone. I'll meet you at the main entrance in a few minutes."

Her mouth tightened. "If you're not there in ten minutes, I'll come for you."

"Deal."

Noor took Harvey's arm. "Let's go."

Gabriel shouldered his way back into the main plaza, then to the western exit of the Lesezelt. This was where he'd last seen the girl with the raincoat. Where did she go?

More shots rang out.

He ducked behind a coffee stand, then searched for the shooter. Something hit the back of his head.

Everything went dark.

CHAPTER NINE

Who might you be?
Where are you from?
What do you know?

—Nezami, *Khosrow and Shirin*

THE SQUEAL OF sirens pierced Gabriel's mind. He groaned, sat up, and winced as lights flashed in his eyes. When someone probed the back of his head, he flinched.

"Easy, sir." A paramedic knelt beside him. The woman gently examined a throbbing spot on his skull. "You fell. Lost consciousness. You should get checked at the hospital."

Fall! He didn't fall. Someone hit him. It was the second time someone attacked him since the girl's warning. Gabriel stumbled to his feet and grabbed a streetlamp for support. "I'm all right. I just need a minute."

"Help! Oh, please help!" a woman cried. Beside her, a man sank onto the sidewalk, clutching his chest. The paramedic hesitated, uncertain what to do.

"Go. I'm fine." He waved her away. Gabriel touched the back of his head as the paramedic rushed to help the couple. Blood coated the tips of his fingers. The cut wasn't deep. When he reached into his coat pocket for a tissue, his hand brushed over a piece of paper. He pulled it out.

The king who upholds justice during his reign,
will watch his kingdom flourish without pain. (Nezami)
Beyond the Heavenly Gates and in the tower,
you will find knowledge and power.

The writing was a hasty scrawl. He wondered how it landed in his coat pocket. *The girl!* She bumped into him on purpose to plant the note. He shoved it back into his pocket and made his way to the main exit.

Police and paramedics had blocked off the entrance to the book fair. Harvey waited behind the barricade. Gabriel joined him, dabbing his head.

Harvey's eyes widened. "What happened to you? Where's Noor?"

Gabriel froze. "She was with you."

Harvey shook his head. "She came after you."

No!

Gabriel sprinted back to the main entrance.

A police officer stepped into his path. "You can't go inside, sir."

"I have to get inside. I was a speaker and my—" He paused. "Girlfriend" sounded childish, and "lover" or "soul mate" were too personal. "My friend is inside. I must find her."

"We have teams checking the buildings. Give me your friend's name. I'll radio it to my superior officer."

Gabriel resisted the urge to shove the man aside. He gave Noor's name, then followed book fair signs until he spotted a small side entrance. A stretch of fence only six feet tall blocked it. Certain no one was watching, he climbed the fence. Slivers of pain pierced his skull when he jumped down. Gritting his teeth, he raced back to the Lesezelt and approached the first officer he saw. "Is anyone inside?"

The officer frowned. "Who are you searching for?" After Gabriel answered, the man said, "You were a guest speaker at the Lesezelt?"

"Yes. Will you please check the tent again? She could be hurt."

"Wait here." The officer went inside with two guards.

Gabriel paced until they returned.

"There's no one inside. What does your friend look like?"

He described Noor while the officer radioed her description to the teams checking the outer buildings. Gabriel raked a hand through his hair. The action sent a spasm of pain through his skull.

The officer motioned to him. "Come with me. We'll check the other buildings."

For the next two hours, they went from venue to venue but found no sign of Noor. Gabriel called her several times, always getting her voicemail.

"Could your friend be waiting at your hotel?" the officer asked.

"She would've called me. Or answered my calls."

"The paramedics would take her to the hospital if she was hurt."

"Where were the wounded taken?"

The officer gave him the names of medical facilities closest to the book fair on the way back to the main entrance. He also took Gabriel's number in the event he spotted Noor.

Harvey was waiting for him. "You didn't find her?"

"No." Gabriel typed on his mobile phone. "There are five hospitals close to the book fair. If she's injured, they'll have taken her to one of them. Let's go."

Three hours later, they arrived at the last hospital.

"Call the hotel again." Dread swelled with every step Gabriel took. He approached the reception desk. A tall nurse with soft doe-eyes listened patiently while he gave Noor's name and description.

"One moment, please." After checking the computer system, she picked up the phone, spoke in rapid German, then replaced the handset. "I'm sorry, sir. She isn't here." Her voice was gentle. "There are other hospitals close to the book fair. Have you checked them?"

Gabriel thanked her. His chest was tight, and the pounding at the back of his skull had worsened.

Harvey paced in the waiting area. "Did you find her?"

"No. The chances were slim, but I had to check." He pushed through the exit, then strode to the main road.

"I don't understand." Harvey hurried to keep up with Gabriel. "She can't have disappeared into thin air."

As the last rays of sunlight surrendered to night, Gabriel's final flicker of hope faded with them. He knew what had happened to Noor, and it made his blood run cold. "She didn't disappear. Someone took her."

Harvey's jaw dropped. "W-what do you mean?"

Gabriel told him about the girl's warning and the note in his pocket. He waved at the line of taxicabs waiting by the station.

Harvey grabbed his arm. "Where are you going?"

"To the police station. Go back to the hotel. I'll call if I find anything."

"I'm coming with you." Harvey's chin jutted out. "She's my friend too."

A cab stopped in front of them. Gabriel asked the cab driver to take the quickest route to the police station. He prayed Noor was okay. Christ, if she was hurt.... No. He wouldn't go there.

He'd remain calm. And he would find her.

THE DOWNTOWN PRECINCT was a modern building with all the commotion of a typical police station. Gabriel approached the front desk. "I'd like to report a missing person."

The officer took down Gabriel's information. "Wait here, please."

Gabriel massaged his neck. Someone had taken Noor. Why? He glanced at his watch. Every passing minute could be the difference between life and death.

He was about to ask how much of a wait there was when an officer approached the reception area. "Mister McKnight?"

Harvey looked up.

Gabriel nodded.

"I'm Officer Muller. Please come with me." When Harvey rose, she said, "I'm sorry. Only Mister McKnight."

Gabriel reassured Harvey it would be okay, then followed Muller past a labyrinth of desks to a conference room furnished with a rectangular table and six chairs. "Have a seat. Detective Jager will be with you in a minute."

Gabriel frowned. He wasn't an expert in German law enforcement procedures, but he knew this wasn't the typical process for reporting a missing person.

The door swung open. Four people walked in—first two strangers, then two familiar faces. The leader's hawk-like eyes homed in on Gabriel. "Are you the author?"

"Yes. Gabriel McKnight."

"I'm Detective Jager of the Frankfurt police." He motioned to the tall redhead behind him. "This is Detective Bruker from INTERPOL." He nodded at a tall man with square shoulders and a petite Asian woman. "I believe you've met Detectives Robin and Hood."

Several months ago, the Washington, D.C. police had discovered Gabriel's name and address on the body of a murdered woman—a government agent who worked with Gabriel's twin brother, Michael. Mike had been missing at the time. Detectives Robin and Hood investigated the murder, and for a while Gabriel was their number one suspect. His brother's disappearance and the murder had sent Gabriel on a hunt, which led him to Noor. He and Noor had collaborated with the police and found the actual killer.

What were Robin and Hood doing in Germany? Did it have anything to do with Noor's disappearance?

Robin of the perpetual buzz-cut and pressed suits scowled at Gabriel. Hood smirked and saluted him.

As if reading the questions in Gabriel's mind, Detective Jager smiled. "Detectives Robin and Hood"—his mouth twitched, then he coughed—"are collaborating with INTERPOL. They came to Frankfurt searching for you. It's fortunate you came to us first."

Detective Hood stared at him. "Why did you come to the station?"

"My friend, Ms. Rahman, is missing. She was with me at the book fair. I think someone kidnapped her after the fake explosion."

"Fake explosion?" Jager's brows arched.

Gabriel forced himself to remain calm. "It was an explosion with small blast radius designed not to kill but to create a distraction."

"We heard," Hood murmured. "What makes you think someone kidnapped Ms. Rahman."

Gabriel needed time to decipher the girl's note, so he didn't mention it. He told the police he was attacked twice and described the man with the beanie hat.

Jager pursed his lips. "Do you know why anyone would kidnap Ms. Rahman?"

Gabriel rubbed his neck. "Noor's father was a powerful Iranian general and advisor to the Persian king prior to the Islamic Revolution of 1979. Several months before the revolution, General Rahman hid some of Iran's valuable antiques and jewels. The items are worth a fortune." He didn't mention the Persian king kept the treasure in a secret vault in Tehran's Central bank.

"The general died during the revolution. Those who knew about the treasure believed the contents were lost. Then, several months ago, rumors floated through the art community insinuating Noor knows the location of the treasures. Her father died before she was born. She doesn't know anything."

Hood tapped her fingers on the table. "She found the famous diamond, didn't she? It's identical to one in Iran's national jewelry collection."

"Yes, but that was by chance." He wasn't going to explain Noor's mother had left clues to the diamond's location and the identity of her father's killer in Rumi's poems. Only a handful of people—including Gabriel, Harvey, and Michael—knew. "I think her abductor believes the rumors."

Robin shut his notebook and scowled. "Here we are again with a woman missing and you involved."

"I wasn't responsible then or now. I came here today to ask for help."

Detective Bruker studied him. "Do you know a Jurgen Mulligan?"

"No."

"When was the last time you were in Paris?"

Gabriel narrowed his eyes. "What does that have to do with Noor?"

"Answer the question, please."

"Noor and I were there this summer."

"And you never met Jurgen Mulligan?" Bruker prodded.

"I already answered that question." Gabriel gritted his teeth. "Is this Mulligan involved with kidnapping Noor?"

Detective Bruker shrugged. "Jurgen Mulligan was a document forger."

Gabriel raised an eyebrow. "Was?"

She nodded. "We found his body two days ago with a flyer for the book fair. He had circled your name."

Gabriel resisted the urge to rake a hand through his hair. "Has it occurred to you it may be a coincidence? Believe it or not, people read my books and attend my book signings."

"The flyer was on a table. Jurgen had cut off the top and hidden the piece with your name in his sock," Bruker said. "We believe he knew his life was in danger and was protecting you."

Gabriel rubbed his temples to soothe the pounding in his head. "This makes no sense. Why would he protect me?"

Bruker studied him. "Do you know a Farid Richter?"

Gabriel frowned. "Only through what I read in the papers."

"We've been watching him for a while," Bruker said. "More than once his competition has died, making it easy for him to dominate specific markets. In the past eight months, two powerful biopharma CEOs were found dead in their homes. Both were healthy and fit. One drowned in his pool. The other had a heart attack. One lived in the United States—D.C., to be exact. The other lived in Munich. They seem like two unrelated, unfortunate incidents. When I researched the German CEO, I learned he had business dealings with Richter. I reached out to the Washington PD. Detectives Hood and Robin were on the case."

Hood nodded. "Our victim also had several ventures with Richter, specifically in the arts."

Bruker leaned forward. "INTERPOL believes Richter acquires stolen artwork for private collectors. The artwork isn't your average hustler's deal. It's priceless art. Richter finds it and, until two days ago, Jurgen Mulligan forged the paperwork establishing its provenance."

Gabriel's stomach dropped. He knew what was coming. "And you believe Noor is somehow connected to this?"

Bruker steepled her hands together. "You're wrong about the rumors. They aren't about Ms. Rahman. They're centered on you."

"I don't understand."

"They say *you* know the location of the artifacts. Now, if anyone wanted to get information from you, Ms. Rahman would be excellent leverage, don't you think?"

Gabriel gaped at the detective who nodded. "Yes, Miss Rahman would definitely be leverage."

The next two hours passed with Gabriel going over every detail of his morning until the explosion. Detective Jager took notes and said his team would look through CCTV coverage. Gabriel answered more questions, provided his hotel information, then left with a headache that was so strong he had double vision.

When Gabriel was finally released, he trudged into the reception area.

Harvey leaped to his feet. "How did it go?"

"Fine." Gabriel didn't want to talk in front of the officer at the desk and steered Harvey toward the exit.

"What do we do now?" Harvey asked.

"We find Noor."

CHAPTER TEN

Shahpour was a painter and Khosrow's closest companion. He told Khosrow of his travels to Armenia and its beautiful mountains and terrain. He praised the Armenian Queen, Maheen Banou, and told Khosrow of her beautiful niece, Shirin. He described Shirin's alluring beauty in detail, from her creamy skin to her sweet lips. "Shirin? Did you say Shirin?" Mesmerized by Shahpour's flattering description, Khosrow decided to find her....

—Nezami, *Khosrow and Shirin*

GABRIEL LED HARVEY to the line of cabs on the other side of the police station.

"Where do we start?"

He massaged his temples. "I can't think with this headache. I need aspirin. Go back to the hotel, Harv. I'll meet you there." In his peripheral vision, he spotted a man in a forest green jacket. He was certain he'd seen him at the Lesezelt. He watched Green Jacket through a shop window's reflection.

The man bought a newspaper, then pretended to read it.

Harvey frowned, making the lines in his craggy face deepen. "How can I help?"

Gabriel texted a picture of the note to Harvey. "Try to make sense of what I just sent you." He watched Harvey get into a cab, then headed to the pharmacy he'd spotted farther down the road.

Thirty minutes later, he dry swallowed two pills while sitting on a bench. Streetlamps lit the park. A crisp wind carried the fresh scent of pine trees, and a mild mist gave the entire area an ethereal glow. He'd chosen this specific bench because he could see anyone enter this secluded area.

Green Jacket rounded the bend.

Hidden by fog, Gabriel waited behind a tree.

The man hesitated. Continued. Halfway to the bench, he stopped. Looked around.

Gabriel stepped in front of him. "Why are you following me?"

The man cursed and jumped. He was American, in his early thirties, with blond hair and shrewd eyes. "My name is Brandon Rohr. I'm a reporter."

The name sounded familiar. Realization dawned. "You wrote the article about Richter's pharmaceutical acquisitions."

Brandon blinked. "You read my article?"

He shrugged. "Why are you following me? And don't give me bullshit about booking an interview with me."

"You're searching for Ms. Rahman. I want to help."

"Why?" Gabriel asked.

"It's the right thing to do."

Gabriel crossed his arms over his chest. "That's not a convincing answer."

Brandon shoved his hands into the pockets of his jeans. "Some people killed a friend of mine. I believe they also took Ms. Rahman. I'll help you find Ms. Rahman, and in doing so, I'll find the people who killed my friend."

Gabriel raised an eyebrow. "What do you plan to do when you find them?"

Brandon sighed. "I want justice for my friend."

"Who are these people?"

Brandon's jaw clenched. "They're connected to Farid Richter."

"Richter?"

A muscle in Brandon's cheek spasmed. "I saw his second in command at my friend's apartment moments before she died."

Gabriel studied the man. "Justice won't bring your friend back."

Brandon looked away. "I'm aware of that."

Gabriel bit back a sigh. The aspirin had dulled the pounding in his head. "I have to get back to the hotel. Walk with me."

Brandon fell into step beside him. "How much do you know about Iran's history?"

"The basics."

"Good." Brandon pulled up the collar of his coat. "In 1925, Reza Shah Pahlavi became the Iranian king. To counterbalance British and Soviet influence in Iran, he established strong trade ties with Germany. By 1940, nearly fifty percent of Iran's trade was with them. Reza Shah then commissioned a German engineer to build a hidden vault for him at the Central Bank in Tehran. It was built in a hidden corridor in the bank's basement. The engineer worked on it for two years. When the vault was complete, Mohamad Reza Pahlavi, Reza Shah's son, had taken over the throne.

"I know about the vault," Gabriel said.

Brandon followed him to the main road. "Nazi leadership showed an interest in art early on and began confiscating works as early as 1938. A large number of stolen pieces was to be showcased at the Fuhrer museum, but the museum was never created, and much of the art is missing. What do you know about the Reichsleiter Rosenberg Taskforce?"

Gabriel massaged the back of his neck. "He's the guy who created the Nazi task force that confiscated art from various countries, correct?"

Brandon nodded. "Rosenberg created a map for each Nazi art stockpile. As further precaution, they wrote the coordinates in code on three different paintings, then separated them. Rosenberg sent one of his top engineers to Iran with the codes. The engineer gave the codes to Reza Shah with a message from Rosenberg to keep them in the vault."

"How do you know this?" Gabriel asked.

"I have the German engineer's diary," Brandon said. "The engineer mentions Rosenberg gave him a document to have Reza Shah store, but when the vault was complete, Reza Shah's son, Mohamad Reza, ruled. The engineer gave the codes to the new king, who placed them in the vault with a series of artifacts." He glanced at Gabriel. "That's where you come in."

"You're saying the people who took Noor want the codes to the map, correct?"

Brandon nodded. "Yes."

Gabriel recalled the girl's warning. *You have the key to the map.* He stopped to face Brandon. "I don't have the map, and neither does Noor." He raised his hand, cutting off Brandon's reply. "Everyone thinks Noor knows where the treasure is. She doesn't. Hell, her father died before she was born."

"Could he have left her the codes without her knowing it?"

Gabriel sighed. "Either way, she knows nothing." He clenched his fists. "I have to find her."

"I have a friend in the German police. He owes me a favor. I'll see if we can get a copy of the security footage during the explosion," Brandon offered.

"Thank you."

They arrived at the hotel. A porter ran up to him. "Mister McKnight, you have a package." He held out a tray with an envelope in it.

Gabriel tore open the envelope, hoping for some news on Noor. A USB flash drive fell into his palm. He turned the envelope over. The stamp was from Paris. The police had said the document forger in Paris was trying to protect him. Did the forger know Noor was in danger?

He didn't know if he could trust Brandon, yet he had no other options. "Come with me."

In his suite, Gabriel inserted the flash drive into his laptop. He clicked on the lone folder and frowned at the screen. It contained three files. The first was a photo of a German newspaper article dated 1963. "Can you read German?"

"Yes." Brandon leaned over Gabriel's shoulder. "It's an article about a Karl von Mayer who died in a car accident. German authorities found him with incriminating evidence. It appears Karl's older brother collaborated with the Nazis to help them hide artifacts they looted during World War II. Karl knew about his brother's activities. Investigators found several valuable documents in Karl's briefcase, which led to the discovery of stolen art in a deserted home's basement. The article labels Karl as a Nazi supporter." Brandon typed on his mobile phone and whistled. "Karl von Mayer was Mina von Mayer's father."

"As in von Mayer Industries?"

Brandon nodded.

Gabriel blew out a breath. "What could Mina von Mayer's family have to do with Noor's abduction?"

"Mina's fortune is self-made. She started von Mayer Industries after college and turned it into a global machine."

Gabriel made a mental note to research the von Mayers and clicked on the next file, hoping to find something that would lead him to Noor. That article showed a courthouse with several people standing outside. A Mr. and Mrs. Lejeune had died in a car accident with their infant daughter. A truck hit their car head on and killed the family. Gabriel enlarged the photo and blinked.

Morris and the Iranian!

Brandon watched him. "You know these men?"

Gabriel pointed at the first man. "Morris is Noor's uncle. He's a family friend who helped Noor's mother leave Iran after her father died. He married Noor's aunt. The man standing next to Morris is his half-brother, Cyrus Rohan. He's a businessman." Gabriel didn't elaborate. Cyrus was powerful, dangerous, and liked to keep a low profile.

He squinted at the blurry photo and tapped on the face of a woman standing between Morris and Cyrus. "It's the girl. It can't be her though." He massaged his temple. The photo was eighteen years old at most. Seeing the confusion on Brandon's face, Gabriel told him about the girl who had warned him at the Lesezelt.

Brandon leaned closer to the screen. "That's Mina von Mayer. The girl you met looked like Mina von Mayer?"

Gabriel studied the mournful eyes in the heart-shaped face. The picture was black and white, yet he was certain Mina von Mayer's eyes were the color of Scottish malt. "Yes, a younger version of her." He rubbed his neck, trying to make sense of the information.

His phone beeped. A text came from Harvey. *Found something on the note. Are you back at the hotel?*

He texted Harvey back. *Come to my suite.* Gabriel clicked on the last file. A photo of a medieval tower filled the screen. Someone had scribbled a note. *Check the tower.* "Do you know where this tower is?"

Brandon's brows furrowed. "It looks familiar."

"I can search for it." Gabriel took a picture of the tower.

A knock sounded on the door. Harvey stomped into the suite, then came to a halt when he saw Brandon.

Gabriel introduced them.

Harvey, ever polite, shook Brandon's hand. "I read your articles. I liked the one about Senator Crawley's interest in biopharma."

"Thanks." Brandon shoved his hands into his pockets.

"Brandon's helping us find Noor," Gabriel said. "Tell me about the note."

"I figured out what it means."

Gabriel pulled out the original note the girl had placed in his pocket.

Harvey pointed to the first two lines.

The king who upholds justice during his reign,
will watch his kingdom flourish without pain.

"This part is a translation of a classic Persian tragedy called *Khosrow and Shirin*. It's a love story between a Persian prince and an Armenian princess. Nezami Ganjavi wrote it."

Brandon grabbed his jacket from the couch, then pulled out a package wrapped in white cloth. A notebook and a pair of cotton gloves lay inside. He put on the gloves, then flipped through the notebook. "Here it is. The engineer refers to Nezami in his diary. He describes miniatures with scenes from *Khosrow and Shirin* and claims the king placed them in the hidden vault with the codes Rosenberg gave Reza Shah."

Startled, Harvey glanced at Gabriel. "Vault? We're back to the vault?"

"It looks like we are." Gabriel relayed what Brandon told him and showed Harvey the pictures on the flash drive.

Harvey pulled a handkerchief from his pocket, then wiped his glasses. "If these people think you have the codes to the map, they'll contact you to bargain for Noor's life. You should call the police."

Gabriel swallowed the fear lodged in his throat. "I'm trying to find something to use as bait while I figure out where they're holding Noor."

"There are parallels." Brandon grabbed one of the complimentary notepads the hotel placed on the consul, then fished in his pocket for a pen. "Noor's father hid a series of codes that unlock a map to artwork the Nazis looted and hid. Mina von Mayer's father was a Nazi supporter who hid the location of the Nazis' stolen artwork."

"That's what the article claims," Gabriel said. "It doesn't mean it's true."

"Agreed," Brandon murmured. "So, what's the common link?"

Gabriel raked a hand through his hair and instantly regretted the action. The movement made his head pound again. "We have three common links. First, there's stolen artwork the Nazis hid. Second, Noor's family's connection to the von Mayer family. Third...."

"What's the third?" Brandon asked, scribbling notes.

"The tower," Harvey answered.

"What?"

Harvey tilted his head at the note. "The last line says, 'Beyond the Heavenly Gates and in the tower, you will find knowledge and power.' The file Gabriel received also has the picture of a tower."

"There's one more thing to consider," Gabriel said. "Nezami's

Khosrow and Shirin is important. The girl used lines from it to warn me, and Brandon has a diary mentioning miniatures from Nezami's tragedy." He began pacing. "I'll research the family angle and the tower." He leaned over to review Brandon's notes. "See if you can make a list of the stolen art that's still missing. Check if there are any rumors on the whereabouts of the stolen pieces."

"I'll research the Nezami angle," Harvey volunteered.

Gabriel nodded. "I'll call Noor's uncle."

Someone pounded on the door. Everyone froze.

Gabriel gestured for them to be silent. He checked the peephole.

Sam, the kid Noor had introduced to him, stood in the hallway, hand raised to knock again.

Gabriel quickly opened the door to avoid the banging. He was about to tell the kid he didn't have time when Sam grabbed his arm.

"I-I snuck out. Mom's asleep." His voice shook. "I saw them."

"Who did you see?"

"The men who took Noor."

Gabriel pulled the kid inside, then shut the door. He took hold of Sam's shoulders. "You saw the men who took Noor?"

Sam bobbed his head.

Gabriel led him to the sitting room. "Tell me everything you can remember."

Sam tilted his head in Brandon and Harvey's direction. "Can I talk in front of them?"

"Yes."

"Okay. I was waiting with Mom for ice cream. The explosion happened, and Mom dragged me to the exit. She"—Sam shook his head—"Noor was running inside when a security guard grabbed her." He wrinkled his nose. "You know what?"

"No, what?"

"She fought him good and hard, but he was bigger. He pushed her against a wall and shoved a cloth over her mouth. No one saw 'cause there were people screaming and stuff. Noor fainted, so the security man carried her to another security person outside. That guy took her to a van, then drove off."

"Can you remember what the van looked like?" Gabriel fought to keep his voice level.

"It was dark blue with a white star on it." Sam lifted his face. "You're Jas—" He glanced at the others, then back at him. "I mean, you're like Jason Vann. You can find her, but I wanted to help. I remember some of the license plate."

"You got the license plate?" Gabriel and Brandon cried at the same time.

Sam's dark curls bounced as he nodded. "I can't remember all of it, but it's got D-N, a symbol like two round green balls, A-R, then numbers. I only remember the last two numbers. One and two."

Gabriel jotted down the letters and numbers.

Brandon pulled out his mobile phone. "I'll call my friend at the police department. He can search with a partial."

Sam tilted his head up to Gabriel. "Was I able to help? 'Cause I wanna be like y—I mean Jason Vann."

"You were a great help." Gabriel reached for his laptop. After typing *blue van with a white star*, he turned the screen for Sam to see. "Did the van look like any of these?"

Sam leaned closer, then pointed to one of the images. "That one."

"It's a security company with offices in Munich and Nuremburg," Gabriel called out to Brandon.

Brandon nodded and continued his conversation in German.

Gabriel patted Sam's shoulder. "Let's get you back to your room."

"Are you gonna make the bad guys sorry they took Noor?"

"Yes."

CHAPTER ELEVEN

Dressed in plain clothes Khosrow traveled to Armenia in search of Shirin. He rode hard until he came upon a pool in a vast green field where a woman bathed. Her beauty stole his breath. Little did he know it was Shirin.

In the water she sat, a lily, graceful and fair,
her mesmerizing beauty for him laid bare.
—Nezami, *Khosrow and Shirin*

CHATEAU GUTSCH, LUCERNE, SWITZERLAND

MINA VON MAYER'S heels clicked on the tiles of the hotel lobby. She caught her reflection in a mirror and slowed, unwilling to display any stress. The cream-colored sheath dress accentuated her slim figure. Her jewelry and makeup were minimal. Her stride was now unhurried.

Satisfied, she paused by the outer terrace to take in the view. Lake Lucerne's magnetic blue waters lay beneath heart-lifting mountains that embraced the city. A steamer cruise passed through the lake, and a young couple walked hand in hand, gazing at each other as if no one else existed. A memory surfaced.

She was eighteen years old. Delighted Mama had allowed her to vacation with a friend in Switzerland, Mina had rented a bungalow in Lucerne. Exhausted after a day of water sports, she swam to the dock at sunset and reached out to climb its ladder.

"Careful." A firm hand gripped hers to help her up.

On the dock, Mina pulled her long hair away from her face and froze.

The young man standing beside her was beautiful. There was no other way to describe him. A few years older than her, he was lean and muscular. Thick wavy hair the color of Italian espresso fell to the nape of his neck. Arched brows graced charcoal-colored eyes. High cheekbones flanked and an aquiline nose. A firm jaw showed strength, and his sensuous lips promised passion. Where had he come from?

"I saw you swimming and thought you were a sea nymph."

Speechless, Mina couldn't help but notice how tall he was.

He extended his hand. "I seem to have forgotten my manners. I'm Cyrus Rohan."

Shaking herself out of enthrallment, she shook his hand. "Mina von Mayer."

His mouth curved up into a full-blown smile. "An intriguing name."

"Why is my name intriguing?"

Charcoal eyes twinkled. "You have a Persian first name and a foreign last name. It makes me wonder."

Her lips twitched. "It's because I'm half-Persian and half—"

"Nymph," Cyrus offered, making her laugh. "I'm Persian too." He motioned to a boy by a boat. "My brother Kameron and I are vacationing here for a few weeks. Do you live here?"

Mina shook her head. "I live in Tehran. This is my last vacation with friends before—" She stopped. What was she thinking? She almost blurted out her plans to a stranger. She looked away. "Before I start university in America."

If Cyrus noticed her discomfort, he didn't comment. He signaled to his brother. "Kameron and I have caught more fish than we can eat. We're going to grill at the picnic area. Will you and your friend join us for dinner?"

"Yes," she said before she could think about it.

The four of them dined on grilled fish, bread, cheese, and wine. After dinner, she and Cyrus took a walk, then sat by the dock looking at the stars.

Mina spent the rest of her vacation with Cyrus and his twin brother. They rode bikes to all the tourist sites, swam in the lake, and visited the neighboring cities. When it was time to go home, Cyrus changed his flight to be with her. His intense charcoal eyes were soft while he whispered promises to her, his lips brushing over her temple and cheek.

The elevator pinged, jolting Mina back to the present. Good Lord, she was rubbing her chest. Mortified, she straightened and focused on the upcoming meeting. Richter wanted her off the Board. He'd gone behind her back to speak with the members. Being underestimated had its merits. Richter was in for a surprise.

A member of the hotel staff unlocked a pair of double doors. Inside, several tables and couches sat haphazardly around a bar. Behind it, a conference room offered a panoramic view of Lucerne Lake.

Seated in the lounge were a group of men and women who looked like consummate professionals. She supposed they were, in essence, professionals, managing not just businesses but international conglomerates. What differentiated them from the average CEO was their level of influence. This group changed the outcome of elections, overthrew governments, started and stopped wars, and stabilized and destabilized the global economy. Their decisions altered societies, economies, and regimes.

Seated at a table beside the bar, Buck Lee and his sister Kim were in deep discussion. Lee was a handsome Asian man with a scar above his left brow. Kim twirled a glass of brandy. If a certain ripple affected Asian politics or finances, the Lees were behind it.

Buck spotted her first and raised his glass in a toast.

Mina smiled in return.

To their right, Yuri Petrov sat across from his second-in-command, Serji. Petrov's jowls quivered as he muttered something in Russian, then downed a shot of vodka. Petrov's business was primarily in Eastern Europe. Serji reminded Mina of a fox. She bit back a smile. She'd acquired one of Petrov's competitors as a silent warning to him. He would not side with Richter.

Adisa Mombasa, the newest member of the Board, sat on a barstool, talking to a server. His muscular arms were folded across his chest. He wanted full control over the African continent. Richter stood in his way.

Two men occupied a table in the left corner. One spotted her and nodded in greeting.

A tsunami of emotion welled from the pit of Mina's stomach to flood her chest. She ignored it and tilted her head to acknowledge him as if he were an ordinary man. As if he couldn't yank out the remaining pieces of her soul and destroy her.

In his sixties, Cyrus Rohan looked better than he did when he was twenty-five. Known in their business circles as the Iranian, he was handsome, classy, affluent, and lethal. Those who knew of him never crossed him. Anyone foolish enough to try paid the price.

A familiar longing tugged at her, followed by a hollowness deep in her belly. The man sitting at the table was a far cry from the jubilant boy who'd biked around Lucerne with her.

Cyrus's brother Morris sat across him. He was a power in his own right. She was surprised to see him because he'd planned on being absent for a couple of weeks.

A tall woman with long auburn hair sipped a martini at the center of the lounge. Magdalena Romano's areas of interest were energy and lovers who enjoyed pain—inflicting and receiving it. She was Richter's current bed mate and a viper to the core. When Mina entered, Magdalena slithered into a seat beside Cyrus.

Mina turned away to hide her disgust. Adisa motioned for her to join him. She ordered a drink and took the seat next to him.

"You were right," he murmured.

The bartender returned with a glass. Mina waited for him to retreat before answering. "I usually am."

Adisa barked a laugh and turned solemn. "Richter wants to meet in private."

The taste of oak and roasted grain coated Mina's tongue. She closed her eyes, savoring the weight and rich flavor of the single malt whiskey. "You should meet with him."

Adisa stared into his glass. "Are you going to vote yes for his move into the biopharma industry?"

Mina bit back her smile. Adisa was already seeking her advice. "Is it up for a vote? From what I saw in the news, it's a done deal."

"The Board can change that." He studied her. "Will you vote yes?"

Mina took another sip. Having reached her self-imposed limit, she set down her drink. "Vote for what you believe is right. I'll do the same."

Lee joined them at the bar. "Is it true Richter is behind the disruption in Africa?"

Mina traced her finger along the rim of her glass. "Who else profits from it?"

Lee ordered a refill. "He should have consulted the Board before moving into biopharma."

She sighed. "He is the Chairman."

"Chairman or not, we vote for any move into new territories." Lee narrowed his eyes. "How do you feel about it?"

Mina shrugged. "It doesn't affect my business."

Adisa grinned. "Speaking of the devil."

Farid Richter entered the lounge with his sallow-faced assistant. Dressed in a grey suit and silk tie, Richter was what many considered a handsome man—tall, athletic, and broad shouldered. His once dark hair was now streaked with silver. Ice-blue eyes searched the room. Upon spotting Mina, he approached the bar.

Richter was caught between a rock and a hard place. Going up against her violated Board rules. His only option was to win her over. This was going to be fun.

"Zauberin"—German for sorceress, a moniker the media had given her because everything she touched became profit—"we missed you at our last meeting." Richter's cultured voice was as smooth and rich as the whiskey. "I purchased a lovely antique book of *Khosrow and Shirin* and wanted to show it to you." He nodded at Adisa and Lee. "Mina and I enjoy Persian literature. Nezami is a poet we both appreciate."

Mina's lips lifted into a smile. "I had business to attend to. You know how that goes. Lee and Adisa were bringing me up to speed."

Richter raised his brows. In a tone used to admonish a teenager, he said, "Why didn't you call me? As Chair, I'd bring you up to speed."

Mina didn't answer. Instead, she met his pallid-blue gaze.

"We were here last session," Lee said, filling in the awkward silence. "You mentioned nothing about biopharma."

Richter sighed. "It's why I asked the Board to gather tonight. Shall we begin?"

Mina joined the Lees at the conference table. Adisa sat on her other side. Cyrus, Morris, Petrov, Serji, and Magdalena sat across from her, while Farid occupied the head of the table.

Richter waxed poetic about an opportunity to boost global economy while strengthening Board assets. His ability to spin lies and twist facts was praise-worthy. After listing several business reasons for moving into biopharma, he concluded with an overall altruistic vision of the future.

He steepled his fingers. "My dear Board members. Now that you have the facts, I'd like to call a vote."

"I vote yes," Cyrus said.

Richter smirked and turned to Magdalena.

"Yes."

He nodded at her benevolently, then moved on. "Yuri?"

"I exercise my one neutral vote for the year." Petrov rushed to explain. "I have assets on the other side of this."

Mina kept her expression neutral. Yes, her latest acquisition had proved beneficial.

The Lees exchanged a look, then Kim said, "It's a no for us."

Adisa sighed. "Sorry. It's a no for me too."

Richter's smile didn't reach his eyes. "That leaves us with a tie. Mina's vote will make the decision. Mina, how do you vote?"

Didn't see that coming, did you? Mina waited several seconds before responding. "I need to consider this. You'll have my answer at our next meeting."

A muscle ticked in Richter's jaw. "The timing is crucial. Our next meeting won't take place until next quarter. If I am to make this move, I must make it within a month."

Mina tilted her head and widened her eyes. "I don't want to impede your business interests." She swept her hand out in a delicate gesture. "We trade and balance power around this table, but power must have limits. There is a line between nudging a country or economy in a direction and eradicating free will. Nonproliferation is essential for the health of our world." She paused and let the significance of her words sink in. "If you must have an answer before our next meeting, then I'm sorry, it's a no for the reason I just stated."

Fury turned Richter's eyes into blue ice chips. He clenched his left fist and blew out a breath. "Very well. I will respect the Board's vote."

CYRUS ROHAN GAVE his driver the destination, then leaned back in the soft leather seat. Defining moments of life weren't gentle droplets of rain helping one grow. They engulfed and obliterated like the tides of a tsunami. His defining moment was the day he'd met Mina von Mayer. Her beauty and light were a beacon, and he a lost ship. What choice did he have but to draw as close as possible? But then, he'd paid the price when life pushed them apart.

Images flickered through his mind. Dreams shared, passion given and taken. Irises that sparkled like topaz when determined, softened to warm caramel when making love. A small hand. Trusting eyes, and the pain. Dear God, the pain of loss.

Cyrus pulled the picture from his coat pocket. He'd lost her, lost all, then drifted through life, acquiring everything except the only thing he longed for. Now, fate offered him another chance. He would not repeat past mistakes.

The car halted outside a large country manor facing Lake Lucerne. Cyrus climbed the stairs.

A mousy woman greeted him at the door. "Good evening, sir. Ms. von Mayer is in the living room."

He handed the woman his coat. "Thank you. How are you, Mercedes?"

She blushed and stammered a response.

Amused at her shyness, Cyrus brushed past her. "I know my way. Don't bother announcing me."

Mina's home was a blend of soft and bold colors mixed in with comfortable furniture. That, or the energy of its owner, made his heart soar every time he visited. After passing through a hallway with views on both sides, he entered a living room facing the lake. Mina hadn't noticed his arrival. He took a moment to study her.

Head bent, she read her favorite poet's work while chewing on her lip, a habit from the old days. Her elegant, upturned nose still wrinkled when she was emotional. She'd taken off her shoes, and her long shapely legs made his mouth water. Over the years, he'd been with other women. None had ignited in him the tumultuous fire Mina did. No one matched her passion or her intelligence. No one intrigued, surprised, amused, and infuriated him the way she did. He cleared his throat.

Mina's head turned up, and her lips parted into a smile. She held out her hands and rose to greet him. "This is a pleasant surprise."

Cyrus took her hands in his. "Are you reading Nezami again? The end won't change no matter how many times you read it."

"It's tragic and lovely."

He lifted her hands to his lips. "I wanted to see you before your trip to New York."

She motioned to the sofa. "Please, sit. I'm glad you came.

Thank you for supporting me this afternoon. Your 'yes' vote gave me the veto."

"I'll always support you."

"Cognac?"

"Thanks." It warmed his heart that she still knew his preferences.

Mina walked to the bar. "I have the financials for the merger. Everything is moving according to our plan."

Was a business partnership all she wanted? Had she really moved on? Cyrus hid his irritation. "I didn't come to discuss business."

"Oh?" She gave him his glass, then waited for him to continue.

He liked that about her. She didn't push. Her face remained impassive. This controlled woman was a far cry from the girl whose eyes told all.

He sipped his drink while she sank into a plush sofa. "What I'm about to say is important, Mina. It changes everything, including our business plans."

A slight wrinkle in her brow indicated he had her attention.

"Your granddaughter lives."

She blinked as if she hadn't heard him. "I'm sorry. What did you say?"

"She's alive, Mina."

Mina shook her head. "No, she isn't."

"The accident." Cyrus swallowed the lump in his throat. "The baby didn't die."

"No." She leaned back to distance herself from him.

Cyrus pulled out the photograph and held it out to her. "Look at her. She's identical to you when you were her age." When Mina didn't move, he shoved the photo into her hand. "Look at her!"

Mina stared at it for a long moment. Her breathing grew shallow. One hand rose to her breastbone.

He didn't touch her or offer sympathy, knowing she'd see it as a sign of her weakness. He waited for her to gether herself.

When her gaze met his, her eyes brimmed with tears. "How? We saw the bodies."

A fire burned deep in his gut. "Richter."

She clasped her hands tightly and sat immobile. "Please explain."

"Richter falsified the documents and bought off the authorities, including our man in the police department. He replaced the child with a dead baby and raised the girl as his ward, keeping her close and hiding her from the outside world." Cyrus raked a hand through his hair. "She's smart and beautiful, Mina. My man inside said she tricked Richter and ran away. She knows the truth."

Her eyes revealed a myriad of emotions, then she looked away. The simple act was a punch to his gut. *Patience,* he reminded himself. What he wanted would take time.

Mina rose and began pacing. "We must find her."

Cyrus tugged her back to the couch. "She's at the Frankfurt Book Fair."

She stiffened. "What's she doing there?"

"Not hiding. She entered the country using her real name. My people spotted her. She went to see Gabriel McKnight."

Mina rubbed her temples. "The author? Why?"

"McKnight helped Noor Rahman find the cigarette case. The one you hid the map in when you were young." He waited for the words to sink in.

Mina gasped.

Cyrus nodded. He couldn't keep the pride out of his voice. "She wants to finish what we started."

She grabbed her mobile phone. "It's dangerous. Richter—"

He took the device from her. "Wait."

"No!" She reached for her cell. "I won't lose her. Not again."

Cyrus grabbed her shoulders. "We're going to find her and keep her safe."

The slight trembling of her lower lip made him ache. He loved this woman with every fiber of his being, but he wouldn't back down. Not this time. "We did it your way last time." When she tried to protest, he gently shook her. "We'll finish what we started. And this time, we'll succeed."

Topaz eyes searched his face. For the first time in decades, he glimpsed the real Mina. The one he'd known.

"We need to change the plan."

He bit back his smile. She used "we" instead of "I." That was a good sign. He loosened his grip on her arms. "Here's what I'm thinking."

CHAPTER TWELVE

Lovely and sweet, her name is Shirin....

—Nezami, *Khosrow and Shirin*

NOOR FLOATED ON undulating waves, body lethargic and eyelids heavy. This haven was peaceful, drawing her into its depth the way the Mediterranean did every time she visited. Mm, she sunk deeper into the blissful oblivion of cool sea waves.

Something jostled her, disrupting her calm. She ignored it. A second shake. Someone called her from far away. A thread of unease coursed through her. *Gabriel!*

Fear gave her another jolt. Someone had hurt Gabriel. Her eyelids fluttered open.

"Ah, you're awake." The man's baritone voice cut through her foggy mind.

She blinked several times, trying to bring her surroundings into focus. The room was dark. A beam of moonlight filtered in through a high window. Noor tried to move and realized she was tied to a chair. Panic set in. She struggled to free herself.

"Don't. The knots are tight. You'll hurt yourself," the man said.

She finally noticed the man. He, too, was tied to a chair. "W-who are you? Why are we here?" Her voice sounded like she had sand lodged in her throat.

He inched his chair closer to her. "Do you remember the book fair?"

The book fair? Yes. She'd run back inside after the explosion. "I went to find Gabriel. The security guard attacked me. He—" She paused, trying to recall what had happened. "He drugged me."

"Are you all right?" he asked, voice gentle.

"Yes. W-who are you?"

"I apologize for my bad manners. My name is Rafael Molina."

"Molina," she repeated. "The famous hotelier?"

He snorted. "I'm not certain about the famous part, but yes, I own a chain of hotels."

"I'm Noor Rahman. I have an author's advisory agency. We do everything from book editing to image development and PR." She didn't know why she was giving this man her professional pedigree. She cleared her throat. "It's the reason I was at the book fair."

"I know who you are, Ms. Rahman. I sat behind you at the Lesezelt."

She glanced around the dark room. Judging from the height of the windows and the musty odor, they were in a basement. "Why did they kidnap us?"

A door swung open before Rafael could answer. Two men lumbered down the steps into the basement.

One approached Noor and shone a flashlight on her face. "*Sie ist wach*," he growled at the other man in German. Noor's German wasn't great, but she understood. *She's awake.*

The other man leaned over Noor. His wide shoulders blocked her view of Rafael. The beam of his flashlight made her eyes water. "Now that you're awake, *fraulein*, we'll chat." His English came with a thick accent. "You will give me the location of the codes. Where are they?"

"I-I don't understand what you mean." Noor failed to keep the fear out of her voice.

The man slapped her.

Stars appeared behind her eyes. Her face throbbed with pain.

"Leave her alone!" Rafael snarled.

The second man punched Rafael in the stomach. He grunted.

The English-speaker bent closer to Noor and grabbed her hair. "If you don't answer, I'll cut your lover into pieces."

"I'm telling the truth." Noor's chest heaved. Her voice shook. "I don't have what you want. I don't even know what you're talking about."

He yanked Noor's head back and raised his fist.

Pain streaked through her skull and tears filled her eyes. She swallowed her cry of fear and remained silent.

"Let her go!" Rafael shouted.

He stomped over to Rafael, then shoved his chair so hard it toppled and crashed to the floor. The man leaned over, froze, then directed his light on Rafael's face. Recoiling, he shouted something in German to the other man. The other man shouted back.

The first man pulled a phone from his pocket, then tapped frantically. His attention bounced from the screen to Rafael to his partner. Another argument ensued, including the words "McKnight" and "Nürnberger." The two men left the basement, still arguing.

She waited until the door slammed behind them. "Rafael, are you all right?"

"Yes." He groaned. "They had me pushed up against the wall so I couldn't tip over." Rafael wiggled and banged his upper body on the floor. The chair finally broke. He continued wriggling until his hands were freed. "Give me a minute. I'll untie you."

Rafael soon removed her restraints. She rose and swayed. He gripped her by the waist. She took several calming breaths until the dizziness subsided.

"Better?" he asked.

"Yes."

"Good. Let's focus on getting out of here." He studied the room. "The windows are too high and small. Our only way out will be upstairs."

Voices on the other side of the door indicated the men approached.

"Stay here," Rafael whispered. He ran up the basement steps

to stand behind the door. As soon as the first man set foot on the staircase, Rafael pushed him.

He tumbled down to the floor and fell unconscious.

The basement lights blazed. The man with wide shoulders stalked Rafael midway down the stairs with a knife. He closed the distance, swinging the blade, and sneered. "I'll enjoy cutting you."

Noor was out of patience. She found a brick and waited for the men to reach the ground level. Rafael dodged the weapon. The attacker spun around and spotted her. She kicked him in the knee. He stumbled. It gave her an opening. She bashed him over the head with the brick. The attacker's leg buckled, and he fell to the ground.

Rafael nudged her. "Let's go."

She didn't need a second invitation. They bolted up the stairs, then locked the door behind them. The main hall was vacant. They creeped to the kitchen. Muted sounds of a man talking on the phone carried to them from another room. They tiptoed into the hall. The man spoke in rapid German. Noor's German was rusty, yet she understood "Gabriel McKnight" and signaled for Rafael to stop.

He squatted behind a cupboard and cupped his ear to listen to the conversation. After the man ended his call, Rafael tapped on her shoulder, then pointed in the direction of the kitchen.

She'd seen an exterior door there. It was their best chance.

They backtracked, then slunk outside into a meadow.

Rafael gripped her hand. "It won't be long before they find the men in the basement and come looking for us."

Together, they sprinted into the tall grass. A full moon lit their way.

Being a runner, Noor easily kept up with his rigorous pace. They stopped at the edge of a cliff with a small foot path carved around it. No safer option appeared. Rafael raked a hand through his hair. The gesture reminded her of Gabriel and sent a pang through her chest.

"They know we're gone by now. We can't go back. Going down the cliff is our only chance." His gaze went from the trail to her feet. "How comfortable are your boots?"

"Very. I can hike down, if that's what you're asking."

"Good. I'll go first," Rafael said. "Follow my footsteps."

The wind bit at her face, and her knit dress offered no protection against the cold. She gritted her teeth and followed Rafael. To call this a path was an overstatement. It was a narrow opening carved around the stone cliff. She turned sideways to inch along the craggy stones. The heels of her boots hung in mid-air.

Half-way down, her foot caught on a rock. She stumbled and was about to tip over the cliff when Rafael grabbed her, pushed her against the craggy wall, plastering his body against hers. Their combined hearts pounded so loud, it took her a while to hear what he was saying.

"Breathe, Noor. Breathe."

She took several calming breaths.

"That's it," Rafael said. "I'm going to move. The path's wider now. You'll need to turn around and inch down with me. Don't look down. Look ahead." He moved away from her and held his arm in front of her waist. "Turn slowly. Once you've got your balance, follow me."

She did as he said. They were both drenched in sweat when the path ended at a country road.

"Thank you," Noor murmured.

"For what?"

"Saving my life." She shivered. "I'm afraid of heights."

He confused her fear for cold and pulled off his sweater. "Here. Put this on."

She thanked him and pulled it on, knowing she'd need it as the adrenaline in her system ran out. "What now?"

"We follow the road until we find civilization."

She fell into step beside him. "I don't understand what those men wanted from us."

"Not us," Rafael said. "You. They confused me with your Gabriel and took the wrong man."

Noor's eyes widened. "We got away in time."

"Yes." He glanced at her. "Where did you learn to fight like that?"

"My uncle Morris taught me." Family made her think of Gabriel. God knew where he was. She hugged herself. "The men mentioned Gabriel."

Rafael nodded. "They want to use you as leverage to get a series of codes from him."

"What codes?" She threw her hands in the air. "None of this makes sense."

He shoved his hands into his pockets. "Actually, it does."

"How so?"

Rafael blew out a breath. "They kidnapped you for the same reason I came to the book fair. I wanted to speak with Mister McKnight about the same codes."

Bewildered, she stared at him.

"How much do you know about the Second World War?"

She blinked. "I'm not an expert, but I've read history."

"Then you know the Reichsleiter Rosenberg Task Force stole valuable artwork from countries the Nazis occupied during the war."

She nodded. "Yes, and some of it is still missing. What does that have to do with Gabriel?"

"Rosenberg made maps of major locations where the Nazis hid the looted artwork. The coordinates are in code. Rumor has it Gabriel has them."

The statement sounded so ridiculous, she laughed. "Why would Gabriel have the codes?"

"He helped you find the famous diamond several months ago," Rafael murmured. "Some say your father had a copy of the codes, and Gabriel found them when he helped you. Others say your father left you the location of the codes, and you told Gabriel."

Noor's heart sank. *The damn vault.* Rafael was watching her. She was grateful the night shielded her expression. "Gabriel helped me find the diamond, but he doesn't have the codes."

Rafael's voice softened. "Are you certain? Could he have found them and not mentioned it?" He paused. "Sometimes men—"

She didn't let him finish. "Not Gabriel. He's not like that."

He raised his hands in a gesture of surrender. "All right. Regardless, those men wanted to use you to get to him. They planned to kidnap both of you and hurt you to force him to surrender the codes. They had to reconsider when they realized I wasn't McKnight."

"How do you know this?"

"It's what the man on the phone said. He was talking to someone about contacting Gabriel to set up a meeting in Nuremberg where they would offer to exchange you for the codes."

"What were they going to do with you?" Noor asked.

"They planned to get rid of me," he said in a matter-of-fact tone.

"We must find a phone and warn Gabriel." She prayed Gabriel was all right.

"Problem is, we don't know where they'll meet," Rafael murmured, more to himself than Noor. "Nuremberg is a big city."

Noor gasped. "Nurnberger. The first man said Gabriel's name with Nürnberger and something else."

Rafael gripped her arm. "Was it Nürnberger Burg?"

"Yes."

"That's the Nuremberg Castle. It's the meeting place." Rafael massaged his neck. "Why do they want to meet at the castle?"

"Why were you looking for Gabriel?" Noor asked. "How are you connected to this?"

Rafael sighed. "Eduardo Molina is the only family I have. My great grandmother, Eduardo's grandmother, was Donna Maria Molina. Donna Maria married a wealthy Jewish Italian. The Nazis stormed into their home one night and took everything, including her husband. They also took a mantilla comb that had been in our family for six generations. The gems on the comb are priceless.

"Donna Maria was a beauty. A Nazi officer became infatuated with her. He told her the comb was packaged with a Rembrandt painting and sent to a secret location. He also said the Nazis shipped the coordinates for the location to a safe place in Iran. I was going to ask Gabriel for the codes so I can find Donna Maria's mantilla comb and restore it to our family."

"I see," she murmured.

"Look." Rafael pointed. Lights of a farmhouse glowed about a mile down the road.

Hope gave her a burst of energy. They ran to the farmhouse. Rafael knocked.

At first, no one answered. Then, a shuffling sound came from inside. An elderly gentleman opened the door.

Rafael spoke in fluent German.

The older man nodded and invited them to enter. The kitchen was clean and smelled of baked bread. A plump lady nodded at them from the kitchen counter.

Rafael bowed in an old courtly gesture and spoke to her. Whatever he said made her smile. She pulled out a basket.

Noor gripped Rafael's arm. "Will you ask them if I can use their phone?"

He asked the gentlemen, who pointed to a phone mounted on the kitchen wall.

She picked up the handset, then dialed Gabriel's number. It went straight to voicemail. What if someone had taken his phone? She tried again. Same result. Noor decided not to leave a message. The hotel wasn't safe either. Someone could listen to their call.

Harvey! She dialed his number. It also went to voicemail, but she felt safe leaving him a message. Sighing, she replaced the receiver, then went to sit at the table, where Rafael and the German gentleman were in deep discussion. A moment later, the older man left the kitchen.

"What did you tell him?"

"We're tourists whose car broke down several miles up the road. I offered to rent his vehicle and leave it for him in the next city. I also asked his wife to put some food together for us."

She patted the sweater's pocket. "I think those men took your wallet. There's nothing in your pocket, and I lost my purse in the explosion."

Rafael grinned. "I never carry a wallet. Life in the streets taught me that." He tucked his hand into the waistband of his trousers and pulled out a stack of euros. "My tailor places hidden pockets in my clothes. That's where I keep my money." He lay several bills on the kitchen table, while the lady filled the basket with baked bread, cheese, slices of ham, fruit, and a thermos of coffee.

The man came back with blankets and a set of keys. He handed them to Rafael, who gave him more money. Noor thanked the lady and took the basket. The couple led them to an old truck.

Rafael opened the passenger door and offered his hand.

"You're not driving." Noor plucked the keys from his hands, handed him the basket, then circled to the driver's door. "Don't ask if I can drive a stick shift."

He chuckled and climbed into the passenger seat. After thanking the old couple, they were on their way.

"We're two hours from Nuremberg," Rafael said. "Let's find a place to crash. We can rent a car first thing tomorrow and drive to the city."

She was silent for a long moment. "Why are you helping me? Gabriel and I don't have the codes."

"I have my reasons."

"Oh?" She raised her brows.

Rafael pursed his lips. "First, these people won't believe Gabriel doesn't have the codes. They'll hound him until he finds them. He'll need all the help he can get, and I have considerable influence. Once he finds the codes, I'll be one step closer to finding my family heirloom. It's a win-win situation."

"And second?" Noor asked.

His mouth curved into a smile. He didn't answer. Instead, he poured each of them a cup of coffee and pulled out the sandwiches. They ate in silence.

It wasn't long before they found a motel in a small town. Noor parked the truck.

"Stay in the car. I'll get us rooms," Rafael said.

"Okay." She waited in the car, wondering where Gabriel was. *Please God, let him be safe.*

Rafael tapped on the window, making her jump. "They only have one room available. I can sleep on the sofa."

She didn't have the energy to do anything but nod.

Rafael guided her up the staircase to a room with one bed. He glanced around and sighed. "This will have to do."

She stood in the middle of the room, clutching the basket. Exhaustion and fear finally caught up with her. Her eyes stung. She squeezed them. How were they going to get out of this mess?

Rafael tugged the basket out of her hand. "We'll find your Gabriel." He handed her a blanket from the closet and nudged her toward the bed. "Get some rest. We'll leave early."

Noor lay on the bed without taking her boots off. *I'm coming, Gabriel.*

CHAPTER THIRTEEN

Intent on finding Shirin, Khosrow rode fast, covering the distance to Armenia in half the time....

—Nezami, *Khosrow and Shirin*

G ABRIEL REACHED FOR the bottle of aspirin. "I emailed a friend and asked him to research the security company. He'll call if he finds anything useful."

Harvey frowned. "Where's your mobile phone?"

"It ran out of battery. I'm charging it." He rose to check it. The screen was still dark. It needed a minimum charge to light up. He rose and began pacing. "The security company has offices in Munich and a warehouse in Nuremberg. I'd say Nuremberg is our best bet."

The screen to his mobile phone lit. Gabriel glanced at it and noticed he had two miss calls from a foreign number.

Brandon paced at the other end of the suite, speaking to his police contact.

Gabriel wrote the numbers and a question on a pad, then took it to Brandon.

Can you ask your friend to trace the location of this number?

Brandon read the note, then spoke in rapid German. A few minutes later, he ended the call, then joined Gabriel. "The number's from Augsburg. It's about two hours away from Nuremberg and an hour away from Munich."

Gabriel clenched his fist. "If it wasn't Noor, it was the kidnappers." He opened his laptop to find Augsburg.

"If it was Noor, why didn't she call the hotel?" Harvey asked.

"She's careful. Someone could listen to my hotel calls." His phone rang, stopping the discussion. He answered with the speakerphone. "McKnight."

"We have something, or shall I say someone, you are searching for." The speaker had a heavy European accent.

"Where is Noor? I want to talk to her."

"The lady is fine. For now," the man answered. *"Come—alone—to Nuremberg Castle, Sinwell Tower, at 9:15 tomorrow morning. Bring the codes, and we will set Ms. Rahman free. If you contact the police, she will die. If you aren't alone, she will die."*

Gabriel forced himself to remain calm. "How do I know she's alive? Let me talk to her."

"Bring the codes." The caller hung up. Gabriel cursed.

Harvey checked his own phone and drew in a breath. "Someone left a message on my phone. I don't know the number."

Gabriel nodded for him to play it. He used the speaker.

"Harvey?" Noor's voice filled the room.

Gabriel's heart slammed against his ribcage, and a lump formed in his throat.

"I'm all right. Tell Gabriel I'll be at Nuremberg Castle tomorrow morning. He'll need help. Oh, and tell him the people who took me were armed. I got away, but they're close by."

"When did she call?" Gabriel asked.

Harvey checked his phone. "Two hours ago."

Brandon narrowed his eyes. "Gabriel just got the call from the kidnappers. Why would they call him if Noor escaped?"

Gabriel pulled the ice tray from the refrigerator. He wrapped the cubes in a towel, then held it at the back of his head. "They're desperate."

Harvey's brow furrowed. "What does that mean?"

"They don't know Noor contacted us," Gabriel explained, trying not to grimace from the pain. "They're gambling I'll be on my way to Nuremberg before she can reach me."

Harvey considered his answer. "If that's the case, why did Noor say she was coming to Nuremberg? All she had to do was make it back to the hotel or tell us where to pick her up."

An invisible fist squeezed Gabriel's heart. "Noor knows I'm the target. She's protecting me." He sighed. "I have to get to her before the kidnappers do."

Harvey held up his phone up. "Now we know what the note meant by 'tower.' This is Sinwell Tower, and it's—"

"The tower in the file sent to Gabriel," Brandon finished, leaning forward to study the image. "I'll rent a car. We'll drive together."

Gabriel shook his head. "I don't want to raise the kidnappers' suspicion. I'll go in a separate car." He continued before Brandon could protest. "I'll need you close by while I search for Noor."

The response satisfied Brandon. "What about the codes? What will you tell the kidnappers?"

"I need to think it through." Gabriel glanced at his watch. "It's past midnight." He picked up the phone, then dialed reception. After a brief discussion, he ended the call and handed a note to Brandon. "I got a room for you. It's down the hall. The bell boy will bring up your key. Get some rest. We'll head out early."

"I'm coming too," Harvey announced.

"No, Harv. I need your help with the Nezami angle."

Harvey shook his head. "I'll ride with Brandon and bring my laptop. I can research Nezami from the car."

"Fine."

"What about you?" Brandon asked. "Don't you need to rest?"

"I'll go to bed soon."

After Harvey and Brandon left, Gabriel retrieved the book of Rumi's poems from Noor's nightstand. Last summer, when he and Noor were chasing a killer, they'd found a clue General Rahman had left for his wife. Gabriel never understood why Noor's father wrote the clue, which was a short line of codes, on a large sheet of paper. He began studying it. "It's now or never."

He went down to the hotel's pharmacy and bought a bottle of liquid iodine. Iodine revealed most types of invisible ink. It also had a pungent odor. He opened the kitchen window, turned on the stove, then poured the liquid into a pot. As soon as the vapors rose, he held the piece of paper over it.

Dark lines and scribbles appeared at the middle of the sheet. He turned off the burner and studied the writing.

Key: a=0, b=1, c=2, d=3, e=4, f=5, g=6, h=7, i=9, L=00, t-01, O=02, U=03 N=04
0-ab, 1=ac, 2=ad, 3=ae, 4=af, 5=ag, 6=ah, 7=ai, 8=aj, 9=ak, .=al

"Shit!"

CHAPTER FOURTEEN

Khosrow was determined....

—Nezami, *Khosrow and Shirin*

GABRIEL PACED AS the implications hit him. He took several pictures of the code, then placed the sheet of paper in a hidden compartment in the spine of Noor's book. Sipping coffee, he studied an online map of the castle and its town. The sun was rising when he lay down for a nap.

An hour later, the trio set out in two cars. They arrived in Nuremberg before the castle opened. After parking their cars in a public lot, they walked to the Old Town, where the castle was situated.

Gabriel looked around. "We separate here."

Harvey nodded. "I'll be at the café across the main square."

Brandon had dressed like a tourist. As they approached the walled area, he pulled his ball cap lower and stepped through the gates, blending in with a group on a walking tour. He wore earphones in case Gabriel called.

Gabriel had also disguised his appearance with a bulky sweater, sunglasses, and a ball cap. Old Town gave him the impression of stepping through time. He found himself in a medieval square with a relaxing atmosphere. Historical buildings and museums sat in a maze of cobblestone streets. A river ran through the center of the town, and vendors were setting up in the market courtyard. The castle loomed ahead. It was the type of place he and Noor loved to explore.

He took a wide cobblestone path to the medieval fortress sitting on a sandstone ridge and followed it to the castle's main entrance, known as the Heavenly Gate. The castle itself was a series of medieval buildings. Sinwell Tower was a tall, cylindrical tower with a viewing platform at the top. He'd read it had two entry points. One was in use.

Gabriel glanced at his watch. They had another hour before the meeting. He took his time exploring the bailey, exit, and entry points. One path led back to Old Town's main café. He chose a corner table inside and watched the castle entrance.

At the top of the hour, nine men built like bouncers gathered outside the Heavenly Gate. They separated into three groups of three. The first trio took the main path up to the castle. The second lingered in the courtyard. The third, wearing uniforms of the security company, took a back road to the castle.

Gabriel dialed Brandon. "Men wearing security guard uniforms are coming your way. Keep a safe distance from them." After ending the call, he went to the bathroom to discard his dark sweater and glasses, then he headed toward the town square and made a show of walking around.

In his peripheral vision, he spotted three men following him into the courtyard. Ten minutes to go, and there was no sign of Noor. He wanted to warn her away from the square. One man separated himself from the group and called someone. The other two continued tailing Gabriel. They were either amateurs or very confident.

Five minutes passed. He was about to check the storefronts on the other side of the main square when a man bumped into him. "Ah. Pardon, *señor*." The man waved a map. "Can you show me which road leads up to the castle?" He pointed to his map and lowered his voice. "I came with Noor. There are two people following you and a third somewhere in the square. They're all armed."

Gabriel maintained a casual stance and glanced at the map. "Where's Noor?"

"She's in an alley on your right behind the café."

The two guards trailing Gabriel moved closer. "Tell her to go to the café by the train station. Our friend Harvey will drive her to the hotel." Gabriel turned and in the reflection of a shop window saw one of the two men pull out his gun. "Go, now! They're coming!"

ZITA STOOD AT the edge of the wide footpath, pretending to take pictures of Old Town. She had followed McKnight to Nuremberg, hoping he would find the clue she'd given him. If he didn't, she planned to help.

She zoomed her camera on the town's square and froze. Gabriel McKnight strolled through the main square. Two groups of men surrounded him. The first unit looked like a team from the wrestlers' club. They split to surround the castle entrance and courtyard. The second team made her blood run cold. Richter's number two, Erik, arrived with a group of six men. Erik brought death everywhere.

Her throat dried. The impulse to run was strong. *Stay where you are. They won't recognize you.* She glanced down at her nondescript leggings, bulky second-hand sweater, and boots. She looked nothing like Richter's fashion-savvy ward.

Through her camera's viewfinder, Zita spotted McKnight talking to a tourist. He grinned and pointed at the castle. The tourist nodded and moved away. Two men from the first group moved closer to McKnight. Didn't the man have military training? How was he oblivious to encroaching danger?

Erik's men branched out. They spotted the first group of men and followed them. McKnight stood at the center of the courtyard like a sitting duck. He turned his head slightly. If she wasn't holding a zoom lens, Zita would've missed the look that passed over his face. She followed the direction of his gaze and spotted Noor Rahman standing behind a tall sign beside an alley café. So, McKnight wasn't clueless. He was protecting his woman.

She turned her camera back to him. His body had gone from relaxed to alert. He moved away from the square. The first group of men followed him. Erik's men followed them. *What the hell's going on?* She turned her camera to Noor, who entered the courtyard in a bright sweater.

Zita zoomed back on McKnight. He was on a footpath. The men behind him rushed to catch up. Erik motioned to his men. Half of them followed Erik up the path. The other half took the second entrance to the castle. A flock of tourists around her talked about a tour of Sinwell Tower. Below her, McKnight strode to the castle. Noor pushed through the crowd, following him.

The air around Zita thickened. Sweat trickled down her back, and she heard nothing but her own heartbeat.

McKnight paused for a moment, as if he too sensed the danger. Shots rang out and hell broke loose.

CHAPTER FIFTEEN

*An embarrassed Shirin rose from the emerald pool. She dwelled
on the handsome stranger while quickly dressing. He resembled the
portrait of Khosrow, but it wasn't him. The stranger wore merchants'
clothes. She continued with her journey regardless of her misgivings.*
—Nezami, *Khosrow and Shirin*

NOOR PRETENDED TO read a menu outside of the Old
Town café. Where was Gabriel? She knew he could make
himself invisible. She'd seen him in action when they were
evading a killer last summer.

She skimmed the crowd. Gabriel appeared out of thin air. In
a pale blue sweater and dark jeans, he strolled through the maze
of stands to shop for baubles. He might as well have carried a sign
with his name on it.

Rafael narrowed his eyes. "What's he doing?"

"He's making sure the kidnappers see him." She bit her lip. "He
looks tired."

"Speaking of the devil," Rafael murmured. "Our friends from
last just night arrived."

The two men who had held them captive arrived with several

others. They split up, some heading to the back of the castle. Three men took the path to the main entrance, and two followed Gabriel.

"Whoa." Rafael squinted. "Who are the other guys?"

"What other guys?"

He tilted his head in the square's direction. "Look behind the men following Gabriel. Group two looks scarier."

"I have to warn him." She jerked away from the sign.

Rafael grabbed her arm. "Are you kidding? You won't help McKnight by waltzing in there."

She pulled away. "I can't stand by and watch him get hurt. I'm going."

"Wait." Rafael glanced back to make sure they weren't heard. "Stay here. I'll go." He strolled through the main square and approached Gabriel, waving a map. Gabriel nodded and tilted his head in her direction. He meant to let her know he got her message.

Rafael walked away. Like other tourists, he took the path around the main square.

The two men behind Gabriel drew closer. Gabriel's body language changed. His shoulders tightened, and he moved away from the square. Both groups followed him as he led them away from Noor. How like him to think of her when his own life was in danger.

The goons who questioned her last night approached him from the footpath on the other side of the square.

Oh, no! Noor patted her pocket and found the cash Rafael had given her. A small shop across the alley displayed trinkets and clothing. She purchased a set of firecrackers, then entered the courtyard. A vendor's cart sat to her right. In went the firecrackers.

Gabriel paused as if sensing her. The men behind him spotted the other group of men. They stopped and studied the others warily. A group of tourists posed by the square to take a photo, and farther off, a man went down on one knee to propose to his girlfriend. The air thickened with tension.

Sweat beaded on her brow. She began her internal countdown. *Five, four, three....*

Cheers went up from surrounding tourists as the girl accepted the proposal.

Bang!

Noor flinched. That wasn't her firecrackers. One man following Gabriel clutched his side and fell. His partners shot back. The other group returned fire.

Gabriel ducked. The girl who had accepted the proposal screamed and bumped into a vendor, turning over his cart. Screams of terror pierced the crisp air, while people ran in various directions. Several fell to the ground covered in blood.

Pop! A man in group two took out another in the first group.

Noor sprinted in search of Gabriel. Blood pooled down the cobblestone. She jumped over a body, then paused where two paths crossed. Where to go?

Someone yanked her back, then dragged her toward a cluster of trees. She kicked and fought, but her assailant was stronger.

"Easy," he crooned in her ear.

Gabriel! With a sob, she hurtled herself into his arms.

GABRIEL HELD HER tight. Her heart pounded fast against his. Grateful his world was right again, he cupped her face. A bruise marred her cheek, her hands were streaked with dirt, and the green dress that peaked out from under the god-awful sweater had tears in it.

She never looked more beautiful.

He was going to ask if she was all right, if they'd hurt her. Instead, he pressed his lips to hers.

Noor returned the kiss with fervor then, reading his mind, whispered, "One man slapped me. That's all."

Thank God. He blinked back the sting in his eyes and leaned his forehead against hers. A hundred ugly scenarios had plagued and tortured him since the explosion at the book fair. He brushed his lips over the bruise on her cheek and rocked her in his arms.

The squeal of sirens brought him back to the present. He gripped her hand, shielding her with his body as he guided to where Brandon waited.

Nuremberg Castle was comprised of three complexes. Gabriel pushed through the mass of tourists fleeing the grounds and veered toward the pentagonal tower, one of the oldest structures in the cluster of medieval buildings. Two men came from the other direction.

Noor gasped. "Those are the men who kidnapped me. They want—"

"I know." He pulled her behind a wall. A bullet pinged off the brick. Two more followed. "Do you see the tall tower with a viewing platform? That's Sinwell Tower. A friend is waiting there for us. He's wearing a red sweatshirt with a matching ball cap. Find him and get to safety. I'll join you as soon as I take care of these guys."

She shook her head.

He squeezed her hand. "Trust me."

Noor hesitated and bit her lip.

He didn't wait for her to decide and hurried in the direction of the imperial stables. The two men pursued him. From the corner of his eye, he saw Noor sprint to Sinwell Tower.

Gabriel took the route around the stone wall. He ducked behind a large sign pointing to Walburgis Chapel, crouched, then waited. When a man ran toward him, Gabriel tripped him. The man toppled to the ground, cursed, then climbed to his feet.

Splat! A bullet hit the sign beside him. He sprinted to the Sinwell Tower, praying Noor made it there safely. *Splat!* Another bullet hit the stone wall beside him. Gabriel ducked behind the closest structure. In his peripheral vision, he saw a beefy man chase Brandon and Noor into the tower.

Brandon confronted him but didn't have fight training. Beefy knocked him down and went after Noor.

Shit! Gabriel sprinted to the tower, then locked the door behind him. Heart racing, he climbed the wooden staircase. Being a runner and in excellent shape, Gabriel was winded by the time he reached the top. Then, his heart stopped.

Noor stood, hands in the air.

A man held a gun on her. Sweat poured down his angular face and through his shirt onto bulging muscles. He panted loudly, telling Gabriel he was more of a gym rat than an athlete.

Gym Rat sneered at Gabriel. "Give me the codes, or I kill her."

Gabriel slowly approached them, hands raised. "Let her go. I brought what you want."

Noor's eyes widened.

"Let her go." Gabriel stepped between Noor and the gunman.

"Go to the platform," Gym Rat snapped.

Gabriel stepped toward the viewing platform, still shielding Noor's body with his body.

Gym Rat stood with his back to the staircase. "I want the codes."

"They're right here." Gabriel reached into his pocket, stalling for time, thinking of how to get Noor to safety. "Here they are." He waved the sheet in front of the man. "Let her go, and it's yours."

Gym Rat used his free hand to wipe the sweat off his face. "I'll decide who lives." He moved closer to them. Gabriel tensed, preparing to take the bullet and give Noor time to escape.

Thud!

Gym Rat blinked, then sank to the floor. Behind him stood the girl from the book fair wielding a large club. Her whiskey-colored eyes darted from the fallen man to Gabriel to Noor. She dropped her weapon, then ran down the stairs.

Gabriel's priority was Noor. He pulled her against him. "Are you all right?" He couldn't stop the tremor in his voice.

She nodded and held him tight. Neither moved for several seconds, then Noor took a deep breath and tipped up her face. "Y-you had the codes?"

He stuffed the note back in his pocket. "These aren't the actual codes." He reached for her hand. "Let's go."

"How long have you had the codes?"

Gabriel moved toward the stairwell.

She pulled him to a stop. "How long have you had the codes?"

Surprised, he turned around. "I found them last night, and aside from you and me, no one knows. Why are you worried?"

She bit her lip.

Was that... *doubt?* Did she doubt him? How could she?

"It's just that Rafael said—"

A knot formed in Gabriel's chest. "Rafael? The guy in the square?"

She nodded.

"Who is he?"

"His name is Rafael Molina. He owns hotels."

Gabriel raised an eyebrow. "Why was he with you?"

She shifted. "The kidnappers mistook him for you. Once they realized who he was, they contacted you."

"Christ." Gabriel raked a hand through his hair. He searched her face for a long moment. "You know I wouldn't lie to you."

Tears clouded her eyes. She wrapped her arms around his waist. "Of course I know."

The knot in his chest loosened, and he held her close. She'd been through an ordeal. He kissed her temple. "Are you ready to leave?"

"Yes."

He brushed his lips over her hair. "Let's check on Brandon."

"Okay."

He took her hand, then froze.

"Gabriel, what's wrong?"

To his left, on the viewing platform's stone wall, an owl was carved into one of the larger stones. He remembered the girl's note. "The girl was right."

CHAPTER SIXTEEN

For his part, Khosrow behaved honorably and
continued with his journey.

—Nezami, *Khosrow and Shirin*

GABRIEL RUBBED HIS jaw. "The girl's note said, 'Beyond the Heavenly Gates and in the tower, you will find knowledge and power.' The Heavenly Gates are the castle's main entrance." He pointed at the small carving. "An owl. They symbolize knowledge."

"Yes."

He studied the carving etched into the wall. Someone had carved the symbol of a hammer into the stone across from it.

Noor joined him. "That's the symbol of Thunar—Thor. It represents power and fertility."

"These signs face each other at opposite sides of a platform." Standing between both carvings at the middle of the viewing platform, he spotted a carving of a tree. "What do oak trees symbolize?"

"Literature claims they contain magical power," Noor said. "What girl? And why is this important?"

He smiled. "We've got some catching up to do." He went to the carved tree, then tapped on the stone. Hollow. He tried to pry it loose, but it wouldn't budge. The note said knowledge and power led to the tree.

The tree? Could it be that simple?

The word tree had four letters in it. There were four stones surrounding the carving. He tapped each until he found another hollow one. When he pried that stone free, he found a lever. When he pulled it, the tree stone swung open. Gabriel retrieved a wooden cylinder from inside.

Footsteps sounded in the stairwell.

He tucked the cylinder under his sweater, then pushed the stones back into place. "Let's keep this between us for now." He pulled Noor to his side as Brandon burst onto the platform.

His right eye was bruising, and blood trickled from the corner of his mouth. He glanced at Gym Rat, still lying unconscious, and shook his head. "You're all right?"

Gabriel nodded and motioned to Brandon's face. "You?"

He shrugged. "I've had worse. Come on. It's crazy out there."

The trio headed down the stairwell.

Outside, police officers guided people out of the castle.

Gabriel took Noor's hand. "Be careful. The kidnappers could be anywhere."

They followed a group of tourists down the cobblestone paths. Noor stopped to search the crowd.

"What's wrong?" Gabriel asked.

"We need to find Rafael."

"Who is Rafael?" Brandon asked.

"A friend," Noor murmured. Her face lit up, and she waved. "Rafael! We're here."

Gabriel studied the man approaching them. Without the sweatshirt and disguise, he was Gabriel's height, with strong Mediterranean features and a five o'clock shadow. Noor's friend was handsome.

She hugged him. "Thank God, you're all right."

Shit. He forced himself to stay where he was when all he wanted to do was yank Noor away from the man.

Rafael held Noor for a moment. "You promised to stay in the café. What happened?"

She beamed and took Gabriel's hand. "I caught up with Gabriel."

Rafael shook his head. He shifted and grinned at Gabriel. "It's nice to meet you again."

Gabriel reminded himself to be polite. The man had helped Noor, after all. "Thank you for helping Noor."

"We helped each other," Rafael said.

Noor tapped on his hand, trying to get his attention. Gabriel realized he was gripping her hand too tight and loosened his hold. He pulled her closer. "Stay alert. The people who took you could be anywhere."

A police officer told them to follow the tourists back to the main square. They fell in line.

Brandon massaged his neck. "Cops have lined up around the town's exits. They're interviewing everyone before they leave. Do you want to talk to the police now?"

"No. I'd rather get out of here," Gabriel said. "I'll call the IN-TERPOL detectives once we're back in Frankfurt."

"INTERPOL?" Noor raised her brows.

Gabriel nodded. "We'll talk on our drive back to the city."

They arrived at the main square where the police set up barricades and divided the crowd into two lines. Gabriel kept a hold on her hand. "Noor and I will take the first line. You take the other. We'll meet at the café where Harvey is waiting."

News vans surrounded Old Town. A crowd had gathered. They found Rafael and Brandon by a stoplight.

Rafael pursed his lips. "I didn't see any of the kidnappers. The—" He paused and furrowed his brows. "Look across the street behind the police car. There's a man in a dark jacket. He was following you back at the castle. Do you know him?"

Gabriel shifted. A tall, muscular man in jeans and a jacket was talking to a woman whose back faced them. He rubbed his chin. "I don't know the man, but I've met the woman. She's a detective with INTERPOL. He's probably her colleague."

"No, he isn't." Brandon clenched his fists. "That's Erik Drussel, Farid Richter's henchman. He's a killer." He pushed away from the group.

Both Rafael and Gabriel blocked his path.

Rafael gripped his arm. "What are you doing?"

"Don't draw attention to us," Gabriel cautioned.

"He killed my friend." The vein in Brandon's neck stood out as he struggled to free himself.

"If you want justice for your friend, you need to set emotions aside and use logic."

Noor touched Brandon's shoulder. "I understand your hurt and anger, but Gabriel's right. Please listen to him."

Brandon's jaw worked for several seconds. He blew out a breath, and his shoulders slumped. "Fine."

Gabriel stepped back. "This is the same INTERPOL detective who warned me against Richter."

"You know what this means, don't you?" Brandon said.

"Right now, getting Noor to safety is my top priority," Gabriel answered. "My car is in the lot behind the train station. Find Harvey and get to the hotel. Noor and I will meet you there."

"Your hotel won't be safe," Rafael said. "I own independent establishments aside from my hotel chains. Allow me to offer you rooms at the Villa Margarite. I can guarantee security there."

THE KILLER BIT into a sandwich and watched Gabriel McKnight and his woman climb into their car. Following McKnight had been an interesting excursion. Slayer had intended to rattle McKnight, but the scene in the square was as captivating as one of Nezami's poems—a gallant Spaniard risking his life for the lovely maiden. The brave and beautiful heroine searching for her lover. Then, there was McKnight, the knight in shining armor, surrounded by Richter's men and the Hungarians. Add to that the detective from INTERPOL, and it was the perfect drama.

Excellent at improvisation, Slayer fired the first shot and shifted the stakes.

McKnight was a key character in the killer's own drama. He had tasks to accomplish before dying, and die the man would. Smirking, Slayer threw the remains of the sandwich into a trashcan, then crossed the street to catch the train to Frankfurt. Timing was crucial in any story.

CHAPTER SEVENTEEN

What is this magic? Shirin thought gazing at Khosrow's portrait.
—Nezami, *Khosrow and Shirin*

GABRIEL GLANCED AT Noor and frowned. "Are you all right?"
She bit her lip. "Why would my father keep the codes in the vault and not hand them over to the international authorities?"

He clasped her hand. "His job was the keep the vault's contents safe."

"We'll never know." She gripped his hand in both of hers. "The girl intrigues me. She's the one who clubbed the guy in the head back in Nuremberg, correct?"

Gabriel nodded.

"Who is she?"

"I think she's related to Mina von Mayer. There's a connection between the von Mayers and your father."

"How do we find her? Can we trust her if we do?"

"That's the million-dollar question." He raised her palm to his lips. "Speaking of trust, are you certain you want to go to Molina's hotel?"

She furrowed her brows. "Why wouldn't we? Rafael says it's safe."

"Do you trust Rafael?"

Her brows rose. "Do you trust that reporter, Brandon?"

Gabriel sighed. "Brandon's interests align with ours. Helping us will help him find justice for his friend. We can trust him for now."

"We can trust Rafael for the same reasons."

He trusted Noor's judgement, yet it bothered Gabriel she didn't elaborate. "What's Molina's skin in the game?"

She stared out the window for a long moment. "The Nazis took an heirloom from his great grandmother. It's important to him, but it's more than that." She paused, as if searching for the right words. "He has old-world values hidden under his successful entrepreneur facade. He's honorable."

"I see," Gabriel murmured. *How much does she like him?* Her face was turned away from him, so he couldn't see what she was thinking.

Frankfurt's south bank wound around the river. They followed it to a sideroad, then Villa Margarite came into sight. It's colonnaded architecture and vast gardens reminded him of a private mansion.

A friendly doorman ushered them into the lobby. The main floor was a blend of gold and white marble, wide archways, and columns.

A receptionist approached them. "Ms. Rahman and Mister McKnight?"

"Yes," Noor said.

"My name is Ingrid. I'll show you to your suite."

They followed her across a cobblestoned courtyard lit with mini lanterns. Large flowerpots and ferns created an atmosphere of privacy. They stopped at a small alcove.

"This entrance is private. You'll have a special key to work the elevator. Your suite is in the western wing."

The elevator opened into a long corridor. Scents of fresh pinecones and wood polish accompanied them to the end of the hallway.

"Here we are." She opened the door to reveal a spacious suite with plush grey and white couches. "The master bedroom is on the right. The bathroom is equipped with a Jacuzzi. On your left is the kitchen and dining area. Mister Molina said your luggage will arrive shortly. In the meantime, I placed some essentials in the closet for you. They're from the hotel boutique. I hope you like the room."

"It's lovely," Noor murmured.

Ingrid handed Gabriel two key cards. "There's a private dining room at the other end of the corridor on your left. Mister Molina asked that you meet him there for dinner at seven."

Gabriel thanked her, then locked the door.

Noor sank onto the sofa. Her face was pale, her pupils large.

He stroked her cheek. "You need to rest."

She leaned into his caress. "I need to bathe."

He carried her to the shower. The adrenaline they'd both been riding on was running out fast. Noor had barely toweled herself dry when Gabriel carried her back to the bed and dropped onto the mattress beside her. They fell asleep as soon as he pulled the covers over them.

He woke an hour later, brewed a cup of herbal tea in the kitchen, then pulled out the cylinder. It took a while to pry open its lid. A piece of paper fell out. Time had turned the page a dull grey. He gently unrolled it on the dining table. A series of numbers and letters covered the front.

00-02-04-6-9-01-03-3-4=ak-.ai-af-ak-ah-af-ah

He pulled up the photo he'd taken of the key codes. Deciphering the writing on the parchment didn't take long. It was a series of numbers with a decimal after the first two. 10.749646.

"What are you doing?" Noor stood in the doorway, cinching the belt on her bathrobe. Her face had regained some of its color.

He kissed her, then poured her a cup of herbal tea.

She sat beside him at the table. "What was in the cylinder?"

"A piece of paper with numbers and codes. I used the map key to decipher the message. If I'm reading it right, they're coordinates."

She drew in a breath. "Could they be the coordinates to the stolen artwork?"

"That would be too easy. Plus, I don't want to assume anything." He rubbed the back of his neck. "I wanted us to talk first because your family is connected to this. If you're uncomfortable sharing information with Brandon and Rafael, we'll find answers on our own. Harvey will help. If not, we'll enlist the others to help too. It's your choice." He waited for her to decide.

"Thank you." She raised her cup to her lips. "I trust Harvey and Rafael. It's the reporter I'm not comfortable with."

Gabriel blinked. When had the Spaniard gotten so close? When he saved her life. *Does she care for him?* Something ugly clawed through Gabriel's chest. Unwilling to examine it, he pushed it back. "I understand."

She sighed and set her teacup down. "You believe Brandon is trustworthy."

"What I think doesn't matter." He cringed at ice in his tone. What the hell was wrong with him?

Noor tugged on his arm. "I'll talk to Brandon and ask him to keep my family off the record." She moved to sit on his lap and lay her head on his shoulder. "It's all surreal and unsettling."

He wrapped his arms around her. "I know, sweetheart." She snuggled closer to him. He brushed several kisses behind her ear. "Mina von Mayer is at the center of this. I searched the internet and found a few pictures of her at charity events. Richter was in some of the photos." His next revelation about Morris's half-brother would surely get her attention. "As was Cyrus Rohan."

She raised her head. "Uncle Morrie's involved in this?"

"There's only one way to find out." He grabbed his mobile phone and dialed a number.

"Who are you calling?"

"Billy. If anyone can dig into someone's past, it's him."

Billy Mason was Gabriel's former SEAL teammate and friend. Billy answered on the second ring. *"You using the chip?"* he barked in lieu of a greeting.

Gabriel refrained from rolling his eyes. "Yes. Are you going to ask me the same question every time I call this line?"

"Probably. What's up?"

"I'm fine, thanks. How are you?"

Billy chuckled. *"If you wanted small talk, you should've called my main line."*

"I need your help."

He grunted.

Gabriel grinned. Billy was brilliant with technology. He also had a mile-wide paranoid streak. In his mind, the less said during any phone call, the better. Hence the economy of words. "I need to know if Mina von Mayer has relatives she's hidden from the public. Specifically, a young girl anywhere from seventeen to her early twenties."

"Got it. Later." The line went dead.

"What did he say?" Noor asked.

Gabriel chuckled. "He's on it." Shaking his head, he put away his phone and glanced at the clock. Why was he sitting in the living room when he should be making love to Noor?

Because Noor has grown fond of Molina. He's decent, and he doesn't have death looming over him like you do. Gabriel ignored his inner voice and rose to change.

CHAPTER EIGHTEEN

The ingenious painter devised a plan.

—Nezami, *Khosrow and Shirin*

G ABRIEL AND NOOR arrived at the dining room. This part of the hotel resembled a medieval castle. Two knights with polished armor flanked the entrance.

Noor brushed a fingertip along the shield of one knight. "I always wanted one of these for my office."

The space was better described as a library suitable for dining. Floor to ceiling bookshelves occupied one side of the room. The other side boasted a large dining table and bar. At the center, leather armchairs with reading lamps clustered around a massive fireplace.

Rafael, Brandon, and Harvey sipped drinks by the bar. Brandon's face sported a rainbow of colors from the bruising.

Rafael came forward to greet them.

Noor embraced him.

He held her a little too long. "Are you settled?"

She beamed. "Yes, and thank you for the clothes."

"I'm glad you liked them." Rafael greeted Gabriel with a handshake.

"I'll stop at the boutique tomorrow and pay for everything," Gabriel said.

Rafael waved away the offer. "There's no need. Would you like a drink?"

Gabriel tried not to sound irritated. "Scotch, please."

Rafael circled the bar to pour their drinks. "May I suggest we postpone business discussions to after dinner? I'm told Maurice, our chef, has worked his magic." As if on cue, servers brought in platters of exotic food and aromatic fresh bread.

They enjoyed the meal in silence. Afterward, they relaxed by the fire, its warmth filling the room as the staff served tea, digestives, and cakes.

Once they were alone, Gabriel said, "Noor and I discussed our options. Either we figure this out ourselves or work with a team we trust. We chose the second option."

The smiles confirmed they'd made the right choice.

"I'd like to set some ground rules for everyone's safety. First, don't share anything we discuss outside this group, unless you clear it with me."

Harvey, Brandon, and Rafael nodded their acquiescence.

"Second, don't chase information on your own. We plan as a group and stick to our plan. That's how we stay alive," Gabriel said.

Rafael raised his coffee cup. "Agreed."

Gabriel let out a breath. "We're all connected to this puzzle. I'll lay out some facts. Each of you can add your information, then we'll try to piece this puzzle together." He glanced at Noor.

She winked her acquiescence.

"This started when the first Pahlavi King of Iran, Reza Shah, commissioned a secret vault to be built in Tehran's Central Bank at the start of World War II. With Iran's strong ties to Germany, the king commissioned a German engineer to design and build the vault.

"The Reichsleiter Rosenberg Task Force was a Nazi organization that looted art from occupied countries during the war. Their goal was to display the stolen works in a museum in Hitler's hometown, positioning Braunau, Austria, as Europe's cultural hub. While the museum was under construction, the Nazis hid the art in secret locations. As head of the task force, Rosenberg wrote the coordinates of each location in code and hid them."

He glanced at Brandon. "Do you want to fill in the next piece?"

"Sure." Brandon swirled his cognac. "The German engineer documented his three-year stay in Tehran. When the vault was complete, Rosenberg gave him the codes for his favorite location, which hid a painting by Rembrandt. He told the engineer to take the codes to the Persian king and ask him to hide them in the secret vault until further notice."

Rafael's eyes gleamed. "How do you know this?"

Brandon produced a velvet pouch from behind him. "I have the engineer's journal."

"May I see it?" Rafael asked.

Brandon handed it and a pair of cotton gloves to Rafael. "It's in German."

"I can get by." Rafael flipped through the journal.

Gabriel continued. "Someone set off a fake bomb at the Frankfurt Book Fair to create chaos. During said chaos, someone attacked me, and a group posing as security kidnapped Noor." He homed in on Rafael. "Why were you at the fair?"

"The Nazis took a valuable family heirloom from my great-grandmother," Rafael said. "A soldier told her it was shipped with a Rembrandt painting. My family has searched for it ever since. A week ago, an informant who worked for Farid Richter told me you have the coordinates to the artwork's location. I came to the book fair to speak with you." He added more logs to the fire. "Richter is no saint. Word is people who cross him either disappear or die."

"That's what the INTERPOL detective warned me about." Gabriel recounted his experience at the German police station.

"I don't understand." Noor scooped up another piece of cake. "Why was the detective talking to Richter's henchmen if she'd warned you off Richter?"

"She's a dirty cop," Brandon growled.

"Speaking of the police." Gabriel glanced at his watch. "I must inform them you're back and safe."

Brandon clenched his fists. "Be careful."

Gabriel massaged the back of his neck. "Noor and I had an encounter with Detective Hood a few months ago. She's a good cop. I'll call her tomorrow."

"Let's not forget there were two different groups following Gabriel back in Nuremberg," Rafael said. "One group came with Richter's man—the one who knows the INTERPOL detective. The others were our abductors."

"Did the kidnappers speak fluent German? Were they locals?" Gabriel asked.

"Hm." Rafael shoved his hands into his pockets. "Come to think of it, no. They had a slight accent, maybe eastern European."

"Let's catalog that for now and move onto the next fact," Gabriel said. "A girl at the book fair warned me I was in danger. She said I had the key to the map, and they would come after me."

Noor leaned her head on his shoulder. "We saw her in Nuremberg." She recounted how the girl had clubbed Gym Rat in the Sinwell Tower.

Brandon touched his swollen cheek. "I must have been out for a while. I didn't see her."

Gabriel pulled out a USB drive. "We come to the third fact. Do you have a laptop on hand?"

"Yes." Rafael reached into a desk drawer for a laptop.

They all gathered around the computer, while Gabriel showed them the three articles. He pointed to the photo of Mina von Mayer in Lucerne. "The girl from the book fair is a younger version of Mina von Mayer."

Rafael leaned forward to study the picture. "Mina von Mayer doesn't dabble in the illegal underworld. I would've heard if she did. Is her father the reason she's connected to this?"

"That's what the article claims." Gabriel sighed. "I don't know if it's true. Noor's uncles are in that picture, and they're both successful businessmen."

Brandon paused mid-stride. "Really? I've never heard of them."

Noor placed a hand on Brandon's arm. "That's because they want to remain inconspicuous." She shared a look with Gabriel. "Anything I share regarding my family is off the record, okay?"

"Of course. Whatever you tell me will stay here." Brandon pointed to his head.

She smiled. "Thank you."

Gabriel strode to the fireplace. "Mina von Mayer and Farid Richter are a common thread. We know Richter has illegal dealings. We know little about von Mayer except what the article says about her father."

"I'll call Uncle Morrie," Noor said.

"He won't be forthcoming." Gabriel squeezed her shoulder. "He'll withhold any information that could put you in danger."

She threw her hands in the air. "We're already in danger."

He kissed her forehead, turned back to the group, then told them about the girl's note, the cylinder he found in Nuremberg, and the numbers he deciphered.

Rafael whistled. "Why hide the coordinates in Nuremberg?"

The fire's warmth flickered over Gabriel's back. "Nuremberg was a logical hiding place, given its importance to the Nazis. It's no surprise Rosenberg hid the parchment there. The problem is, we don't know what the numbers are."

Brandon scribbled more notes. "Is there anything else?"

"You forgot Nezami," Harvey said.

Gabriel showed Noor a photo. "Harvey researched the poem. It's from *Khosrow and Shirin*."

Brandon flipped through the journal. "The engineer said the king placed Rosenberg's codes behind two miniatures depicting Nezami's *Khosrow and Shirin*."

Harvey adjusted his glasses. "You're the expert on Persian literature. Tell us about *Khosrow and Shirin*."

Noor leaned into Gabriel. "It's the story of Persian Prince Khosrow and Armenian Princess Shirin, whose love is doomed by fate. It's Persia's *Romeo and Juliet*."

Brandon tapped his finger on a page in the diary. "Here's the first mention of the miniatures. The king placed the first line of codes behind a miniature depicting a naked woman in a pool. It's a scene from Nezami's *Khosrow and Shirin*."

Noor nodded. "Khosrow's friend, Shahpur, was a talented painter. He went to Armenia and left portraits of Khosrow for Shirin to find. When she saw them, she fell in love and asked about the man. Shahpur described Khosrow and their destined love, revealing he was Khosrow's emissary. He gave Shirin Khosrow's ring and told her it would guide her to the palace. The next morning, she rode off to find him."

Rafael grinned. "The princess went after her man, eh? Good for her."

"What's the scene with a nude woman in the lake about?" Harvey asked.

A smile played on Noor's lips. "The lovers first crossed paths at a pool. After traveling day and night, Shirin reached a lush field with a gleaming pool and bathed, thinking she was alone. Meanwhile, Khosrow's enemies tricked his father into believing he'd plotted against him."

"Like Shakespeare," Harvey murmured.

Noor refilled her tea. "A sage advised Khosrow to flee. Disguised, as a merchant, he rode to Armenia and stumbled on the same pool where Shirin was bathing."

Rafael leaned in. "Interesting. What happened next?"

"Khosrow was awestruck by Shirin's beauty, but he was on a quest to find his love." Noor shrugged.

Brandon skimmed through the journal. "Ah, here we are. The second miniature was of a man riding a black horse. It's another scene from *Khosrow and Shirin*."

Noor nodded. "The lovers keep missing each other between Persia and Armenia. When Khosrow's father died, he rode back to Persia to claim the throne and found Shirin's horse, Shabdiz, in his stables. He rode his beloved's horse until they could be together."

Gabriel added more logs to the fireplace. "I wonder why the Persian king placed Rosenberg's codes behind the miniatures?"

Noor drew in a breath. "I bet he had the codes copied into the miniatures."

Brandon frowned. "That would ruin the artwork."

"The miniatures could be copies for all we know," Gabriel said.

"If that were true, there will be two sets of codes showing the location of the hidden artwork," Brandon said. "The first set are the original codes Rosenberg sent to Iran in the note. Gabriel found half of them at Nuremberg, which means at some point the king sent them back to Germany. The second set was embedded into two miniatures of Khosrow and Shirin."

"Why would there be two sets of codes?" Rafael asked.

Noor glanced at Gabriel. "Last summer, Gabriel and I found a famous diamond. During our search, we gained a bit of insight into how the Persian king's mind worked. I believe he copied the codes in case he needed to negotiate or bargain with the German authorities at some future date. He put copies of the codes behind the miniature."

Brandon flipped Rafael's laptop around. "In 1978, the Iranian Ambassador to Germany donated two miniatures depicting scenes from Nezami's *Khosrow and Shirin* to a German museum in Frankfurt."

Gabriel checked the date of the article. "That was six months before the Islamic revolution in Iran. Can you find where they are today?"

Brandon smiled. "One miniature is on loan at the Liebieghaus Museum, and the second one is on loan at the Stadel Museum. We should check them out."

"It's not like we can pluck them off the wall," Rafael grumbled.

"We may not need to." Gabriel paced in front of the fireplace. "We just need to see if the codes are embedded in the miniatures."

"What if they were carved behind the paintings instead of being part of them?"

"You can always go through the museum authorities," Harvey said. "I can say you're doing research for your next book and want to inspect the miniatures."

"Let's visit the museums first," Gabriel offered. "Noor and I will go to Liebieghaus. Brandon and Rafael can go to the Stadel Museum."

Rafael's mobile phone rang. He answered it, nodded, then ended the call. "Your luggage has arrived. The porters will bring it up. Let's head out after breakfast."

CHAPTER NINETEEN

Khosrow informed his servants he'd be hunting for a fortnight.
—Nezami, *Khosrow and Shirin*

THE NEXT MORNING, Gabriel woke to the sound of voices. After showering, he joined Noor in the living room.

She beamed. "Rafael called. They're waiting."

He kissed her. "Let's go."

At breakfast, Brandon poured syrup over his pancakes. "I looked into von Mayer last night."

Gabriel sat beside Noor. "What did you find?"

Rafael occupied the other seat by Noor. They spoke quietly as Brandon explained von Mayer's involvement in biopharma before the Richter Holdings merger.

Rafael whispered something. Noor chuckled.

Gabriel's appetite vanished.

"So, what do you think?" Brandon asked.

Gabriel blinked. "I'm sorry, what?"

Brandon sipped his coffee. "What do you think about me traveling to Lucerne?"

Noor was in deep discussion with Rafael.

Gabriel set aside his plate. "Let's check the museums first."

Noor and Rafael were still talking. Rafael shared a look with Noor. Both laughed.

She prefers to spend time with him. Gabriel waited until he had their attention. It hurt, yet he made himself say it. "Brandon and I will go to Liebieghaus, Noor and Rafael to the Stadel Museum, and Harvey will stay here to research Mina von Mayer. Be careful. Richter's men and the kidnappers are out there."

Noor's brow wrinkled. She opened her mouth to say something then decided against it.

Gabriel glanced at his watch. "We'll meet back here at noon." He rose to get his coat from their room.

Noor followed him back to their suite. "Gabriel, what's wrong?"

He's a better man than I am. You already see that.

"Nothing." He shrugged on his jacket.

"Then why are you going to Liebieghaus with Brandon?"

"I know Brandon better, and you seem to know the hotelier. I figure we can each keep an eye on the others while we're investigating."

She narrowed her eyes. "His name's Rafael."

"Okay, you can keep an eye on Rafael."

She sighed. "Why are we arguing?"

"We aren't."

"Fine." She pulled on her coat, then pecked him on the cheek. "I'll see you at noon."

They parted ways at the entrance. He watched Rafael offer her his arm, then the two departed in the other direction.

A streak of pain shot through his chest.

"THE LIEBIEGHAUS IS a nineteenth century villa." Brandon read what he'd found about the museum on his phone. "The structure is a mix of several architectural styles and even has a tower. It has an impressive sculpture museum with artifacts over five thousand years old. The miniature is in the eastern art exhibit."

They entered a garden with paths running up to the main building. They continued to a rectangular exhibit hall with paintings on one side and sculptures and pottery on the other.

Gabriel nudged Brandon. "There it is."

Glass encased the miniature mounted on the wall. He got as close as he could to study it. Vivid colors and delicate lines showed a woman bathing in a pool. Her ebony hair fell around her like a curtain.

"The craftsmanship is beautiful."

"I can't see any numbers or codes," Brandon mumbled, squinting at the miniature.

Gabriel checked the miniature from every angle. "Neither can I. Stand in front of me. I'm going to get a closer look."

Brandon moved to stand in front of him.

Gabriel used his phone's flashlight to check the artwork from several angles "I don't see any numbers or signs."

A man in a leather coat approached a sculpture across the hall. He gestured to a museum guard. Gabriel bent down on the pretense of tying his shoelaces and twisted slightly. The guard closed the exit doors, locking them into the building.

Gabriel rose and spoke in a low voice. "Look at this painting."

Brandon followed him to the next painting. "What are you—"

"Get ready to run."

Brandon blinked. "Huh?"

"The guard just locked the exit. I don't know how many others are working with him. I'll divert the guard by going into the other exhibit hall. Get out of here."

Brandon's eye twitched. "I won't leave you here on your own."

"I'll meet you at the metro station." Gabriel approached the guard, whose eyes widened. "Hello, where are the restrooms?"

The guard glanced at the man in the leather coat and muttered, "Out the hallway to the right."

Once outside the exhibit, Gabriel ran into the men's restroom and climbed up onto the toilet seat. Above him, thick pipes ran along the ceiling. He reached for one that wasn't hot, then tugged to test if it would hold his weight. Satisfied it would, he gripped it. Footsteps announced at least two people entering the bathroom. Gabriel held his breath.

The stall door flung open.

He swung on the pipe and kicked a man in the face, knocking him to the floor. Gabriel stepped over the unconscious man as another muscular guard approached with a bat.

They circled each other. Muscle Man swung. Gabriel ducked. The bat whiffed through the air and shattered a mirror above the sink.

Gabriel dodged one blow after another, trying not to lose his balance. Muscle Man panted as his movements grew slower. Gabriel kicked him in the knee. Muscle Man crumpled. He pried the bat from Muscle Man's hand, then drove it into his stomach. Muscle Man curled into a ball and groaned.

Exiting the bathroom, Gabriel sprinted toward the main tower. Suddenly, the fire alarm's ear-splitting blare surged through the building. Lights blinked, and the sprinkler system turned on. Museum visitors fled under the guards' direction.

He reached the courtyard as Brandon dashed out of another exit. "This way." They followed the throng of visitors to the main gate. "Good thinking, setting off the fire alarm."

Brandon blinked. "I didn't. I thought you did."

Crack! Something zipped by Gabriel's ear. He pulled Brandon behind an oak tree. "Someone's shooting at us." *Vzztt!* Another bullet streaked by. Gabriel peered around the tree to check how far they were from the exit. "There's a gate behind the trees. We'll climb it. Ready?"

Brandon bobbed his head.

"Three, two, one. Go!" They sprinted to the gate, climbed it, then dropped onto the sidewalk on the other side.

Thump, thump! Gabriel turned. The men following them landed on the sidewalk.

A silver Mercedes screeched to a halt in front of him. "Get in." The woman behind the wheel gestured frantically. They dove in. She whirled the car around.

Clang! A gunshot hit the fender.

"Hold on." She veered onto the Autobahn after a couple of sharp turns.

Gabriel grabbed the dashboard for support and glanced at the driver. She had long tawny hair and a delicate face with high cheekbones and an upturned nose. Who the hell was she?

She glanced at the rear-view mirror. "We're safe."

"Thank you," Gabriel managed. "I take it you triggered the alarms?"

"You're quite welcome, Mister McKnight. And yes, the alarm was my little ploy."

"You have the advantage," Gabriel said. "I don't believe we've met."

"It's Fan Bau for you." She burst into laughter. "And didn't that sound like a line from one of your Jason Vann movies?"

Brandon gaped at the woman. "You'd pass for a Jason Vann girl." He held up his palms. "Whoa, that came out wrong. I meant that in the best possible way and with no disrespect to women."

Gabriel couldn't hide his smile. The incredulity of the situation hit him. "Where are you taking us, Ms. Bau?"

She flicked a glance at him. "Somewhere we can talk."

What if the people who followed him and Brandon were also following Noor? He reached for his mobile phone.

Fan pursed her lips. "You can put away your phone. My brother isn't far from the lovely Ms. Rahman. He'll help if she and Mister Molina run into trouble."

Gabriel narrowed his eyes. "Why are you helping us?"

Fan turned off the Autobahn into a suburb outside of Frankfurt. She wound the car around several streets before screeching to a halt in front of a small café. "I enjoy driving in Germany." She pulled a tube of lipstick from the console. After applying enough to tempt any hot-blooded man, she stepped out of the vehicle and strode into the café.

In unspoken agreement, Gabriel and Brandon followed her.

Every head in the café turned toward her. Fan ignored the appreciative looks and slid into a booth.

Gabriel and Brandon followed.

Her sharp gaze homed on them. "What will you have?"

"Coffee please," Brandon said.

"Same," Gabriel agreed.

She nodded and placed their order in fluent German. When the server left, Fan's head tilted to the side. "Your photos don't do justice to your eyes, Mister McKnight. They're an interesting shade of aquamarine."

Gabriel crossed his arms over his chest. "Why are we here?"

The server arrived with three cups of coffee and a plate of strudels. Fan waited for him to retreat. "I want to help you find the codes."

Brandon stiffened.

Gabriel sent him a warning glance. "What codes are you referring to?"

"Let's not play games, shall we?" She stared at her cup. "My brother and I are half-French, half-Chinese. Grand-Mère, our French grandmother, widowed young, had several lovers, including an Italian count whom she said was the love of her life."

Gabriel felt a pang. Noor called her grandmother Grand-Mère. Had he done the right thing by sending Noor out with Molina?

"You were at the book fair, weren't you?" Brandon asked, bringing Gabriel back to their conversation.

"Yes. I came to speak with Mister McKnight, but the smoke bomb went off." Fan pursed her lips. "The Count gave Grand-Mère a Rembrandt. The painting hung in her country house until the Nazis confiscated it. Two weeks ago, I received information regarding the locations of their stolen artwork and the codes that would reveal their storehouses. The codes were locked in a secret vault in Tehran." Fan kept her gaze centered on Gabriel. "The Persian king copied the codes into three Persian miniatures. My informant said you have the key to the codes."

Gabriel studied the woman. He'd bet Fan Bau could handle herself in any situation. "If what your informant said was true, why would I share them with you?"

Fan looked like the cat who had swallowed the canary. "Because I have the first set of codes to the locations. If we collaborate, we can find the second set. The miniature you and Mister—" She glanced at Brandon.

"Rohr. Brandon Rohr," he murmured.

Fan nodded. "The miniature you and Mister Rohr were studying was an original and not the one with the codes." She pulled a folder out of her tote bag and handed it to him. "Consider this an olive branch."

Gabriel pulled out a miniature identical to the one they'd seen in the museum.

She handed him a magnifying glass. "Take a look."

Gabriel leaned forward and spotted the line of numbers etched into the blue hues of the pool.

Brandon leaned closer. "Incredible."

Fan rose from her seat and pulled her tote bag over her shoulder. "Keep it and consider my offer." She turned to leave, then stopped. "There's a train station across the street. The last stop is two blocks from your hotel." They watched her glide—the only way to describe her movements—toward her car.

"Wow." Brandon muttered. "Fucking wow."

"Let's get back to the hotel." Gabriel couldn't wait to tell Noor about Fan Bau.

CHAPTER TWENTY

Dressed in hunter's clothing, Shirin rode to Persia....
—Nezami, *Khosrow and Shirin*

NOOR FOLLOWED RAFAEL to the Stadel Museum's lower level. Her thoughts shifted to Gabriel. What had happened that morning to make him withdraw from her?

Rafael rubbed his chin. "This museum houses over three thousand paintings. The miniature is in Gallery Y1."

She didn't respond.

He tilted his head. "Is everything all right?"

Noor forced herself to pay attention. "Yes, of course. This is the museum's latest addition. I read about it. They've added an underground gallery that creates a dome-like wave in the courtyard with a blend of skylights and artificial lighting."

He grinned.

"What?"

"This thing you have with Gabriel, is it serious?"

She remembered the overwhelming love she'd felt when she realized he was safe. "Yes."

They passed a photo gallery, then entered a long hallway of paintings.

Noor stopped by a miniature. "Here it is."

The art showed Khosrow on horseback, surrounded by riders. Shabdiz's mane shimmered in shades of midnight blue, gray, and ebony.

Rafael scratched his chin. "I don't see any numbers or codes."

"Maybe with different lighting."

"I'll switch off the lights in the electric closet outside the exhibit," Rafael said. "You keep an eye on the painting in case codes appear in the dark."

She grabbed his arm. "Wait. There are cameras everywhere."

"The camera in the main hallway faces the gallery, not the closet," he whispered.

"Be careful."

Rafael nodded.

A museum volunteer guided a group into the exhibit hall. Noor felt a tingle of unease and scanned the room. An Asian man stood by a painting—Gabriel had mentioned a similar person watching Rafael at the book fair. As she adjusted her position, the lights in the gallery went out. Skylights kept the room dimly lit. She moved closer to the miniature. No numbers or symbols appeared.

Oomph! A museum volunteer bumped into her.

"Pardon." The volunteer moved toward the center of the exhibit.

Noor caught the woman's profile. Her pulse quickened. It was the girl who helped them in Nuremberg. The girl left through the exit at the end of the hall.

Rafael would worry if she disappeared, but she couldn't lose this opportunity. Noor followed the girl.

The lights flickered back on. She stepped into a new exhibit area in time to see the girl step between sculptures. A shiver ran down her spine as Erik—Richter's henchman—entered the hall. Noor hid behind a Greek sculpture, hoping he hadn't noticed her.

He moved toward the eastern paintings, while the girl slipped out through a side exit. Noor waited for Erik to pass by, then hurried after the girl.

A "Staff Only" door clicked shut. Noor pushed it open and entered a dimly lit stairwell. Her museum map showed the stairwell led to two exhibits, with H3 leading to a main road. She raced up to the H3 exhibit, where rows of impressionist art sat behind glass cases. Inside the next stairwell, she came face to face with the girl.

"I won't hurt you," Noor whispered. "I just want to ask you some questions."

The girl's face remained expressionless.

Noor's heart constricted. She was too young to have learned such control. "Are you in danger? Is there anything I can do to help you?"

The girl's eyes widened slightly. "No."

Noor raked a hand through her hair. "No, you're not in danger? Or no, you don't want my help."

The girl's lips twitched.

"Is Mina von Mayer after the codes? Is that why you're helping us?"

"You're looking for answers in the wrong places. Look closer." The girl glanced at her watch. "Get out while you can."

The stairwell lights went out, plunging the space into darkness. Noor fumbled for her mobile phone. When she turned on the flashlight, the girl was gone. Sighing, she made her way back to the YI exhibit hall.

A crowd had gathered outside its doors. Noor craned her neck to see what was happening. The INTERPOL detective from Nuremberg entered the exhibit with several officers.

Where was Rafael? Had the police spotted him?

She squeezed through the crowd to get closer when someone grabbed her arm. Startled, she spun around.

Rafael's eyes flashed with anger. "Where the hell have you been?"

"It's a long story. I didn't see any codes, and Richer's men are here. They—"

"I saw them," he growled. "They're taking down the miniature. Let's get out of here." On their way toward the main entrance, Rafael pulled her behind a statue. "Richter's men have the exits covered. We need another way out."

She linked arms with Rafael as they turned back into the exhibits. "I found a staff-only stairwell upstairs. Let's try that."

They took the stairs to the terrace at the back of the museum, where another flight of stairs led to staff parking. As they reached the lot, a shot rang out. A car's windshield cracked.

Rafael pulled her behind an SUV. "Two armed men are coming. I'll handle them. Follow the signs to the main road."

Noor had learned several tactics from Gabriel. She pulled a compact mirror from her purse and threw it in the opposite direction of the road.

"What are you doing?" Rafael hissed.

"Saving us."

Both men ran toward the sound. The second—a bald man with a tattoo on the back of his neck—stayed farther behind, while the first one went ahead.

Noor scooped a large rock from the ground, crept behind Neck Tattoo, then bashed him on the head. He crumpled. She grabbed his gun. As the second man swiveled, she shot him in the knee.

Rafael raked a hand through his hair. "You scare me." He took her gun and wiped it with his sweater. "No prints."

"Shouldn't we call an ambulance for the bad guy?"

He shook his head. "Museum staff heard the gunshot. They'll be here any minute. Let's go."

They followed the signs to the main road, then hailed a cab.

CHAPTER TWENTY-ONE

When Khosrow and Shirin finally meet, Khosrow had left home because of Bahram Chobin, a sly general who schemed to take over the Persian throne. Khosrow pleaded for physical intimacy with Shirin. She didn't give in and subtly reminded him he had to win back his kingdom and good name before they could be wed. Energized, Khosrow traveled to Constantinople where the emperor of Byzantium resided.
—Nezami, *Khosrow and Shirin*

FRANKFURT, GERMANY

MINA VON MAYER shivered and pulled her cashmere shawl around her. Her silk dress offered little protection against the brittle fall air. She was to meet Cyrus and several business associates at her favorite Moroccan restaurant prior to attending Richter's party.

A staff member opened the door for her. "Are you Herr Rohan's guest?"

"Yes."

The woman nodded. "The Blue Lounge is on the top floor."

"Thank you." She took the elevator with a family. The father smiled and held the hand of a chattering young boy, while the mother cradled a baby in her arms and hummed a German lullaby. The song brought back a memory.

Mina cradled her daughter in her arms. Swaying on her feet, she hummed the song her mama sang to her when she was little. It didn't take long for her daughter to succumb to sleep. She lay her cheek against the infant's soft forehead. "This won't be forever. It's only until mommy and daddy get settled. I love you, my Sarah."

Cyrus entered the cottage. His eyes softened at the sight of Mina and the infant. "My two favorite people in the world." He leaned down and kissed the top of Sarah's head. "Are you certain you want to do this? I can keep you and Sarah safe."

Mina blinked back her tears. "No. Richter will find out. He'll hurt her to get to us." She crooned at the baby. "Hiding isn't the life I want for her. Sarah deserves better. Once I expose Richter and set things right, we can all be together."

"We will set things right. My brother's fiancée is General Rahman's niece. Her name is Leila. She'll help get the map out of the vault, and it will prove Richter and his family are guilty."

"Can we trust this Leila?"

"Cameron vouches for her." His eyes moved back to Sarah. "I don't like this."

Mina swallowed the lump in her throat. "Neither do I, but it's the only way to keep her safe."

"You're certain the woman you chose is reliable?"

Mina inhaled the sweet scent of baby shampoo. "Yes. Mariam is my former nanny. She and her husband will care for Sarah until we claim her." Little Sarah wiggled in her arms. A pair of charcoal eyes very much like her father's stared up at her. Mina resumed humming. Sarah's angelic smile tugged at her heart.

Pain shot up Mina's breastbone. She clutched the metal bar in the elevator for support. *Dear God. Not now, not now.*

The woman looked up at Mina and smiled. "The baby likes it when I sing to her."

Mina's hands tightened on the metal bar. She ground her teeth together, hoping she wouldn't be sick. The elevator pinged, and the family exited. The walls tightened around her as the doors swung shut. Sweat formed on her forehead. Memories of Sarah filled her mind, pushing the pain from her breastbone to her throat. She wanted to scream. What came out was a whimper.

The shawl hung from her shoulders. She threw back her head, trying to draw air into her lungs. The elevator arrived at the top floor. Mina stumbled onto the landing. Air, she needed air. She clawed at her chest, trying to breathe.

Cyrus stood by the entrance of the lounge. He was handing his raincoat to one of the wait staff. His eyes widened. "Mina?"

Oh, no. She didn't want him to see her like this. She turned away.

He gripped her arm, concern etched in his handsome face. "What's wrong?"

She tried to speak. Her chest heaved, and tears made her vision blur.

Cyrus put an arm around her waist and led her to an outdoor terrace. Outside, the crisp fall air greeted them. Mina gripped the railing and gulped fresh air.

"That's it, Pepper. Breathe deep."

He hadn't called her that silly endearment in decades. The ache in her chest deepened. She turned away, willing herself to gain control. She couldn't let him see how broken she was, not after everything between them. Clinging to what little self-respect remained, Mina drew more air into her lungs and went through her deep breathing routine.

Cyrus stroked her back. His touch sent shivers down her spine. He wrapped his coat around her. Eventually, her body settled. Gripping the railing, she slowly straightened. "I'm better now."

Charcoal eyes studied her, eyes that could be cold as onyx or warm as embers.

She wanted to reach out and run her hand along his smooth jaw. Instead, she returned his coat. "Thank you."

He kissed her palm, letting his lips linger on her skin. It felt like he'd seared her hand. "We're all allowed a moment. Do you want to tell me what happened?"

Did she? A part of her missed the intimacy—not just physical intimacy, but the sharing of hopes, fears, and dreams. They had once been two bodies with one soul, and it had almost destroyed them. Years of habit made her draw back. "I'm tired, that's all. Nothing a good night's rest won't cure." It was a poor excuse, and they both knew it.

His eyes flashed with emotion, gone as fast as it had appeared. He shrugged on his coat. "You trust me with business."

Business won't obliterate what's left of me. She forced herself to smile. "I'm fine. Really, it was nothing."

"Are you ready to join the meeting?"

His curt tone hurt. What did she expect? They'd erected too many barriers between them.

"Yes. Go ahead. I'll be there in a minute."

He hesitated, his eyes hard as tourmaline. "I'll see you inside."

Mina waited till he left the balcony, then slumped into one of the lounge chairs. That split second of emotion she'd glimpsed conjured another memory.

"Is this a joke?" Cyrus roared. "You got married over the weekend? Married!?"

Mina raised her chin. "Please understand. This is for the best. Richter—"

"To hell with Richter! You should have talked to me. Or am I nothing to you?"

"Cyrus, will you please listen?"

His eyes turned bleak. She felt like she was staring into an abyss. "Congratulations on your wedding." He turned and left.

Mina rubbed her chest. It had been years since she had a panic attack. Why had they come back now?

Because your granddaughter lives. Because you can right all the wrongs and maybe... maybe redeem yourself.

She straightened her shoulders. Moving forward with her plan was the only way to correct the past. Composed and focused, she joined the group in the lounge.

The Blue Lounge paid homage to Morocco's blue city, Chefchaouen. Decorated in multiple shades of blue, it gave one the impression of dining in the city's main square.

Yuri Petrov spotted her first. He motioned to Serji, who jumped up to hold out a chair for her. Adisa waved in greeting. Cyrus merely nodded.

She took her place at the table and ordered a ginger ale. "Sorry I'm late."

Petrov sipped his drink. "Let's get down to business."

Mina met Petrov's placid stare. "I asked to meet with this group because Adisa and Cyrus have an interest in the pharmaceutical industry. I also bought out the last company you had an interest in and wanted to make it up to you by offering an opportunity to invest in this venture. I have several companies working on a solution for trauma, specifically psychological trauma. It's a breakthrough drug that surpasses anything on the market. It's in the manufacturing phase. Several governments are ready to sign agreements with me." She distributed reports, then walked them through the information.

Petrov piled his plate with appetizers. "What about Richter?"

Mina kept up the appearance of eating. "Richter didn't speak to the Board when he entered biopharma. Besides, his attention is occupied elsewhere." She clasped her hands together. "Let me know by next week if you want to be part of this. I'll proceed either way."

Cyrus gazed at her untouched plate with a frown. "Is this drug patented?"

"Yes."

Adisa dipped a slice of pita bread into a bowl of hummus. "Can we shift the timeline?"

"The timeline affects revenue. I've offered two timelines as options and added financial forecasting to each. It's in your packet."

"Aren't you doing the same thing Richter did?" Petrov asked

between bites of food. "This could push your revenue and reach beyond the other Board members."

"That's why we're holding this meeting," Mina said. "I talked to the Lees. They prefer to focus on their assets in Asia, and Magdalena wants to invest in Alum. She's waiting for Richter to announce the merger."

"Which you have delayed," Petrov finished, scratching his chin.

Mina shrugged. "I believe in nonproliferation. Too much power is dangerous in any hands." She wondered how long it would take for Petrov to ask the inevitable question.

"Do we need to take this to the Board?" Petrov asked.

"No, the pharmaceutical industry is one of mine. It's not a new venture."

Petrov grunted. She could see him mentally calculating profits. A grin spread across his face. "You'll have my answer by the end of the week."

Adisa picked up his folder. "I want to control the distribution in Africa."

Mina nodded. "We can work that out." She glanced at her watch. "If you have no more questions, I must leave."

Adisa grinned. "Are you going to Richter's shindig?"

Petrov scowled. "What are you talking about?"

Adisa spread out his palms. "Richter's hosting a shindig at a fancy hotel. Didn't you know?"

Petrov's scowl deepened.

Cyrus gave Petrov his most winning smile. "It's for investors with an interest in biopharma, specifically Alum Pharmaceuticals. Richter is dangling something similar to Mina's offer."

"I wanted to give every Board member an opportunity before I proceed." Mina rose to leave.

"Let me walk you out." Adisa accompanied her to the elevators. He waited until they were away from the others. "He'll tell Richter."

"I hope he does."

Two hours later, she paced in her hotel suite. It wouldn't be long before Cyrus landed on her doorstep. He'd want answers.

"Ms. von Mayer." Mercedes's gentle voice broke through her thoughts. "Is there anything else I can do for you?"

Mina glanced up at her assistant. Despite her shyness, Mercedes's intelligence and capability made her invaluable. "Have the financials for the latest acquisition come in yet?"

"They'll be in tomorrow."

"Thank you. Take the night off. I'll be back late."

Mercedes bid Mina goodnight, then left.

A moment later, a knock sounded on the door. Bracing herself, Mina went to answer it and frowned when a porter handed her an envelope. "Good evening. Your granddaughter left this for you in the lobby."

Mina reached for the envelope with shaky hands.

CYRUS FUMED WHILE his driver maneuvered through Frankfurt traffic. Memories he had long ago buried surfaced.

Morris paced back and forth. "We'll continue to protect Missus Rahman and her daughter. Paris is safe, but you never know."

Cyrus grinned. "You've developed a soft spot for young Noor."

Morris shrugged. "Kid's innocent."

He thought of his own daughter and granddaughter in Lucerne and felt a jolt of longing.

The phone rang.

"I'll get it." Morris grabbed the receiver on his desk. His face paled, his features turned to stone, and he cleared his throat. "You're certain?"

The hair behind Cyrus's neck prickled. Dread skittered up his spine. He held out his hand in a silent gesture.

Morris handed him the phone.

Mina was on the line, her voice flat. *"She's dead, Cyrus. They're all dead—Sarah, the baby, and her husband."*

They hadn't gone through the motions other couples did. There was no blaming each other, quarreling, or grief counseling. They'd buried their daughter and her family in polite silence, creating a chasm between them that was so wide, only a miracle could obliterate it. After that, they'd become broken halves of a canvas drifting through life, tethered by the goal of bringing down Richter.

Cyrus rubbed a hand over his face. He'd planned to take it slow with Mina—to focus on their plan first and then on their relationship. The wall she'd thrown up earlier infuriated him. The driver stopped in front of her hotel. He told his driver to wait in the lot.

Mina opened the door on his first knock.

He strode in, shoving his hands in his pockets. "Normally, I'd begin with a greeting or some nonsense about our meeting. I'll skip that for now. What happened today?"

Mina raised her chin. "Nothing, I—"

"Enough!" He grabbed her by the shoulder and shook her. "I am done listening to you. I'm done catering to you."

"What are you talking about?" She wrenched free from his grasp. "I haven't asked you for anything."

"Exactly," he cried. "You've never asked for anything. You just pushed me aside."

Her chin jutted up. "You didn't have a problem with it."

Is that what she thought? He took a step forward. "What did you expect? You married that man."

"It was a marriage in name to confuse Richter." She hugged herself. "We planned to divorce in a year. I tried to explain, but you wouldn't listen."

"Did you consider how it made me feel? Did you consider what it did to me?" Somewhere in the back of his mind, Cyrus was aware he was shouting and strove for control. He clenched his fists. "You threw up barriers, and I respected them. You decided for Sarah, and I went along."

Mina's lower lip trembled, and the tears in her eyes made his heart clench. "Cyrus—"

He raised a hand to stop her. "I'll ask one more time. What happened today?"

Her shoulders slumped. "You blame me for Sarah's death, and you're right. I-I was a careless mother. I didn't deserve her."

He gaped at her. This was what she was carrying? "I never blamed you for Sarah's death. We both loved her, and we both decided to have her raised in Lucerne."

Mina beat her chest. "She died because of me."

"No. She died because Richter killed her." He paused and raked a hand through his hair. "You were the best mother. You loved her unconditionally, as did I."

"I was busy building an empire and didn't see it coming. I didn't protect my daughter." Her voice shook, and her eyes gleamed with tears.

"Neither did I." His own voice sounded hoarse. "It wasn't your fault, Mina." He would have to say it more than once for her to believe it.

Her gaze met his. "I had a panic attack. I've had them for years. That's what happened today." She stood there, letting him see her vulnerability.

Cyrus wanted to reach for her, but she wasn't ready. He stayed where he was. "We can make it right."

"I don't know how to go back to what we were."

Hallelujah. He let out the breath he didn't know he was holding. Gently, he took her hands into his. "We've changed too much to go back. We can move forward and become what we want to be. Part of that means being open with one another." He waited for his words to sink in.

"Okay."

Okay. He didn't know one word could bring him so much joy. He raised her hands to his lips. "Part of being open with each other is to share how we feel. It means we discuss more than day to day business, agreed?"

She drew in a breath. "Yes." Her gaze strayed to the coffee table. "She left this for me in the lobby. A porter brought it before you arrived. It's the article the Lucerne press ran when Sarah died. There's a flyer for the Frankfurt Book Fair behind it."

Cyrus reached for the clipping. "I've sent men to look for her."

Mina nodded. "I sent someone too. She's in danger."

"Forgive me for repeating myself. We are no longer inexperienced kids. We'll protect her."

Mina squeezed his hands. "She involved Gabriel McKnight. We must find him and warn him."

"I'll find him." Cyrus sighed and glanced at his watch. "We should get to the dinner party."

"Give me a minute." She turned to leave then stopped. "If I could go back in time, I'd change many things. But not us. I wouldn't change us for anything, Cyrus."

Aah. Just when he thought he didn't have a heart, she reminded him she held it. "Neither would I."

CHAPTER TWENTY-TWO

Meanwhile, Shirin's thoughts were with Khosrow....
　　　　　　　　　　　　—Nezami, *Khosrow and Shirin*

NOOR HELD HER temper as Gabriel paced like a caged tiger. "I saw an opportunity and took it. The girl wanted to talk to me."

A vein in his neck bulged. "You could've been hurt. Or killed."

"That's what I said." Rafael smirked, leaning against the bar in the hotel's private dining room.

"It was a gutsy move." Brandon said. The comment earned a glare from Gabriel.

"She is gutsy," Rafael murmured. "You should've seen her shoot Richter's man."

"Noor is incredibly brave," Harvey added.

Though everyone else defended her, Gabriel's reaction stung. Didn't he trust her? "Thank you. I did what I thought was best."

Gabriel's voice softened. "In the future, please don't take unnecessary risks."

She nodded. "The girl said we're looking for answers in the wrong places. She said to look closer."

Brandon narrowed his eyes. "Closer? Does that mean the codes are in Frankfurt?"

Gabriel strode to the window and stared outside. She wanted to go to him and wrap her arms around his waist but didn't. He'd erected a barrier between them.

"Maybe we've gone at this the wrong way." His aquamarine eyes homed in on Rafael. "Does your pharmacy carry iodine?"

Rafael picked up the phone. "I'll ask. Shall I have them deliver some if they do?"

Gabriel nodded.

Rafael put in the order. "May I ask why we need iodine?"

Understanding dawned. She smiled. "Is there a private kitchen here? Gabriel wants to check if the rest of the codes were written with invisible ink."

They gathered in the small kitchen behind the dining area. Brandon and Rafael opened windows and turned on the vent, while Gabriel warmed the iodine.

As it evaporated, he held the other side of the note above the iodine fumes. "And voila."

Covering her mouth with a cloth, Noor leaned in to study the document. A line of code appeared behind the note.

00-0-01-9-01-03-3-4=afai-al-ag-ag-ai-ai-ae-ac

They followed Gabriel back to the dining room, where he grabbed a piece of paper and pen. "I have the map's key on my phone." He deciphered the code with the key. "Here's the entire note. Longitude equals 10.749646. Latitude equals 47.557732." He typed on his phone. "It's Neuschwanstein Castle. Why does that sound familiar?"

"It's the Disney castle," Noor exclaimed. "Well, it's a castle in Bavaria. Disney based its famous Cinderella Castle on Neuschwanstein. The Frankfurt Book Fair is holding a gala there in two days. We're attending it. That's why it's familiar."

"We should all go," Brandon said.

Gabriel rubbed his chin. "Why this specific castle?"

"It makes sense," Harvey murmured. "The Germans catalogued the artwork they looted in the Neuschwanstein Castle during the Second World War."

Brandon typed on his mobile phone and whistled. "Thirty-nine albums of artwork were found in the castle after World War II."

"Noor and I booked rooms at a resort by the castle. Shall I book rooms for you and Brandon?" Harvey asked.

Rafael went to the phone. "Give me the name. I'll have my assistant take care of it."

"Do we know what we're looking for?" Brandon asked.

Noor inched closer to Gabriel. He moved back, pursing his lips. "The castle will have tours. They all do. Let's check it out first. It may point us in the right direction. Meanwhile, we'll carry on with our business plans as if nothing happened."

Harvey rose. "In that case, I need to make a few calls. There are a couple of producers and publishing houses that want to speak with us."

She straightened. "Three of my clients will be there. I'll have business meetings too."

Gabriel sighed. "There's more we need to discuss." He told them about his and Brandon's morning at the museum and Fan Bau.

Anger heated Noor's cheeks. She crossed her arms over her chest. "It's okay for you to deviate from the plan and jump into a stranger's car, but it's not okay for me to follow a girl whom I knew could give us answers?" She held her hand up before Gabriel could respond. "I'd like to point out we found the second set of codes because of my decision to follow her."

Gabriel shoved his hands in his pockets. "You're right. I'm sorry. We didn't have time to think. Men were coming at us with guns, and jumping into the car seemed like a good idea."

She bit her lip. Why had he reacted that way?

"There's also the minor matter of the police," Gabriel said. "Detectives will want to talk to you."

Rafael straightened. "What are you planning on telling them?"

"As little as possible." Gabriel glanced at her—met her gaze for the first time since they reconvened. "I'll tell Hood we want to talk to her and no one else. I think it's best to tell her you didn't see the kidnappers and escaped with Rafael. If that's okay with you?"

She glanced at Rafael. "This affects you too. Are you okay with it?"

Gabriel turned to get a bottle of water. She caught a sudden flash of emotion in his eyes before it disappeared.

Rafael shrugged. "Gabriel says this detective is trustworthy. I'll take his word. I agree with providing minimal information to the police for now."

She sighed. "All right, then. That's what we'll do."

A porter entered the dining hall and went to Rafael.

Gabriel dialed a number on his phone, then motioned to Noor, who joined him by the fireplace. He held his mobile phone out to her. "Detective Hood wants to speak with you."

She took the phone and cleared her throat. "Hello, Detective."

"Are you all right, Ms. Rahman?"

"Yes, thank you."

Detective Hood sighed. *"I'll be at the hotel tomorrow morning to speak with you and McKnight."*

"Sounds good." Noor would have to coordinate her story with Gabriel and Rafael before they met with Hood.

Silence.

"You're sure you're, all right?" Hood asked.

"Yes. I'm tired, that's all."

"I won't take up more of your time. Since you're at Mister Molina's hotel, please let him know I'd like to speak with him as well."

"I will." Noor handed the phone back to Gabriel.

The porter handed an envelope to Gabriel after he ended the call. "A messenger brought this for you and Ms. Rahman."

"Thank you." Gabriel ripped open the envelope. His brows rose. He handed her the note.

"What is it?" Brandon asked.

She read the message. "It's an invitation from Farid Richter. He's invited Gabriel and me to a private dinner party tonight. How does he know we're here?" She glanced up at Gabriel. The ice in his eyes had disappeared.

"His people are watching us. I'd say a visit to Villa Margarite's boutique lies in our future."

"We're coming with you." Brandon snatched the note out of her hand. "I can pretend to be your driver or something."

"No, Richter's men will recognize you," Gabriel said. "He won't try anything at a public event. Noor and I will be fine."

"Why does Richter want to meet with us?" Noor wondered out loud.

Gabriel shrugged. "There's only one way to find out."

ZITA ADJUSTED THE frames of her glasses and watched Mina von Mayer enter with a handsome man. Who was he? Hovering behind a marble column, she watched the couple make their way to the elevator. The first part of her plan had worked. The information she gave to Noor Rahman would redirect Gabriel McKnight's efforts. Knowing Richter, and no one knew him as well as she did, he would initiate contact with McKnight. It was just a matter of time. Now onto the next part.

She straightened her wig and checked her appearance. No one would recognize her. Not Mina von Mayer, not Gabriel McKnight, and least of all Richter. Turning, she took the stairwell to the kitchens, then joined the group of servers gathered for the evening. The manager had ordered the staff to arrive before the dinner guests. Several executives of Alum Pharmaceuticals were expected. It was interesting that Richter Holdings had announced a delay in the merger. Zita would bet Mina von Mayer was the reason for the delay.

She mentally reviewed her plan while the manager finished giving out assignments. The surprise she had prepared would be the first nail in Richter's coffin.

Zita patted her apron and began dinner preparations.

CHAPTER TWENTY-THREE

Shirin's speech spurred Khosrow into action....
—Nezami, *Khosrow and Shirin*

NOOR STUDIED HER reflection. The gown she'd chosen was sapphire blue. It covered one shoulder and left the other one bare. The material clung to her upper body, then flared below her waist. She'd styled her hair into dark waves and even applied some makeup. Satisfied, she stepped into the living room, where Gabriel waited.

His gaze roamed over her like a warm caress. "You're stunning."

"Thank you." She kissed his cheek. "We need to talk."

He stepped back, wary. "About what?"

She tried not to show her exasperation. "About what happened today."

"Several things occurred today."

She searched his face. "You were angry at me this morning. Why?"

A tick worked in his jaw. "You were kidnapped. I don't want it to happen again."

Was that what was wrong? Was his fear of someone harming her making him act out of character? She stood on tiptoe and kissed his lips.

He pulled her close and returned the embrace. "We're going to be late."

She sighed. "Lead the way."

They took a cab to the hotel, where a doorman gave them directions to the party.

Gabriel gripped her hand. "Two security cameras face the elevators. They'll capture anyone getting in and out of them."

"Is that good or bad?"

His eyes twinkled. "That depends on the situation."

They took the elevator to an elegant reception hall. Tables piled with flowers and crystal glasses stretched wall to wall. Musicians played soft jazz, while servers circulated with drinks and hors d'oeuvres.

Noor took a quick count. "There are at least a hundred people here."

The maître d' guided them to their table, where two were already seated.

"Mister McKnight." A woman in a figure-hugging bronze dress smiled. "I'm pleased our little escapade hasn't worn you out."

Surprised, Noor glanced up at Gabriel.

The lines around his eyes tightened. "Noor, meet Fan Bau. She's the lady who helped Brandon and me at the museum this morning. Ms. Bau, this is Noor Rahman."

Fan raised her glass. "It's a pleasure." She waved at the man sitting beside her. "My brother, Alex."

Oh. Alex was the man she'd seen at the museum earlier today.

Gabriel pulled out a chair for her then seated himself beside her. "Did you ask Richter to invite us to dinner?"

Fan's gaze raked over Gabriel with obvious approval. "Like you, we are guests." The music changed into a bluesy melody. She reached for Gabriel's arm. "Let's dance."

Gabriel glanced at Noor apologetically and followed Fan to the dance floor.

Noor turned her head away from the sight of Gabriel holding the beautiful woman. Fan Bau wanted to provoke her. She wasn't in the mood to accommodate the woman.

Alex chuckled then held out his hand. "My sister can be harmless when she puts her mind to it. Let's even the odds with some dancing of our own."

She allowed him to lead her to the dance floor. "I saw you at the museum today."

Alex's mouth curved into a smile. "Yes, all the running back and forth was quite the diversion." He bent his head close to her ear, fingers caressing her back. "Molina almost lost it when you disappeared. Can't blame him. Where did you run off to, Noor?"

His breath made her shiver. "I thought I saw a colleague. I was wrong."

A tawny brow rose. "Is that so?" His gaze lifted then hardened. "Be careful."

She was about to ask him what he meant when a man said, "May I cut in?" The smile on his unyielding mouth was a humorless lifting of the lips, and the pale blue of his eyes reminded her of glaciers. He bowed in an old courtly gesture. "I am Farid Richter. It's a pleasure to meet you, Ms. Rahman."

Icy fingers crawled up her spine. She forced herself to smile. "The pleasure's mine, Herr Richter. Your invitation was both a surprise and delight."

He pulled her into the dance. "I have an interest in the publishing industry." He glanced at Gabriel, who still danced with Fan Bau. "Much as I appreciate Mister McKnight's novels, I'm more impressed with your work."

The music ended. Richter motioned to a server, then handed her a glass of champagne. "I see Mister McKnight has disengaged himself from his dancing partner. Shall we join him?" He introduced himself to Gabriel, then plucked another glass from a nearby tray for him. "It is crowded in the reception hall. Would you care to join me in a more secluded setting?"

He guided them to a lounge with plush sofas and velvet drapes. Richter waited until she and Gabriel settled onto the sofa, then took a seat beside the fireplace. "You are wondering why I asked you to join me here?"

Noor refrained from rolling her eyes. What was he waiting for, a drum roll?

Gabriel glanced at her, and the corners of his mouth twitched. "The thought has occurred."

Richter steepled his fingers and stared at the fireplace. "My father was a patron of the arts. After the Second World War, he partnered with multiple international groups to recover artwork the Nazis looted and hid. Father believed art must be cherished and shared with future generations. I hold the same perspective. As a concerned global citizen, I support the effort to retrieve artwork the Nazis stole." He paused, and his predatory eyes homed in on Gabriel. "Rumors suggest you have a series of codes leading to their location. Is that true?"

Noor repressed a shudder. But Gabriel didn't seem affected by Richter.

"It's become a popular question. And no, it's not true."

Richter rubbed his chin. "May I ask who else asked you this question?"

Gabriel grinned. "An INTERPOL detective."

Richter studied Gabriel. He pursed his lips as if considering something, then nodded. "If you hear anything, kindly inform me. I'll notify INTERPOL and the groups I work with to search for the art." His gaze bounced between her and Gabriel. "You'll find my influence will affect your careers."

She stared. He'd threatened them and boasted of his influence in one sentence. A surge of anger coursed through her. Before she could reply, the doors to the lounge swung open. "Uncle Cyrus." She jumped up to greet the man she loved as family.

He enveloped her in a hug. "I thought I saw you and Gabriel and came to check." He shook Gabriel's hand. "I didn't know you were in Germany." His brow wrinkled. "Ah, the book fair, of course. My apologies. Old age affects my memory."

Noor bit back a giggle. Uncle Cyrus had an intellect she'd seen in few people and the looks of a movie star. Old wasn't a word one would use to describe him. "Have you heard from Uncle Morrie?"

"No, but then one doesn't expect to hear from honeymooners."

Richter raised a brow. "You know Ms. Rahman and Mister McKnight?"

The smile did not reach Uncle Cyrus's eyes. "They are my extended family."

The lines around Richter's eyes tightened. "I see."

Uncle Cyrus chucked her under the chin. "Did I interrupt your conversation?"

"Not at all," Richter replied. "I heard Mister McKnight may have information that would help find lost artwork. You are aware I support the endeavor."

"Ah, yes." Uncle Cyrus said. "Farid is a patron of the arts."

The door to the lounge opened, and a woman stepped in. "Oh. I'm sorry. I thought the lounge was vacant."

Noor turned at the sound of the velvety voice. The woman in the doorway reminded her of the old-world movie stars, captivating and elegant. A simple black sheath emphasized her trim figure. Dark hair fell into a graceful bob below her chin and, despite her age, her skin glowed. She moved forward with the grace of a dancer. Mina von Mayer. Noor was certain because of the strong resemblance between her and the girl she'd met in the museum earlier that day.

Uncle Cyrus beamed. "Come in, Mina. I want you to meet members of my family." He introduced them.

Mina's topaz-colored eyes softened. "Your mother and I served on several charity boards in Paris. She was a lovely person, inside and out. You look like her."

Noor smiled. "Thank you. It's nice to meet you."

Mina complimented Gabriel on his books.

The door to the lounge swung open again. An African gentleman with a crop cut sauntered into the lounge. "Am I late?"

"No, no, Adisa." Richter motioned for the man to join them. "We haven't started yet."

"We should get back to the party." Noor kissed Uncle Cyrus's cheek. "Will we see you later?"

He grinned. "Definitely."

MINA WATCHED THE young couple leave. Anger heated her entire body. Richter had them under his radar. She would discuss it with Cyrus. She forced her features to remain impassive and glanced at Richter. "Your assistant mentioned you wished to speak with me."

"Yes." Richter motioned to the room's conference table. "Please have a seat. We're waiting for a last-minute guest."

The door opened. Petrov lumbered inside, drink in hand. Richter's assistant handed each of them a folder.

Richter's chest jutted out. "As chairman of the Board, it is my business to know about every transaction between members. Earlier today, Mina made a business proposal to this group regarding a breakthrough drug."

"Why shouldn't I?" Mina asked. "Being in the industry, I don't need the Board's permission."

"You had every right to make the proposal," Richter said. "As most of the Board plans to invest in this business, it is my duty to notify you of any risk."

Mina's brows rose. "I've completed every kind of risk management study for the venture. The numbers and forecasting are accurate."

Richter smirked. "The owners of this venture are the Abromowski family. Their grandparents and family members died in the Holocaust. They won't do business with anyone involved in the crimes that took place back then." He cleared his throat. "If they discover your father's connection with the Nazis, they'll cancel the agreement."

Bastard. Mina ground her teeth. "I am not responsible for the sins of others."

Richter raised his hands in a gesture of surrender. "Of course not, and I'm not insinuating you are. Since this pharmacy venture is lucrative, the Board members must understand what's at risk."

Adisa crossed his arms over his massive chest. "And why would they check Mina's lineage?"

Richter set his folder down. "They conduct background checks on everyone they do business with."

Mina clenched her fists under the table. She wouldn't allow Richter or anyone to see her pain.

Cyrus flicked a glance at her. "What are you suggesting, Farid?"

Richter shrugged. "You can cancel the venture—"

"No." Adisa interjected. "Billions in profits are at stake. Not to mention we'll control the entire market."

Richter pursed his lips. "I propose a solution. Allow me to run the venture instead of Mina. I will become the major shareholder, and everyone's shares will stay the same. Except Mina's." His face took on a solemn look. "The Abromowskis will back out of the deal once they run a background check on you."

Petrov was silent. The rat had colluded with Richter.

When Mina spoke, her voice remained steady. "I signed a letter of intent with the Abromowskis."

"Their board won't approve the sale of shares." Richter held his palms out. "I am only trying to help."

Mina tilted her head to the side. "Even if you convince them to allow you to take my place, the terms of the contract are leave them ten percent of the business. My ninety percent was divided into thirty percent ownership for me, and twenty each for Adisa, Yuri, and Cyrus. Would you honor the same conditions?"

"I will draft papers with the same conditions," Richter assured.

"I went after the opportunity," Mina argued. "I did the research. I convinced the Abromowskis to sell. What happens to my cut of the profit?"

Richter pursed his lips. "You believe in the balance of power. I will sign over the equivalent in my merger with Alum over to you. We can announce you have taken it over."

There it was—Richter's revenge for her stopping the merger.

Mina ground her teeth. "The profits aren't the same. You would have to hand over most of your shares, making me the major shareholder."

Richter shrugged. "I'll do that. After all, fair is fair, cousin."

She hated it when he referred to her as cousin. She had nothing in common with him—this murderer who had killed her sweet, innocent daughter. The image of Sarah, lifeless in a morgue, made it hard to breathe.

Cyrus's dark eyes bore into hers with concern. "Farid is offering a fair exchange. Why don't you consider it?"

"There's no time," Adisa cried. "She is supposed to sign the deal tomorrow."

Mina cupped her chin in her hands and closed her eyes, trying to stop another panic attack. To the others, it would seem she was pondering the issue. She counted backward from fifty and forced her body to settle. "I'll call the Abromowskis tomorrow and tell them you're replacing me as major shareholder. It may take a few days to draft the paperwork. If you honor the previous terms, I'll ensure they work with you."

Richter beamed. "To show my good faith, I'll wait until you are the major shareholder in the Alum merger before I sign with the Abromowskis."

Mina nodded. "With your family's impeccable history, it won't be hard to convince them."

Richter leaned forward. "The Board is family, Mina. That's what truly matters."

Sarah's laughter filled her mind. Bile rose to her throat. "Thank you."

"Let's celebrate with champagne." Richter motioned to a server.

Mina was about to excuse herself to go to the restroom when a shrilling scream shook the lounge.

CHAPTER TWENTY-FOUR

While blood smeared over necks like ornamental chains, ruby droplets adorned blades and plains.

—Nezami, *Khosrow and Shirin*

ZITA CIRCLED THE reception hall with a tray of drinks. Mina von Mayer stood in the periphery talking to a wide-shouldered African gentleman. The man's rigid posture broadcasted he was military. Her companion, whom Zita had nicknamed Hollywood, mingled with the guests.

Richter, McKnight, and Noor Rahman left the dining hall. *Be careful, McKnight.*

Hollywood turned. Zita picked up an empty glass. Hollywood's attention was on the trio.

She'd initially thought Hollywood was an upper-class blueblood. Thirty minutes of serving tables corrected that misconception. The man missed nothing. Even Richter was deferential to him.

Zita served guests. Hollywood left the dining hall, while von Mayer spoke with Military Man. It was now or never. Heart pounding, she zig-zagged through the tables, stopping here and there to refill glasses. She approached von Mayer's table. Mina's purse lay on a chair.

A sudden light-headedness made her pause. Her mouth went dry. If circumstances were different, she would be with her family. Shaking herself out of childish thoughts, Zita bent to pick up an empty champagne glass. *Get the job done.*

After setting down the tray, she unclasped Mina's purse, dropped a thumb drive inside, then moved to the next table.

Snakey arrived and positioned himself by the exit. She quickly backtracked, trailing another server as they filled their trays with empty glasses. Keeping her head low, she headed for the kitchen, passing the exit where Snakey stood.

The first server passed.

"Wait," Snakey called out as Zita tried to pass him. Had he recognized her?

Her throat tightened, choking off her breath. Blood roared in her ears and pounded so loud, she could barely hear what he was saying. Zita gripped the tray, every muscled coiled—one move from him, and she'd fling it in his face.

Snakey straightened a tilted champagne glass on her tray. "You don't want any accidents."

She thanked him in a hoarse voice even she didn't recognize.

A sudden scream shook the entire hallway.

Snakey bolted to the reception area.

Zita placed the tray on a nearby table, then hastened to the exit. As she moved through the hallway, chaos erupted.

People ran toward the dining hall. Turning to avoid the commotion, she slammed into a solid chest—Hollywood. He steadied her, eyebrows raised in polite concern.

Startled, she glanced up at him, then spoke in fluent German. "My apologies. I must find my manager. There seems to be a problem."

Hollywood responded in German, bowing slightly. "It's I who apologize. Can I help?"

She avoided his gaze, grateful for her glasses. "No, thank you." Without waiting for a reply, she brushed past him into the stairwell, then dashed down to the ground floor.

Richter's men guarded the exits. Panting, Zita scurried to the kitchens. The entire space bustled with commotion. Pushing into a locker room, she pulled on a cleaning crew's uniform, shoved her dark hair into a yellow cap, then made her way past the servers with the trash cart.

"Pickup's early tonight," a staff member commented.

Zita shrugged. "There's an event at the reception hall."

A crowd blocked the employee exit, while security screened IDs. Snakey hovered nearby.

Zita kept her head down and pushed the cart toward the dumpsters.

A guard followed her. "What are you doing?"

She gestured to the cart. "Taking out the trash."

He opened a bag and grimaced. "Make sure you re-enter through the employee entrance."

"Got it." Once he left, she shed the yellow overalls, then slipped through the line of vehicles in the parking lot to the main road. Only then did she allow herself to breathe.

GABRIEL PULLED NOOR behind a stone column and kissed her, drinking in her muffled gasp of surprise. She tasted like spring flowers. He raised his head, pleased at the bemused look in her eyes.

Her mouth curled up. "Let's—"

An earsplitting scream shook the hallway.

Gabriel bolted to the reception hall, Noor at his heels. The music had cut off, and the musicians stood like statues. Guests retreated from the dance floor, gazes fixed on the eastern wall. White linen draped the dessert table. From underneath, a body had tumbled out.

Noor gasped. "Oh, no."

"Stay here." Gabriel approached the body—a man in a dark suit, his angular features distorted. One hand was closed in a fist. The other lay flat at his side, his left index finger missing.

"Is that Darren Johannsson?"

A woman shrieked.

"It's him."

"Call the police." Gabriel leaned closer to the body. The blood on the man's suit was dark. He'd been dead a while. He scanned the dining hall. The Bau siblings were missing. The door marked "Staff Only" stood wide open, and several servers stood there, staring at the gruesome scene.

Richter arrived with his security team. His jaw clenched.

Cyrus and Mina von Mayer came next. Cyrus gripped Mina's hand in his. The two stared at the body and exchanged a look.

"We've called the police, sir," a security guard announced.

Richter addressed the crowd. "My friends, this incident is a shock to us all. There are several lounges outside the hallway on your left. If you would kindly proceed to one of them and wait until the police arrive."

The reception hall erupted into whispers as guests filed out.

The guard with the snake tattoo said something to Richter, who nodded and followed him outside.

Noor signaled to Gabriel. She was with Mina and Cyrus.

He pulled her against him. "Are you all right?"

"Yes."

Mina's face had lost its color. Cyrus took her hand into the crook of his arm. "Let's find a quiet place." They chose a lounge occupied by a handful of couples. He signaled a server for bottles of water.

Gabriel waited until they settled at a table. "Someone said the man's name was Darren Johannsson. Do you know him?"

Mina nodded. "I've seen him at charity functions. I believe he had several ventures with Richter."

"Did they have some kind of falling out?"

She shrugged. "Richter wouldn't kill someone at his own party."

Gabriel leaned back in his seat. "Would he kill elsewhere?"

Mina's eyes went from honey to dark copper. "If Richter wanted someone dead, he would make sure there were no connections to him."

Voices rose in the hallway. The door to the lounge swung open. Detective Jager of the Frankfurt police arrived with Detective Bruker and several police officers.

Noor gripped Gabriel's hand. He squeezed it, letting her know he'd seen them.

Gabriel wanted to warn Cyrus, then checked himself. Cyrus Rohan could handle more than local law enforcement.

Bruker spotted Gabriel and narrowed her eyes. She said something to Jager, who turned and blinked. The duo approached their table.

Gabriel stroked the back of Noor's hand to reassure her.

Jager cleared his throat. "Mister McKnight, I didn't expect to see you here." He studied the others. "I'm Detective Jager from the Frankfurt police, and this is Detective Bruker from INTERPOL We'll be taking your statements."

Cyrus's brows rose. "INTERPOL?

Jager nodded. "INTERPOL has been searching for Mister Johannsson for over a week. We contacted them after hotel security notified us someone had identified the body."

Gabriel wondered if that was true, or if Richter had called them.

Jager pulled out a small notepad and pen from his coat pocket. "May I have your names, please?" His eyebrows rose when Noor gave him her name.

"I called the station and left you a message when Ms. Rahman came home." Gabriel didn't offer more explanation.

The man Brandon had pointed out at Nuremberg as Erik Drussel handed Jager a clipboard. "Here's the list of tonight's guests and hotel staff on shift."

Jager thanked him and introduced Bruker to Drussel. "This is Mister Richter's head of security."

Bruker shook hands with the man as if she'd never met him.

"Did any of you know the deceased?" Jager asked, turning his attention back to them.

"Ms. von Mayer and I met him at a few functions," Cyrus answered.

Jager took notes, then homed in on Gabriel. "My team informed me you've checked out of your hotel, Mister McKnight. Kindly provide me with your contact information as well as the address of your current lodgings."

Gabriel nodded. "Of course."

"Mister Rohan and Ms. von Mayer, my colleague at the next table will take your statements. You may leave after." His attention shifted back to Gabriel. "I'll take yours."

Cyrus rose, and in a voice that broached no arguments said, "I trust the Frankfurt police will not detain my niece or Mister McKnight for long."

Jager bowed his head.

Satisfied, Cyrus nodded at them. "I'll call you tomorrow."

Jager pulled out a chair. "All right. Let's start with Ms. Rahman. Mister McKnight reported you missing after the bombing at the book fair. Please describe what happened."

Gabriel squeezed Noor's knee under the table, hoping she would understand what he was asking.

Noor fiddled with her necklace. "It's hard to remember what exactly happened. One moment I was speaking with Gabriel's agent, and the next people were screaming. The tent went up in smoke, and Gabriel"—she patted his arm—"helped me get out. That's when I remembered I'd left my purse with my passport inside. Gabriel went to get it while I waited." She paused and tapped her finger to her lips. "Someone shoved me. I fell. Everything was hazy for a while."

Jager's brows rose. "How long is a while?"

She lifted her shoulders. "I'm not sure. Half a day, maybe more. The shock made things fuzzy."

He resumed taking notes. "Where were you?"

"That's just it. This is my first time in Frankfurt. I don't know where I was. I found myself in the same area as Rafael Molina. He procured a car and dropped me off at the hotel." She grasped Gabriel's hand. "I lost my phone in the chaos and couldn't call Gabriel."

"Mister Molina will confirm this?"

"Yes. We've moved to his hotel."

Gabriel suppressed a grin. Noor was one of a kind.

"What happened tonight?"

Noor lifted her shoulders. "Gabriel and I had a chat with Mister Richter and my uncle in the private lounge. On our way back to the party, someone screamed. We arrived at the main hall and saw the body."

"Did you recognize the deceased?" Jager asked.

Noor shook her head.

"What's your connection to Herr Richter?"

"I don't have one. He knows my uncle and invited us."

"Thank you, Ms. Rahman. We'll call if we have more questions." Jager's gaze shifted to Gabriel. "What did you and Mister Richter discuss?"

"Writing. Art. Mister Rohan and Ms. von Mayer joined us. Noor and I returned to the reception hall for another drink. You know the rest."

"Did you know the deceased?"

"No." Gabriel glanced at his watch. "If that's all, Detective, we'd like to get back to the hotel."

Jager scowled. "Don't leave Frankfurt before notifying us."

Gabriel ground his teeth. "Consider this formal notification. Noor and I plan to leave Frankfurt in two days. We're traveling to Bavaria for a gala the book fair organized. I must fulfill my commitments."

"My agency handles Gabriel's promotions," Noor interjected. "I'll send you our agenda and itinerary." She took the card Jager offered her and rose.

They took a cab back to Villa Margarite.

The receptionist smiled when they entered the lobby. "Mister Molina asks that you call him when you get to your suite." She handed Gabriel a small package. "This came for you earlier this evening."

The hair on Gabriel's neck prickled. He thanked the clerk.

Noor peered over his shoulder. "Who's it from?"

He scanned the lobby for threats, then checked the exits. Rafael had placed security at the exits. Good thinking.

Sensing the change in his mood, Noor waited until they were back in their suite. "What's wrong?"

Gabriel raked a hand through his hair. "I think I know what's in this package."

"I don't understand."

He used a tissue to unwrap the bright blue velvet box. A man's index finger lay inside.

CHAPTER TWENTY-FIVE

Bahram Chubin plotted against Khosrow to seize the throne. He spread rumors across Persia that Khosrow killed his father.
—Nezami, *Khosrow and Shirin*

GABRIEL USED A pen to pry a note out of the box.

"Gabriel?" Noor's voice held a slight tremor. "Why would anyone send that to us?"

"Not us. The sender wanted *me* to receive this."

"What does the note say?" she whispered.

"'As spears rose with fallen heads, the morning breeze unfurled the prince's flag.'"

Her brows furrowed. "Hmm."

He took her hands. "Do you want to leave? We can fly home tomorrow."

"I can handle danger."

She had that look in her eyes. He kissed her forehead. "That's not what I meant. I'm asking if you want us to leave?"

"Oh." Pacified, she bit her lip. "I think we need to stay and find answers."

"It may get ugly. Hell, it's already ugly."

Eyes green as the hills he'd trekked in Ireland met his. "I know."

He dialed Rafael. "Find Brandon and Harvey and meet us here in ten minutes." He hung up. "Let's get out of these clothes."

When Harvey, Brandon, and Rafael arrived, Noor's eyes brightened at the sight of the hotelier. Gritting his teeth, Gabriel went to the kitchen to brew tea, while she told them about Richter's party.

Brandon scratched his chin. "Darren Johannsson. Why is his name familiar?" He typed on his phone. "He was part of a joint venture with Magdalena Romano and Richter. Johannsson was the major shareholder at OilStat. He facilitated the merger with Global Energy Services. They named the new company 'Global Energy.' Romano runs the show, and Richter is a shareholder." He pursed his lips. "Maybe there's an internal power struggle between Richter and the Global Energy executives."

"Or someone's trying to sabotage the company or Richter," Harvey said.

Gabriel brought out the tea. With no segue into the next topic, he said, "The body at the party didn't have an index finger. When Noor and I arrived tonight, the clerk said someone left us this package."

"What?' Rafael bounded out of his chair. "I told the clerk to notify me and security if anyone asked about you."

"Technically, no one asked about us." Gabriel handed out mugs. "There's a man's index finger with a note in the package."

Harvey paled. "Good God. Why would anyone do that?"

Gabriel moved aside to let Brandon and Rafael study the package. "Whoever sent it wanted to intimidate me."

"Well, that's too bad," Noor snapped.

Rafael glanced at her with a frown. "What does the note say?" Gabriel read the message.

Noor gripped her mug with both of her hands. "It sounds familiar."

"I'll have my security team review footage to see who delivered the package," Rafael said. "We can talk to the clerk tomorrow morning."

Gabriel met each man's gaze in turn. "We've reached a whole new level of danger. I don't want to make you targets. It's safer for you to leave Frankfurt."

Rafael snorted. "I'm not going anywhere."

"Neither am I," Brandon chimed in.

Harvey polished his glasses with his handkerchief. "I've considered the danger since Noor was kidnapped. I too shall stay."

Rafael crossed his arms. "Aren't you extending this warning to Noor?"

"He knows better," Noor said.

Brandon reached for the box.

"Don't touch it. I left it there for the police." Gabriel sighed. "I've gone about this entire thing the wrong way. I know the ugly side of human nature. Instead of using my experience, I've reacted to everything. That will stop." He paced in front of the fireplace. "I always research the subject I want to tackle. It's time we hunt down some facts." He stopped beside Brandon. "I need you to travel to Paris and find everything you can on Jurgen Mulligan. We know he forged documents for Richter. Check if he had any connection with Mina von Mayer or Cyrus Rohan." His gaze flickered to Noor.

She gave him an almost imperceptible nod.

"Find out if he had any dealings with General or Shiraz Rahman."

Brandon nodded. "I'll fly out tomorrow."

Gabriel set aside his resentment for Rafael. "Can the man who told you about me get close to Richter's inner circle?"

"No. He's not high on the food chain." His brow furrowed, then he grinned. "I know someone who can."

"Good. Richter told us his father helped locate artwork the Nazis stole. He claimed it made him unpopular with his family. See if your contact can dig up information about Richter Senior's connection with von Mayer's father, specifically after the war."

"What can I do?" Harvey asked.

"Nezami," Gabriel murmured. "I keep going back to Nezami."

"That's it," Noor said. "The note in the package is from Nezami's *Khosrow and Shirin*. A general named Bahram Chubin spread rumors against Khosrow to take over the throne. Khosrow sought the aid of the Byzantium emperor to win back Persia. It's a war cry. Whoever sent this is warning the enemy."

"So, whoever murdered that man believes Gabriel's the enemy?" Brandon asked.

"Not necessarily." She pushed a strand of hair out of her face. "Sometimes a war cry is to gather troops. The killer may be calling Gabriel to the battle."

Brandon threw his arms in the air. "What's the battle? Why does the killer think Gabriel can help?"

"Gabriel's right. We don't know enough," Rafael said.

"Nezami's important." Gabriel resumed pacing. "Didn't the German engineer mention in his diary the Persian king hid the codes behind the miniatures?"

"He did," Brandon confirmed.

"Why Nezami's miniatures? He could've hidden them behind other paintings." He glanced at Noor. "When you think of me, what kind of food comes to your mind?"

Her eyes widened. "I think of Chinese food, kebabs, and pizza. You're saying there's a connection between Nezami's poems and Germany."

"Yes."

Harvey nodded. "I'll research it."

"Perfect. We'll all regroup in Bavaria." Gabriel glanced at his watch. It was past midnight. "It's best if you return to your rooms. Noor and I will call the police. They'll want to talk to Rafael."

"That's fine," Rafael said. "I can answer their questions without giving anything away."

"Can your team make an extra copy of the security footage? The police will take the original."

Rafael rose. "I'll go talk to them right now."

CHAPTER TWENTY-SIX

At a young age, Khosrow mastered the art of war.
—Nezami, Khosrow and Shirin

JAGER ARRIVED AT the hotel with a team of forensic experts. The lines around the detective's eyes looked more pronounced than they had at the hotel. "Is this the package?"

"Yes."

Jager pulled a pair of gloves from his pocket and nudged aside the lid. "When did this arrive?"

"The clerk said a courier brought it after Noor and I left for the dinner party, which was around seven."

Jager read the note in the package. "Does this make sense to you?"

"It's a poem from a Persian poet," Noor explained. "It's a war scene."

"War scene, huh?" Jager called to one of the uniformed officers. "Get Rafael Molina in here." The officer nodded and retreated. "We'll need both of your fingerprints so we can separate them from other prints on the box, if any." He scanned the suite. "When did you switch hotels?"

"Yesterday."

"Who knows you're staying here?"

Gabriel decided not to mention Brandon's name. "My agent, Mister Molina, Mister Richter, and a friend of mine."

"Are you certain?"

"Yes."

The uniformed officer came back with Rafael, who arrived in rumpled hair, a battered sweatshirt, and jeans.

He had the appearance of someone who had been roused from sleep. "What's going on?"

Jager told him about the package.

Rafael showed an appropriate mix of surprise and outrage. Gabriel had to admit the Spaniard was good.

Forensics bagged the package. Jager accompanied them to the door and spoke in low tones with the group leader. "Mister Molina, we'd like to speak with the clerk who received the package."

Rafael glanced at his watch. "The clerk's shift ended before midnight. I'll check schedules and let you know her next shift."

"We'd also like to review your security footage."

"Very well." Rafael pulled out his phone. "I'll call security."

Jager grunted his thanks. "I realize it's late, but I'd like to speak with you once I've finished here."

"Of course. There's a private dining room down the hallway to your left. I'll wait there for you with fresh coffee."

The comment elicited a smile from Jager. Yep, Rafael knew how to schmooze.

Gabriel hid his amusement as the hotelier offered him and Noor his help and support. He bid them goodnight then left.

Gabriel followed Rafael's example. He put an arm around Noor and invited Jager to sit. "Can I get you anything?"

"No, thank you." Jager lowered himself into an armchair. "Why would someone send you a severed finger? Would it have anything to do with the rumor claiming you know the location of valuable artifacts?"

Gabriel massaged his neck. "I doubt it. All they'd have to do is ask me. I'd give them a true answer."

"You're certain you never met Mister Johannsson?"

"Never."

Jager's hawk-like eyes homed in on Noor. "Is there anything you would like to add to Mister McKnight's statement?"

Noor pulled the blanket around her. "No."

"All right. I'll assign a couple of plain clothed officers to the hotel." Jager rose to leave. "You still planning to travel to Bavaria?"

Gabriel accompanied him to the door. "Yes."

"Be careful."

Gabriel locked the door behind him. Noor opened her mouth to speak. He held a finger to his lips and motioned for her to follow him into the bedroom. "You realize what it means if forensic finds the finger belongs to Johannsson?"

Noor sank into the bed. "It means whoever killed Johansson sent us the package."

He squatted in front of her. "I don't want you going out alone." Harvey didn't have defense training. Rafael, on the other hand, could handle himself if someone attacked. He heaved out a breath. Damn it to hell and back. He hated the thought of Noor alone with Rafael, but her safety was more important. He took both of her hands in his. "You only go out with me or Rafael."

"Okay."

"We need to talk to your uncle."

She eased out of his grip. "You want to ask Uncle Cyrus about Johansson?"

"I want to ask him about Mina von Mayer and Farid Richter. They have history, and it's more than business."

She lay back and tucked a pillow underneath her head. Shadows had formed under her eyes. "What about Detective Hood? What should we tell her?"

He pulled the cover over her. "We'll tell her everything except for finding the codes." When Noor stifled a yawn, he traced the shadows beneath her eyes with his finger. "Get some rest."

Her eyelids fluttered. "Aren't you coming to bed?"

"In a bit." He closed the door, then reached for his laptop. Time to do some research.

MINA KICKED OFF her shoes and leaned her head against the door. Cyrus had insisted she go back to her hotel. He'd come by when he finished answering INTERPOL's questions.

She flung her purse on the couch, then went to change. She'd heard of conflict between Johannsson and Magdalena. Did Magdalena kill him? Killing Johannsson would implicate Richter in the murder. That didn't make sense.

After donning comfortable pants and a sweater, she returned to the living room to pick up her purse. The gleam of a metal object caught her attention. Frowning, she removed a thumb drive. How had it wound up in her purse? She inserted it in her laptop. A file appeared on the screen.

"Dear God." Mina flicked through the images with trembling hands. How could this be? Leaning back against the couch, she tried to think who else knew about her and Cyrus's plans.

A knock sounded. *Cyrus.* Mina flung open the door.

The smile on his face froze. "What's wrong?"

"Come see this." She dragged him to the couch.

He raised an eyebrow when she nudged him to sit and handed him the laptop. After flicking a glance in her direction, his gaze settled on the screen. The slight tightening in his shoulders betrayed his surprise.

She fought the urge to fidget while he clicked through the images in slow precision.

"How did you get this?" He continued studying the images.

"I found a thumb drive in my purse." She spoke before she lost her nerve. "I think Sarah's daughter was at the dinner and left it for me."

"Richter would have spotted her, unless—" He paused and raked a hand through his hair. "Of course. The server. I should've known."

"What are you talking about?"

"When we heard the scream, I first thought it was Noor and went to find her. I bumped into a server outside the lounge. Something about the girl seemed familiar." A hint of a smile appeared on Cyrus's lips. "It was her eyes. She'd disguised them with bulky glasses, but they reminded me of yours." He shook his head. "She must have placed the thumb drive in your purse when we were with Richter." Cyrus grinned. "Richter couldn't create a media circus for his missing ward because he doesn't want the media to know she exists."

"She's not his ward." Mina raised her chin. "She's our... granddaughter." There, she'd said it aloud.

His expression softened. "Yes, Pepper, she is. She's intelligent and a survivor, like her grandmother." He set aside the laptop. "We can use this to our advantage."

One of the good things about being a business partner with the man one loved was knowing how his mind worked. Mina bit back a smile. "Since Richter kept her existence under the radar, he won't seek help from the authorities to find her."

Cyrus nodded. "He'll hire a private team for that. We'll get to her before Richter does. I'll also talk to Gabriel and Noor." His eyes narrowed. "What?"

"If the information on the drive is true, we can push up the timetable and help Gabriel and Noor."

"I see what you mean." He rubbed his chin. "I'll travel to Vienna tomorrow. I believe a visit to an old friend is in order."

She allowed herself to hope.

Cyrus leaned close, so close she could see the silver streaks in his eyes. "We will give our granddaughter what Richter took from her—took from all of us. We won't let her down."

Her pulse stuttered. This man could pierce her heart with one look and make it soar with a few words. She smiled. "No, we won't."

He stroked her cheek, watching her with those burning eyes. His fingers traced her jawline.

She could pull away. One move from her and Cyrus would step back, respecting her decision. He would be polite and distant, like he had all these years. Was that what she wanted?

His gaze stayed glued to hers while his fingers traveled to her lips, tracing them.

Her heart thundered, and her chest constricted. His breath feathered her face as he lowered his lips to hers. Oh, his scent—that unique mix of aftershave and Cyrus—brought to surface feelings she had buried deep. Love, laughter, anticipation, trust, pain, and hope merged into a cauldron of emotions close to boiling over. This was them—an intense tangle of highs and lows. Ignoring the past was no longer an option. It was a weapon to build a future on.

She didn't pull away. This time, she held on and kissed him back.

CHAPTER TWENTY-SEVEN

Bahram Chubin gathered his legion of men and prepared for war against Khosrow.

—Nezami, *Khosrow and Shirin*

NOOR PAID FOR the postcards. Grand-Mère and Moira, Gabriel's mother, would appreciate them.

Her gaze slid toward the hotel's reception desk. The clerk who had been on duty when the package for Gabriel arrived was speaking with an older couple. Rafael and Gabriel had questioned her earlier. She claimed she hadn't seen who had left the package.

Noor studied the clerk. The combined interrogation by Rafael and Gabriel had to be intimidating, not to mention anticipating a discussion with the police. Jager wouldn't get more out of her. A more subtle approach was necessary.

She glanced at the courtyard café, where Gabriel was reading the paper, and decided to try her own hand at interrogation. Pinning a smile on her face, she approached the clerk. "Good morning, Ingrid."

Ingrid's smile faltered. "Good morning, Ms. Rahman." She gripped a pen. "I–I'm sorry to hear what happened last night."

Noor kept her tone light. "It was awful." She sighed. "You'd think a writer could travel inconspicuously. The fans always find him."

"You think it was a fan?"

Noor shrugged. "They love his books. Have you read any?"

Ingrid's shoulders relaxed. "Oh, yes. And watched the movies. They're great."

Noor leaned forward and lowered her voice. "Once when Gabriel and I were on vacation, a fan came to our room pretending to be hotel staff."

"Oh, no." Ingrid's blue eyes grew round as saucers. "That won't happen at Hotel Margarite. We value our guests' privacy."

"I agree. The staff here is wonderful. Including you."

A blush spread over Ingrid's cheeks.

"I hate you're involved in this," Noor murmured.

"Oh." She looked away. "I'm afraid I wasn't much help."

"Women are always trying to meet Gabriel. Do you think it was a woman?"

Ingrid's knuckles grew white. "I couldn't say. The courier wore a black jumpsuit. One of those unisex ones with a helmet and gloves."

"Did you notice cologne or perfume?"

Ingrid blinked several times. She blanched and looked away. "I-I'm sorry. I didn't."

Hmm, interesting. Noor didn't push. The girl would clam up. "No problem. I thought I'd ask."

Ingrid's smile looked forced. "I must work through lunch. Is there anything else I can assist you with?"

Noor thanked her, then made her way to the café.

Gabriel held a chair for her, eyes twinkling. "Did you get anything out of the clerk?"

"Her name is Ingrid, and she's terrified of something."

"Is that so?" He knitted his brows. "What did she tell you?"

"She said the courier wore a unisex jumpsuit with a helmet and gloves. When I asked about cologne or perfume, she remembered something. I'm sure of it."

"Hmm." Gabriel frowned. "Rafael and I reviewed the security footage. A shuttle of tourists arrived around seven-thirty. The courier waited to walk in with them. The clerk barely glanced up when the package was left."

"I'll ask Rafael to speak with her again. He's good with people. Ingrid may confide in him."

Gabriel opened the newspaper. "Hood will be here any minute."

The abrupt change in topic along with his brisk tone surprised her. "What's wrong?"

He didn't raise his eyes. "The authorities are saying two women died during the Nuremberg shooting. That's not accurate. I checked the pulse of three dead men that day."

Either he misunderstood her or was evading her question. "Maybe they're keeping the details quiet because the shooting is under investigation."

"Maybe." He turned the page.

She placed her hand over his. "That's not what I asked."

"Oh?" He met her gaze, his eyes dark like stormy seas.

She loved this man with all her heart and wanted to heal the fracture in their relationship. She stroked his cheek. "I care about us more than anything else. If you want to leave, I'll come with you."

He shook his head, as if trying to rid it of something distasteful, then brushed a kiss across her cheek. "I care about us too."

"Aw, it warms the cockles of my heart to see you two lovebirds going strong." Dressed in head to toe in black, Detective Hood stood by their table in a long coat, leather pants, and Dr. Martens. Her dark hair was tied back from her face, and the nose ring she'd recently added made her look more like a teenage goth girl than a thirty-something-year-old Washington, D.C. cop.

Noor beamed. "Hello, Detective."

Hood slid into a chair at their table. "I gotta give it to you two. If there's trouble within fifty miles, you'll land in it."

"It's good to see you too," Gabriel muttered.

"Did you expect a hug?" Hood's chocolate-colored eyes traveled over Noor. "You look a little peaked."

She lifted her shoulders. "Being kidnapped will do it for you."

"Uh-huh." Hood pointed a blue-tipped fingernail at her. "You said you were going to rest at the hotel." She glowered at Gabriel. "Instead, you take her to a party where a dead body rolls in with dessert and bring her back to a severed finger. You sure know how to show a girl a good time, McKnight."

"Let me explain."

"Please do." Hood crossed her arms.

He walked her through the explosion at the book fair, his hands clenching into fists.

Noor knew the ordeal had been torture for him, making him relive a painful memory. Early in his military career, he had befriended a young Afghan girl who'd provided intel on terrorists. When the Taliban found out, they killed her and most of her village. Her death had hit him hard, leaving a guilt that drove his overprotectiveness.

She recounted her version of the kidnapping. "The kidnappers took us to a farmhouse out of town. They had mistaken Rafael for Gabriel and intended to use me as leverage."

Hood raised her brows. "Leverage for what?"

She and Gabriel had agreed to tell Hood everything except about finding the codes. "They wanted the location to certain artifacts and were going to hurt me to make him talk. They quickly realized they had the wrong man, so they tried to set up an exchange—me for Gabriel."

Hood watched her closely. "How do you know this?"

"Rafael and I heard them talking to each other."

The server arrived with their coffee and a plate of marble cakes.

Hood sipped her espresso. "Damn, why do the Europeans make better coffee than we do?" She transferred her gaze to Gabriel. "Did the kidnappers contact you?"

"Yes. They wanted me to take the codes for the location of the artwork to the Nuremberg Castle in exchange for Noor."

Hood narrowed her eyes. "Tell me you didn't go to Nuremberg."

Gabriel spread his palms. "The boyfriend or husband is the number one suspect in every disappearance. I wasn't going to wait for the police to make up their minds about my innocence. I wouldn't risk Noor's life." There it was again, that tremor in his voice.

She reached for his hand.

He gripped hers. "I went there to find Noor, and before you ask, I had nothing to do with the shooting."

Hood's eyes had a hard glint. "How did you find Noor?"

"Rafael and I rented a farmer's truck and drove to Nuremberg to warn Gabriel."

"That's where I found her," Gabriel finished. "I ran into her and Molina during the shooting."

Hood began ticking off her fingers. "First, you withhold information from authorities. Second, you go vigilante to confront a group of kidnappers. Third, you're involved in a shooting and didn't bother to tell Detective Jager. Christ, McKnight, this isn't one of your action novels. You could've been hurt. You could have died." She glared at them. "You're lucky this isn't my jurisdiction. I'd have hauled both of you in for obstructing a police investigation."

"I'm sorry, but I had no other choice. There's more." He told Hood about spotting Detective Bruker with Richter's henchman at Nuremberg.

A muscle twitched in Hood's face. "Has it occurred to you Bruker may have an informant in Richter's empire? You can't go pointing fingers at a detective without proof."

"I'm not willing to take a chance with Noor's life." He raked a hand through his hair. "We trust you."

Her brows rose. "Not Robin?"

Gabriel's jaw tightened. "His dislike of me colors his judgment."

Hood threw her head back and laughed. The action caused the people at the next table to stare at her. "Robin dislikes everyone, McKnight. He's solid." She tilted her head and studied them. "What are you not telling me?"

Noor could see Gabriel's internal struggle. He rubbed his chin. "Everything else is mere conjecture. When I confirm something, I'll let you know. You have my word."

"Fine. What's next for you two?"

"We'll stick to our itinerary," Noor interjected. "We're traveling to Bavaria tomorrow. If we follow our schedule, whoever thinks Gabriel has the codes will see it's all rumor."

"That's a very Pollyanna way of looking at it," Hood muttered.

Noor shrugged. "These people could follow us back to America where we have family. We'll stay in Europe until this clears up."

Hood nodded. "Describe Erik Drussel."

While Gabriel answered, Noor's attention strayed toward the lobby.

Ingrid jumped every time the phone rang. The girl was afraid of something, no doubt.

Noor smiled at Hood. "If you don't have questions for me, there's something I saw at the boutique I want to buy for my grandmother." She ignored Gabriel's questioning look and strolled into the hotel boutique while keeping Ingrid in sight.

Ingrid checked her phone, then frowned. She said something to the other clerk, picked up her purse, then left the reception area.

Interesting. Ingrid said she was on lunch duty.

Noor headed to the reception desk. "Hello. Where is Ingrid?"

The clerk smiled. "She left to run an errand."

"Which direction did she take?"

"She left that way." The clerk pointed to an employee exit behind the elevators. It opened into an alley beside the hotel.

She bit her lip. Gabriel didn't want her to go out alone. Where was Rafael? She texted both. *Ingrid at reception just left. Am going to follow her via alley by the hotel.*

Noor rushed after Ingrid without waiting for a response. She caught a glimpse of Ingrid's coral blouse as the girl turned the corner.

Her phone rang. *"I'm two blocks away from the hotel,"* Rafael said. *"Where's Gabriel?"*

"He's talking to Detective Hood."

"Wait for me. Don't—"

She hung up. A shiver ran down her spine—a warning time was running out. The men would catch up soon.

The alleys twisted into a maze, the dim light adding to her unease. "Hurry, Gabriel."

The hair on the back of her neck prickled as she navigated the streets. Behind her, the stomp of footsteps echoed. She broke into a run, not knowing which was louder—the footsteps or her pounding heart. The *tap-tapping* behind her grew louder. Sweat trickled down her back. She ran faster until the waterfront came into view. Panting, she burst into a secluded area by the Rhine River, with a scatter of buildings on each side.

The gentle swoosh of the river broke the silence. Her muscles tightened. Where was Ingrid?

Metal clanked. Sounds of a scuffle drifted from a nearby building. An engine roared, then a motorcycle shot out of a side alley, heading straight for her. The rider, in a black jumpsuit and helmet, drew a gun.

Time slowed. The stench of old trash and river water choked her. Blood pounded in her ears, matching the frantic rhythm of her pulse. Wind whipped at her face.

The rider aimed.

Noor searched for cover.

A metal bin rolled in front of her as the gun fired. Bullets pinged off the steel. The rider sped off across the bridge.

Strong arms gripped her. *Gabriel.* A muscle twitched in his face. "Are you hurt?"

"N-no. I'm fine."

"Thank God." He held her tight. She thanked her lucky stars he'd arrived in time.

She pressed a fleeting kiss to his shoulder before looking up. "Ingrid received a text message and left her shift. Something felt wrong, so I followed her."

His gaze flicked past her, and his body went rigid.

Dread curled in her gut as she turned and followed the direction of his gaze.

A woman's leg jutted out from behind the building.

Like a moth drawn to the flame she stepped forward. "Oh, no. Please, no."

CHAPTER TWENTY-EIGHT

Not every gem can be unveiled,
Not every thought should be voiced

—Nezami, *Khosrow and Shirin*

GABRIEL STEPPED CLOSER, his stomach twisting. Ingrid lay crumpled behind a trash can, a lifeless heap, a bullet hole in her skull. Poor innocent kid. She'd got caught in something she didn't understand. And now, she'd paid the ultimate price

He gritted his teeth and glanced around. Ingrid's purse lay open beside her. Her mobile phone stuck out of it. He used a handkerchief to retrieve it, then pocketed it, careful not to leave fingerprints on her bag.

"Is she—"

He nodded. "She's dead."

Noor's lower lip quivered.

He took her into his arms and led her away from Ingrid's body.

Rafael burst from the alley, then came to an abrupt halt when he spotted them. Panting, his gaze landed on the body. The color drained from his face.

Gabriel kept his voice even for Noor's sake. "I'm sorry. We didn't get to her in time."

Rafael clenched his fists, eyes glued to Ingrid's lifeless form. "She was just a kid."

"We should call the police." Gabriel didn't offer words of comfort. Nothing he said would change the ugly truth. "I'll make the call."

"No." Rafael turned. "Take Noor back to the hotel. I'll deal with this."

"Let me help."

Rafael's eyes blazed. "She was my responsibility! Besides, you can't get involved in another murder." He ran a hand through his hair. "I'll tell the police I went after Ingrid because Detective Jager wanted to speak with her. When staff informed me, she took an early lunch, I tried to find her and instead found her body."

He didn't like it but Rafael made a good point. "All right. We'll wait at the hotel." Gabriel took Noor's hand, then led her back through the alley.

She was quiet—too quiet. Her breathing grew shallow as they drew near the hotel.

He tilted her chin up. "Do you need to sit for a moment?"

"No." Her voice was tight. She stayed silent until they reached the suite. The moment the door shut, she was on him, tugging at his buttons with desperate fingers.

Conflicted, he caught her hands, pressing a kiss to her knuckles. "Easy, sweetheart. Do want to talk about it?"

"No." She pulled free and covered his mouth with hers.

It had been a close call, and adrenaline surged through them like a volatile current. His own need slammed into him, just as raw, just as demanding. Harnessing his willpower, he made another attempt to talk to her. "Noor—"

She bit down on his lip.

Hell. A jolt of heat ripped through him. Fire ignited in his veins, burning away the last of his restraint. He crushed his mouth to hers, as his hands, rough and relentless, roamed over her body. Clothes tore away in frantic pulls until there was only skin on skin, and the raw, unspoken hunger pulling them deeper, consuming them both.

The bedroom was too far. They wouldn't make it. With a swift pull, he drew her down to the carpet, their bodies merging with undeniable urgency.

Later, he carried her to the bedroom, then held her close. "You can't go vigilante on me. If I hadn't arrived in time—" He tightened his arms around her.

Noor kissed him. "I won't do anything like that again."

"Thank you."

She nestled against him, eyelids fluttering, adrenaline crashing.

He stroked her hair until her breathing grew even and she fell asleep. Careful not to wake her, he dressed then returned to the living room.

The carnage of their discarded clothing and toppled armchair made his mouth twitch. He put things in order, brewed a cup of tea, then grabbed Ingrid's phone.

What had the girl seen? No, not seen. What had she remembered? It was important enough that she'd died for it.

Gabriel retrieved the small chip he kept in his wallet, then attached it to his phone. Satisfied the device was working, he dialed an overseas number.

"Yo," Billy boomed. "I just sent you an email about the security company you asked me to research. It belongs to a Swedish man named Darren Johannsson. The company is registered as a German corporation, but it's a front. The staff aren't legitimate security personnel. Rumor says Johannsson's in the illegal arms business."

"I can't say I'm surprised." Gabriel jotted notes. "Was Johannsson the sole owner?"

"No, he had a partner. Francisco Oliveira. You know who that is, don't you?"

"The Brazilian entrepreneur?"

Billy chuckled. "None other. Daddy Oliveira was a powerful crime lord. Raised his three daughters to run his illegitimate businesses and groomed Francisco to be the face of the Oliveira empire. It's very Godfatherish. Oliveira and Johannsson were tight. Why are you interested in this company?"

"It's a long story—not one for the phone."

Billy's penchant for security would stop the barrage of questions. He grunted. *"Need anything else from me?"*

"Actually, yes." Gabriel stared at Ingrid's phone. "I need to get into someone's phone."

"Do you know who the phone belongs to?"

"Can you get into it?"

Billy chuckled. *"Can birds fly?"*

Gabriel bit back a smile. "It belonged to a local girl named Ingrid Alter." He spelled her name. "I need to see every text message she received in the past forty-eight hours."

Computer keys clicked in the background. *"Text me a picture of her phone. I'll find her phone company. German data retention laws allow for storage of data for a certain time. I'll let you know when I have what you need."* He paused. *"You need me to fly out there?"*

Gabriel smiled. "You're needed at home."

"Fine. Send Noor my best." He ended the call.

Noor stepped out of the bedroom and flushed as her gaze skimmed over the tidy living room.

He opened his arms, and she slid onto his lap. Gabriel kissed her brow. "Now that you've taken advantage of me, do you want to talk about Ingrid?"

Her mouth turned up for an instant. She fiddled with the buttons on his sweater. "If I'd pushed Ingrid harder for answers, she would be alive now."

"The killer is responsible for her death, not you." He held her gaze until her shoulders relaxed.

She snuggled against him. "Who were you talking to?"

"Billy. I asked him to get into Ingrid's phone."

Her gaze jumped to his. "What if the police find out?"

"They won't. I'll place it somewhere for the hotel staff to find later." He pressed his lips to her temple. "Rafael's right. We can't get involved with Ingrid's death. I don't want to risk the police detaining us. It's best to leave for Bavaria tomorrow."

Gabriel's phone beeped. He checked it, then rose to open the door.

Harvey strode in. A grin deepened the lines on his craggy face. "I found the Nezami link." His smile faded. "What's wrong?"

Gabriel told him about Ingrid while Noor brewed tea.

Harvey sank into an armchair. "This is terrible."

Noor returned carrying a tray with tea. "Rafael will give us an update once he's done talking to the police."

"What did you find?" Gabriel asked.

Harvey pulled two copies of old articles from a folder. "I found these in a German cultural database."

Gabriel studied one. "As part of improving relations between Iran and Germany, the Iranian culture center held a musical of Nezami's *Khosrow and Shirin* in Berlin before the Second World War. Hitler enjoyed it so much, he purchased three *Khosrow and Shirin* miniatures from Iran."

Harvey tapped his finger on the second article. "I tracked them. The Nazis kept all three at the Neuschwanstein Castle. Two have traveled among various museums through the years. The last never left the castle. They don't move it."

Noor brushed at a stray strand of hair. "You think the Nazis kept that specific miniature at Neuschwanstein because it's connected to the codes?"

Harvey beamed at her. "I cross-checked several data bases and scrolled through the catalogs found after the war. There was no mention of the miniatures."

"If it's connected to the codes, they wouldn't catalog it," Gabriel said.

"Exactly. I also checked online videos of the castle. I found the miniature in the castle's main ballroom."

"Great work, Harv."

"Have you heard from Brandon?" Harvey asked.

He scrolled through his messages. "He's meeting with a source today."

Another knock sounded. Rafael came in, his dark eyes haunted. "The police took Ingrid's body. They'll be back tomorrow to question the staff."

Noor's eyes filled with tears. "I'm sorry, Rafael. Ingrid didn't deserve that."

"No, she didn't."

Gabriel patted him on the shoulder. "We'll find the killer."

He nodded and sank into an armchair. "What happened?"

Noor relayed everything until the moment they found Ingrid's body.

"The rider had a gun with a suppressor," Gabriel said. "If I hadn't arrived in time, he or she would have shot Noor."

"You went toward the noise despite our warnings?" Rafael stared, incredulous.

Two spots of pink appeared on Noor's cheeks. "I was trying to help."

He looked like he was going to argue. Instead, he paced in front of the fireplace. "The police asked about you, Gabriel. I made sure they understood neither you nor Noor were anywhere near her when she died."

Gabriel nodded. "I checked the waterfront area. There are no CCTV cameras, which is why the courier wanted to meet her there."

"What do we do next?" Harvey asked.

"You all go to Bavaria," Rafael said.

"I want to speak with Noor's uncle first," Gabriel said.

"I'll call him." She checked her phone. "He sent a text an hour ago. He'll be out of town for a few days and will see us in Bavaria."

Gabriel raked a hand through his hair. He didn't want the police to delay their departure, but leaving Rafael on his own wasn't right. "We can stay to help."

Rafael shook his head. "No, I can handle the police."

"You're certain?"

"Yes."

Gabriel nodded. "We'll leave first thing tomorrow."

CHAPTER TWENTY-NINE

Khosrow sought the emperor's help in getting back his kingdom. The emperor was shrewd and agreed to aid Khosrow on the condition he marry his daughter, Maryam. Caught in a dilemma, Khosrow knew if he didn't win back his kingdom, he would never have Shirin. So, he married Maryam.

Heartbroken, Shirin couldn't believe what Khosrow had done....
—Nezami, *Khosrow and Shirin*

NOOR BURROWED INTO her coat. She had planned a work week in Germany, then hoped to whisk away with Gabriel to Paris before returning home. Instead, they were once again embroiled in danger.

Her gaze drifted to the platform. Passengers milled about, ready to board the train. A guide led a group of tourists to their car, and a lady paid a porter to board her carry-on. A typical train station with the usual scuttle of passengers. How did Gabriel spot danger in public places?

He arrived with the tickets, followed by Rafael, who had insisted on accompanying them to the platform.

She took the tickets. "Why did you cancel the rental car?"

Gabriel's gaze skimmed the platform. "Public transportation is safer."

Hm. He made a good point. "Why did you ask Harvey to take a later train?"

"Because we're not going to Bavaria."

She gripped his arm. "Where are we going?"

"Nuremberg."

Rafael turned. "Why?"

Gabriel waited for a couple to pass. "There's a Nazi Museum in Nuremberg. Mina von Mayer's father was a Nazi supporter. The archives should have information on him."

The PA system crackled to life. *"Train A343 to Bavaria is now boarding. Passengers to Bavaria, please board the train."*

"We should go," Gabriel murmured.

Dear God, the man confused her. "You said we're not going to Bavaria."

His aquamarine eyes twinkled. "We'll board the train, get off, and change platforms."

"Were we followed?" Rafael scanned the platform.

Gabriel took her carry-on. "Caution doesn't hurt. Let's go." He shook hands with Rafael. "Stay safe."

"I need a minute," Noor said.

His jaw ticked. He drifted toward the next platform but kept her in sight.

Rafael shuffled his feet and tilted his head in the train's direction. "I'll repeat what Gabriel said. Stay safe."

"Of course." She bit her lip, feeling guilty about leaving him to deal with the police. "What are you doing today?"

Shadows flitted through his eyes. "Helping Ingrid's parents make funeral arrangements."

"Oh, Rafael." She hugged him.

He stiffened, then held her tight.

She leaned back and patted his arm. "I can stay."

His mouth turned up. "No. Go with Gabriel. I'll see you in Bavaria."

She hugged him again, then joined Gabriel, who stood scrolling through his texts.

His cheek twitched, and he blinked several times.

"Gabriel?"

He looked up. His eyes were red.

"Are you all right?"

The muscle spasmed again. "Yes, why wouldn't I be?"

"Your eyes." She leaned forward. "They're red."

He pulled a tissue out of his pocket and wiped at them. "It's the damned smell of train stations. I hate it."

Uncertain whether it was true to not, she left it alone. "What do you hope to find on von Mayer?"

His eyes hardened. "It's what I believe we won't find. Nuremberg has one of the largest archives on the Nazi era culture and property. If von Mayer supported them, there'll be information pointing to it."

Trust Gabriel to wade through the fabrication to find the truth. "And if there isn't, you believe he was innocent of the charges?"

"It's a possibility."

Two hours later, they arrived at the rally grounds, where several kilometers of unfinished buildings, barracks, and parade grounds had held Nazi party rallies.

"The city council of Nuremberg established the Documentation Center in 1994," Gabriel said. "An Austrian architect, Gunther Domenig, designed a diagonal glass-and-steel passageway on the northern head of the unfinished conference hall to house the museum, making the documentation center part of the rally grounds."

She followed him into the building, where echoes of the past cast a somber atmosphere. The primary exhibit, *Fascination and Terror,* displayed pictures and information depicting Nazi culture.

Noor repressed a shudder. "They do a good job of showing the regime's megalomania."

"They do." Gabriel studied photographs of German fighter planes and soldiers. "Officers of the Luftwaffe, Germany's air defense during the war." He pointed to the names printed under the picture. "This must be Richter's father."

Noor examined the picture. Farid Richter resembled his father. She lifted her head.

Gabriel was staring at her, eyes blazing with emotion. He looked away. "Let's find the archives."

They came to a brick tunnel, where an attendant greeted them.

Gabriel smiled and introduced himself.

She blushed and stammered.

Noor pitied the girl. The McKnight smile was a powerful weapon. She remembered their intense lovemaking after Rafael and Harvey had left last night, and her cheeks heated. *Get a hold of yourself, Noor.*

"I'm doing research for my next novel," Gabriel said. "My friend and I are looking for information on Nazi supporters who assisted with the Reichsleiter Rosenberg Taskforce, specifically ones the hunters discovered after the war."

The attendant beamed. "I'll bring up the catalog."

Noor bit back a smile. No doubt the girl would tell her friends she helped Gabriel McKnight with his next novel over beer tonight.

The attendant typed on a computer. "We have two catalogs. One is a photo archive. You may print any information you need."

Noor glanced in the direction of the computer stations. "Divide and conquer? I'll take the photo archive if you want to look through the other information."

"Sounds good." Gabriel seated himself behind a computer and avoided looking at her.

She rubbed her temples. *What's bothering him? Why won't he talk to me about it?*

A thought occurred to her. "Is anyone following us?"

"Hm." He raised his head from the screen and glanced over her shoulder. "No. We're safe for now." He nodded to the computer beside him. "The attendant has the photo archives on this one."

Feeling like a chastised child, she sat. Once she accessed the photos, her worry dissipated. Fascinated and immersed in the terrifying World War II era, her personal worries took a back seat.

They spent the rest of the morning in the archives. Gabriel print-ed articles of Hans Richter with various Nazi officials. She found nothing on von Mayer but discovered a photo series titled *Young Officers of the Luftwaffe* and scrolled through pictures of German soldiers attending parades until one title jumped out at her.

"Gabriel, look at this." He joined her at the computer. "It's Karl von Mayer. This says he graduated from pilot school that year. They flew the planes for the rally."

Gabriel enlarged the photo. "A staunch Nazi supporter who attended one rally."

She rubbed her brow. "Wasn't he a general?"

"That happened after the war."

The attendant ushered a middle-aged man with shaggy blond hair into the archives. He took a seat behind a computer and drew out pince-nez glasses to focus on the monitor in front of him. He seemed familiar.

Gabriel checked his watch. "Print the picture. We should leave."

Outside the archives, she took his arm. "Do you think the story about Mina's father is false?"

"There isn't much about him, yet he was labeled a Nazi supporter."

She considered this. "What if Mina's father had found the loca-tions to the looted art and was going to notify authorities? What if he was innocent of the allegations made against him?"

Gabriel stopped by some type of coding machine. His jaw tight-ened, and he leaned forward to study the machine.

"Gabriel?"

"We're being followed."

Startled, she put the folder in her purse. "Are you certain?"

"Yes. Follow my lead."

He guided her out of the exhibits and into the courtyard. She resisted the urge to glance behind her.

"There are two men heading toward the bench by the exit. Are they your kidnappers?"

She glanced to her left. "No."

Gabriel stopped by a newspaper stand, pretending to search through a rack of postcards with a mirror on its top. He used it to check on the men behind them. "Two more are coming from the other exit."

She gulped. "Do we run?"

"I have an idea." He approached a tour group and introduced himself to the guide. "Can my friend and I join you? I'll pay for tickets."

The guide rubbed his chin. "You'll have to pay for the entire day, even though you missed the tour of the documentation center. We're going to the Nuremberg Castle next."

"No problem. We'll join you." He paid the guide. They climbed onto the bus.

"What now?" Noor settled into a seat.

"Do you have a mirror?"

She retrieved her compact from her purse.

He tilted the mirror back and forth. "There was a man in the archives."

She rubbed her brow. "Yes. He looked familiar."

"He's in a car with the muscle following us. We have a good chance at losing them once we arrive at Old Town." He returned the compact, then squeezed her hand to reassure her.

The bus, like most tour buses, trudged along the city, pointing out noteworthy sites and buildings. It was hard to sit still when all she wanted to do was run. It stopped outside of Old Town Nuremberg.

"Tie your hair back and leave your coat on the bus." Gabriel peeled off his own jacket. They joined other groups outside of Old Town's entrance. The crisp October wind made her shiver. He lowered his voice. "See those trash cans beside the entrance? When we reach them, we'll jump into the other lane and leave with the tourists exiting the castle."

The line progressed until they reached the trashcans.

"Go now."

She ducked under the rope, then ran to a cluster of tourists and struck up a conversation with a young couple. It was hard not to look back.

Just when she thought she'd scream, a hand gripped her upper arm. "I'm here." Gabriel fell into stride beside her, and they exited Old Town. "Keep to the crowd. The train station isn't far."

She spotted one of the men following them. "Gabriel?"

"I see him." Gabriel gripped her hand. "Run."

They sprinted across the street toward a bridge by the river. She kept up with him, racing through the crowd in line for cruises. They turned into a side road. Two more men came at them from the northern end of the bridge.

Gabriel slowed his pace. "I'll distract them. Get to the train station. If I don't make it, I'll take the next train."

"I won't leave you."

His expression faltered, and his voice took on a hard note. "Yes, you will."

She froze. What was he talking about?

"Go," Gabriel urged.

Noor dashed to the bridge, while he took a left into a back alley. Every step away from him hurt. She couldn't leave him. Circling around the bridge, she ran back to the alley, grabbed the metal lid of a trashcan for a weapon, then crept forward. Three men lay unconscious at the end of the alley.

Gabriel jumped down from behind a trashcan. He saw the lid in her hand, and the corners of his mouth twitched. "Let's go."

The man from the archives stepped out from behind the trashcans. He had a gun in his hand. "Not yet, if you please."

Noor gripped Gabriel's hand. She'd fight beside him.

The man glanced at the unconscious goons. "Impressive."

Gabriel shifted his body to shield hers. "What do you want?"

"I ask for a few minutes of your time, Mister McKnight."

Gabriel nodded. "Fine, let my friend go."

The man chuckled. "We're not negotiating." He paused as more footsteps approached. Another gunman appeared. The older man smiled. "I would like to ask you some questions."

Gabriel didn't move. The man held his gun steady.

Noor refrained from rolling her eyes and stepped around Gabriel. "How about you quit aiming guns at us for a start?"

The man's grey eyes twinkled. He motioned to the guard beside him. Both lowered their guns.

"I'm Stefan Johansson. Darren Johannsson was my brother."

So, that was why he seemed familiar.

"You were headed to the train station. Allow me to give you a lift, and we'll talk on the way."

It wasn't as if they had a choice.

Gabriel shrugged. "Fine."

They followed the men to the to the riverside, where a luxury yacht sat at the dock. Johannsson's muscle guided them aboard then to a sitting room.

Johannsson waited for them to settle onto the sofa. "I was out of the country when I heard of my brother's demise."

Gabriel nodded. "I'm sorry for your loss."

Johansson accepted this by lowering his chin to his chest. "Darren had a passion for art and artifacts. He told me you have the location of artwork the Nazis took during the Second World War. He attended Richter's dinner party to approach you."

"I never spoke to your brother," Gabriel said.

He raised his brow. "Herr Richter is also an art enthusiast."

"If you say so."

Johannsson's eyes gleamed. "What is your impression of Richter?"

Gabriel rubbed his chin. "I believe he's a man who gets what he wants, no matter the price."

"Did Herr Richter approach you for the artwork?"

"I don't know the location of missing artwork. Herr Richter is aware of this."

Noor ducked her head. Gabriel had avoided giving a direct answer.

Johannsson waved his hand. "I want to find who killed my brother. You have a military background. You notice things others don't. Did you spot anything out of the ordinary?"

Gabriel met his gaze. "The blood on your brother's clothing was dry. He was killed elsewhere."

Johannsson's nostrils flared. "Someone sent you a package the same evening."

Gabriel rubbed his chin. "Yes. We tried to identify the courier and were unsuccessful. An innocent clerk died because of it."

"Is that so?"

"That's all I know," Gabriel said.

Johannsson shifted his gaze to Noor. "Where are you headed?"

She followed Gabriel's tactic. "We came to Germany for business. We're following our itinerary."

Johannsson steepled his fingers together and considered this. "And where would that be, Ms. Rahman?"

"Neuschwanstein."

"I will come to Bavaria in the event the courier makes another visit." Johannsson produced a card from his pocket. "This is my private line. You will let me know if that happens?"

Gabriel took the card. "Of course."

The server cleared his throat. At Johannsson's nod, he approached and murmured something in a low tone. "We have arrived at the train station. Thank you for your time. My man will accompany you to the dock."

Noor waited until they were on the train. "Do you believe him?"

Gabriel sighed. "He seemed sincere."

THE CAB DRIVER dropped them off at a place Noor could describe as a fairytale. Nestled in a valley between Hohenschwangau Castle and Neuschwanstein Castle, the hotel was a majestic traditional structure with an enchanting forest for its backdrop.

She had barely a minute to take in the scene when Gabriel touched her arm. "Noor, I think it's best if we stay in separate rooms."

What? "I'm sorry, what did you say?"

He shoved his hands in his pockets. "It's best to stay in separate rooms. We should, ah... give each other space."

Space? He wanted space? She gaped at him. Was this why he'd been acting strange? Had he tired of their relationship? Was this how relationships worked? She didn't know because he was the first man she'd loved. She couldn't believe it. "Gabriel if this is about Ingrid's murder—"

"No."

"Then what is it?"

He didn't answer. Her chest felt like someone had ripped it open and clawed through her heart. Her eyes stung. She gripped the handle of her carry-on.

He took a step toward her. "I'll always be your friend, and we agreed a separation wouldn't affect our working relationship." He was reminding her of a conversation they had at the start of their relationship. She had promised him if they didn't work as a couple, she would continue to work with him professionally. *And he said he was in it for the long haul.*

Pain morphed into anger. They had spent the past months together, sharing dreams—sharing their lives. She'd given her body and soul to him. He'd given his to her. How could he casually discard all that? Like lava, her anger bubbled up from her stomach to her chest, making it hard to breathe. *Don't cry.*

"Noor—"

She lifted her chin. "You don't need to explain. I'll see you tomorrow morning at the opening breakfast." She picked up her carry-on, then headed to the reception area. *Don't you dare cry.* She repeated the mantra until she arrived at her own suite. Only then did she allow the tears to fall.

CHAPTER THIRTY

Caught between his love for Shirin and doing the right thing, Khosrow's pain was great....

—Nezami, *Khosrow and Shirin*

IT WAS FOR the best. She cared for Rafael. He'd seen it in the way she'd held onto him at the station. What other choice did he have but to step back? *Let her go. She deserves to be with a good man, not a broken one.* Gabriel rubbed his eyes with the heels of his hand.

"Are you crying?"

He swiveled around. The kid he'd met in Frankfurt. What was his name? Sam.

Sam stood beside him, holding a pair of binoculars. "Are you crying because you fought with Noor?"

"I didn't fight with Noor."

"Then why are you crying?"

Gabriel clenched his jaw. "I have allergies."

Sam wrinkled his nose. "Jason Vann doesn't have allergies."

He picked up his carry-on and headed toward the hotel.

Sam followed. "Mom said you and Noor were joining the mystery convention. I was waiting for you to arrive."

Gabriel liked children, but his patience was low at the moment. He needed a moment to gather himself. And several years for his heart to quit bleeding.

Oblivious to his mood, Sam chattered on. "Since we arrived earlier, I checked the hotel grounds for you. And you know what?"

Gabriel didn't take the bait.

"The men who kidnapped Noor are here."

He came to an abrupt halt. "What?"

Sam bobbed his head. "I saw the man who put the cloth on her mouth."

He gripped the kid's shoulders to stop him from squirming. "You're certain they're here?"

"Yeah." Sam wiggled free from his grasp. "He's in a bungalow behind the golf course with others. I can show you."

"Come with me." Kid in tow, he checked into the hotel. With a mighty effort, he held onto his patience while the receptionist welcomed him. When she reached for a brochure to give him a speech on the hotel's amenities, he plucked it from her hand. "I know my way around, thank you."

Sam followed him to his suite. Behind the lake, a golf course sprawled into the Bavarian Forest. The boy pointed to a patch of trees where the forest began. "There are cottages back there. I saw the man coming out of the second cottage. He was with people I didn't recognize."

"Give me those." Gabriel motioned to the binoculars. Sam handed them over. He zoomed in on the forest until spotting the thatched roof of a cottage. "What does the man who took Noor look like?"

Sam's forehead wrinkled. "He's tall and has long, brown hair. The left side of his face has a scar." Sam ran his own hand in a diagonal line across his face. "Right here."

Gabriel headed to the door.

"Where are you going?" Sam ran after him.

He returned the binoculars. "Thank you for your help. Go back to your room."

"But—"

"No buts."

"What if you need help?" Sam cried.

"I'll manage."

Sam's chin jutted out. "I'll stay until you're back."

If the kid was right, Noor was in danger. He took the elevator down to the gym, grabbed a bag of golf clubs, then wandered onto the course. By blending in with different foursomes, he made his way to the edge of the forest. A trail opened at the edge of the woods. He hid his golf clubs, then followed it.

Cottages sprawled through the trees. No doubt hotel staff lived here. Two vans sat behind the second cottage. How close could he get to it? A scuffling sound made him duck behind a fir tree.

The door to the cottage swung open. Erik Drussel stepped out, followed by two men carrying something wrapped in blankets.

Gabriel craned his neck for a better view.

The edge of the blanket fell away. Christ, it was a body. The dead man had dark hair. A diagonal scar ran down the left side of his face.

"Careful," Erik snapped. "Don't leave a mess." The men loaded the body into the vehicle, then drove off.

Gabriel waited until they left to approach the cottage. He peered through each window to make sure no one was inside. Satisfied, he fiddled with a window latch, then climbed in. He wandered through the kitchen into the cottage's small living area. A letter of resignation and a map of the hotel grounds lay sprawled on a table. Beside the map lay pictures of himself and Noor at Richter's dinner.

Shit. He shuffled through the pictures and found several photographs of her. A quick search of the cottage revealed nothing else.

Together or not, he wouldn't let anyone hurt Noor.

"MS. VON MAYER?" Mercedes's gentle voice carried into the study.

Mina glanced up from the spreadsheet on her computer. "Yes."

"Mister Richter and Messrs. Abromowski are in the lobby. They'll be up shortly."

Mina ignored the slight jump in her stomach. "Show them into the formal sitting room, please."

"Shall I prepare a tea tray?"

"Yes, thank you."

Mercedes turned to leave then stopped. She clasped her hands together and stared at her shoes. "Is... is everything all right, madam?"

Hard as Mina tried to hide her apprehension, the girl had sensed it. She managed a smile. "I'm just tired. I'll rest once we complete our business in Germany."

Mercedes nodded. "Maybe you can take vacation in Lucerne."

"That's a good idea."

Her shoulders relaxed. "I'll get the door."

Mina straightened the pleats on her skirt. Preparedness was the key to success in business—that and a knowledge of human psychology. The Abromowskis would balk if they glimpsed uncertainty from her. Straightening her shoulders, she went to greet her guests.

"Ah, Zauberin. You are lovely as usual." Richter beamed.

"Thank you." She pasted on a smile. "You're looking fine yourself."

He chuckled and patted his flat stomach. "It's the intermittent fasting. You should try it."

"I don't know. I like my mid-morning snacks." She greeted the Abromowskis.

As always, Mina was struck by the contrast between the brothers. David, the older brother, wore a yarmulke, the brimless cap a traditional head covering for Jewish males. Somber by nature, he preferred to dress in dark colors. In business, David was risk adverse. Asher, his brother, enjoyed risk. Dressed in a pale grey suit with a bright purple tie—and no kippah on his head—his hazel eyes twinkled.

"It's always a pleasure to wield magic with a sorceress," Asher said.

They exchanged pleasantries, while Mercedes brought in a tea tray.

"Your assistant makes the best tea," Richter announced.

Mercedes blushed and almost tripped over herself. Had Richter not caught her, she would've fallen on the tea tray. She stammered a thanks before leaving the room.

Richter rubbed his jaw. "Is she like this with everyone? Or should I be flattered?"

Mina sighed. "She's shy."

David cleared his throat. "Herr Richter mentioned something about a change of plans."

Mina nodded. "You are aware the authorities claim my father worked with the Nazis?"

He nodded gravely.

"I believe the authorities accused my father incorrectly, but I cannot change history." Her voice came out steady. "I appreciate the trust you and Asher have in me. Your board, however, will not allow you to carry out the merger with me in the picture."

Asher's eyes clouded. "Some of the board members are more modern thinking. They don't believe one should pay for the sins of their fathers."

"I agree, but you and I know you're the minority."

"It is disappointing," David murmured, staring at a space over Richter's shoulder. "I was not aware of your father's past until we ran the background checks." He steepled his fingers. "You know I admire and respect you, Ms. von Mayer." David was proper. No Zauberin nicknames from him.

She nodded.

"Then, I hope you will understand why the board won't proceed."

"I do." *Keep your cool.* She raised her chin. "I'd like to suggest an alternative solution, one that will allow the business venture to go through. Herr Richter will take my place as major shareholder." She let it sink in. "His family is above reproach. The other details will remain the same. It's a win-win situation for everyone involved."

Asher rubbed his chin. "Yes, for everyone except you."

Keep your calm. She spread her palms. "I'm not suggesting a partnership I wouldn't consider."

Richter coughed. "Zauberin and I have come to an arrangement. We will partner on another venture, which will compensate for her losses in this one."

"Biopharma." Asher leaned forward. "Is that why you delayed your merger with Alum?"

She allowed the corners of her mouth to turn up. "I can't discuss it."

Asher grinned. "I won't breathe a word."

David had been silent until this moment. "The suggestion has its merits. I'll take it to the board. We'll have an answer for you by the end of the week."

Asher smiled at Mina. "To make amends for our board, may I suggest you invest in Kroner's stock?"

David glared at his brother.

Richter furrowed his brows. "They're a small pharmaceutical company. Why would their stock go up?"

"Is the new cancer drug working?" Mina asked, unable to mask her interest.

Asher's eyes twinkled. "It's been out for a year now and... er, it's just my opinion."

"I'll keep that in mind." Richter pursed his lips.

She knew that look. He would research the company.

The brothers rose and bid them goodbye.

Richter waited until she was back in the living room. "I'd say that went well."

"I agree. The vote with the board is a formality. If David's on-board, which he was, they'll all vote to proceed."

"How would Asher have insider information on the cancer drug?"

She considered it. "He's friendly with a certain female VP at the organization."

"Ah." Grinning, Richter went to the liquor cabinet. He poured two glasses of brandy, then brought them over. "I've talked to the

Alum executives and let them know my capital is tied up with another venture. I informed them you will replace me as the major shareholder. They agreed with the switch. Your legal counsel will have the paperwork tomorrow."

She nodded and accepted the drink.

Richter's eyes fell on the book sitting at the coffee table. "Do you like Nezami's *Khosrow and Shirin*?"

"Yes."

His eyes grew distant. "My father saw the musical in Frankfurt prior to the war. He made me learn Farsi so I could read the work in its original language."

"Did you enjoy it?"

"Very much." His eyes shifted back to her. "What do you like best about it?"

"Their love was strong," Mina said.

He watched her the way a predator watched prey.

"What about you? What did you like best about it?"

Richter considered her question. "Aside from its beautiful prose, it shows intelligence combined with power gains the upper hand. For example, Khosrow gave Farhad, a man enamored with Shirin, an impossible task. When Farhad almost accomplished it, Khosrow sent him word Shirin was dead. It caused the young fool to throw himself off the Bistun mountain and die."

It was a subtle threat. He was warning her from making alliances on the Board. She bit back a smile. She really was a thorn in his side.

Richter raised his glass. "Shall we toast to our future?"

She clinked her glass against his. "To the future."

He leaned back in his chair. "Your help with the Abromowskis saved me grief."

"Grief?" She shook her head. "You're the man who starts catastrophic wars with a phone call."

He raised his brows. "You're the woman who stops them. You've cost me money and grief, Zauberin."

She mimicked his gesture and leaned back in her chair. "I saved you from yourself. Nonproliferation is essential for our Board. The balance of power pushes us and our world forward."

He tilted his head. "Have you considered the future?"

Where was this going? "In what way?"

His eyes grew distant. "Someday you and I will tire of this. Have you chosen who you want to replace you at the Board?"

"No. Have you?"

"Not yet." He pursed his lips. "The others have chosen their replacements. Petrov has that nephew of his. Magdalena is grooming her niece. Cyrus has Morris, and Lee is grooming his children."

"I thought Lee's boys were running his casinos."

"I was referring to his illegitimate offspring." Richter chuckled. "Have you met them? They're quite resourceful." He leaned forward. "You and I are alike, Zauberin."

No, we're not. "Oh?" She took another sip of her drink. "How so?"

"For starters, we're both from Persian-German descent. Neither of us married—well, you were wed for a short while, but that doesn't count. We both built empires our fathers dreamed of." He grinned. "I consider you family, and family looks out for one another. Don't you agree?"

Is that why you killed my daughter, kidnapped my granddaughter, and hid her from me all these years? She made certain her smile wasn't strained. "Yes. Family looks out for one another."

CHAPTER THIRTY-ONE

Shirin's unhappiness was extreme....
　　　　　　　　　　　　—Nezami, *Khosrow and Shirin*

NOOR RAN FASTER, taking the route through the forest. Running cleared the mind. She'd spent most of the night in alternate states of shock and hurt. Gabriel loved her. She didn't doubt it. However, loving someone and wanting to be with them were two separate things.

She circled the trail around the hotel, slowing to admire the view. The lake's sparkling waters reflected the golden rays of sunlight. The forest trees, cloaked in the rich colors of autumn, rose gracefully over the hills where the Neuschwanstein Castle, with its turrets and towers merged with blue skies.

Noor transitioned to a walk, giving her body time to adjust. If being lovers wasn't what Gabriel wanted, she would respect that. Besides, he was her client, and work was top priority. She glanced at her watch. The convention would kick off in an hour. Gabriel and two other clients were speakers on panels. She pushed back the pain. It was time for business.

Back at the hotel, she caught her reflection in a mirror. Her cheeks had gained back some color, and her eyes—well, skillful makeup would hide the redness brought on from all the crying. She reached for a sore spot behind her shoulder and came to an abrupt halt in front of her suite.

Gabriel stood waiting outside her room. The red rim around his eyes indicated he hadn't slept either. His gaze skimmed over her. "You're all right."

No, I'm not. "Yes."

He raked a hand through his hair. "You didn't answer when I knocked."

She swallowed the lump in her throat. "I went for a run."

His eyes darted to the emergency exits before settling back on her. "I'm glad you're all right. I—"

Noor held up a hand. "You don't need to worry. We're adults, Gabriel."

His cheek twitched, and shadows flitted through his eyes. He looked away. "Of course." Shaking his head, he stepped closer. "That's not why I'm here." His eyes turned a deep aquamarine, and his posture was stiff.

She knew that look. "What's wrong?"

"Erik Drussel is here. I saw him transport the body of one of your kidnappers."

"What? How—"

He glanced down the hallway. "I'll explain when the others are here. Be careful."

She suddenly felt queasy. "Okay."

Gabriel checked his phone. "Brandon arrived last night. Rafael is on his way. Don't go anywhere on your own. I can't—" He raked a hand through his hair. "I don't want you to get hurt."

A shiver crawled up her spine. She lay a hand on his arm. The contact sent a jolt of electricity through her. "I don't want you to get hurt either."

He felt it too. His eyes softened. "I'll be careful." He traced a finger down her cheek to her jawline, then stepped back. "I'll meet you up here in thirty minutes. We'll go down together."

An hour later, the conference hall was in full swing. Writers, editors, critics, consultants, and representatives from the publishing and entertainment industries mingled. Gabriel kicked off the morning panel. When several women threw admiring glances in his direction, she tried not to be bothered by it.

"Hi, Noor."

She whirled around.

Sam smiled up at her. "Did I scare you?"

Noor ruffled the boy's mop of curls. "What are you doing here? Your mother said you had golf lessons this morning."

He grimaced. "Golf is so booooooring. I came here to spy for Gabriel."

She lifted her brows. "Does Gabriel know?"

He shrugged, and a dark curl fell across his forehead. "He needs my help." Sam pushed away the wayward lock. "We won't let anyone kidnap you again."

"Is everything all right?" Harvey murmured. Concern deepened the lines on his forehead. "Gabriel seems perturbed."

She ignored the question. "I'm free after lunch. If you have nothing scheduled, we can tour the castle."

Harvey didn't comment on her change of subject. "I have meetings with a production company for Gabriel's new book."

Her mouth turned up. She couldn't wait to see his new series on the silver screen.

Brandon strode into the convention. Taller than most people, he was easy to spot. He wove through the crowd to join her. "It's packed in here. Next time someone says books are dying or publishing is in trouble, I'll correct them."

"You can write an article about it."

Brandon had dark circles around his eyes—another member of the miserable and sleep deprived. He had lost someone dear, and if he'd loved his friend half as much as she loved Gabriel.... No. She wouldn't go there. It occurred to her she hadn't trusted Brandon because he was a reporter. It wasn't like her to stereotype people.

Ashamed of her behavior, she strove to be cordial. "How was your trip to Paris?"

"Informative. I'd rather recount it once. Where are Gabriel and Rafael?"

"Rafael will arrive soon. Gabriel's speaking with an editor." She checked the time. "I have a meeting at the pavilion. Gabriel and Harvey are meeting with a publisher at the same place. Let's gather at the hotel café in an hour."

"Shouldn't I come?" Sam pushed into their circle. "You'll need my help."

She patted his arm, feeling guilty she'd forgotten about the boy. "We'll find other activities to keep you busy."

Sam scowled. "I can handle danger."

"Look, kid," Brandon began.

Sam glared up at Brandon, which was a feat because he had to crane his neck. "I'm almost ten." Muttering something about clueless adults, Sam stomped off to the young adult section of the convention.

She turned to follow him.

Brandon gripped her arm. "He'll be safe. Rafael's here."

Rafael weaved through the booths. He greeted the men then leaned down to kiss her cheek as his eyes skimmed over her face. "Everything okay?"

"Yes. It's been a busy morning." She'd said the last part with a forceful cheer.

He glanced at her dress with approval. "It's good to see you."

She blushed. She'd worn the fitted black and emerald dress with the matching pumps because Gabriel liked it. Apparently, he wasn't the only one. "Thank you. It's good to see you too." And she meant it.

She was about to ask Rafael about Ingrid's funeral when she spotted Stefan Johannsson several booths away.

"Stefan Johannsson is here," she murmured to no one in particular.

Brandon furrowed his brows. "Who?"

"Noor, my darling." A woman swept into their circle. Tall and full figured with an ample bust and generous hips, her sweet perfume wafted in the air.

"Hello, Hema."

"Am I early?" She tucked a strand of ebony hair behind her ear and gave Noor air kisses. The movement caused the fur shawl dangling from her shoulder to hit Brandon in the face.

"No, you're on time."

She smoothed her figure-hugging dress. "It's sweet of you to make time for me."

"I always have time for my clients." Noor faced the men. "This is Hema Guvari, a gifted writer, friend, and client." She motioned to the men. "These gentlemen are my friends. This is Brandon Rohr, Rafael Molina, and Harvey Cornwall."

Hema beamed. "So, you're Gabriel's super-agent?"

Harvey blushed and stammered a greeting.

Hema's dark eyes skimmed over Rafael. "Molina, as in the Molina hotels?"

Rafael bowed his head. "*Sí, señora.*"

. "It's *señorita*." Hema batted her lashes. "Such a gentleman and so handsome." Her voice crooned on the last word. She swiveled around and homed in on Brandon. "Are you in the hotel business too?"

"No, ma'am," Brandon said. "I'm a journalist."

"Ah, a fellow writer." She heaved a long sigh. "Writing requires both heart and mind to be engaged."

"What do you write?" Brandon asked.

"Romance," Noor said.

Hema's mouth turned up. "I write *erotic* romance. Steamy, makes your toes curl and your body burn erotica." She sighed heavily. "I'm searching for my next muse. It's been a frustrating search."

Brandon and Rafael stepped back, distancing themselves from anyone using the words muse, romance, and search in one sentence.

Harvey, ever the gentlemen, cleared his throat. "There's quite a market for romance novels."

"Hema's won two RITA awards for contemporary romance," Noor chimed in. "Her books fly off the shelves."

"My novels inspire women to not only seek but demand what

they desire in their mates. A strong relationship is a healthy mix of love and lust." Her lips turned down. "Finding my muse is essential. If I don't burn, I can't make my readers burn." She tapped her index finger on her lips while her eyes skimmed over Brandon. "Is my muse a Viking warrior?"

Brandon's eyes widened. He took another step back.

Hema's gaze drifted over to Rafael. "Maybe he's a Latin sex god."

Rafael's mouth twitched.

Hema blew out a breath. "It's why I came to the convention. I have a bone deep feeling I'll find him here. One must venture away from the laptop to meet the muse."

"*Latin sex god?*" Rafael mouthed to a grinning Brandon.

Noor frowned at them. "Hema and I have business to discuss." She steered Hema toward the pavilion.

"Noor, dear, what do I do?" Hema trailed after her. "My writing is as tepid as lukewarm tea. I want true love, not some short-term ba-ha people call a relationship."

You and me both.

"I broke up with Ray. Now he's heartbroken and miserable."

Noor didn't doubt it. Both Ray and his predecessor had adored Hema. She wondered what the woman did to encourage such devotion. Maybe she should be the one seeking advice from Hema.

Hema's eyes glistened with tears. "What should I do?"

She rubbed her temples, wondering what to say. Hema needed inspiration. "You'll find your muse. Don't give up, and don't settle for anything less. Until then, keep writing. It's the best advice I can give you."

Hema sighed. "You're right."

Feeling the need for a caffeine jolt, Noor rose. "I'll get coffee."

She rushed to the small booth set up beside the pavilion and thought about what she'd said. *Don't give up.* Should she follow her own advice and not give up on Gabriel? But what if Gabriel didn't come to his senses? Funny how she'd helped solve murders yet had no clue how to fix her love life.

"What'll you have?" the barista asked, interrupting her train of thought.

She placed her order.

"Hello, beautiful." A man's breath tickled her ear.

She whirled around and bumped into Alex Bau. He was close enough for her to see flecks of gold in his irises. "What are you doing here?"

"You can ask better questions than that." He leaned forward. "You look enticing."

She rolled her eyes.

His mouth twitched. "We need to talk."

"I can't right now. I'm working."

Alex chuckled and bent his head. His breath tickled her ear. "Make time. This is important."

She was about to tell him to go to hell when Hema sidled up beside them. "Noor, darling, shall we order some pastries with our coffee?"

Noor turned to tell Alex she would talk to him later, but he'd disappeared. Another unwelcome addition had joined the gathering at the castle. She made a mental note to tell Gabriel about Alex and Johannsson.

Hema frowned. "Who were you looking for?"

"Hm? Oh, I thought I saw someone I knew."

Hema smiled at the barista. "Please add two slices of your most decadent chocolate cake to the order."

"Oh, no, I'm not—" Something cracked above them and rumbled. Noor glanced up to see what the noise was.

Someone yanked her backward, slammed her to the ground, shielding her with his body. A deafening roar echoed through the pavilion as a massive light fixture crashed down beside them.

The collision of metal against concrete sent people screaming in all directions. Dust rose, tickling her nostrils. The ringing in her ears made it hard to concentrate.

The man shifted away from her chest, and her breath rushed back. Dizzy, she sat to find Detective Robin staring down at her.

"You all right?" he growled.

Dear God, if he hadn't jerked her away, she'd be dead. "Y-yes."
He helped her up.

"Thank you." Her voice sounded like she'd swallowed sandpaper.
"Y-you're bleeding." She pointed to the trickle of blood streaming
down his bicep.

"I've had worse." He tilted his head to study her. "Do you
need a doctor?"

She rubbed her sore back. "N-no, I'm fine." Awareness flooded
back, and she whirled around. "Hema!" The action made her dizzy.

Hema groaned and opened her eyes.

Robin nudged her aside, then picked up Hema like a child. "Are
you hurt?" He gently shook her.

Her eyes fluttered. They widened when she saw who held her.
She licked her lips. "I-I think so."

Robin grunted and put her down, keeping an arm around Hema's
waist until she could stand on her own. Satisfied they were fine, he
waved at a member of security. "Close off this area."

"Hema, shall I take you up to your room?" Noor asked.

Hema didn't answer. Hands clasped, she stared at Robin and
murmured something under her breath.

Uh-oh. Noor knew that look.

"What the hell is going on?" Detective Hood made her way
through the crowd. Her eyes landed on Noor. "Of course, you'd be
here. Where's McKnight?"

"He and Harvey are meeting with a production company," Noor said.

Hood studied Hema. "Are you all right, ma'am?"

"Yes, thank you," Hema answered, not taking her eyes off Robin.
"That brave man covered Noor and me with his body. Who is he?"

"My colleague," Hood said.

"Are you staying for the convention?" Hema asked.

"Oh, yeah. We're big fans of Mister McKnight."

Hema's dirt-streaked face lit up. "Wonderful. Will you be at the
dinner tonight?"

Hood glanced at Robin, who was talking to security. "Looks like we will."

Hema drew herself up. "I must get ready for dinner. One must meet the muse prepared." She tottered off in her high heels.

Hood frowned. "Is she all right?"

"I don't know," Noor answered truthfully.

Robin joined them. He held gauze over the cut on his arm. "Security has closed off the area. They'll check the other light fixtures."

"Did you see the one that fell?" Hood asked.

Robin's mouth flattened into a thin line. "I did."

They exchanged a look.

The lines around Hood's eyes deepened. "The Frankfurt police believe McKnight is involved in the murders. They have no proof, or they would've arrested him." She raised a hand before Noor could speak. "I don't believe he killed anyone. So, Robin and I took some personal time to keep an eye on you in Bavaria. It's a good thing we did." Her almond-colored eyes shifted to the ceiling. "This wasn't a coincidence."

Noor shifted. Her right side was sore from the fall and the impact of Robin's weight. "I don't understand."

"Someone tried to kill you," Robin said.

CHAPTER THIRTY-TWO

Grand counsels were held in Khosrow's court....
—Nezami, *Khosrow and Shirin*

G ABRIEL LEAPED OVER chairs as he raced to the pavilion. Why was Noor alone? Why hadn't he kept a closer eye on her? Dodging two security guards, he ducked under the tape placed around the meeting areas.

Clouds of dust thickened the air, making it hard to see. He squinted through the haze. When he spotted her, the world stopped.

She was talking to a security guard. Grime covered her dress. Her hair was a mess, smudges of dirt stained her face, yet she stood tall. He gripped the back of a chair, willed his heart to slow, then made his way to her. He gripped her hand, not trusting himself to speak. The security guard said something and bid her a good day.

She patted his arm. "I'm fine, Gabriel."

He couldn't hear her over the pounding in his ears.

Noor winced and patted his arm again.

He eased his hold on her. "W-what happened?"

She glanced up at the ceiling and wrinkled her nose. "The light fixture fell."

He closed his eyes for a moment and forced his emotions under control.

"I was lucky Detective Robin was there to push me out of the way."

"Robin's here?"

"And Detective Hood." She favored her right side.

Gabriel circled his arm around her waist so she could lean into him. "Do you need a doctor?"

She shook her head.

He guided her to a bench where she could sit. "You're sure you're all right?"

"Yes."

The mix of broken glass and metal occupying the center of the pavilion chilled him. "Wait here. I'll be back." Careful not to trip over the detritus, he approached the fixture's support chain.

This was no accident.

Heat bubbled up from his stomach. Calm. He must remain calm. Gabriel returned to the bench and offered Noor his arm. "You should go to your room and rest."

"No, we need to talk to the others." She raised a hand before he could protest. "It was a shock, that's all."

Familiar with her stubborn nature, he accompanied her to her suite and waited for her to change. While part of his brain processed what he'd seen, every cell in his body was aware of the enormous bed. He wanted to drag her under the sheets, and make love to her. He wanted to hold on to her for days. Forever. For as long as it took his heart to settle.

Instead, he paced in the living room, wondering who had tried to kill her.

"I'm ready." She'd changed into slacks and a silk shirt. Her mass of sable hair was pulled back into a knot. Damp tendrils framed her face. He knew from experience how soft the silky strands were.

He pulled his gaze away from her mouth. "Let's go."

She lingered, fidgeting with her purse. "Detective Hood said the Frankfurt police believe you're involved in the murders."

He shrugged. "I'm the common factor."

"She said they don't have proof, or they would have arrested you."

"They won't find any."

She bit her lip. "The detectives believe someone wants to kill us."

His blood boiled. He tried to keep the anger out of his voice. "I'll find who it is. No one will hurt you."

"I'm not worried about myself." She sighed. "Is it because my father knew where the codes to the artwork are?"

"No. At least, I don't think so." He'd been asking himself the same question. "I first thought whoever's after the artwork wants to hurt you to get to me." *Because you're my soul.* "These people exploit their target's weaknesses."

"Weakness?" Her brows rose. "I'm a weakness?"

He flinched at his choice of words. "What I meant to say is, if they kidnapped or hurt you, I'd hand anything over, including my life, to get you back."

"Is that so?" Her eyes hardened into chips of emerald glass. "Since I'm able to take care of myself and don't plan to let anyone hurt or kidnap me, there will be no risk to your life."

He knew better than to respond.

She sniffed. "You said first. Does that mean you don't think that's the reason anymore?"

He blew out a breath. "That light fixture would've—" He gulped, unable to continue.

Her features softened. "I'm fine, Gabriel."

"I'm uncertain which of us was the intended target since I had a meeting there too. All I know is we're in a tangle we don't understand."

Her shoulders relaxed. "Let's find the others."

He scanned the corridor, then motioned for her to follow him. If anyone wanted to hurt Noor, they'd have to get through him first.

At the hotel café, Harvey rushed to greet them. "I'm glad you're all right." He patted Noor on the shoulder several times.

Rafael hugged her and asked if she needed to see a doctor. Gabriel refrained from rolling his eyes. Did the man think he was the only one who'd thought of it?

Noor assured him she didn't, and Brandon pulled out a chair for her. Everyone seemed determined to pamper her.

He scowled. He should be doing these things, not them.

A server approached. He gathered his thoughts while the others ordered. There were several crises to deal with. None came before Noor's safety.

He'd start there. "Someone tampered with the light fixture. I don't know if the intended target was Noor or me."

Rafael furrowed his brows. "Are you certain?"

"A major chain holding the fixture had a break, and there was no erosion on it."

"Shit," Rafael muttered.

"My exact sentiments." Gabriel paused. "We need help. I'll call my brother, Michael, and ask him to join us."

Rafael pursed his lips. "Does your brother have experience in this kind of thing?"

"Oh, yes," Noor murmured. "Both he and his fiancée have experience in this kind of thing."

Gabriel massaged his neck and moved to the next crisis. "Erik Drussel is here."

Brandon straightened. "Are you sure? Where did you see him?"

Gabriel told them about the cottages in the forest and the body he'd seen Drussel transfer.

"Whoa. Give me a minute to digest this." Brandon leaned forward. "What about the kid? Did Drussel see the kid?"

"Oh, no, Sam!" Noor rose. "I'll warn his mother. I'd never forgive myself if—"

"Easy." Gabriel tugged on her hand and pulled her back into the chair. "Sam's safe. He's at the golf course. I'll keep a close eye on him."

Noor nodded and leaned back against the chair.

Rafael rubbed his jaw. "If Drussel killed one of our kidnappers, is it safe to assume Richter isn't working with them?"

"That, or he ordered Drussel to kill them so there won't be a link connecting him to the kidnapping," Brandon said.

"Theories and assumptions won't get us anywhere," Gabriel said. "We don't have a clear picture because we don't have all pieces of this puzzle. Each one of us had a task. Let's go over the information first, then we'll place it against the facts and see what we come up with."

Harvey cleared his throat. "I researched Nezami. He's one of the giants of Persian literature. Scholars claim his poetry merges romantic human emotions and heroic elements seen in Ferdowsi's poems with the spirituality of Rumi's poetry. He has other works, but none connect to what we're dealing with."

"Thank you." Gabriel pulled a sheet of notes. "Let's move to Brandon. What did you find in Paris?"

The server arrived with their orders. Brandon reached for his coffee. "Jurgen Mulligan was a German-Dutch national who moved to Paris to become an artist. He wasn't talented enough to make it, so Mulligan took a job in an antique shop in the Marais. That's when he started a little side business of forging documents. A decade later, he bought the store from its owner and used it as the legal front for his illegal business. He became a top document forger with select clientele. My contacts in art insurance and the French police believe Richter was one of them." Brandon pulled out a small notepad, then flipped through its pages. "Mulligan had an apprentice in the nineties—Claire La Roche. I found her." His eyes gleamed. "She was in hiding after Mulligan's murder. It took some persistence, but I got her to talk to me."

Rafael saluted him. "Viking warrior's charm, no doubt."

"A fancy dinner and bribery." He flipped to another page. "Claire said a little over eighteen years ago, a young couple went to Mulligan. They wanted fake IDs to get married. The girl, who was pregnant, showed Mulligan her original birth certificate. Mulligan panicked when he realized who she was and tried to convince her to go back home to Switzerland. They persisted, so Mulligan gave the work to Claire, who by then was an associate. She worked on birth certificates and passports for a Mister and Missus Lejeune."

"Lejeune?" Harvey tapped his forehead. "They're the family in the article someone sent Gabriel back in Frankfurt. The ones who died in a car crash, correct?"

Brandon leaned forward. "Correct. Claire saw the girl's original birth certificate. The names of her parents surprised her. The girl's mother was Mina von Mayer, and her father—" His gaze slid to Noor. "She didn't remember the first name clearly. It was Cyrus or Sirius Rohan."

Noor blanched. "Are you sure?"

"Yes."

Noor's lower lip trembled. "Uncle Cyrus lost his daughter."

Brandon nodded. "There's more. Two months later, Richter showed up on Mulligan's doorstep with an unusual request. He claimed a friend of his died in an accident, leaving an infant girl behind. Richter wanted a fake ID and fake guardianship papers for the baby. He gave Mulligan a bogus story about raising the child to protect her from her father's enemies. The baby's name was Zita Lejeune."

"No!" Noor's eyes filled with tears. She covered her mouth with her hands. "The girl, the one who helped us in Nuremberg. She's—"

"Your Uncle Cyrus and Mina von Mayer's granddaughter," Gabriel finished.

Rafael whistled.

"Exactly," Brandon said. "There's a rumor that Richter's ward has fled the nest. Claire believes Richter killed Mulligan because Mulligan helped his ward by creating false paperwork for her. Claire doesn't want Richter to think she was involved."

Rafael furrowed his brows. "Why would Richter raise von Mayer's granddaughter?"

Gabriel rubbed his chin. "He did it to use the granddaughter as leverage."

"Leverage for what?" Harvey asked.

Brandon reached for a pastry. "Mina von Mayer is a powerful mogul. Richter would see her as competition."

Noor raised her chin. "Uncle Cyrus is honorable. He doesn't kill or use children for his personal gain."

Gabriel bit back a smile. Noor was loyal to a fault. She'd said Cyrus wouldn't kill children, and that was true. However, Cyrus

Rohan was nobody's fool. He wouldn't hesitate to obliterate anyone who threatened his family, and Richter had done just that.

"That doesn't explain why the girl is helping Gabriel," Rafael said.

The server brought a plate of chocolate truffles. Noor reached for one. "That shouldn't be hard to guess. Richter is cold and uncaring. The poor girl must have realized he's evil. She discovered who her actual parents were and rebelled by helping Gabriel."

"If that's the case, she knows something about the codes," Harvey said.

"Makes sense," Brandon murmured.

"I'll call Uncle Cyrus," Noor said.

"Wait." Gabriel pulled the phone out of her hands. "Let's finish our discussion first. I researched the von Mayer family. Mina's father was a young pilot in the Second World War. Afterward, he met and fell in love with a Persian student, whom he later married. When Mina was a child, the couple traveled to Tehran to visit Missus von Mayer's cousin, Queen Farah of Iran. Half-way into the trip, Mina's father traveled back to Germany, presumably for business, and died in a car accident in Bavaria. Authorities found evidence in his vehicle pointing to a location where the Nazis hid stolen artwork. They labeled him a Nazi supporter.

"Mina and her mother stayed in Iran after her father's death. Missus von Mayer gave one interview to a Persian journal several years later. In the interview, Kiana von Mayer claimed the allegations against her husband were fabricated and insisted Karl was innocent."

Gabriel motioned to the server, pointing at a display of pastries. Noor had eaten nothing that morning. He'd gladly keep talking if it meant she would eat something. "Noor and I checked several Nazi databases, including the one in Nuremberg Nazi Museum. Aside from the evidence found in Karl's car, there's little to suggest von Mayer was a Nazi supporter."

"Was Karl von Mayer framed for a crime he didn't commit?" Brandon asked.

Gabriel shrugged. "It's happened before."

The server brought an assortment of freshly baked goods. Rafael reached for a muffin. "So, you're saying the girl, Zita, is helping you prove her great-grandfather wasn't a Nazi supporter."

"I don't think she'd risk her life for someone she didn't know." Gabriel blew out a breath. "I think the girl is helping me find the codes because the answer will harm Richter."

Harvey narrowed his eyes. "That makes little sense. The only way it could harm Richter would be to prove he framed von Mayer. Farid Richter must have been a child when Karl von Mayer died."

Gabriel's lips lifted into a smile. "Farid Richter was a child. His father, Hans Richter, wasn't. He could've done it."

Harvey shook his head. "Richter and von Mayer were cousins. Why would Richter frame his cousin?"

Noor reached for a sweet cake. "For the same reason his son killed Mina and my uncle's daughter—greed."

"This is where my research comes in," Rafael announced. "Gabriel asked if I could get into Richter's inner circle. My uncle Eduardo has a special friend." The corners of his mouth twitched. "She's a vivacious matron who has connections with most of Europe's powerful families. Let's call her Natasha.

"Natasha remembers a rivalry between Hans Richter and his cousin Karl von Mayer. Both men fell in love with a Persian student. Hans had lost his first wife to cancer and went after the girl first, but she met von Mayer at a social function and fell for him. They wed several weeks later."

"Must have put a strain on the relationship," Brandon said.

Rafael grimaced. "Natasha claims Richter didn't stop him pursuing Kiana even after she married Karl."

Noor slammed her coffee cup on the table. "Richter framed von Mayer to marry his wife?"

Gabriel smiled at her outrage. "It's not the first time it's happened."

The group fell silent.

Brandon fidgeted. "Where do we go from here?"

Noor shook her head. "My uncle needs to know his granddaughter is alive. He can protect her from Richter."

"I tried calling him when you were changing," Gabriel said. "It goes straight to voicemail. I sent him a text letting him know we want to speak with him and Mina."

A porter joined their table. "Ms. Rahman, this came for you."

Noor reached for the envelope then tore it open. She skimmed through the letter, then handed it to Gabriel. "It's a message from Uncle Cyrus. He says he'll be in Bavaria tomorrow."

Brandon rose. "I'll go change and take a hike in the forest trails. I may get lost and wander toward the cottages." He glanced at Rafael. "Wanna join?"

"I do." The two departed the café.

Noor glanced at her watch. "I signed up to tour the Neuschwanstein Castle. I want to find the miniature." Her gaze locked onto Gabriel's. "Are you free?"

The hope in her voice confused him. Didn't she want to spend time with Rafael? He cleared his throat. "I can't. I'm meeting with the Italian publisher. You arranged it, remember?"

She smiled. "It's not a problem."

"I'll accompany you on the tour of the castle." Harvey rose. "Give me fifteen minutes to change into something comfortable." He rushed back to the hotel.

Noor bit her lip. "It will shock Uncle Cyrus to learn his granddaughter is alive."

He massaged his neck. "He may already know."

She sighed. "I wonder where he is."

"Wherever he is, I'd bet my life Mina von Mayer is with him."

CHAPTER THIRTY-THREE

Khosrow faced Bahram in this field of war....
—Nezami, *Khosrow and Shirin*

HEIDELBERG, GERMANY

FARID RICHTER SURVEYED his guests with satisfaction. Some socialized and drank, while others played cards or smoked cigars. The whores were plenty, offering tantalizing glimpses of the satisfaction awaiting guests who chose more intimate pleasures. In this company of relaxed people, millions of dollars changed hands through private deals.

Magdalena slid her hand up a whore's skirt. With practiced movements, the whore shifted and tilted her head back in exaltation. Magdalena's sexual appetite was as voracious as his own. The only difference between her and the whore was Magdalena expected more after sex. He'd satisfied his hunger for the Italian and was ready for another bedmate. He'd pick one before the night was over, but business came first.

Where was Cyrus Rohan? Richter furrowed his brows. He needed Rohan's support if he were to get rid of Mina von Mayer once and for all. Anyone else, and he would've arranged for a discreet accident. Killing Mina would be no easy feat. Through the years, her power and influence had grown to rival his own. Plus, it would set the Board on edge. No, he'd have to convince the members one by one that she was a poison they'd have to discard. He'd taken the first step by pushing her out of the agreement with the Abromowskis. His mouth curled up. That was her first step into descent.

He didn't mind doing business with women, so long as he could control them. Magdalena, he controlled with sex. He'd tried that with Mina long ago. Bitch had ice in her veins. He'd taken another route to get at Mina, but just when it was time for payback, his leverage escaped, which meant she'd planned it for a while. How much did the girl know?

It didn't matter. Mina didn't know the girl existed, and that bought him time. He'd find her, and when he did, more than one generation of von Mayers would pay for inconveniencing him.

Cyrus finally arrived. Farid studied the elegant blond accompanying him—he always brought his own playmates—and bit back his amusement. She tipped up her head and whispered something. He plucked a drink from a passing server's tray and handed it to her.

Farid wove his way around the crowd and mingled until he reached Cyrus, who was talking to a stockbroker. "Glad you made it."

Cyrus shook his hand. "It's always a pleasure to attend your gatherings."

The blond beside him shifted, and her blue eyes settled on Farid.

Cyrus chuckled. "Lola, this is Herr Richter." He gave a lopsided "what can you do" look. "My friend, Lola Lamar."

Farid took the beauty's hand and brought it to his lips. He complimented her and made the required small talk, making her preen and purr. "I'd like to borrow Cyrus for a few minutes, if that's okay with you." He called over to a whore. "Gemma will entertain you until we're back."

He led Cyrus into his study, then poured two glasses of his best bourbon. "Your bird is lovely."

"Yes, she is."

"What happened to the last one?"

"My interest waned. The escort service provided me with a new one," Cyrus said.

Farid shook his head. "How is it a man with your financial power and looks needs an escort service?"

"I'm not the relationship type."

"Neither am I." He sipped his drink. "Mina and I met with the Abromowskis to discuss the switch."

"I trust it went well."

"I signed a letter of intent with them today."

"Good. I imagine we'll hear from them soon."

Farid bit back his frustration. Most people were simple to read, but not Cyrus. "Asher Abromowski hinted one pharmaceutical company is about to announce a breakthrough drug, which means its stock will raise."

Cyrus raised a dark brow. "Did he? Which one is he referring to?"

"Kroner."

"Didn't that belong to Johannsson?"

Farid nodded. "He was one of two partners." Cyrus showed no reaction, so he extended an olive branch. "It's a good idea to invest in Kroner."

Cyrus raised an eyebrow. "You mean you and Mina haven't bought the entire stock yet?"

Perfect segue. Farid chuckled. "I do research. Mina...." He paused, making a show of choosing his words carefully. "She dives into things without considering the risk to her or others."

Silence.

Farid put on his PR smile. "I worry about her."

"How so?"

"Inadequate research will hurt her, and consequently the Board. The case with the Abromowskis is a prime example. If I hadn't done my research, we'd have irritated members when the deal fell through. We can't have disruption among our members."

Cyrus didn't comment.

He rubbed his chin. "How much do you know about her personal life?"

"Not much."

Farid nodded. "She married long ago, but it was short-lived. They couldn't have children and divorced six months later. She brings it up occasionally. More often in our recent conversations."

"I see," Cyrus murmured.

Farid let the seed he'd planted sink in. "Maybe I'm overthinking things. I don't want my family ties with her to affect my role on the Board. If you do witness her making hasty decisions or taking un-necessary risks, I ask you be patient and let me know. I'll intervene. I don't want the Board to think she's unstable."

"Certainly."

THE COLD FURY pumping through Cyrus's veins blurred his vision. Aware of Richter's sly move on Mina, he made a mental note to meet with Adisa and the Lees for damage control. God, he wanted to erase the smug smirk on Richter's face. He forced himself to swallow the bourbon. The tables would change in less than a week. For now, patience was essential. It was time to dangle the bait.

"About the Kroner stocks. If you don't mind, I'll run an analysis. If it yields the results we hope, I'll purchase the company. It'll be another company under the Board's influence."

"I already placed a bid on it." Richter gave him a benevolent smile. "If you like, I can pull out of the deal."

Cyrus waved a hand. "No, no. I have several other ventures on my plate. My intent is to keep it under the Board's influence in the event it generates global profit."

Richter bowed his head. "That's why I placed a bid on it. I'll notify the Board once I purchase it."

Time for his second shot. "Noor and Gabriel are at the book convention in Bavaria. I plan to join them for some family time."

Richter's face remained impassive. "You mentioned the lovely Ms. Rahman is a member of your family. How did you meet Gabriel McKnight?"

Cyrus hid a smile. "Noor and Gabriel are in relationship, which makes him family."

"Until he breaks your lovely niece's heart," Richter finished. "I've researched him. He hasn't had one long-term relationship. What then?"

And Richter just fell into his trap. His focus was on Gabriel, not Noor. That meant Gabriel either had the codes or knew how to access them. He shrugged. "We'll cross that bridge when we get to it." He stayed and talked nonsense with Richter for a while, then checked his watch. "Thank you for your hospitality, Farid. If it's all right, I'll join my escort. We won't stay long. I'd like to work off some work-related stress."

Richter chuckled. "There's a lovely redhead who has a high threshold for pain. I plan to play a bit myself."

Thirty minutes later, he climbed into his car with the escort. He waited for the driver to pull away from Richter's palatial home, then handed the girl a stack of cash. "Thank you for your time. My driver will take you to wherever you need to go." Once they were a few blocks from the hotel, he exited the car. After flipping up his collar against the brittle wind, he dialed a number on a burner phone.

Mina picked up on the first ring. *"Hi."*

His insides warmed at the sound of her voice. "Hello, yourself. How was your evening?"

"Oliveira is in. How was your evening?"

He heard a slight tremor in her voice. "What's the matter, Pepper?"

She sighed. *"My sources spotted our... our granddaughter in Bavaria. She's at the convention."*

"I expected that. I'll call Sheila. She'll watch over her while we take care of business."

"Do you think she'll accept us after everything that's happened?"

He considered her question. "Blood runs deep. She's ours, and I believe in time, we'll be hers."

Mina blew out a breath. *"You're right."*

"You'll do well to remember that." He strove to lighten the mood. "What are you doing?"

"I was reading Khosrow and Shirin."

"I never understood your obsession with it."

She was silent for several seconds. *"They remind me of us."*

"We're not them, Mina. Our ending will be what we want, not a tragedy. Tell me you believe that."

"I believe it."

He heard the smile in her voice. "What?"

"You're bossy, Mister Rohan."

"You like it."

She laughed. *"Yes, I do."*

They'd come a long way in a few days. He gripped the phone. "I've missed us, Mina." Cyrus bit back a curse. He couldn't believe he'd blurted it out like some inexperienced kid. He'd planned to say it when they were together in a romantic setting, not like this, and not over the phone.

"I've missed us too." She sighed. *"I'll see you in Bavaria."* The line went dead.

Cyrus grinned. He had no self-control when it came to her. Shaking his head, he dialed Sheila's private line.

Sheila was a vigilante who exacted punishment on human rights violators. Her influence was considerable and her reach far. Most interesting was that no one, including Cyrus, had seen her in person. She was a ghost who dispensed swift justice, then disappeared into thin air.

Through the years, he and Sheila had developed mutual respect. Both believed in taking matters into their own hands when man-made laws came short of or violated ethics. Cyrus had hired Sheila for such projects in the past.

She answered after the first ring. *"It's always a pleasure to hear from the Iranian."*

Was this her authentic voice? He doubted it. "We've done business long enough for you to call me Cyrus."

"*I wouldn't dare,*" Sheila murmured.

He smiled. "Do you have eyes on my granddaughter?"

"*Yes. She's in Bavaria.*"

"I need her out of there twenty-four hours after my arrival. The timing is crucial."

"*I see.*" Sheila's voice lost its playfulness. "*Who am I protecting her from?*"

"Farid Richter."

Silence.

"Can I count on you?"

Sheila didn't hesitate. "*Yes.*"

The wind bit his face. He crossed the street and reached his hotel. "I have the information you seek. Yuri Petrov ordered the kill on the woman you were looking for. He'll be in Bavaria with Richter in two days."

"*Thank you,*" Sheila murmured. "*I'll call you when I have your granddaughter.*"

Sheila's word was as good as his own. His granddaughter would be safe. Now onto finalizing his plans, part of which meant protecting Noor and Gabriel.

CHAPTER THIRTY-FOUR

The palace Shirin took up residence in Persia was surrounded by pastures with poisonous weeds.

—Nezami, *Khosrow and Shirin*

NEUSCHWANSTEIN CASTLE, BAVARIA, GERMANY

N OOR GLANCED UP at the at the majestic structure perched on the hill. Multiple towers gleamed, rising into the sky against a backdrop of colorful hills. "It's like stepping into a fairytale."

"It's breathtaking." Harvey blotted his beet-red face with a handkerchief.

Guilt consumed her. She'd been restless since Gabriel broke up with her. The climb up to the castle was an excellent excuse to walk off the excess energy. She'd begged Harvey to take the shuttle, but he'd insisted on accompanying her.

Grateful for his friendship and company, she stopped by a large boulder beside the outer wall. "Let's sit and admire the view for a while."

Harvey joined her.

She pulled two bottles of water from her backpack, then handed him one. "Hearing about Neuschwanstein Castle isn't the same and experiencing it."

Harvey gulped down half his drink. "King Ludwig II of Bavaria ordered it to be built on a hill because he liked the view. 'Fairy Tale King' is one of the generous names history gave him."

She studied Neushwanstein's stone facade, then shifted her attention to Hohenschwangau Castle on the opposite hill. "I wonder what drove him to build it."

"What drives people to do incredible things? Love, passion, and dreams make the impossible possible." Harvey pursed his lips. "I'd say you've given all three to Gabriel, and he's a better man for it."

She blinked back the tears pricking her eyes. "You give me too much credit."

Harvey used his handkerchief to wipe a smudge off his glasses. "Minor setbacks are not life's outcomes." He patted her shoulder. "Shall we join the tour?"

She followed him to the line gathered at the castle's entrance. "The crowds are at a peak at midday. No one will notice if we wander off."

They made their way through the castle's elaborate rooms. The main throne hall occupied the entire west side of the third and fourth floors of the castle. A massive chandelier hung from the ceiling, its intricate artwork and churchlike dome reminiscent of Byzantium churches.

Harvey typed on his phone. "The last view of the miniature was in Singer's Hall."

She checked the map bought from the ticket stand. "That's on the eastern side of the fourth floor. It connects to Throne Hall through an upper corridor."

They squeezed through throngs of tourists until they arrived at a long rectangular hall.

Harvey beamed. "This is it."

Enormous, gilded candelabras glowed on murals framed in gold, and plush burgundy seating occupied the space between the walls.

Noor tilted her head up. "It's like hundreds of paintings are mounted into the ceiling." Her eyes scanned both sides of the room.

Every inch of space was a work of art. The western side had a singer's bower separated by steps, three arches, and a small gallery above it.

Another tour group arrived, crowding the hall.

She lowered her voice. "You take the right side. I'll go left. We should also check behind the pillars in the gallery."

"Got it."

They separated. Every muscle in her body froze when Erik Drussel arrived in the hall.

What was he doing here? She pulled her ball cap lower and kept a safe distance from him. Drussel's attention centered on a man. She texted Harvey.

Richter's henchman is here. Be careful.

Noor rose on tiptoe to see who Drussel had in his sights. It was one of her and Rafael's kidnappers. Common sense ordered her to stay away. She followed Drussel through a marble portal to the upper hallway.

He waved at a thick-necked man in a grey sweatshirt. Grey Sweatshirt turned around.

Noor shifted and asked a woman the time. Several seconds later, she hurried to pursue the men. Drussel and Sweatshirt were parallel to her kidnapper. Her kidnapper, a beefy man with a ponytail, knew he was being tailed and pushed through another marble portal.

Drussel followed him.

What were they doing? Several tourists bumped into her. She wiggled through the group, passed through the next portal, then arrived at the upper balconies of the main throne hall.

Farther off, her kidnapper broke into a run. Sweatshirt pursued him. A man swore. Scuffling sounds came from ahead. A couple stopped in front of her. Noor sidestepped them and craned her neck to see what the commotion was.

A loud thud reverberated through hall, then a woman shrieked.

More screams followed. Security guards ran to the lower floors. Drussel and Sweatshirt disappeared into the crowd.

Noor pushed through the horde onto the balcony. Her kidnapper lay dead below, blood pooling around him. Someone had pushed him over the railing.

She gripped the railing. *Oh, no.* The tangy odors of sweat and fear overwhelmed her. People shoved one another to reach the exits, but her legs were rooted, and her body didn't cooperate. The surrounding chaos blurred, voices dimmed, and the roar in her ears grew louder.

Someone gripped her waist, then pulled her into the crowd. Screeching alarms made her ears ring, and glaring lights made it difficult to concentrate. She tried to wriggle free but couldn't get loose. Then everything dimmed, and the cold stone pressing against her back replaced the suffocating confines of the hall.

"Easy." The man helped her stay upright.

She took several deep breaths and let her eyes grow accustomed to the darkness. "Alex? What are you doing here?" She put some distance between them.

He leaned against the wall beside her. "They tailed you from the hotel."

"I checked to make sure I wasn't followed."

Alex chuckled. "Wild elephants could tail you, and you wouldn't know it."

"Where are we?"

"In a hidden compartment between Singer's Hall and the upper corridor. The Mad King wouldn't build a castle without some safety measures."

"I have to go. I—"

He shook his head. "You're going to wait until it's safe."

"It all happened so fast," Noor murmured.

"Which part?"

She rubbed at her temples. "I-I'm not certain what happened."

"The man with the ponytail was following you," Alex offered. "He had a knife, which I assume was meant for you. Richter's men followed Ponytail."

"Richter's men killed Ponytail?"

"I killed Ponytail. They're still trying to figure it out. It was that or he'd kill you," Alex explained.

"I don't understand."

He leaned closer. The amusement gone from his voice. "Are you working with Richter?"

Noor pushed away. "Are you crazy?"

His hold tightened on her arm. "Why were Richter's men watching out for you?"

Noor yanked her arm free, then began searching for an exit.

"We need to talk."

"No. I have to find Harvey," she said.

Alex didn't move. "Does McKnight know they're trying to hurt you to get to him?"

A lump formed in her throat. "Yes."

"And he let you come here alone?"

Her heart constricted. "Lower your voice. I'm standing beside you. Besides, I can take care of myself." She poked him in the chest. "You better not roll your eyes."

"If you were mine, I wouldn't leave you alone." His muscular arms held her in place, while his lips skimmed from her cheek to her ear. Amusement laced his voice. "Tell McKnight we know he found the second set of codes. We'll help him if he helps us. He doesn't need more enemies."

"I—"

He stiffened then cupped his hand over her mouth. "Quiet."

Voices drifted into the enclosure. Someone cursed in German.

Alex pushed a small stone out of the way. Light filtered in. The opening offered a view of the balconies over Throne Hall.

Drussel and Sweatshirt searched behind the marble pillars.

"Where did she go?" Drussel snapped. "She was here."

"She may have left the castle," Sweatshirt muttered.

Alex lowered his head to her ear. "Wait here."

"No—" Something shifted, and he disappeared.

Irritated, Noor dug out her mobile phone and turned on the flashlight. The enclosure was a decently sized rectangular room. She searched the walls for a lever or a doorway when a series of carvings caught her attention.

There was a verse in Farsi with a series of numbers etched beneath it. *"Farhad carved the beloved image of Shirin on the stone and began his labor."* This was important. What had Gabriel done at Nuremberg when he saw the carvings?

She tapped the stones around the carving, hoping one would sound hollow. It didn't work. Noor took a picture, then inched forward until she spotted a lever. "Ah, here we go."

Part of the eastern wall opened into the gallery of Singer's Hall. So, this was how Alex had found the enclosure. There had to be a similar lever in the gallery.

Security guards guided the remaining tourists out of the castle. One motioned for her to follow them. Outside, some headed down the hill, while others waited to take the shuttle.

While scanning the masses for Harvey, she bumped into a solid chest. "Where the hell have you been?" Rafael snapped.

"Have you seen Harvey? I lost him, and Richter's men are here."

He pulled her behind a tour bus. She tried to move away, but he gripped her arms. "Harvey's with Brandon. They're waiting at the bottom of the hill."

"Thank God. Erik Drussel was here with another man. So was one of our kidnappers. He's dead now." She couldn't control the tremor in her voice.

Rafael pulled her into his arms. "I heard."

"No one deserves to die like that," Noor whispered.

He said nothing.

Mortified at her own lack of control, she stepped out of his arms. "Thank you. I'm better now."

"Good." Rafael guided her toward the path leading down the hill as he scanned the crowd. "Did Drussel kill the man?"

"No, Alex Bau did."

He came to an abrupt halt. "The Asian man?"

"Yes."

He waited for a couple to pass them. "Start at the beginning."

They were halfway down the hill when she finished her story.

Rafael cursed in Spanish. "Why didn't you leave when you spotted them?"

She rubbed her temples. "I wanted to find out what they were up to. I didn't find the last miniature, only a series of numbers and a line of poetry."

They arrived at the mid-point of the hill. A shuttle sat in the middle of the road because of a flat tire. Passengers milled, some waiting for another shuttle and others walking the rest of the way.

They were making their way through the throng of people when something sharp pressed into Noor's back.

A man in a T-shirt and ball cap stood behind them. "I have a knife at the lady's spine. If you want her to live, come with me."

Rafael's jaw tightened, yet he acquiesced.

Ball Cap led them away from the crowd into the cluster of trees behind the hill. He shoved her against a rough-barked trunk. "What did you find?"

"I don't understand," Noor said.

"I want the truth." Ball Cap held the blade to her neck.

"Whoa." Rafael raised his palms in a gesture of surrender. "I'm the one who found something." He made a pretense of pulling a folded note out of his wallet. "If this is what you're looking for, you can have it. Just back away from the lady."

Ball Cap inched toward Rafael. As soon as he drew close, Rafael kicked the knife out of his hand. A scuffle followed. Rafael punched Ball Cap hard in the jaw. The man went down.

He wrapped an arm around Ballcap's neck. "Who are you?"

"Urgh!" Their assailant tried to shake free.

Rafael held him in place. "Who sent you?"

"I... I...." Ball Cap's face turned red. He coughed and spluttered. "Missus McKnight. Gabriel McKnight's wife sent me."

CHAPTER THIRTY-FIVE

Khosrow used hunting as an excuse to ride to Shirin's place....
—Nezami, Khosrow and Shirin

"YOU'RE LYING." RAFAEL tightened his grip on the man's neck.

"I swear," Ball Cap croaked. "I was supposed to get answers from the lady and warn her off McKnight."

Noor rubbed her temples. "What did Missus McKnight look like?"

"She's a beautiful half-Asian with hazel eyes."

"Alex's scary twin," Noor muttered. "Let him go, Rafael."

Rafael eased his hold.

Ball Cap sprinted down the hill.

"Let's find Gabriel."

GABRIEL WANDERED THROUGH the streets of Fussen. Everything seemed dim without Noor. He missed being with her. He missed her unique taste of sunshine and honey that made his mouth water.

She'll be happier with Rafael.

Didn't loving someone mean you let them go when they had better options? Problem was, his heart couldn't accept it. Everything inside him had frozen the moment he broke it off with her.

He'd kept busy the previous day, and when sleep evaded him at night, he tried to write. The ice in his soul had bled into his work, so he gave up. At dawn, he'd gone for a run only to end up outside her hotel room. When she stepped out of the elevator, it took all his willpower not to pull her into his arms.

He bought a burner phone from a store he'd found on the internet and dialed Billy.

Billy picked up on the first ring. *"Hey, Fa."* Alpha and Beta were nicknames his SEAL teammates had given to Gabriel and his identical twin Michael. In time, they had shortened the monikers to Fa and Be.

"Hi. Before you ask, I put the chip on the burner phone. The fact that I travel with the damn thing says a lot about my sanity."

"Doesn't hurt to be cautious."

Gabriel snorted. "Says the man with a mile-wide paranoid streak."

"Paranoia keeps you alive." Billy chuckled. *"You should order a bumper sticker with that slogan."*

"Did you get into Ingrid's phone?" Gabriel asked.

"Do bears take a dump in the woods? Of course I did. Most of it's the usual stuff. The last forty-eight hours on her phone show several texts between Ingrid and someone labeled 'Lover' in her contacts list. Lover appears to be a fan of yours and asked for access to your hotel room to sneak in a present. Twenty-four hours later, Ingrid sent several frantic texts asking if Lover had planted the box—with a finger, of all things—in your room." Billy sighed. *"What the hell is going on?"*

"I'll tell you later. Did Lover answer?"

The clicking of a keyboard reverberated into the phone. *"Yes. Sent some reassuring nonsense and asked Ingrid to come to their usual meeting place. That's the last text on the phone. I traced Lover's phone. It belongs to a Karl Hagden, who died in a hospital several weeks ago."*

A dead end. "Thanks, Billy."

"No problem. Do you need help taking care of your secret admirer?"

"No, thanks. I'll call you if I need anything else." He disconnect-ed the call, then threw the pre-paid phone into a trashcan. Gabriel raked a hand through his hair. Harvey and Noor had finished their tour by now. Maybe they'd found something.

He was about to cross the street when his mobile pinged with a message. After glancing at the screen, he ran to the line of cabs outside the hotel.

Thirty minutes later, Gabriel pounded on the door to Noor's suite. Harvey answered. "She's fine. She—"

Gabriel stepped around him, desperate to see for himself.

Rafael stood by a window, staring outside. Brandon was on his cellphone, speaking in low tones. Noor huddled in a loveseat, hug-ging her knees to her chest.

He crouched in front of her. "What happened, baby?"

Her bottom lip quivered. "It was awful."

Gabriel glanced at Rafael.

Rafael shrugged. "Brandon and I arrived after the fact."

He went to the kitchen to brew tea, then brought her a steaming mug.

"I'm all right—just sad." She told him what had happened at the castle.

He forced himself to think objectively. "Alex Bau said the man following you wanted to hurt you?"

She nodded. "Richter's men pursued him. Alex thought I was working with Richter."

Brandon pocketed his phone "Something's changed."

Gabriel massaged the knotted muscles behind his neck. "Cyrus warned Richter away from Noor by letting him know she was family. He'll think twice before he tries to harm her."

"The kidnappers—the ones who took us—are still going after her," Rafael said. "It's you they really want, Gabriel, not Noor."

"I don't understand." Noor shook her head. "If they want to use me as leverage, why try to kill me?"

"Maybe they didn't want you to identify them," Brandon said. "Maybe Alex made a mistake, and the kidnapper didn't have a knife."

"Alex said he did." She gripped Gabriel's arm. "He wanted me to tell you they—he and his sister—know you have the second set of codes. He said you didn't need more enemies."

Brandon's brows rose. "He threatened Gabriel?"

"Not exactly. He said it in the flirty way he and his sister have, all up close and personal."

Heat traveled from the depths of Gabriel's chest to his fingertips. He wanted to break Alex's neck. With effort, he kept his voice steady. "Did he touch you?"

Noor blinked several times. "W-what?"

The beast inside him raged. His fingers curled into a fist. "Did he put his hands on you?"

Noor gulped. "Oh, um, no. Not like that."

He studied her for a long moment.

Brandon and Harvey exchanged worried glances.

"There's more." Rafael told them about the man with the knife. "He said your wife sent him."

The pounding in Gabriel's ears lessened. He shifted his attention to Rafael. "What?"

Amusement lit Rafael's eyes. "Noor believes Fan Bau posed as your wife and hired Knife Man."

"Not to hurt me," Noor explained. "He wanted to know if we'd found anything at the castle."

Gabriel raked a hand through his hair. "That makes little sense. Alex would tell his sister if you'd found something."

"I found something, and neither Alex nor Fan know." She showed him the photos on her phone. "I found some numbers and a line of poetry in the hidden room at Neuschwanstein."

Gabriel enlarged the photos on her phone. "I can—"

"No." Harvey crossed his arms over his chest. "The author's dinner is in one hour. We need to stay on schedule to keep up appearances. Look at the clue after the dinner."

"Harvey's right." Noor rose. "My clients rely on me."

Brandon waved his phone. "I've bought two tickets to tonight's dinner. Rafael and I will join you."

"Fine." Gabriel pocketed the sheet of paper. "We go in pairs or as a group. None of us should be alone."

Rafael nodded. "I'll be here in thirty minutes to pick up Noor."

Brandon clapped Gabriel on the shoulder. "Harvey and I will come get you."

Rafael's cheer grated on Gabriel's nerves. "We'll meet in my room and go down together." He was still fuming when he unlocked the door to his own suite. God help him if he saw Alex Bau.

"Hello, handsome." Fan Bau beamed at him from the couch.

He raised a brow. "How did you get in?"

She shrugged. "Locks don't stop me from going where I want."

"What do you want?"

She rose and floated—the only word to explain how she moved—to him, then traced a line from his shoulder to his elbow. "Someone's touchy."

"Did you send a man to threaten Noor?"

Her lips curved. Her fingers traced up toward his neck. She was close enough for him to see the gold and green specs in her pupils. "Threaten, never. I sent a warning." Her hand moved up to his jaw.

He grabbed it. "Why?"

She pressed her body against his. "You don't want me as an enemy." She moved fast, raising her leg to kick him.

He caught her ankle, then pulled off her stiletto.

She fell on her rear, blinking in surprise.

He yanked her to her feet, then shoved her against the wall. "You and your brother don't want me as an enemy." He closed his hand around her throat. "Play anymore games with Noor, and I'll break both your necks. Understand?"

Fan didn't flinch. "I'm not here to quarrel. I have a proposition for you. It would help if you let me go."

He loosened his grip on her neck. "I'm listening."

CHAPTER THIRTY-SIX

Have mercy on my broken heart! Save me from this flood of pain....
—Nezami, *Khosrow and Shirin*

A KNOCK SOUNDED on Noor's door. She glanced at her watch. Rafael was as punctual as Gabriel. *Stop moping.* She joined him in the hallway.

Rafael whistled. "You look beautiful."

She took his arm. "Thank you. I hide behind makeup when I'm nervous."

"There's no need to be afraid. You won't be alone."

"Oh, I'm not worried about myself. It's Gabriel I'm worried about."

"Why is that?"

"He's going to try to protect me by making himself the target." Her stomach lurched at the thought.

Rafael furrowed his brows. "Is that why you're in separate rooms?"

To her horror, tears pricked her eyes. She swallowed several times, unable to speak.

Rafael squeezed her hand. "Sorry. I shouldn't have asked."

She shook her head. "No, it's—I can't talk about it right now."

They met Brandon and Harvey outside of Gabriel's suite.

Harvey raised his hand to knock when Gabriel joined them, Fan Bau hanging on his arm. The fact that Fan looked fabulous in a scarlet dress didn't improve Noor's mood.

Fan beamed. "It's nice to meet the rest of Gabriel's friends." She winked at Noor. "You and Alex had quite the adventure."

A cold hello was all Noor could muster. The rest of the group seemed at a loss for words.

Rafael patted her arm and pulled her toward the elevators. He started a conversation and kept up the chatter until they reached the octagon-shaped dining hall.

Fairy lights hung from the ceiling and outside patio, where guests wove through the space like colorful threads in a tapestry. A server guided them to their seats.

Fan sat with Gabriel on the eastern side of the hall. Rafael accompanied Noor to a table several feet away. Brandon and Harvey joined a group close to them.

Marci Saleh, Sam's mother, jumped up to greet Noor. "It's been so busy we haven't been able to catch up."

She embraced Marci. "We'll catch up tomorrow. I was thrilled with how many people attended your panel."

"The cozy mystery genre is growing."

"Where's Gabriel?" Sam cupped his eyes and swiveled around to check the dining hall. "How come he's over there with that lady?"

She glanced over. Fan leaned into Gabriel and whispered something. Noor turned away. "He's working."

Sam scratched his head. "Who is that lady?"

"Sam," Marci admonished.

"It's all right." Noor leaned down to Sam. "Go talk to Gabriel. He won't mind."

"I will." Sam veered toward Gabriel's table. Was it childish of her to appreciate Sam for nudging Fan's arm out of the way? No, it wasn't.

"He idolizes Mister McKnight." Marci glanced meaningfully at Rafael.

Noor introduced them. Rafael kissed the back of her hand, and Marci's cheeks turned bright pink.

A woman joined them. Blonde waves reached her shoulders. Iceberg blue eyes took in the rest of the guests at the table.

Noor rose. "Doctor Reich, I didn't see you this morning."

"My flight was delayed. I arrived this afternoon."

"Doctor Reich is a new client," Noor explained. "She's written several books on the impact of the Second World War in German culture, politics, and economy."

Reich shook hands with her and Rafael. "Are you a writer, sir?"

"No, I'm in the hospitality industry."

"Molina, as in the Molina hotels." Hema pulled back a chair and beamed. "Hello, table mates."

"I thought you looked familiar." Marci clasped her hand together. "My son and I stayed at the Molina in Dubai last winter. It was a wonderful experience."

Rafael soon had the group involved in a lively discussion about best and worst vacation experiences. Noor's attention strayed to Gabriel. Sam sat between him and Fan. Gabriel had an arm around the boy's shoulder and was holding a serious conversation with him. Her heart twisted. How was she going to move on?

Gabriel's head came up, and his gaze sought hers.

She looked away, pretending to study the crowd.

Rafael squeezed her hand. "Noor is a better authority on mysteries than I'll ever be."

She forced herself to pay attention. "Sorry, what was the question?"

"I asked if mass market fiction sells?" Dr. Reich said.

"Oh, yes. It's a thriving global market."

Dr. Reich sniffed. "Tells you a lot about the nonsense the average reader admires."

"I disagree." Noor tried not to be critical of her client. "You learn new things even when reading fiction. All books have something valuable to offer readers."

"My readers become friends with my characters," Hema chimed in, searching the crowd. "There they are." She waved her napkin in the air.

Detectives Robin and Hood entered the dining area. Hood was in her signature black. Robin wore a suit without a tie.

"Looks like we're joining you for dinner," Hood said.

"How wonderful." Hema preened and patted the seat beside her. "Have a seat, Detective."

Robin sat beside her.

Hood scanned the dining hall. "Why is lover boy at another table?"

"He's working."

She glanced at Gabriel's table, and her brows arched. "Is that so?"

Hema motioned to a server, who brought champagne to the table. Everyone took a glass except Detective Robin.

"Don't you like champagne, Detective?"

"I don't drink," Robin announced.

Hema placed a glass in front of him. "Make an exception tonight."

"Are you with the Bavarian police?" Reich asked.

Robin glared at the glass Hema set in front of him. "No, I'm a detective with the Washington D.C. Police Department."

"We're book nerds on vacation," Hood added. "What better way to spend your vacation than at a book convention?"

"Do you read erotic romance?" Hema gazed up at Robin through hooded lashes.

"I, uh, well—" Robin cleared his throat.

"Detective Robin saved my life this morning," Hema announced. "If it wasn't for him, the light fixture would've crushed Noor and me."

"How terrible." Marci reached for Noor's hand. "I didn't know."

Hema scooted her chair closer to Robin. "Is the Washington D.C. Police Department appreciative of the fearless Adonis working for them?"

Adonis? Had she called him that?

Hood's eyes twinkled. "Oh, yeah. We're tickled we've hit the testosterone jackpot of sacrifice and courage."

Robin glared at Hood.

Rafael covered his laugh with a cough.

Hema raised her glass. "Let's toast our gorgeous hero."

Everyone raised their glasses. "To our hero."

The tips of Robin's ears turned red. He shifted to say something to Hema. She smiled up at him and patted him on the cheek. Robin blinked several times. His color heightened, and he reached for the champagne glass.

Noor wondered if she should take notes from her vivacious client. Hema barely knew Robin and had him tongue tied, while she couldn't keep the man she loved at her side.

As if reading her thoughts, Rafael bent his head toward hers. "Stop worrying. Everything will be all right, *mi querida*."

"Hm?" She glanced up.

He kissed her forehead. "I said stop worrying."

Everyone at the table stared at them in fascination. Blushing at what the others were undoubtedly thinking, she wracked her mind to say something.

Marci saved her. "Your work sounds fascinating, Doctor Reich."

Reich nodded. "The impact of the Second World War is vast and continues into our present times. For example, there are people searching for artwork the Reichsleiter Rosenberg Taskforce hid during the war. The Germans created codes to pinpoint every location."

Butterflies flitted in Noor's stomach.

Rafael stiffened, and Robin, who'd been in discussion with Hema, paused to listen.

Reich fiddled with the string of pearls at her throat. "Noor, will you introduce me to Mister McKnight?"

Was it coincidence that Reich wanted to meet Gabriel?

Rafael rose. "Excuse me, I see an acquaintance I must speak with." He joined Brandon and Harvey, no doubt to relay the message to Gabriel.

Hood nudged her and lowered her voice. "Who is this woman?"

"Noor, what a pleasure," a man called out before she could reply.

"Arthur." She rose to greet the man with the painted face and dark suit, stunned the reclusive author had left his home to attend the convention. "It's wonderful to see you. I hear your second book will be out soon."

"Yes, and I believe it will be a bestseller." The white of his teeth gleamed against the black-and-white paint on his face.

She embraced him. "Everyone, meet Arthur Trells, also known as Paradox. Arthur's first book *Questions* was on the *New York Times* bestseller list."

"I read it," Detective Robin said. "It's a series of questions a young man asks himself while searching for the meaning of his life. He visits all the places he'd been to as a child to find answers. In the end, he learns he had the answers all along."

Arthur, or Paradox as the world knew him, chuckled. "That's what he thinks. My second book *Answers* gets into all that."

Hema ran a finger down Robin's forearm. "Are you on a journey of self-discovery, Detective?"

"No, I—" Robin gulped. "I know who I am and what I want."

She leaned toward him and whispered something. His eyes widened.

"I was talking to someone about you." Arthur scratched his chin. "Can't remember the fellow's name, though. I have the devil of a time remembering things." He patted Noor on the shoulder, then strolled to another table.

"Good evening, Detective Hood." Gabriel took Rafael's vacant seat.

"Hello, yourself." The corners of Hood's mouth twitched. "Are you enjoying the dinner?"

Gabriel shrugged. "As much as you are."

The comment elicited a grin from her.

Noor gripped her clutch. The scent of Gabriel's aftershave brought back memories of heated lovemaking. Her throat went dry. She reached for her champagne and risked a glance at him. Those blue eyes burned with... what? She'd give anything to know what he was thinking.

Sam sidled up to Marci. "Gabriel says I can spend time with him tomorrow. I'm going to help him do research for his next novel. Can I, Mom? Please?"

Marci smoothed a wayward curl from his face. "What about your golf lessons?"

"It's Jason Vann," Sam cried. "I'll take golf lessons later."

"If Mister McKnight says it's okay."

"I'll make sure he's all right," Gabriel assured her.

Marci kissed Sam's forehead. "Remember to mind your manners."

Sam wiggled the way boys do when parents show their affection in public. "I'll be there at eight sharp, Gabriel."

Marci rose. "It's getting late. Sam and I came down to meet everyone. We're planning to have dinner in our room, then go to bed."

"Aw, Mom, it's not bedtime yet." So began the age-old argument between every parent and child. Funny how the young avoided sleep. Noor wanted to crawl under her bedcovers and sleep for a week.

Marci bid everyone goodnight while maneuvering Sam out of the dining hall.

Gabriel rose. "Detective, Noor and I have a mutual friend who would like to see you. Can you spare a few moments?"

"Sure." Robin and Hood both rose. They followed Gabriel to a table on the outside terrace where Harvey waited.

"You heard about the incident at the castle?" Gabriel asked.

"Yes," Robin said. "Were you there?"

"No, Noor was." His gaze locked with hers for an instant.

Noor knew the look. He didn't want her to talk about the hidden chamber at Singer's Hall or Alex. She nodded. "The man who died was one of my kidnappers."

Robin patted his coat pocket as if searching for a notepad, then remembered he was in evening attire. "Did you see who killed him?"

"No." She blew a tendril of hair out of her face. "I was distracted because Richter's main man, Erik Drussel, was at the castle."

"The same guy you saw talking to Detective Bruker?" Hood asked.

"Yes. He was looking for something or someone."

Robin furrowed his brows. "What makes you think that?"

"Drussel was looking at the crowd, not sightseeing." She bit her lip. Gabriel had taught her to stay as close as possible to the truth while omitting what didn't need to be said. "The artwork distracted me. I heard a commotion, then ran into the upper hall of the castle.

That's when I heard someone scream. The man on the floor—" She willed her voice to remain steady. "Even with the blood, I recognized him. He was one of our kidnappers."

"Were you alone?" Hood asked.

"No," Harvey interjected. "I accompanied Noor on the tour."

"That's two times an incident occurred in your vicinity," Robin muttered.

She reached for the locket around her neck. "They can't be connected. I didn't see my kidnapper at the convention."

Hood drummed her fingers on the table. "You may have missed him."

Had she? She thought she paid careful attention.

"What about this Drussel guy? Have you seen him at the convention?" Hood asked.

"I saw him at one of the staff cottages behind the golf course," Gabriel said.

Robin and Hood exchanged a look. "When does the convention end?"

"Three more days," Gabriel answered.

She pursed her lips. "Robin and I have vacation to burn. We'll stay for the convention and keep an eye on things."

Gabriel nodded. "Thank you. I won't turn down your help."

Hood lowered her chin. "You don't need me to warn you to be careful. So, be careful." She followed Robin and Harvey back inside.

Noor found herself alone with Gabriel. Unable to meet his gaze, she stared at the forest. "Bavaria is beautiful, isn't it?"

He searched her face. "How are you feeling?"

"I'm fine." Did he think she was weak?

He raked a hand through his hair. "Look—"

"Here you are." Fan joined them. "I've been looking for you. Let's dance." Fan tugged on Gabriel's arm. "Come on, I love the song they're playing."

Noor moved away. "Go dance."

She was on her way to the dining hall when Rafael intercepted her. "Let's dance, *carina*." He all but dragged her to the floor. The tune gave way to a slow melody. Rafael pulled her into his arms.

Her gaze strayed toward Gabriel. Fan had plastered herself to him.

Rafael's arms tightened around her. "I'm sorry things aren't working out between you and Gabriel."

She rolled her eyes. "Gabriel's flirting with Fan to divert attention away from me. He's being noble."

Rafael shook his head. "You're incredible."

"What do you mean?"

"Any other woman would breathe fire, yet you're understanding and accepting."

"I never said I accept his behavior. I'm just explaining why he's behaving this way."

He searched her face. "You know him that well?"

"I thought I did." Tired of games and too drained to do anything but take a long bath, Noor stepped back. "I'm tired. Detective Hood is calling it a night. I'll go up with her."

She was half-way to the exit when Arthur stepped into her path. "Noor, my dear, I must speak with you."

"Can we meet tomorrow over breakfast?" She kept her gaze on Hood.

"They were talking about you."

"I'm sorry. I don't understand."

"T-they talked about y-you." Arthur's voice slurred, and he bobbed his head several times for emphasis. "Your client, the historian, and the other one. It-it conce-concerned me."

"Who was the other person?"

He mumbled something she couldn't hear above the music. Arthur blinked. "It was years ago. Besides, the rumors aren't true."

"What rumors?" Noor asked, gripping his arm.

He shook his head. "Breakfast is a good idea. I'll meet you at the café first thing tomorrow." Arthur wandered off, drink in hand.

Exhausted, Noor left the dining hall with Hood. Back in her room, she discarded her heels, then opened the door to the terrace. The silver moon glowed in a star-studded sky. The golf course had transformed to a maze of golden lights, and the outline of Neus-chwanstein gleamed against the forest.

It wasn't unusual for conference attendees to speak of her. The Rahman Agency had made a name in the publishing industry. Part of her wondered if something more sinister was at play. Then she saw them. Several figures in dark clothing streaked across the golf course.

There wasn't time to call anyone. She peeled off the dress, tugged on black leggings and a black sweater, then sprinted down the emergency stairwell.

The figures took the running path. She followed, staying in the shadows.

"We'll spread out," Erik Drussel said. "I'll take the first path. You two try the other one."

"It's an old well. It may not even be here. Besides, you don't know the woods," one man cautioned.

"Fine, we'll stick together," Drussel snapped. "Turn off the flashlight. We don't want to attract attention."

She ran back to the hotel to find Gabriel.

CHAPTER THIRTY-SEVEN

Some warriors swung their weapons
while others bore lacerations....

—Nezami, *Khosrow and Shirin*

GABRIEL CHECKED HIS phone. Noor hadn't responded to his text. *She's probably asleep.*

Fan sidled up to him. The spicy scent of her perfume tickled his nostrils, and her bow of a mouth turned up for a kiss. His body hardened.

Annoyed at his reaction, Gabriel pushed her away. "You said you wanted to discuss business in private. That's the only reason we're in my room."

She pouted. "Why not mix pleasure with our business?"

"We'll stick to business."

"You love her, don't you?" Fan asked.

He didn't answer.

"Fine." She pouted. "If finesse won't work, I'll be direct. I want the second set of codes."

"Why?"

A tawny brow rose. "Why not?"

"That's not an answer."

She perched on a chair and crossed one long leg over the other. "I'll tell you mine, if you tell me yours."

Irritation gave way to anger. He gripped her arm and dragged her to the door. "I won't play your games. Leave."

"All right, we'll do it your way." She yanked her arm free and went to the fireplace. "Close the door."

"Why do you want the codes?"

"Shut the door first." When he complied, Fan's bottom lip curled. "I told you about my grandmother and the Rembrandt painting her lover gave her. It's called *An Angel with Titus Feathers*. Alex and I want to take it back to the family home where it belongs."

"Let's say I have the codes and find the artwork. You can go through the legal channels to get it back."

Fan snorted. "Please, I wasn't born yesterday. It'll take years to go through legal channels. Odds are the authorities will find some loophole to keep it." She ran her fingers over a glass piece sitting on the console. "No, we'll take the painting home, where it belongs, then my mother's spirit will rest in peace." She raised her chin. "Now, please give me the codes or—"

"No." Gabriel crossed his arms over his chest. "Threats won't get you anywhere. If I find the artwork, and if the painting is there, I'll bring it to you. That's all I'm willing to give. Take it or leave it."

Her eyes narrowed. "I don't trust anyone outside my family."

He found his first genuine smile. "There's always a first."

She contemplated for a moment, then held out her hand. "If you trick me, I'll hunt you down and kill you slowly."

"Deal." He shook her hand.

Fan reached for her shawl and sauntered to the door. "Good luck with the delectable Ms. Rahman." He let out a breath when she was gone.

Harvey would be asleep, so he texted only Brandon and Rafael. *My suite, if you're still up.*

Gabriel changed into jeans and a sweater while contemplating his talk with Fan. There were too many people entangled in this mess.

Rafael and Brandon showed up in short time.

"What's up?" Brandon asked.

Gabriel brought out mugs of tea. "Have any of you heard from Noor?"

Rafael reached for a mug. "She's probably asleep."

"Fan Bau was here."

Brandon arched a brow. "Do we want to know why?"

Gabriel massaged his neck. "She wants to get her grandmother's Rembrandt back."

"Of course she does," Brandon laughed.

Rafael rubbed his chin. "You believe her?"

"She seemed sincere," Gabriel murmured.

"Come on." Brandon sank into an armchair. "The woman has her own agenda."

"I agree. However, Gabriel's instincts are solid." Rafael grinned. "Before you ask how I know, I'd say if they weren't, Fan Bau would be sitting here and not us."

It occurred to Gabriel, if it weren't for Noor being half in love with Rafael, he'd enjoy getting to know the hotelier.

"She a beautiful woman," Brandon murmured.

Rafael stared into his cup. "When I lived on the streets, I shared the space behind an alley with a viper. It was a beautiful creature, and it taught me a valuable lesson."

Brandon leaned forward. "Yeah, what was that?"

"No matter how alluring, a viper's nature is to bite." He shrugged. "It's best to stay clear of Ms. Bau."

"Hell, I thought I was skeptical," Brandon muttered.

"It's called being practical." Rafael raised his cup in a toast. "Gabriel believes Ms. Bau is sincere. Let's go with that for now."

"I wanted to regroup," Gabriel said. "There are—" A pounding on his door had all three of them swiveling around. Gabriel reached for his knife then checked through the peephole. "What the hell?" He opened the door.

Sam stumbled into the room. "She's gone. Noor—I kept an eye

on her like you told me to. When Mom went to bed, I placed a chair by the door and kept watch on her room. She went back to her suite, then left wearing burglar clothes. She took the emergency stairs.

"The stairwell faces the eastern side of the forest," Brandon said.

"Let's go." Gabriel dragged Sam with him to the corridor. He punched the elevator. "Brandon, make sure Sam gets back to his room. Rafael and I will search the premises."

"Aw. I wanna help."

He leaned down until he was at eye-level with the boy. "You did. Now go back to your room and get some rest." He gave the boy a gentle nudge in Brandon's direction.

The elevator door opened. Noor dashed out.

"Oh, thank God." A pink flush covered her cheeks. "They're on the trail. If we hurry, we'll catch them."

"Who's on the trail?" Gabriel, Brandon, and Rafael asked simultaneously.

"Drussel and two men. They're looking for something." She turned back to the elevator.

Gabriel grabbed her arm. "Wait. We can't go running into something we don't know."

"They're searching the property. They're on the longer running trail. We can take the shortcut to find them."

"Go ahead." Brandon nudged Sam into the elevator. "I'll catch up to you."

Gabriel patted his pocket. "I have a knife."

"I brought one too," Rafael said.

They took the emergency stairwell and kept to the edge of the property.

Gabriel pocketed his phone. "Don't use your flashlights. There's enough moonlight."

The wind hissed and bit his skin as they sprinted to the running trails. There were two—a longer one that circled the hill and a shorter one that went up the center. The two met at the top.

"This way." Noor pointed to the trail, then stumbled on something. "Argh!" She toppled to the ground. She'd stumbled over a bowler hat. Behind it, a crumpled form lay at the foot of the trail.

Rafael cursed.

Gabriel helped Noor to her feet. "Wait here." He approached the figure. The man with face paint—the one Noor had talked to at the dinner—lay on his side. An axe protruded from his back.

CHAPTER THIRTY-EIGHT

Khosrow was restless. He still loved Shirin....
—Nezami, Khosrow and Shirin

GABRIEL APPROACHED THE body, careful not to touch or disrupt anything. The man's lifeless eyes stared ahead. The black-and-white paint crisscrossing his face gave him a garish look, and the terrain bore the dark stains of his blood. Behind him, the wooden sign post lay flat on the ground.

"Arthur!" Noor sank to the ground beside him. "Oh, no."

Gabriel scanned the immediate area. A piece of paper lay under a stone at the foot of the trail.

Having eliminated the marauder, Khosrow, the blessed, won the war.

Another Nezami poem.

He dialed a number.

Hood's sleepy voice answered. *"This better be good, McKnight."*

"We found a body."

"What? Where are you?" Sleep evaporated from Hood's voice.

"By the running trail east of the golf course."

"On my way."

Hood and Robin arrived in short time.

Robin circled the body, then glared at Gabriel. "Why is there always a corpse when you're around?"

Gabriel massaged his neck. "I've been asking myself the same question."

Hood studied the body. "Did you call the police?"

"Not yet."

She shone her flashlight on the victim's face. "Do you know the victim?"

"Noor did. She talked to him at the dinner."

"Wonderful," Hood muttered. "Call it in, Robin."

An hour later, Gabriel stood by a tree stump with Noor, Rafael, and Brandon while the forensics team started their routine. The police had secured the area and set up several night lights.

A stocky man with a rumpled suit and short grey hair approached them. "I'm Detective Wagner of the Schwangau Police. May I have your names, please?"

They gave the detective their names. Gabriel ground his teeth. His life had become a never-ending series of deaths and police interviews.

Wagner posed the pen on his notebook. "Which one of you found the body?"

Noor straightened her shoulders. "I fell over his bowler hat. Gabriel helped me up and—" Her voice quivered. "We found him."

Wagner scribbled on his notepad. "What were you doing here?"

"We went for a walk." Gabriel wrapped his arm around Noor. "We're attending the book convention, and it's a beautiful night."

The detective made a sound between a snort and a cough. "Do any of you know the deceased?"

"I do," Noor said. "His name is Arthur Trells. He's a writer with the pen name Paradox."

The detective's brows rose. "And the paint on his face? Was it because of some event at the convention?"

"No." Noor kept her face averted from the trails. "It was part of his persona. Few people saw him without the makeup."

"Were you alone when you found the body?"

"We were also here," Hood chimed in.

To Gabriel's astonishment, Robin didn't contradict Hood. "We had too much to eat and went for a walk. We heard Ms. Rahman scream and arrived at the scene. I called it in."

Wagner rubbed his blood-shot eyes. "Did any of you see or hear anything unusual on your walk?"

Gabriel made a show of thinking about it. "No, I didn't."

"Did any of you have a conversation with the deceased tonight?"

Noor shifted. "I did. He came to my table to say hello."

The detective's brows rose. "What did you discuss?"

She rubbed at her temples. "We talked about his upcoming book, and I introduced him to the guests at my table. Mister Molina and Detectives Robin and Hood were there."

"Did you notice anything unusual about him?"

"You mean aside from the painted face and Paradox signs on his suit?" Rafael asked.

Noor sighed. "You should speak with his agent." She gave him the agent's name.

Wagner pocketed his notebook. "Our officers will take your statements. You may go back to your rooms. We'll call you if we need anything else."

They were about to leave when Wagner called out to Gabriel. "How long does this convention last?"

"Two more days," Gabriel answered.

He nodded. "Let me know if you plan to leave Bavaria." He handed them each a business card, then waved at the hotel manager, who stood behind the police tape, wringing his hands.

Hood and Robin exchanged glances. No one said anything until they were back in the hotel. Gabriel wondered what had compelled the detectives to vouch for them.

Hood's head swiveled between him and Noor. "You two will join us for a nightcap and conversation." She nodded at the others. "Get some rest, gentlemen."

"Wait a minute," Brandon objected.

Rafael was more subtle. He raised an eyebrow.

Gabriel nodded, confirming they would be okay.

Rafael slapped Brandon on the shoulder. "Let's go." He squeezed Noor's hand, then followed Brandon to the elevators.

Hood watched the interchange with arched brows.

Gabriel and Noor followed the detectives to the small lounge behind the lobby.

Hood straddled a chair. "Tell us what you didn't tell Wagner."

Gabriel answered her question with a question of his own. "Why did you tell the detective you saw the body with us?"

It was Robin who answered. "Someone killed three people in the past week. You're not on my list of favorite people, but you should—" He glanced at Noor.

Noor clasped her hands. "Go on. I can handle the truth."

Hood blew out a breath. "What Robin means is your luck will eventually run out. We want to catch this killer before anyone else, including you, gets hurt." She waved her hand in a "there you have it" gesture. "Now start from the beginning and leave nothing out."

Noor bit her lip. "He tried to tell me something."

Hood frowned. "Who? The victim?"

"Yes. He cornered me when I was leaving the dining hall. He said he overheard Doctor Reich speaking with someone about me. It's not unusual. I was a speaker at the convention. Whatever Arthur overheard bothered him. I asked him if we could meet for breakfast tomorrow." She fidgeted with her locket. "I didn't think he was in danger."

"What do you know about this Doctor Reich?" Robin asked.

"She's a professor at a Swedish University. We checked her out before taking her as a client."

Gabriel made a mental note to contact Billy.

"Did the victim seem agitated or afraid?" Robin asked.

"No." Noor stared at the tabletop. "I don't understand why anyone would kill Arthur."

Robin tapped his fingers on the tabletop. "Each murder tells us more about this killer. The first one was planned. The other two happened on the spur of a moment. Our killer is getting desperate, which means they'll make a mistake."

Hood pursed her lips. "McKnight's the common factor."

Gabriel shook his head. "Something else connects these murders." He needed time to think. "I have bits and pieces of information, nothing concrete. If I connect the dots, I'll call you."

Robin nodded. "That's fair. How did the four of you wind up at the walking trails?"

Noor told them about Drussel and friends.

Robin scowled. "I thought you would have better sense after what happened this morning."

"I went with my gut," Noor said.

Gabriel rubbed his chin. "I don't think Drussel and his goons did it."

Robin narrowed his eyes. "Why do you say that?"

"Because Noor saw them take the longer running trail. It winds around the hill and goes up to the hilltop. There's no way they made it up there and back down the other side in time. I'll bet anything Drussel and his men were on the running trail when the victim was killed."

Hood rose. "I'll see if I can charm Detective Wagner into sharing the medical examiner's report with me."

Noor leaned her head against the chair. Deep shadows had formed under her eyes.

"Are we done?" Gabriel asked.

Hood sighed. "Yes. Call if you need anything."

Gabriel accompanied Noor up to her suite. He cleared every room before signaling for her to enter.

The fact that she didn't argue spoke volumes about her exhaustion.

He tilted her chin up. "I'll sleep on the couch." *I don't want Rafael spending the night here.*

"Okay." Was that hope he saw? No, it couldn't be. She was into Rafael. Even Detective Hood had noticed.

She disappeared into the bedroom, then returned with two blankets and a pillow. Her face had no makeup, and the ridiculously large silk pajamas couldn't hide her beauty. Longing traveled through his entire body. She was and would always be his Noor.

"Thank you for watching over me." She didn't make eye contact.

He wanted to tell her he'd always be there for her. "You're welcome."

She bit her lip. "Gabriel?"

"Hm?" He busied himself by reaching for a bottle of water. He couldn't look at her. Not now, not here. He'd lose control if he did.

"Regardless of what happens. I don't regret our time together."

He clenched his fists. "Neither do I."

Gabriel waited until she'd gone to her room, then dialed a number. The call went straight to voicemail. "Mike, it's me. I need your help."

CHAPTER THIRTY-NINE

Khosrow summoned his advisors....

—Nezami, *Khosrow and Shirin*

G ABRIEL SANK INTO a chair at the Fussen café. News of Arthur's murder had spread. The convention had shifted its opening to noon because of it, and the hotel manager sent guests notes, assuring them of doubled security.

"Everyone is talking about the murder," Brandon announced.

Noor cupped her chin. "People have shown one of two reactions. They either won't leave their rooms or are out to solve the case."

"Is that what they're doing?" Rafael asked, glancing at the convention attendees huddled around one of the café tables with notepads.

Gabriel leaned forward. "I wanted to have breakfast here to avoid interruptions." He waved off a server approaching to refill their coffee. "Detective Hood said something last night that got me thinking. Three people were killed last week. The first, Darren Johannsson, a Swedish entrepreneur. The second, Ingrid, a German receptionist. The third, a reclusive American writer. Hood claims I'm the common thread in the murders. I disagree.

"Let's try a different perspective. Every incident has a backstory, a chain of cause and effect leading to its ultimate moment. The beginning sets everything into motion. For each of us, the beginning was different. Brandon's beginning was when his friend gave him a German engineer's diary two weeks ago. Rafael's was when his uncle told him about his grandmother's mantilla on his sixteenth birthday. For Noor, Harvey, and me, the beginning was the Frankfurt Book Fair. Each beginning has a different timeline, all incorrect, which is why we're running in circles." He tapped his fingers on the table. "The correct beginning is the key to the puzzle."

Brandon pursed his lips. "Maybe ground zero is eighteen years ago, when Richter killed Mina von Mayer's daughter."

"I considered it. However, several recent incidents don't connect to her daughter's death. Why would Richter kill Mina's daughter in the first place? Mina wasn't an international business tycoon then. She wasn't in Richter's league."

"Why would Mina's granddaughter want to help Gabriel?" Noor asked. "He has nothing to do with the family."

Rafael rubbed his jaw. "It also wouldn't explain why a group of people want Gabriel to find looted artwork the Nazis hid. From what I've read, von Mayer's interests lie in theatre and literature, not the art Richter's after."

Gabriel pulled a sheet of paper from his coat pocket, then spread it on the table. "I put what we know into three separate columns. The first is a list of facts. The second is a series of incidents that have occurred to the people connected to this mess. I used each incident as ground zero and tried to connect it to the facts and people involved. Only one makes sense to me." He pointed at a third column. "What if the true beginning was when an innocent man was accused of being a Nazi supporter? We know Karl von Mayer had a strained relationship with his cousin, Hans Richter, because they both fell in love with the same woman."

Gabriel checked off the first line. "Kiana von Mayer gave one interview to a Persian newspaper years after her husband's death. She acknowledged Karl had been a German soldier during the war, but he, like many others, didn't appreciate Hitler's policies."

"Interesting." Harvey steepled his fingers together. "How old was Mina when her father died?"

"Five," Brandon said.

"She was just a baby," Harvey murmured.

"Children are aware of what happens around them." Rafael's tone was flat. "Adults forget that."

"Exactly." Gabriel noticed Noor had eaten nothing and pushed a plate of muffins toward her. "Even if Mina didn't know about her father as a child, she would've heard the accusations growing up. Add in her mother's aversion to Richter Senior, and—"

"She'd want to prove her father's innocence," Noor finished. "I spent a decade trying to find my mother's killer. If I were Mina, I'd look closely at the Richters. They had motive and means."

Gabriel checked off the second item. "One way for Mina to prove her father's innocence would be to find the missing artwork."

A slow smile spread over Brandon's face. "Mina would go after the artwork to kill two birds with one stone. She'd prove her father was innocent and expose the Richters as Nazi supporters."

Gabriel leaned forward. "Suppose Richter Senior told his son where the Nazis hid some of the artwork. Farid Richter could sell pieces in the black market. If authorities discovered he sold looted art, they would prosecute him."

"Not only would his reputation go to hell, but it would also impact his business–another win for Mina," Brandon finished.

Rafael whistled. "That gives Richter motive for killing Mina's daughter and kidnapping her granddaughter."

Brandon waved his fork in the air. "In all my research on Richter, there's no mention of a ward. He must have kept the girl locked away where no one could find her."

Harvey fiddled with his glasses. "Following this chain of logic, Mina's granddaughter learns the truth about Richter and escapes. Instead of going to her grandmother, she reaches out to Gabriel to help bring her mother's murderer to justice."

Gabriel smiled. "Therefore, I'm not the common thread."

"No." Rafael rubbed his chin. "You were the catalyst."

"Exactly."

"Wait." Noor furrowed her brows. "You lost me."

"Eat. I'll explain," Gabriel said.

Scowling, she broke off a piece of muffin, then popped it into her mouth.

Satisfied, he continued. "Jurgen Mulligan forged documents for the baby Richter kidnapped. However, the best forgery won't stand in court today—not with modern technology."

Brandon plucked a muffin off the plate. "There are consequences for kidnapping the grandchild of Mina von Mayer and Cyrus Rohan."

Gabriel agreed. "Once Cyrus realized his granddaughter was alive, he'd use every ounce of his power to ruin Richter. And because Richter didn't have actual custody of the girl, he couldn't notify the authorities when she escaped. His only option was to capture her before Mina discovered her granddaughter is alive then find the rest of the hidden artwork before Mina does."

Noor gasped. "Richter started the rumor you have the codes. He knew about the miniatures in Iran and knew who my father was."

Gabriel smiled. "That's my theory. Richter's plan triggered a chain of events. Brandon, Rafael, and the Bau twins came to the book fair to find me. The kidnappers took you and so forth." He paused and reached for Noor's hand. "I had Billy check your client's background. Doctor Reich is the illegitimate daughter of Farid Richter."

Noor's jaw dropped. "Is that why she became my client?" Her eyes filled with tears. "She asked if I would introduce you to her. I'm so sorry. I didn't—"

"Easy." He squeezed her hand. "You couldn't know. The only reason I checked into her background was because of what Arthur Trells told you."

Rafael drummed his fingers. "What about the murders? How do they connect to this?"

Harvey toyed with his napkin. "They're connected because of the artwork. Everyone else associated with this puzzle has a reason to find it." He patted Noor's hand. "Since Doctor Reich is Richter's daughter, I'd say she's trying to help her father by getting close to Gabriel. Mina von Mayer and your uncle also have their reasons."

Rafael sighed heavily. "This convention is a veritable snake pit."

"Before we get to the last fact, I know parts of Nezami's *Khosrow and Shirin*. Tell me the whole story" Gabriel said.

All gazes turned to Noor, who stared into her cup. "After obtaining his father's forgiveness for a night of wild revelry with his friends, Prince Khosrow of Persia dreamed of his grandfather, who made four predictions, the last being Shirin, the woman he was destined to love.

"Khosrow had a friend, Shahpour, who told him about the Armenian princess, Shirin. Hearing Shahpour's description of Shirin, Khosrow fell in love with her." The corners of Noor's mouth turned up. "Here's where it becomes complicated. Shahpour traveled to Armenia and showed Shirin a drawing of Khosrow. Shirin fell in love with Khosrow and decided to visit him at his capital. She tricked her aunt and rode to Mada'in to find him. Meanwhile, some treacherous people told the king Khosrow was rebelling against him.

"To escape his father's wrath, Khosrow wore merchant's robes and rode to Armenia to find Shirin. They meet each other by chance when Khosrow came upon her bathing in a pool. Neither one knew the other, so they moved on. Khosrow arrived at Armenia and was welcomed by the queen. He heard Shirin was in Mada'in and ordered Shahpour to bring her back.

"When Shirin reached Armenia, she learned Khosrow returned to Mada'in because of his father's death. The two lovers kept going in opposite directions until Khosrow was challenged and overthrown by an evil general named Bahram Chobin."

Rafael shook his head. "Christ, that's complicated."

She nodded. "Khosrow fled to Armenia. The lovers finally met. Khosrow wanted intimacy with Shirin, yet she wouldn't marry him until he gained his kingdom back. He rode to Constantinople and sought the emperor's help. The emperor agreed to aid him if he would marry his daughter, Maryam. Khosrow married Maryam."

Noor pushed aside her unfinished muffin. "When Shirin heard of the marriage, she was devasted. Khosrow should have found an alternate solution, one that involved the prince getting his country back and marrying the woman he loved as opposed to leaving her."

"What happens in the end?" Brandon asked.

She shrugged. "Khosrow's wife died. After an appropriate mourning period, the lovers married."

Rafael blew out a breath. "Hallelujah."

"They lived happily, but Shiruyeh, Khosrow's son from Maryam, also loved Shirin. He killed his father to marry her. Shirin pretended to accept his proposal and asked to say goodbye to her dead husband, then killed herself to avoid marrying Shiruyeh. Khosrow and Shirin were buried together. And that is the difference between Shirin and Khosrow," Noor finished as her voice trembled with emotion.

Gabriel blinked. Whoa, was she referring to him? No, it couldn't be. He hadn't left Noor. He'd stepped back to give her the opportunity to be with a man she clearly preferred—Rafael. "Okay. The story gives us some context, which leads us to the last fact on my list." Gabriel placed a check on the last item in the column. "The numbers Noor discovered at the castle are latitude and longitude pointing to the valley between the two castles."

Rafael narrowed his eyes. "That's where our hotel is. Was the hotel around during the war?"

"I don't know," Gabriel said.

Noor tapped a finger to her lips. "There's something important in this area, or Drussel and his men wouldn't be searching for a well. The verse I found at Neuschwanstein is from *Khosrow and Shirin*. After Khosrow's marriage, Shirin lived in a palace shrouded with poison plants. Shahpur engaged an engineer named Farhad to create a channel from a distant pasture so shepherds could pour milk into the trough for Shirin. Farhad fell in love with Shirin. Khosrow heard of this and summoned Farhad to his court. He gave Farhad the impossible task of cutting through a mountain and said he could marry Shirin if successful.

"When Farhad almost succeeded, Khosrow's court advised him to tell Farhad Shirin was dead. Khosrow did, and Farhad threw himself off the mountain. Khosrow regretted this because he didn't intend for Farhad to die."

"Is that a clue to dig through something? Or are we supposed to find some secret tunnel?" Brandon asked.

"Hi." Sam skipped up to their table and sidled up to Gabriel. A pair of binoculars dangled from his neck. "How come you didn't let me come with you? I missed the murder."

Gabriel patted the boy's shoulder. "You helped keep Noor safe."

Noor kissed the boy's cheek. "You're a hero."

Sam blushed. "Cause Jason Vann and I, we're—" He slapped a hand over his mouth and glanced at Gabriel. "I mean, I read all the books and stuff."

Rafael grinned. "So, where's this secret location we must cut through?"

Sam scratched his head. "Are you talking about the old well—the secret one the Mad King made?"

Everyone stared at Sam.

"You know about a secret well on the castle grounds?" Gabriel asked.

Sam bobbed his head. "The Mad King made it when he made the Neuschwanstein. It's really a secret tunnel between the two castles. The hotel brochure says so."

Rafael whistled

"Sam! There you are." Marci joined them. "I told you not to stray from my sight." She ran a shaky hand over her son's curls.

"I want to stay here with Gabriel," Sam announced.

Marci shook her head. "Sorry, bud. You're coming with me."

Gabriel smiled. "Go with your mother. I'll be back at the hotel soon. We'll go for a hike if your mother allows it."

Sam turned his doe eyes to his mother. "Can I hike with Gabriel? Please, Mom? Can I?"

Marci bit her lip.

Noor patted Marci's arm. "He'll be safe with Gabriel."

She sighed. "Very well."

Sam grinned.

"What's next?" Brandon asked.

"It's time Noor and I talked to Mina von Mayer."

CHAPTER FORTY

As dawn broke, the lovers were finally united.
—Nezami, *Khosrow and Shirin*

LUCERNE, SWITZERLAND

CYRUS LAY FLOWERS on his daughter's grave just as the first rays of sunlight streaked through the cemetery. His eyes stung with unshed tears. *My sweet Sarah, I'm sorry I wasn't there to protect you. I'm so sorry.* He traced his fingers over the cold tombstone. "I'll protect your daughter. Your mother and I will make it right."

A sniffle caught his attention. Farther off, an elderly couple huddled by a grave, holding onto each other. The woman sobbed, while the man kneeled to kiss a tombstone. They bid goodbye to their loved one, then made their way to the exit.

Cyrus stepped aside to let them pass.

The woman tilted her head. "May your loved one rest in peace."

Unable to speak, Cyrus nodded at her.

A wrinkled hand motioned to the cemetery. "My husband and I lost our firstborn when he turned five. We visit him on his birthday every year."

"I'm sorry," Cyrus murmured with feeling. "It must have broken you."

The woman's snowy brows drew together. "It broke our hearts, not us." She sighed. "We were blessed with five more children, ten grandchildren, and six great grandchildren. Life gives you pain. It also gives joy."

Her husband wiped his eyes with his handkerchief, then hobbled over to his wife. "The children want to take us out for breakfast. Are you up to it?"

The woman's wrinkled face broke into a smile. "Of course." They bid him good day and hobbled out of the cemetery.

Cyrus stared at the group waiting for the couple. They ranged from adult to young children. The ashes of his anguish sparked fire. His blood boiled. He called Mina.

"Cyrus? Where are you?"

"I visited Sarah."

Silence.

Cyrus balled his fist. "We finish it tomorrow night."

"What about our granddaughter?"

"I'll get her out by then."

"All right."

"Mina?"

"Yes."

"We're going to talk."

He ended the call, then dialed his assistant. "Have the plane ready in thirty minutes. I'm going to Bavaria."

WHEN THE KNOCK sounded, Mina opened the door with a steady hand, then moved aside to let Cyrus enter.

He threw an envelope onto the breakfast table. "I've got proof. The adoption paperwork is Mulligan's forgery. I have a signed statement from his assistant and a confession from the retired assistant to the coroner." He nudged the envelope toward her. "Go on. Open it."

Mina reached for the document, fingers trembling. "Thank you." They needed to talk, and she tried to speak, yet the pounding of her heart made it impossible.

"I saw an older couple—" His mouth turned up. "Well, older than us. It hit me more than ever what Richter took from us."

"Cyrus—"

He reached for her hand. "We are not characters in a tragedy, Mina. We're powerful, intelligent adults. My father never loved my mother. Theirs was an arranged marriage. He traveled for his trade and fell in love with a woman on one of his trips. He was going to divorce my mother when he realized she was pregnant."

She didn't move. This was the first time Cyrus had shared his childhood with her.

"Dad kept his marriage and loved my brother Cameron and me. He spent half the year in Tehran and traveled to Italy several times a year. Every time he came back, there was a light in his eyes, but even as a child, I noticed it dim every day." His hold tightened on her hand. "I don't want to live a half-life and steal a few moments in private with you. I want a full life with you and our granddaughter."

Mina felt as if she stood on the edge of a cliff, deciding whether she should jump. It was now or never. Her shoulders straightened. "When my father died, Mama lost her light and became a shell of her former self. I didn't want to become like her. I didn't want to love someone with every fiber of my being because I couldn't bear the loss." She touched his jaw. "Part of the guilt I felt all these years is because I kept back part of me, while you gave yourself wholeheartedly. I didn't deserve you or Sarah." She touched his lips to stop him from speaking. "I was wrong. The best moments of my life were with you and Sarah. "You've owned my heart since the day I met you. I'll stand for us and our granddaughter. I love you, and I hope you'll forgive me."

"You're going to marry me." His voice came out stern.

Her heart soared. "Yes, I am." She pulled out a chain hanging from her neck. On it sat a ring with a rectangular topaz. He'd given it to her when he learned she was pregnant years ago.

His eyes widened. "You kept it?"

"I never let it go."

He took the ring, then placed it on her finger. His mercurial eyes turned to molten ash when he pulled her into his arms.

She tilted up her head, basking in the unique exotic sweetness of his kiss. Stroking his back, reveling in the muscular contours—familiar and new.

His skillful hands roamed over her, branding, igniting. Loving. "Bedroom?" he whispered.

"To the left."

A while later, they lay in each other's arms, satiated.

Cyrus kissed a trail down her neck to her shoulder. "Not bad for a pair of senior citizens."

She laughed and snuggled closer. "I love you."

He grinned. "I love you too."

The clock on the nightstand chimed. There was work to do if they wanted to right Richter's wrongs. Mina sighed. "We should talk to Gabriel and Noor before sunset. Let's finish this once and for all."

CHAPTER FORTY-ONE

The task was so difficult, Khosrow was certain Farhad would fail.
—Nezami, Khosrow and Shirin

NOOR STUDIED THE brightly painted buildings of Fussen. "This is lovely."

Gabriel smiled. "We'll come ba—" He looked away. "Sorry."

Falling into their old habits was easy. She'd stopped herself from reaching for his hand several times. Her heart clenched. Once this was over, she wouldn't see him. Her eyes stung with unshed tears.

They arrived at a building painted in bright yellow. A doorman in finery greeted them. Inside, burgundy walls held bookshelves, and armchairs sat scattered around the lobby, creating an atmosphere more like a drawing room than a hotel.

"How did you know Mina von Mayer is here?"

"Your uncle sent me a text." Gabriel approached the reception desk and flashed a bright smile. "Please inform Ms. von Mayer Gabriel McKnight and Ms. Rahman are here to see her."

The clerk blinked. "Sir, we don't—"

His voice shifted into his "don't mess with me" tone. He didn't use it often. When he did, it yielded results. "You can contact her or Mister Rohan and let them know we're waiting."

The clerk's eyes widened. "Sir—"

"Never mind." Gabriel's went after a woman with a baggy brown dress.

"Gabriel?" Noor rushed after him.

He caught up with the woman as she reached the elevator. "Miss?"

She jumped and dropped the binder she was carrying.

Noor picked it up and handed it to her.

"T-thank you." Up close, she looked younger. Her chestnut hair fell below her shoulders. Pale blue eyes dominated a pointy face. The brown dress hung loose on her slim frame, and she shifted from one leg to another like a skittish colt. "I have butter fingers."

Gabriel kept his tone gentle. "I saw you back at Mister Richter's party in Frankfurt. You're Ms. von Mayer's assistant."

A pink stain covered her cheeks. "Her financial analyst."

"Apologies. My name is Gabriel McKnight, and this is my friend, Ms. Rahman."

"I read your books. They're very good." She sucked in a huge gulp of air, as if talking to strangers had drained the oxygen from her lungs. "I'm Mercedes."

Noor smiled to put the woman at ease. "It's nice to meet you."

Gabriel took half a step toward her, then stopped when she flinched. "We must speak with Mister Rohan or Ms. von Mayer. It's urgent."

Mercedes straightened. "I see. I'll, um, ask her." She motioned to a sitting area in the lobby. "Would you have a seat while I check with her? It won't—"

He didn't let her finish. "We'll come up with you." Gabriel nudged Mercedes into the elevator and motioned for Noor to follow.

She bit back a smile and stepped in after them.

"I don't know if she can meet with you right now," Mercedes murmured. They exited on the top floor. Mercedes stopped outside what had to be the luxury suite. "Please wait here."

Gabriel stepped around her.

"No! Wait, please. You can't just barge in."

But barge in they did.

Mina von Mayer stood by the fireplace, deep in discussion with Uncle Cyrus. Her face was turned up to his. Neither one seemed surprised to see them.

"I'm sorry, ma'am. I tried to stop him."

Mina smiled at the quivering woman. "It's all right, Mercedes. Will you kindly order tea for our guests?"

She bobbed her head, then fled, shutting the doors behind her.

Mina waved an elegant hand toward the sitting area. "Please have a seat."

Gabriel crossed his arms over his chest. "Did you turn Noor and me into targets to lure your granddaughter away from Richter?"

What? Noor hadn't considered that angle.

Apparently, Gabriel had, and he wasn't happy about it. He also didn't back down. "Did you?"

"No," Cyrus and Mina answered simultaneously.

Cyrus frowned. "I would never put Noor at risk."

"Of course not," Noor began.

"I know you," Gabriel said to Uncle Cyrus. "It's Ms. von Mayer I don't know."

Cyrus was about to say something.

Mina laid a hand on his arm. "Let's sit down and discuss this."

Gabriel was in alpha-male mode. Noor dragged him to the sofa. Mina sat beside them. Uncle Cyrus stood behind her, placing a hand on her shoulder. So, they were still a couple. She sneaked a glance at Gabriel. If he was surprised, he didn't show it.

Mina patted Cyrus's hand. "As much as I'd love to see my granddaughter, I would never put you, Ms. Rahman, or anyone in harm's way"

Gabriel studied her for a long moment. His shoulders relaxed. "I had to ask."

She nodded. "I understand."

Mercedes came in with a server bearing a large tray of tea with an assortment of pastries.

Mina waited for them to leave before pouring. "How did you know about my granddaughter?"

"I'm good at research."

A smiled tugged at Mina's mouth. "I see." She handed him a cup.

Gabriel declined an offer of milk. "Are you two going to tell us what's going on?"

Mina clasped her hands together. "Why don't you start by telling us what you know?"

"Richter Senior framed and killed your father. Richter Junior arranged for a car accident and killed your daughter and son-in-law. You believed your granddaughter died in the accident. She didn't. He kidnapped her and raised her as his ward, likely to use her against you at some point. His plan backfired. Your granddaughter learned the truth and escaped. Have I got it right so far?"

"Yes."

Gabriel tilted his head and watched Mina. "This past summer, Noor and I found a jewel-encrusted cigarette case and a diamond, both part of a collection once housed in Tehran's Central Bank. Cyrus took a sheet of paper from the case. He claimed it belonged to a friend of his and not the people of Iran. I assume you are the friend."

"That, too, is correct," Mina confirmed.

"What do you have on Richter that's driven him to such lengths to destroy you? What was in the case?" Gabriel asked.

Mina was holding back. Noor could see it.

She rose, went to the man she loved as family, then wrapped her arms around him. "I'm sorry you lost your daughter, Uncle Cyrus."

He lay his cheek on top of her head. "Thank you."

She stepped back and smiled down at Mina. "Uncle Cyrus is family, which makes you and your granddaughter family. Gabriel and I want to help you."

Mina's eyes softened. "You're very much like your mother." She exhaled slowly. "It's safer for you to not know details."

Gabriel raked a hand through his hair. "We're already in danger. What was in the case?"

Cyrus started to answer.

"It's all right, Cyrus." Mina's golden eyes skimmed over them. "It was a note from Alfred Rosenberg, chief Nazi ideologue, to Farid's father. Rosenberg thanked him for his help in hiding the artwork stored at Neuschwanstein. Behind the letter is a map with locations of the artwork and a list of coordinates, in code, for each location. Farid's father left a stamp from his coat of arms at several of the locations. My father was going to take it to the authorities."

Gabriel's eyes gleamed. "You have the locations of the artwork."

"Not all," Cyrus answered.

Mina shifted. "The list I have includes eight locations, all within several miles of the castle. Richter Senior hid artwork in twenty plus locations, one being the location the Nezami miniatures indicate."

Gabriel rubbed his neck. "We're hunting a killer connected to this. We can't help you if we're flying blind."

In a rare display of affection, Uncle Cyrus clasped Gabriel's shoulder. "Richter hasn't come after you or Noor because he's convinced you don't know the location of the artwork. The best way I can protect you is by keeping you in the dark. I know it's not easy, but I need you to trust us. Everything will... change in the next twenty-four hours."

Noor could see Gabriel's internal struggle.

He raked a hand through his hair. "All right."

Uncle Cyrus beamed. "You mentioned you want to catch a killer. Tell me what you're planning, and I'll help you."

They talked for another hour.

ZITA DUCKED BEHIND a stone pillar and watched Gabriel McKnight weave through the crowd at Fussen. What was he doing wandering around the city like a tourist? He should be at the castle.

Being out in the open was a risk for her. She'd spotted Snakey and his goons earlier that morning. Zita shifted her sunglasses and followed McKnight.

He bought a cup of coffee before circling back to the town square to sit on a bench.

The sun was out, drawing crowds into the main square. Biting back a sigh, she bought an ice cream cone from a stand, then pretended to window shop while keeping McKnight in her line of sight.

Several minutes later, he rose and headed down an alley. She followed him, then came to an abrupt halt when there was no one in the alley. Where was he? Muttering something under her breath, she turned back.

"Not so fast." A man firmly gripped her arm.

Shock pushed her muscles into action. Her leg came up in a kick.

McKnight caught it mid-air, then whipped her around. "Why are you following me?"

"I-I—" She was at a loss for words. He'd made her. No one had ever done that.

His grip tightened, but she refused to wince.

"I warned you at the book fair back in Frankfurt. Why are you wasting time?"

He yanked her ball cap off and leaned forward. "Answer my question."

A flush heated her cheeks. If Richter couldn't break her, McKnight certainly wasn't going to. She raised her chin. "I'll scream rape if you don't let me go."

He pulled out his wallet and threw it into her bag. "Thief!" he yelled, hauling her forward. "Someone, call the police. This woman tried to steal my wallet." He dragged her toward the town square.

Oh, no. The noise would attract attention. Richter's men would recognize her. Snakey would find her.

"Okay," she cried. "Stop shouting. I'll answer your questions."

He shoved her against the wall and leaned over her, crowding her space. His eyes reminded her of blue marble, deep and unyielding.

Zita licked her lips. "I'm trying to help you." She was pleased her voice came out steady. "You need the clues to beat him."

A dark brow rose. "Beat who?"

Was he kidding? She scowled. "Richter, who else?"

McKnight studied her for a moment, then dragged her toward the town square. "You're coming with me."

She didn't struggle while he shoved her into the cab. The last thing she wanted was for people to notice her. Why hadn't she'd worn contacts or a wig?

They arrived at the hotel in less than ten minutes. Gabriel dragged her to the front desk. She'd watched him for days. He hadn't seemed like a hard man, but then people rarely showed their true colors in public.

He turned on the charm for the poor receptionist. "I think I lost my key card. Would you kindly give me another one?"

The girl blushed, stuttered, and rushed about to reprogram another card. "Here you go, sir."

He beamed at her. "Thank you."

"Will you loosen your hold? I'll have bruises on my arm," Zita muttered.

They waited for a couple to exit the elevators. He nudged her inside. "Consider yourself lucky to be breathing." They arrived on his floor. "Come on."

Panic settled in her chest. "Why are we going to your suite?"

"We need to talk, and I won't risk you screaming or running away."

"We can talk in the café."

He chuckled and slid the key card into the door. She was about to protest when he dragged her into the room, then locked the door.

"No room service, please," a man called out.

A doppelganger of the man gripping her arm came through the bedroom door. Zita gasped. He looked exactly like Gabriel McKnight, though he wore sweatpants, no shirt, and held a mug of coffee to his lips.

The man beside her grinned and let her go.

The two men hugged and slapped each other's backs. She watched in fascination.

The man who had brought her chuckled. "I came as soon as I could." He tilted his head in her direction. "I brought you a visitor."

Her head swiveled back and forth between them. "You're identical." How had she missed that? Her research hadn't turned up an identical twin.

The bare-chested one studied her. He had an impressive upper body. Now that they were side to side, she conceded they both had impressive physiques.

Bare Chest—likely the real Gabriel McKnight—smiled. "Excuse me for a moment." He retreated to the bedroom, then returned wearing a T-shirt. He approached her and held out his hand. "Miss Zita, we didn't have time to talk at the book fair. I'm Gabriel McKnight." He glanced over his shoulder. "That's my brother, Michael."

Michael grinned. "We've met."

She was too stunned to do anything but stare. Gabriel's eyes reminded her of the Mediterranean Sea.

"Can I get you anything to drink? Coffee or tea?"

She shook herself out of her stupor. "N-no, thank you."

Michael stomped over to the kitchen. He returned with a bag of chips, plopped onto the sofa, and stretched his legs. "What's going on, Gabe? I get a cryptic message from you, then Noor's uncle Cyrus called and left me a similar message."

She sank onto the edge of a chair. She hadn't planned for this. What to do?

Gabriel went into the kitchen and came back with a bottle of water. "Drink this."

Zita gulped the water. Gabriel and his brother watched her the way two jungle cats homed in on prey did. She gripped the bottle and waited.

Gabriel pulled a chair beside her. "I'll help you prove Richter killed your mother."

The familiar burning moved through her. "It's not enough. Richter's evil. I want to destroy him."

"Richter's men aren't the only danger here. There's a killer running loose."

Michael paused in the act of eating chips.

Gabriel's voice was gentle, as if he was talking to a child. "Your grandmother wants to meet you. Go to her."

She raised her chin. "Not yet. I—"

A chilling scream came from the hallway.

CHAPTER FORTY-TWO

Khosrow prepared his men for war....

—Nezami, *Khosrow and Shirin*

WHAT THE HELL? Gabriel burst into the corridor.

A woman dashed from a hotel room. "There's blood all over the bed!"

The elevator dinged. Noor stepped out. Her eyes widened as a crowd gathered. Brandon, Rafael, and Harvey came running from Harvey's suite.

"Blood!" the woman shrieked.

Gabriel brushed past her and entered her room. A large red stain covered her bed. Droplets of red dripped onto the carpet. He sniffed, bent, then touched the stain. "It's paint. Someone played a cruel prank on you. Call the security desk to notify them."

The harried woman scurried back to her room.

"False alarm. Everything's fine." Gabriel raised his voice for the hotel guests to hear.

Noor pushed through the thinning crowd. "Why would anyone do that?"

"Hello, beautiful." Michael held his arms open.

"Michael." Noor embraced him. "When did you arrive? Is Aliza coming too?" Aliza was Michael's fiancée and an agent at the National Security Agency.

Michael kissed her cheek. "I just arrived. Aliza flies in this afternoon."

Gabriel cupped Noor under the elbow. "Your uncle's granddaughter is in my room. Come talk to her."

"Sorry, bro," Michael said. "She bolted when we rushed outside."

"Damn it." Gabriel raked a hand through his hair.

"Where did you find her?" Noor asked.

"I found her and brought her to Gabe. She can't have gotten far." Michael kept his arm around Noor's shoulders. "Where were you when the hullabaloo started?"

"In my room."

Michael's eyebrows shot up. His gaze traveled from Gabriel to her and back.

Gabriel mouthed, "Later." He signaled for Brandon, Harvey, and Rafael to join them.

Harvey greeted Michael warmly. Gabriel introduced the others.

Rafael chuckled. "It's impossible to tell you guys apart."

"Not once you know us better." Michael laughed. "I'm the fun twin."

Noor patted Michael's arm. "The convention starts in fifteen minutes. I'll see you later."

"I'm coming with you," Rafael announced.

Gabriel forced himself to stay where he was, while Rafael accompanied Noor out the door.

Michael blinked.

Harvey and Brandon made excuses and left the brothers alone.

"What's going on between you and Noor?" Michael asked.

"Nothing. Come on." Gabriel handed him a ball cap and sunglasses. "I want you to stay inconspicuous."

Michael took the ball cap. "Where are we going?"

"To meet a kid."

～

"I WISH I had a brother who looked like me." Sam hopped from one foot to the other and chattered nonstop while guiding them through a worn-out path behind the running trails.

"You're sure you know where the well is?" Gabriel asked.

Sam nodded then glanced at Michael. "How come Jason Vann doesn't have an identical twin?"

Michael pushed a tree branch aside. "Good question for the genius writer."

"You know what? I bet it's 'cause he doesn't need one. 'Cause he's Jason Vann."

"Kid's chatty," Michael muttered, moving around a thicket of thorn bushes.

"I'm not a kid," Sam snapped. "Jason Vann's perfect. He doesn't need a grumpy brother."

Michael chuckled. "You got it right. Jason is perfect."

Gabriel thought of Noor alone at the convention.

She's not alone. Rafael's with her.

He wondered if she thought of him as much as he did of her.

Sam glanced up at him. "Does he know?"

"Hm? Sorry, what did you say?"

Michael gave him a knowing look. "If the woman I loved was spending the day with a good-looking Spanish billionaire, I'd be distracted too."

"Who's the billionaire?" Sam asked.

Michael sighed "Look, kid—"

"If you call me kid, I won't show you the well. Besides Gabriel's like Jason Vann. All the women love him. Noor loves him."

Michael threw his head back and laughed. "Is that why she's in a separate room?"

Gabriel held up his hand before Sam could reply. "Enough, Mike."

Michael waited for an explanation.

"Rafael saved her life."

"And?"

He rubbed the back of his neck. Michael wouldn't stop until he had an answer. "She cares about him."

Michael threw his hands in the air. "I care about many people. Doesn't mean I want to spend the rest of my life with them."

How could he explain Noor lighting up every time Rafael was near? That thought didn't improve his mood. He forged ahead.

"I don't get it. You're okay with her spending time with the hotel king, while you look for a stupid well? What gotten into you?" Michael gripped his arm. "Damn it, Gabe! Stop for a minute."

Gabriel whirled around. "What the hell do you want me to say? You think I want this? He's a better man than I am. He saved her life when I couldn't even find her. What else could I do but let her go?" He hated that his voice shook, hated the sudden blur in his vision.

Michael crossed his arms. "First of all, you're the best man I know. Second, did she say she loved the hotel king?"

"That's not the point."

"Yes, it is," Michael snapped. "Did she say she loved him?"

Gabriel glared at his brother.

Michael smirked. "That's what I thought."

He brushed past Michael. "How much farther, Sam?"

Sam pointed to the left side of the trail. "It's behind the trees."

The inaudible murmur of voices reached them.

Gabriel shoved Sam behind him. He pressed his forefinger to his lips, signaling the boy to be quiet.

Eyes wide as saucers, Sam bobbed his head.

The brothers moved up the path in unison, careful not to make noise.

Erik Drussel searched a clearing between trees with two men, whom he glared at. "It has to be in this area. Keep looking."

He'd seen enough. Gabriel pointed to the path. Michael nodded. Gabriel picked Sam up, then ran back to the hotel. At the golf course, he put the boy down, then strode toward the hotel.

Sam ran to keep up with him. "Were they the bad guys? If they were, how come you didn't punch them like Jason Vann punches bad guys?"

Gabriel shared a look with Michael. "Go to the suite with Sam."

"Where are you going?" Michael asked.

"I'll find Noor and the others. We need to talk."

"I wanna stay with you," Sam said.

"I wanna stay with you too," Michael mimicked Sam.

Gabriel pulled out his phone. "I'll ask the others to join us in my room."

"Ah, there's Gabriel." A familiar voice rang through the hotel lobby.

"Looks like Michael is with him," boomed another man cheerfully.

"Are you certain, Mustafa? Your eyesight isn't what it used to be." The third man's voice carried despite being raspy.

"Are you kidding me?" Michael muttered.

Gabriel followed his brother's gaze and came to an abrupt halt. He blinked to make sure he wasn't hallucinating.

Three men stood in the lobby. The first was craggy-faced with wisps of silver hair. His wrinkled priest's frock had seen better days.

The second, slim and tall, wore a loose white shirt over his trousers. His eyes danced with amusement as he stroked his beard.

The last was slightly bent over, with fragile bones and a long silver beard. A yarmulke sat askew on his head. He peered at Gabriel then stomped his cane. "Ha! It's him."

Michael glared at his brother. "You called them?"

"I'm not that desperate," Gabriel growled. Resigned to the inevitable, he approached the priest. "Father Pierre, what a surprise."

"Surprise?" Rabbi Abarron stomped his cane. "We came looking for you." His head swiveled toward Michael. "And you."

"Rabbi." Michael nodded his head.

Mustafa slapped Gabriel on the shoulder. "How are you, son?"

"I'm fine, thank you. What brings you here?" Gabriel was pleased his voice didn't betray his irritation.

Father Pierre, Rabbi Abarron, and Mustafa were friends of Noor's mother. The trio had stepped in to help when Noor and Gabriel had tangled with a killer several months ago.

Abarron leaned on his cane. "You're in trouble."

"Now, now, Abarron. The man has his pride." Mustafa beamed. "We heard you had some... complications and came to offer our help."

"Mustafa?" Noor stepped into the lobby. "Father Pierre, Rabbi Abarron! What brings you to Bavaria?" Her gaze shifted to Gabriel.

He lifted his shoulders and shook his head.

"Your uncle Cyrus called us," Mustafa said.

"Of course he did," Michael muttered.

Rabbi Abarron adjusted his glasses and hobbled closer to Michael. "When's the wedding? Aliza said you haven't finalized a date."

Michael shuffled his feet. "We've been busy."

The lobby doors swung open. Brandon and Rafael froze as Aliza, a stunning brunette with silky hair and golden cat-eyes, surveyed the lobby with effortless confidence before her gaze landed on Noor. Smiling, she strode in.

"Aliza!" Noor embraced Michael's fiancée.

"I missed you, sister-friend." Aliza returned the hug. Her exotic features, enticing curves, and generous smile could—and often did—mesmerize others.

Aliza kissed Michael, then hugged Gabriel. "You look good, brother of mine."

He kissed her cheek. "So do you. Thanks for coming."

"And miss the party? Never." She greeted the beaming rabbi. "Rabbi, hello."

While Rafael and Brandon stood dumbfounded, Gabriel gritted his teeth. "Let's gather in my suite." He prayed for patience while the rag-tag group made their way to his sitting room and settled in.

Sam sat between Mustafa and Father Pierre. "Are you a priest too?"

Mustafa chuckled. "Muslims don't have priests. I'm a humble scholar."

"He's an outstanding scholar," Abarron offered. "I've known him for years."

"Are you a Jewish priest?"

Abarron peered down at the boy. "We have rabbis, and yes, I'm a rabbi."

"How come we can't call all of you the same thing? It's the same God, isn't it?" Sam asked.

Mustafa scratched his beard. "Hmm, that is a suitable topic for our podcast. What say you, Abarron?"

Sam's eyes widened. "You have a podcast?"

Abarron's mouth curved up. "We'll have one soon. We'll call it 'Baking Cakes with Uncle Mustafa and Rabbi Abarron.'"

Noor tapped the boy on the shoulder. "Your mother's here to pick you up."

"Aw," Sam groaned.

Gently, Noor cajoled the boy and led him from the room, while Gabriel helped Michael and Aliza serve tea.

Aliza handed Rafael a mug. He took her hand and kissed the back of it.

Michael jammed his elbow into Gabriel's side. "Smooth, isn't he?"

"Smooth and likeable." Ignoring the familiar sense of loss, Gabriel strode to the middle of the room. All eyes turned to him. "Thank you for coming. Noor and I have found ourselves in a tangle. Our problem is two-fold. First, we have a series of incidents which took place after an innocent man was framed for crimes he didn't commit. The second is a trail of murders that have followed us here from Frankfurt. I believe the two are connected."

"Cyrus Rohan and I trust you. Therefore, I'll share information with you no one outside of Cyrus's immediate family knows." He recounted everything from the moment Karl von Mayer died up to his and Michael's hike with Sam.

Concern deepened the lines around Father Pierre's eyes. "Where is Cyrus's granddaughter?"

"Cyrus will get her to safety," Gabriel said. "If you spot her, let me know. I'll convince her to join her grandparents." He shoved his hands into his pockets. "Noor and I met with Cyrus and Mina earlier today. They've planned something for Richter tomorrow night."

"How's that possible?" Harvey pointed to a German newspaper. "This says Mister Rohan and Ms. von Mayer are attending the opening night of Nezami's *Khosrow and Shirin* in Berlin. They'll be miles away, while Richter is here opening the ball."

Gabriel blinked. "Ball?"

"It's a costume ball. We signed you up for it when we accepted the invitation to the convention, remember?" Noor said.

Gabriel's mouth fell open. "You signed me up for a costume party?"

Harvey tugged on his collar. "Actually, I did. You're going to open the event with Richter. It's an excellent opportunity to keep an eye on him."

"A fucking costume party?" Gabriel roared.

Abarron thumped his cane on the floor. "Don't curse, boy!"

Brandon and Rafael exchanged glances.

"We'll search for the well while you're at the ball," Brandon offered.

"If I'm going to a damned ball, you're going, too," Gabriel snapped.

"Are you going, Noor?" Rafael asked. "I'll accompany you."

The comment had everyone glancing between Rafael and Gabriel.

"Gabe." Michael's tone shifted Gabriel's attention from Rafael's grin. "This could be a good thing. It'll provide cover for what you're planning."

"What's the boy planning?" Abarron asked.

Gabriel gritted his teeth. How had his life spun so out of control? He forced himself to be objective. Michael was right—the ball did provide distraction. He raked a hand through his hair. "I don't want to sit around and wait for another murder. I want to trap the murderer, and I think I can find the artwork. I have a plan."

"What about the Bau twins and the two detectives?" Brandon asked.

"I'll speak with each separately." Gabriel walked the group through his plan.

Noor sprang from her chair, fists clenched. "No!"

Brandon crossed his arms. "You're putting a target on your back."

"No!" Noor glared at the group. "Tell him it's dangerous."

"She's right." All traces of humor had vanished from Rafael's voice. "You of all people know the risk."

Noor's lower lip trembled.

Gabriel sighed. "Please excuse us." He took her arm and led her into the kitchen.

Her chin jutted out. "I won't let you put yourself in danger."

She still cared for him. His chest ached. He pushed a strand of her hair away from her face. "We had a similar conversation several months ago when we were tracking down your parents' killer. You said it was your choice. You said I was there to keep you safe and reminded me you weren't alone."

"I—"

"I'm giving you all the same answers. Whether we're in a relationship or not, you'll have my back, and the people in the sitting room do too."

Her voice shook. "I don't like the plan."

"Neither do I." Come to think of it, he liked nothing about his life at the moment. "We have a brief window and need to act fast."

CHAPTER FORTY-THREE

Torn between love and anger, Shirin welcomed Khosrow....
—Nezami, *Khosrow and Shirin*

NOOR GLARED AT her reflection in the mirror.

Aliza stepped into an evening gown. "What's up with you and Gabriel?"

"He called quits on our relationship." She kept her voice steady. "We'll continue to be friends." She began pulling her hair up into a loose ponytail.

"He wanted to break up, and you agreed?"

"What was I supposed to do?"

Aliza's golden eyes met hers in the mirror. "Fight back."

"But he doesn't—"

"Have you seen how he looks at you?" She waved Noor's answer away. "Do you believe Gabriel loves you?"

Tears welled in Noor's eyes. "I thought he did. One moment he's the Gabriel I know, and the next he's cold and distant."

Aliza furrowed her brows. "When did this start?"

"After the murders."

A slow smile spread over Aliza's face. "Did it start after the murders, or after your friendship with Rafael?"

"What are you talking about?"

She took hold of Noor's shoulders. "Has it occurred to you Gabriel is insecure when it comes to your friendship with Rafael?"

"What? No."

Aliza rolled her eyes. "Have you noticed how the incredibly hot Rafael looks at you?"

"Rafael's a friend, that's all."

"A friend who, from Gabriel's perspective, is handsome, successful, and whole," Aliza finished.

"What do you mean?"

"How much do you know about Gabriel's experience in the military?"

"If you're referring to the girl who died in Afghanistan, Gabriel told me about her," Noor said.

Aliza plucked the blush from the vanity, sat Noor in front of her, then began working on her makeup. "Michael told me Gabriel blames himself for the girl's death. It's hard to recover from a scar like that. If Gabriel saw himself as unworthy, he'd convince himself you'll be happier with Rafael. His reaction isn't surprising." She studied her work, then nodded. "He stepped back because he loves you, not because he doesn't."

Could that be true? A hundred butterfly wings fluttered in Noor's stomach, and hope shone bright in her heart. "Fan Bau flirted with Gabriel. I ignored it because I believed he loved me. Gabriel's intelligent. Why would he be insecure?"

Aliza brushed mascara on her lashes. "We come from different backgrounds. Our experiences, triumphs, and scars differ. Hence, our reactions differ. You were confident in your relationship. That doesn't mean Gabriel was."

Unable to sit longer, Noor rose and paced. Aliza had a point. Gabriel acted strange every time she was with Rafael. Did he believe she felt anything other than friendship for Rafael? How had she been so blind?

Anger whipped through her like lightening. She whirled around. "What gives Gabriel the right to decide who I should be with?"

Aliza smirked. "Exactly."

Noor resumed pacing. "I bet you don't have this problem with Michael."

"Michael has different issues." Aliza laughed. "We have wild sex, then once he's calm enough to talk, we talk through it. One thing we don't do is give up on each other."

"I'm going to beat some sense into Gabriel," Noor growled.

"Atta girl." Aliza examined Noor's gown. "Let's find something else for you to wear. You want to make him drool before giving him hell."

Thirty minutes later, she entered the ballroom with Aliza. She felt like she'd stepped into a party from the Gatsby era. Tables with crisp white linen and intricate flower arrangements filled the dining hall. Pyramids of champagne glasses sat on each end of the ballroom. Musicians occupied a large stage, while couples danced and mingled. They passed several Miss Marples and a few Sherlocks until they reached their table.

"Ladies." Rafael wore an old-world tuxedo. He'd been talking to Marci, who had dressed as the main sleuth of her books—a chef.

Noor introduced Aliza to Marci.

"Shall I fetch you champagne?" Rafael asked.

"Yes," she and Aliza responded simultaneously.

Noor watched Rafael walk away. "He is handsome."

Marci giggled. "You just noticed?"

Detective Hood arrived in a black suit and top hat.

"You're dressed as Arsen Lupin," Noor said.

Hood chuckled. "I thought a gentleman thief would be a good change." Her gaze swept through the ballroom. "Where's McKnight?"

Noor scanned the ballroom. "He'll be here soon."

Rafael returned with the champagne. She took a fortifying sip.

Michael arrived with Detective Robin. Both men had black and white paint on their faces and the sign of Paradox pinned to their lapels.

Hood laughed. "I can't tell you apart."

"I can." Hema arrived at their table wearing a 1920s evening gown with a jeweled headband. "One can't miss the detective. He's so"—she batted her lashes—"manly."

Michael grinned.

Hood placed her top hat beside her chair. "What's the big surprise Gabriel mentioned?"

"You'll have to wait and see," Michael answered.

"Detective." Hema trailed her hand up Robin's arm. "Can you tell who I'm dressed as?"

Robin shook his head.

"I'm a private detective from a historical series." Hema's eyes gleamed. "The character and the police detective are lovers."

Robin tugged at his collar.

She whispered something in his ear, then veered toward the champagne.

Hood watched Hema sashay away. "Play your cards right...."

"Play?" Michael laughed. "All jarhead has to do is show up to the party. The rest is guaranteed." He clapped Robin on the shoulder, earning another scowl from the detective.

Harvey and Brandon arrived. Brandon wore a suit with a mustache.

Marci furrowed her brows. "Who are you supposed to be?"

"Watson." Brandon shrugged and headed straight to Michael. "Gabriel's talking to the Bau twins. He'll be down soon."

"Let's dance." Michael led Aliza to the dance floor.

Noor set down her glass, hand shaking. The thought of confronting a killer made her stomach twist.

"You owe me a dance." Rafael pulled her to the dance floor and into his arms. His hard frame pressed against her. "Are you nervous?"

"I'll be glad when this is over."

He guided her to the edge of the ballroom. Distracted with catching a killer, she didn't notice they had moved into one of the sitting rooms. She looked up at him. Goodness, he was beautiful with those coffee-colored eyes, ridiculously long lashes, and contagious smile.

She wanted to review the plan with him. Instead, she blurted something else. "Tell me about your childhood."

His eyes widened a fraction. "I was a homeless kid until Eduardo, my mother's first cousin, came to find me. The rest is history."

Her brows arched.

Rafael blew out a breath. "My mother was a bit of a rebel. She eloped with a musician against her family's wishes. They disowned her, and the musician left before I was born. She resorted to drugs and died of an overdose when I was nine. I lived in the streets for a year."

"I'm sorry. That must have been rough."

He shrugged and pulled her into the shadows of the dimly lit room. His hand ran up and down her back. "Can I ask you a question?"

Her mouth went dry. Unable to speak, she nodded.

"Can you open your heart to someone other than Gabriel?"

"I-I don't know."

"He makes you sad." When she looked away, Rafael tipped up her chin. His seductive eyes focused on her. "Come with me. Be with me. We can go anywhere you like."

He was a man who didn't give himself easily. When he did, he would give generously, and he'd expect nothing less from his lover. Any woman would be lucky to have Rafael. He was kind, intelligent, and honorable. She imagined being with him, building a future with him.

No! Every fiber of her being revolted at the thought. She stepped back. "I-I'm sorry, Rafael. I love Gabriel."

Something shifted in his eyes. He lifted her hand to his lips. "I'd be a fool not to ask."

She took a deep breath. "I don't want to lose your friendship. It means a lot to me."

His irises darkened, but his expression remained unchanged. He kissed the back of her hand and tucked it into his arm. "You won't."

GABRIEL SPOTTED NOOR dancing with Rafael. The floor length silky number she wore was demure in front and open in back, giving him and the entire ballroom a tantalizing view of her smooth skin. She'd pulled up her sable hair, leaving tendrils to frame her face. And her mouth—Christ, what had she done to it? It beckoned the way a lighthouse drew boats to shore. His hands itched to yank her away from Rafael, who was steering her to one of the sitting rooms.

He kept them in his line of vision while he mingled with others until he was close enough to hear their conversation.

"Come with me. Be with me. We can go anywhere you like," Rafael urged Noor.

The beast inside him raged, crying for blood. His muscles coiled and his pulse thundered in his ears. Fresh air. He needed the cool, biting air—something to keep him from shattering. Balcony doors on his right stood ajar. He stepped outside. The muted notes of jazz music mocked him, distant and hollow. A bitter wind nipped at his face, while pain traveled from his heart to his temples. Watching her walk away would tear him apart. He bowed his head and blinked away the tears. Noor deserved to be happy. She deserved a good man. He couldn't have her, but he could and would make sure she was safe.

He forced the pain down, shoving it into the recesses of his soul. One by one, his fingers released the railing he'd gripped. Licking his wounds would come later. Tonight, he'd focus on his part. He reentered the building through an adjacent sitting room.

"*Gabe, where are you?*" Michael's voice cackled in his earpiece.

"*Yes, where are you?*" Mustafa repeated.

"I'm in a lounge by the ballroom." Christ, was that his voice? He cleared his throat. "Is everyone in place?"

"*Check.*" Brandon said. "*Rafael's on his way.*"

"*We're in the main lounge, monitoring everything,*" Rabbi Abarron answered.

"*You should hide the radio.*" Father Pierre's voice carried into Gabriel's microphone.

"Where's Noo—"

"There you are." Noor strode toward him. Her eyes like chips of glass—hard and unyielding.

He blinked. "You're-you're here?"

The green in her irises darkened. "Yes."

Gabriel shook his head to make sure he heard her. "You... didn't go with Rafael?"

She crossed her arms over her chest. "Obviously not."

She hadn't gone with Rafael. She was here with him. A flicker of light pierced his dark soul. Had something happened? Was that why she'd come looking for him?

Noor poked him in the chest. "We're going to talk." Hands balled into fists, she stepped closer. "You do not choose for me. I choose who I want to be with. I choose the man I love. How dare you—"

She didn't go with Rafael. She's right here with me. Hope warred with disbelief. His world tilted, shook, shifted, then fell back into place. The ice in his chest evaporated the way mist does under sunlight. His shoulders loosened and his life went from desolate to bliss in a nanosecond. He couldn't speak. She, on the other hand, had plenty to say. He didn't hear it. An idiotic grin spread across his face. He wouldn't live another second without her. Gabriel reached out.

Noor stepped back. "No! We will not have sex. You're not Michael."

He froze. "I beg your pardon?"

Michael's laughter pierced his ear. *"I am flattered and fascinated."*

Noor scowled. "You're not Michael. We're going to talk and re-solve our problems first."

"She said first, bro. Get it over with and—"

"Shut up, Mike."

Noor blinked. "W-what?"

"Don't snap at your brother," Abarron's raspy voice pierced through the earpiece. *"Now finish your talk with Noor."*

"You have sixty seconds," Michael announced.

The hurt in Noor's eyes tugged at Gabriel's heart. Where to be-gin? What to say? *Hell.* "I fucking love you." He buried his hands in her hair and kissed her.

She tensed for a heartbeat before melting into his embrace.

Light. He inhaled pure light and sweetness. Reveling in her response and desperate to show her the depth of his feelings, Gabriel poured everything into the kiss, while his hands roamed and stroked, then ultimately crushed her to him.

"*What happened?*" Father Pierre asked.

"*She's probably angry,*" Abarron muttered. "*The boy wasn't eloquent, was he?*"

"*Young people,*" Mustafa sighed. "*Mayhap we offer a podcast on communication skills.*"

"*He did fine.*" Michael chuckled. "*He's kissing her.*"

"*Ahh.*" Everyone fell silent.

Noor's scent filled him. Her taste was an aphrodisiac he couldn't get enough of. Her hands slid under his coat, sending ripples of heat down his spine. His body tightened with need as his hands explored the soft skin of her back. He wanted to haul her away and spend a month in bed with her. He wanted her all to himself.

"*Gabe, we need you back in the ballroom. Richter's here,*" Michael announced.

"*Focus on the plan, boy. You can talk to Noor later,*" Abarron chided.

"*Yes, do hurry,*" Brandon urged.

Ignoring the chorus of voices talking at once, Gabriel lightened the kisses until his pounding heart settled and their lips brushed against each other. He leaned his forehead against hers. "We have to go."

"Mm." Noor wobbled and clung to him.

It made a man feel invincible to see his woman lose control in his arms. He brought her hand to his mouth and pressed his lips to her knuckles. "We have to go, sweetheart."

"What? Oh, yes." She reached up to push her hair back into place.

"*Show's over,*" Michael announced. "*They kissed and made up.*"

"*She's not wearing his ring,*" Abarron pointed out.

"*The boy will get to it in his own time,*" Mustafa chuckled.

Noor narrowed her eyes. "We're not done, Gabriel."

"*Good girl.*" Abarron snickered.

Gabriel sighed. There was no privacy with this lot. He leaned down and kissed Noor's forehead. "We'll talk later. I promise."

CHAPTER FORTY-FOUR

Khosrow and his army marched toward Persia.
—Nezami, *Khosrow and Shirin*

GABRIEL TAPPED HIS earpiece. "We're in the ballroom."
Noor stiffened and mouthed, "Could they hear us?"
He grinned and nodded.

She clapped a hand over her mouth to stifle a giggle.

He kissed her forehead and mouthed, "I love you."

Her eyes softened. "I love you too."

His heart soared. "Game on, Ms. Rahman."

"Game on, Mister McKnight." She waved her fingers at him before disappearing into the crowd.

On stage, the host tapped the microphone. Conversation died as he introduced Richter. The audience applauded as Richter greeted guests, then drew them in with a story.

Gabriel searched the audience. Harvey and Brandon were in place. Rafael stood by one exit, while Aliza and Noor covered the other. Detective Hood waited in the back, a puzzled expression on her face. Where was Michael?

Richter beamed. "Now, I'd like to welcome a talented writer whom I consider a friend."

Gabriel spotted his twin. Satisfied, he took the microphone, then began in a somber tone. "One of our own died two days ago. Arthur Trells was a kind man and brilliant writer. His death hits us all." Heads bobbed in affirmation. "Before passing, Arthur made an important discovery. He found an old tunnel on the hotel grounds where the Nazis hid art during the Second World War. I believe his discovery resulted in his murder."

Whispers filled the ballroom.

Gabriel paused to extend the tension. "We changed tonight's agenda to honor Paradox. Instead of a staged murder mystery, we will search for Arthur's tunnel. You have two hours to explore the grounds and report your findings back to our judges. If anyone's successful, we'll notify local authorities. The winner will receive fifty thousand dollars from the Richter Foundation."

The crowd erupted into a frenzy.

Gabriel was half-way across the room when Richter caught up with him. "What the hell are you doing?"

"Arthur confided in me the night he died," Gabriel said. "Crowd-sourcing will achieve two objectives. First, you'll have an army of people scouring the grounds. Second, it will keep Noor safe by clearing any rumors that we know where it is."

The frost disappeared from Richter's eyes. "Has anyone bothered Ms. Rahman?"

"Squashing the rumors keeps her safe."

Richter nodded. "I understand."

ZITA WOVE THROUGH the crowd. The entire convention, along with a cesspool of criminals, was searching for the tunnel. One McKnight and the reporter rushed to the hiking trails. The second McKnight spoke to a priest and—was that a rabbi? She shook her head. The one on the trails must be Michael, the evil twin. Where was Noor? Richter would go after Noor.

She ran up the stairwell, then peered down the corridor. All clear. Zita arrived at Noor's room and was about to knock when someone grabbed her from behind.

"MS. RAHMAN?"

Noor turned away from the exit.

A bulky man with a pugnacious nose approached. His beady eyes roamed over her, making her skin crawl. "My name is Yuri Petrov. I am an associate of your Uncle Cyrus."

"What can I do for you, Mister Petrov?"

Petrov stepped closer. "I would like to discuss the tunnel Mister McKnight mentioned."

She straightened her shoulders. "If Gabriel or I knew anything about the tunnel, we wouldn't be here."

A trio in costume brushed past them, forcing Petrov to step back.

"Here you are." Aliza beamed. "Excuse us. Noor and I are going to help Gabriel with the hunt." Aliza dragged her away without waiting for Petrov's response. "Stay clear of that man. He's dangerous."

"You don't need to warn me twice."

"Ready?" Aliza asked.

"Yes." She took Aliza's outstretched hand and joined the clusters of convention members until they reached the elevators. "We'll change in my room."

They'd just dressed when a knock sounded. Noor checked the peephole.

Father Pierre stood outside with a young woman in a blue cat mask. Her dark hair and slim frame were familiar.

"It's all right," she called to Aliza before opening the door and ushering the couple inside.

"This young lady saw us talking to Gabriel and sought our help." He patted the girl's arm. "You'll be safe here."

Noor beamed at Uncle Cyrus's granddaughter. "I'm glad you came to us."

Father Pierre nodded. "I'll go back to my post in the lounge."

Noor locked the door. "Make yourself comfortable. I'll call your grandmother." She picked up her phone.

"Put it down." The voice didn't belong to the girl she'd met at the museum.

Noor froze.

The barrel of a gun pressed against her temple.

CHAPTER FORTY-FIVE

And the battle began.

—Nezami, *Khosrow and Shirin*

MICHAEL AND BRANDON sprinted to the running trails. Brandon began their rehearsed conversation. "Did anyone follow you?"

"No, I'm clear."

"My source said the tunnel is at the top of the trail," Brandon said.

They took the longer route up the hill. Moonlight cast the forest into shades of silver and grey. The clearing at the top wasn't large.

Michael wiped the sweat off his brow. "I counted three men behind us. We—" He came to an abrupt halt and cursed.

Brandon bumped into him. "Sorry." He drew in a breath. "Is that—" A man lay motionless under the moonlight. A hunting knife protruded from his throat. "That's one of Erik Drussel's men."

Michael cocked his head to the side. A faint rustling came from behind the boulders in the clearing. He dragged Brandon behind a tree as their pursuers arrived at the clearing.

"What the—" one man cried.

"Watch where you're going," the second growled.

"It's Frank. Someone killed Frank," the third man said. "Call Erik."

"I can't." Goon Two glared at his phone. "There's no reception."

The faint pattering of pebbles made the hair behind Michael's neck stand. He peered around the tree.

Goon One sank to the ground, clutching his throat. A patter of bullets fired through suppressors pierced the night. Someone was shooting at Drussel's people, and they fired back.

Michael pointed to a side road cutting through the hill. Brandon nodded. He ticked off his fingers—*three, two, one.* They sprinted back down the hill to the golf course where Michael switched trails.

"Where are you going?" Brandon cried.

"To find Gabriel. Something's wrong."

FAN BAU SEARCHED the files on Noor's laptop. Nothing. She raked a hand through her hair. McKnight had given his word. "I won't take any chances."

Muffled voices came from the hallway. The click of a cardkey being inserted in the lock signaled her to retreat behind a pillar in the shadows. She reached for the small pistol in her clutch.

Noor and the NSA agent rushed to the bedroom to change.

Another knock sounded on the door. Noor spoke to a priest, then greeted a woman with a cat mask.

As soon as the priest left, Cat Mask pulled a gun on Noor. "You're coming with me."

Fan considered intervening, but she wasn't certain which party would help her attain her goals. Instead, she watched. NSA didn't live up to her reputation. Instead of putting Cat Mask down, she raised her hands in surrender.

After the trio left the suite, Fan counted to ten, then sprinted to the employee elevator at the end of the hallway. She arrived at the garage in time to see Cat Mask force Noor and NSA into a tour van.

ZITA SPOTTED THE snake tattoo and struggled harder.

Snakey dragged her to the emergency stairwell, then shoved her against the wall. One hand circled her throat. "Don't make a sound."

Like hell. She tried to kick him.

His hold tightened, cutting the air from her lungs.

"Easy, Asher," a woman said.

The words penetrated through Zita's fear. She cringed when the tall figure in the burka approached her. Black cloth covered the woman's entire body except her moss green eyes. "Asher and I won't hurt you, sweet." Her voice was throaty and soothing. "He will release you, but you must not scream. Richter's men are everywhere. Do you understand?"

Zita blinked to answer.

Burka lady nodded. Snakey released her.

Zita clung to the iron rails of the stairwell to keep from falling over. "W-who are you?"

"I'm Sheila. Your grandparents sent me."

"Grandparents?" Zita gaped at the woman. The man Mina had married and divorced died years ago.

"Yes. They are eager to see you." Sheila sat on a step and patted the space beside her. "Join me, sweet."

Zita sank down beside the woman before her shaky legs gave out.

"Come with me. Leave Richter to his fate."

"Fate?" Tears flooded Zita's eyes. "Fate serves Richter the way everyone else does. Someone must stop him."

Sheila's gloved fingers brushed a tear from her cheek. "Someone will." Flecks of brown warmed her green irises. "Fate has a way of throwing us into fire, precious. Those of us strong enough to withstand it transform into priceless gems. What's important is what happens after one's transformation. What will you do now that you're no longer a prisoner? Will you waste your freedom by stooping to Richter's level? Or will you take what's rightfully yours and leave your mark in this world?"

Zita rubbed her forehead. "Gabriel McKnight and Noor Rahman are in trouble. They need help."

Sheila gave a throaty chuckle. "They have friends assisting them, and they, too, will leave their mark." She rose and held out a hand. "Ready for the future?"

Was she? Taking a deep breath, Zita placed her trembling hand in Sheila's. "Yes."

Snakey—Asher—covered her front and Sheila her back as they took the stairs to an exit. He drove them to a private hanger where a plane waited on the runway.

A muscular man with dark shaggy hair descended the air stairs. His dark eyes scanned her from head to foot, and he broke into a smile.

Sheila greeted the man. "Asher will take you to the hotel."

The man climbed into the car. Snakey drove away.

Zita followed Sheila to the stairs and froze, uncertain. What if this was a prison worse than life with Richter? What if her grandparents were just as cruel? Could she ever trust or love anyone?

"Now, now." Sheila came up behind her. "You've come this far. Don't fear the last step."

Zita straightened her shoulders, gripped the railing, and began to climb the stairs. Beads of sweat trickled down her back, while her heart hammered in her chest. At the top step, she stopped and peeked inside. *Here goes.*

A couple rose. Her grandmother stood with—oh! The good-looking one, the man she'd nicknamed Hollywood. Both held out their arms.

A sudden rush of emotion engulfed her. Zita took one step, another, then ran into their embrace.

CHAPTER FORTY-SIX

Riding ahead, Khosrow confronted Bahram Chubin.
                                    —Nezami, *Khosrow and Shirin*

GABRIEL SPRINTED UP the hill to the opening Drussel and his men had searched. The kid said the well was in a stone structure behind a cluster of birch trees. He glanced at his watch. *Where were Noor and Aliza? They should be here by now.*

A twig snapped. Gabriel whirled around.

Rafael stepped out of the shadows. "It's me." He glanced around. "Where is everyone?"

Michael and Brandon broke into the clearing.

"Where are Noor and Aliza?" Michael asked.

Icy fingers crawled up Gabriel's spine. "They weren't on the trails?" His stomach twisted when Michael shook his head.

"Ah, thank God." Father Pierre and Harvey arrived. The priest latched onto Gabriel's arm and bent over, trying to catch his breath. Gabriel held him steady while he regained his breath. "I t-took a y-young woman up to Noor's suite. I thought she was Cyrus's granddaughter." He coughed. "Morris found us in the lounge, and after I explained what I'd done, he said that was impossible. He'd delivered the granddaughter to Cyrus at the airport over an hour earlier." The priest broke into another coughing fit.

Gabriel cupped his hand under the priest's elbow. "Where's Morris now?"

"I don't know."

"Brandon, help Father get back to the lounge." He didn't wait for an answer and sprinted back to the hotel. Bile rose in his throat when he found Noor's door ajar and the suite empty.

Rafael came up behind him. His eyes mirrored Gabriel's horror.

Two mobile phones sat side by side on the coffee table.

Michael pushed past Rafael and Brandon. When he spied the phones, his jaw tightened.

Fear clawed at Gabriel's chest. He raked a clammy hand through his hair. Who could the costumed woman be?

"Security may have footage of what happened," Michael said. "I'll ask TCU to get a copy."

"Call Billy. Ask him to hack in and send us a copy."

"What's TCU?" Brandon and Rafael asked simultaneously.

"The Clandestine Unit. It's a branch of the Bureau of Counter Terrorism. Mike works for them," Gabriel answered.

Brandon and Rafael gaped at Michael.

Gabriel's phone rang. The number was blocked. He answered on the second ring.

"Are you missing your lady, lover boy?"

He put the call on speaker. "Who are you? Where are Noor and Aliza?"

"I have someone—actually two people—you want." Her unhinged giggle made the hair on the back of his neck stand. *"Be good, and I'll give you both women with body parts intact. Did you like the gifts I left you in Frankfurt?"*

Gabriel's stomach lurched. "You killed Johannsson and the receptionist?"

Another giggle followed. *"You're forgetting the writer. I killed him right under your nose."*

"Let me speak with Noor and Aliza. I'll do whatever you want."

Several seconds of silence ensued. *"You have the codes to the missing art. Find it. There is a jeweled photo frame mounted on a wall where the art is hidden. Bring me the frame, and you get the women back."*

The voice was familiar. Where had he heard it? "I need proof Noor and Aliza are alive."

A shuffling came from the background. *"Gabriel."* Noor's steady voice wound around his heart. His beautiful courageous Noor was alive.

Another shuffle sounded, then Aliza spoke. *"We're all right."*

He shared a look with Michael, who stood with clenched fists.

"You have two hours to bring me the frame," the woman said. *"I'll call to arrange a meeting. If you don't have what I want, both women die. Call the police, they die."* The line went dead.

"How do we find the artwork?" Rafael growled, pacing back and forth.

Gabriel massaged his neck. "The killer won't let Aliza and Noor live. They can identify her."

"So, what do we do?" Rafael asked.

Gabriel fought the panic rising in his chest. *Think, don't feel.*

He stared out the window. He would not lose Noor. The only way to defeat this killer was to push aside all emotion and focus. He called on years of combat training to do just that. His thoughts sharpened, and his resolve was absolute.

"There was no background noise during the call." His voice was steady—cold and flat—when he spoke.

Michael's head swiveled around. "They can't have gone far. Father Pierre said he brought the woman upstairs at seven."

"Do we call the police?" Brandon asked.

"No," Gabriel answered. "I'll call Detective Hood. She'll contact the local authorities. The killer wants me to deliver a frame." He shared a silent message with Michael.

Michael's blue eyes turned stone cold. "Let's do it."

Rafael stared, and Brandon blinked. The world rarely glimpsed this side of them—relentless warriors intent on defeating an enemy.

"There are several groups after the artwork," Gabriel continued in his matter-of-fact voice. "First, there are the Europeans who kidnapped Noor in Frankfurt, likely Richter's rivals. There's Richter himself. And Stephen Johannsson, who believes Richter killed his brother. We also have the Bau twins, and one of Richter's daughters—a German professor who got close to Noor through her writing." He pursed his lips. "They'll follow us. We'll have to lose them. Here's what we'll do."

Several minutes later, Gabriel exited through the hotel's employee exit with Mustafa, Father Pierre, and Abarron. He held a map and pointed to it. Father Pierre then joined Harvey in the lounge, while Mustafa and Abarron followed Gabriel to the walking trails at the edge of the golf course. They took one leading into the backwoods. Gabriel signaled for them to stop when they arrived at thick foliage. The crickets stopped chirping.

Someone had taken the bait and followed them.

His voice was barely above a whisper. "You and Abarron continue along the path. I'll catch up with Michael and the others." He darted into the bushes, cut through trails, then arrived at the hotel. He dialed Detective Hood.

"Where the hell are you?" Hood snapped.

"She has Noor and Aliza."

"She?"

"The killer is a woman. Father Pierre took her to Noor's suite, mistaking her for someone else."

Hood cursed. *"I'll call the local police."*

"Tell them there's a body at the top of the hill. They can get there by taking the longer running trail."

"What?"

"I have to go."

"Wait. What are you doing, McKnight?"

"Harvey's in the lounge. He'll bring you up to speed." Gabriel ended the call, then ran past several groups of convention attendees scouring the golf course for the tunnel. At the eastern border, two trails diverged.

Michael, Brandon, and Rafael waited for him there.

"What do we have?"

"Two groups," Michael answered. "The first group is with Drussel. I don't know who the second group is."

Gabriel glanced at his watch. "Rafael and I will take the right. You and Brandon take the left. Wait a few minutes before you head out. We'll meet by the well in ten minutes." He and Rafael were half-way up the hill when Gabriel stopped. "We'll hide here." They crouched behind the bushes.

Several convention attendees searched the trails. Their voices grew fainter as they meandered off, then a trio of men approached.

One, panting, said, "Where did they go?"

"They must have gone that way," another answered.

Gabriel waited until the men continued up the hill. "Let's go." They sprinted back to the cluster of birch trees Sam had shown him. Gabriel stepped behind them. "The kid was right. There's an old stone structure attached to the hill."

"Look." Rafael pointed to a carving of a man cutting through a mountain with a chisel. "Isn't that Farhad cutting through the mountain?"

Gabriel nodded. "Michael and Brandon will be here any minute."

The night expanded, drawing an ebony veil over them. Gabriel counted every passing second, praying Noor was all right.

Rafael shuffled his feet. "Noor loves you."

Something shifted in Gabriel's chest. "I love her too."

"I asked her to be with me." Rafael straightened his shoulders. "You broke it off with her. So, I asked."

Gabriel nodded. "I see."

"I'd be furious if anyone went after the woman I loved," Rafael muttered.

Gabriel's respect for the man increased. "I thought she would be happier with you. It's why I stepped back. I was wrong. Try again, and you'll get a different reaction."

"I don't chase other men's women." He sighed. "You're a lucky man."

"I know." Gabriel held out his hand.

Rafael hesitated, then shook it.

A low whistle pierced the night.

"They're here."

Michael and Brandon arrived.

Mike said, "We have ninety minutes."

"The structure has a stone door. Let's try to push it open."

The four tried but were unsuccessful.

"Wait." Gabriel shone his flashlight on the carving. A compass was engraved in the stone with a series of numbers. "Read the numbers and direction, Rafael."

"Eight steps north, three west, and one south."

Gabriel followed the directions. The ground changed on his last step—metal. He shoved aside the foliage. An old trapdoor. It took several tries to yank it open. "It's a stairway."

"Very good, Mister McKnight."

Gabriel froze.

A bulky man with a bulbous nose strode into the clearing. Three men accompanied him. All carried guns. "You're going to lead me to the artwork."

"No, he isn't." A woman with Amazonian stature stepped into the clearing. Her fiery hair gleamed under the moonlight. Several men filed into the clearing with her, all armed. These had to be the men Michael and Brandon had run into. They surrounded the first group of men.

"You're not going anywhere, Petrov."

Yuri Petrov made a sound like a pig's snuffle. "Does Magdalena know you're here?" Another snort. "Of course she does. Your aunt fucks everyone."

"My aunt, as you indelicately put it, fucks consenting adults. You, on the other hand, are a sick bastard." The woman raised her hand. Her men pointed their guns.

Petrov's men aimed back.

Gabriel gritted his teeth. He couldn't die. Not now. Noor was counting on him.

Safeties clicked off.

His muscles stiffened, and the countdown began. *Three... two... one.*

CHAPTER FORTY-SEVEN

Farhad hammered away at the mountain, thinking of Shirin.
—Nezami, *Khosrow and Shirin*

"DUCK!" GABRIEL SHOVED Rafael behind a boulder as shots exploded like patters of rain. The *thuds* of bodies hitting the ground made him grit his teeth. Certain he was all right, Gabriel glanced at Rafael, who nodded to indicate all was well. Michael had dragged Brandon behind a tree. Both were unharmed.

Petrov's men lay dead. One of the Amazon's men was down. She nodded to a muscular bald man with a snake tattoo.

He grabbed Petrov. "You're coming with me." He dragged the cursing Russian away.

Amazon swung her flashlight between Gabriel and Michael. "Which one of you is Gabriel McKnight?"

Michael stepped forward. His tone of voice and body language mimicked Gabriel's. "I'm Gabriel."

Gabriel shrugged and stepped forward. "No, I'm Gabriel."

The woman's gaze swung back and forth between them. She scowled. "I don't have time for games. We're all going into the tunnel."

Gabriel led them down the stairs into the tunnel. Several kerosene lamps and a box of old matches sat outside its entrance. He lit one. Swastikas had been carved into and painted on the walls. He began lighting lamp wicks. How could he rid himself of these people?

"You're Magdalena Romano's niece," Michael said.

Amazon didn't answer.

"Why do you want the art?"

"Shut up." She jammed her gun into Michael's back.

Michael shrugged and followed the others. The tunnel widened into a circular opening. Several empty crates sat by a sledgehammer. Two paths lay in front of them.

Amazon pointed her gun at Gabriel. "Where do we go from here?"

"I don't know."

She shoved her gun at Brandon's temple. "Answer me, or your friend dies."

"Easy." Gabriel raised his hands. "The codes led us here. We have to figure out the rest out."

"You two take the first path with McKnight Number One and the blond," Amazon barked. "I'll take the second path with McKnight Number Two and the darker one." She shoved her gun between Gabriel's shoulder blades. "Move."

They took the path to the right. The tunnels opened into natural caverns. Continuing on, they wound up in the same clearing.

"We're back where we started," Amazon growled.

The sound of footsteps echoed in the tunnels. Michael, Brandon, and the other men returned.

"It's a circle," one of Amazon's men called out.

Sweat trickled down Gabriel's back. Team Amazon was in the way.

Michael tapped two fingers on his leg. His head tilted subtly to the men beside him. One had a scar running on the side of his face, and the other one was thick in the middle. He was saying he'd take those two.

Gabriel studied the other two men in his peripheral vision. One was bald, and the other had a military crew cut. He dipped his head to let Michael know he'd take the other two. That left Amazon.

They'd have to risk it. Hopefully, Rafael or Brandon could help.

Gabriel pretended to stumble on a stone and fell. Rafael leaned forward to help him up. Crewcut shoved Rafael aside, giving Gabriel the opening he needed. He pulled Crewcut down, grabbed his gun, then shot the weapon out of the bald man's hand. Baldy tripped and fell, hitting his head on the stone floor. He was out.

Michael kicked Thick Man in the stomach. Thick Man went down. He snatched Thick Man's gun, then shot Scar Face in the leg. Scar Face fell.

Rafael tackled Amazon. As they wrestled, Gabriel shot the gun out of her hand. She kicked Rafael, who cursed then hesitated, not wanting to hurt her. Amazon kicked him in the groin. Rafael doubled over.

Michael hit Amazon on the head with the butt of his gun. She sank to the ground.

Cursing in several languages, Rafael slowly straightened.

Michael patted him on the shoulder. "An icepack will fix it." He dragged Thick Man's heavy frame to the wall, where chains had been mounted. After securing Thick Man's hands, he stuffed torn pieces of his shirt into the man's mouth.

They did the same with the other men and Amazon.

Michael checked his watch. "We have seventy minutes."

Gabriel raked a hand through his hair. "Let's try the paths again. Check the walls for symbols, carvings, or any clue." They found nothing.

"Damn it! We're going in circles," Michael growled.

Footsteps echoed. Gabriel and Michael raised their guns.

Three figures ambled into the clearing.

"Have you found anything, my boy?" Abarron asked, leaning on Mustafa.

Harvey followed, panting.

"What are you doing here?" Gabriel asked.

Harvey blotted his forehead with a handkerchief and waved a sheet of paper. "Farid Richter has a home five miles from the hotel.

It's built into the side of the mountain with a drop on one side and a winding road leading to the peak on the other. I printed a map of the property."

Gabriel took it. "That must be where the killer took Noor and Aliza."

Michael narrowed his eyes. "The killer works for Richter?"

"Maybe. She could also be one of Richter's rivals, which would explain why Magdalena's niece is here."

Thick Man moaned.

Harvey's eyes widened as he noticed the people chained to the wall. "What's going on?"

"The usual. Criminals looking for stolen art." Michael punched Thick Man in jaw.

He slunk back into oblivion.

Abarron sat on an empty crate. "Mustafa and I must rest our weary bones. We'll watch them for you."

Mustafa rubbed his chin. "We may persuade them to change the direction of their lives and find faith. God forgives those who repent."

Crewcut rolled his eyes.

Abarron banged his cane on the man's knee, then spoke over his muffled cry. "My legs are weary. My hands aren't."

Michael checked his watch. "We have forty-five minutes. What are we missing, Gabe?"

Gabriel closed his eyes. The shape of the two paths reminded him of something, but what? He let his mind wander. "New York City."

Several pairs of eyes stared at him as if he'd lost his mind.

"Have you ever seen the trick where a guy hides a ball under three cups? There's one at every corner in New York City."

A grin spread across Michael's face. "Ah. I see."

Brandon threw his hands in the air. "I don't."

"There's a scam where a guy has three cups and hides a ball under one. He moves the cups around, and people bet on which is covering the ball. The guy lifts whatever cup people point out, but the ball isn't there, but it's rigged. He's cut a slit into one of the cups. It captures the ball when he covers it, so even if someone chooses correctly, the ball remains hidden when he lifts the cup. That's why people always lose."

Rafael scratched his ear. "I don't understand."

"Think of each path here as one of the cups. There must be a third cup, or path, hiding the ball, or artwork, and it's here." Gabriel shone his light on the ceiling.

"There." Michael pointed.

On the eastern corner wall of the cavern, someone had carved the number eight and an arrow pointing west.

Gabriel stood under it, then took eight steps to the west. He stopped by the sledgehammer. "There's a reason the sledgehammer's here. The verse about Farhad cutting through the mountain was our cue. We'll have to knock down this wall. Unless I'm wrong, it won't be hard." He picked up the tool, then set to work. The stone easily crumbled, revealing a path. "Hallelujah." He dropped the sledgehammer, then stepped into the tunnel.

Michael, Rafael, and Brandon followed. The path widened, ultimately ending in a cave.

Boxes, piled high on crates, stood around the cavern. Pottery, bronze statues, and several rows of paintings lay in neat rows against the walls. Beside the entrance, three open barrels sat side by side. The first two contained jewelry. The last one brimmed with pieces of gold.

Brandon whistled.

Rafael inched toward a collection of jewelry boxes on a crate. He stopped by one with a crest, muttered in Spanish, dusted off the box, then opened it. "My great grandmother's mantilla comb." His hoarse whisper betrayed his emotions.

Gabriel walked among various pieces of art—paintings, wood carvings, stone statues, sketches, watercolors, rugs, tapestries, and jewelry—until spying one particular piece, which he set aside.

"The Rembrandt?" Brandon asked.

Gabriel nodded. "We're taking it with us."

"Gabe, over here." Michael reached over a crate to take down a jeweled frame.

Gabriel studied the photo of four people standing in the very same cave. Hitler, Alfred Rosenberg, Richter Senior, and a little boy—Farid Richter, next to his father. "This will ruin Richter."

"I'll take that." Stephen Johannsson stepped into the cavern as his gaze scanned the art.

"I need it to bargain for Noor's life," Gabriel said. "You can have it once Noor's safe."

Johannsson's brows rose. "Richter has Ms. Rahman?"

Gabriel nodded and held out the frame. "Take a picture of the photo. Once we stop Richter, I'll leave this for you at the reception desk."

Johannsson rubbed his chin. "I'll come after you if you don't."

"I keep my word." Gabriel extended his hand.

Johannsson shook it. "Can I assist you?"

"No, thank you," Michael snapped.

Johannsson nodded, then left with his men.

Gabriel tucked the frame under his shirt and picked up the Rembrandt. "How much do we have?"

"Not long." Alex Bau stepped through the opening. His tawny eyes landed on the painting. "You are a man of your word."

Gabriel frowned. "You doubted it?"

"I'm the skeptical twin."

"You and me both," Michael muttered.

"Ah, you found it." Abarron entered the cavern with Mustafa and Harvey.

"Unbelievable." Harvey straightened his glasses and did a full circle, studying the cavern.

"For a secret tunnel, there's a lot of traffic here," Michael growled.

Mustafa's gaze skimmed over the cavern, then landed on one barrel. "Are those gold nuggets?"

"Gold fillings." Abarron's thin shoulders slumped. "From victims' teeth."

Mustafa lay a hand on his shoulder. "Ah, Abarron. We'll pray for their souls."

Alex stared, then shook his head. "Fan said a woman took Noor to a house several miles away from the hotel. It's up a hill." He threw two pairs of keys at him. "Our cars are in the back parking lot."

Gabriel handed him the painting then stepped into his space. "If you ever go near Noor, flirt, or try to put your hands on her, I'll hunt you down and kill you." He paused. "You know I'm a man of my word."

Alex nodded.

"Good." Gabriel glanced at Harvey. "Detective Hood called the authorities. They'll be here soon. Tell them the people chained to the wall killed the men outside and show them the artwork. I'm going to get Noor."

CHAPTER FORTY-EIGHT

Khosrow had a son named Shiruyeh from his marriage to
Maryam. Shiruyeh wanted Khosrow's throne, and he wanted Shirin....
—Nezami, *Khosrow and Shirin*

NOOR WONDERED IF she could distract the killer long
enough for Aliza to find help.

"Make one wrong move, and I'll put a bullet through you."
The woman shoved the gun into her back. "Get in the elevator."

Her voice was familiar. Where had she heard it?

Aliza followed her into the elevator. The killer entered behind them.

"Wait!" Hema pushed into the elevator before its doors closed.
"You changed into comfortable clothing too." She smiled at the
costumed woman, her ebony eyes twinkling. "Hello, I'm Hema,
Noor's client. I love your mask."

The killer didn't answer, but silence never deterred Hema.

She beamed at them. "Isn't my muse delicious?"

"Are you pairing up with Detective Robin to find the tunnel?"
Noor hoped the answer was yes.

Hema patted her hair. "I'll search for the tunnel with you. One
must toe a fine line when seducing the muse."

"Detective Robin's waiting for you." Noor tried to keep her voice steady. "Go with him."

Hema's eyes lit up. "Is that so? He'll have to wait. I'm with you."

"But—"

The killer aimed her gun at Hema. "Since you insist on accompanying us, I'll oblige. Now shut up."

Hema's eyes widened. "I-Is this a joke?"

Noor met Hema's gaze, silently pleading for her to comply.

Hema bit her lip and said nothing.

The elevators opened into the garage. Cat Mask motioned to a van. "Get in." She shoved Aliza. "You open the door."

Aliza pulled it open.

Their assailant handcuffed them to the seat railings. "Good thing I brought an extra pair. Don't bother trying to break out of them. They're a special model." She slid into the driver's seat, then pulled away from the parking lot.

When the bus exited the hotel, Noor asked, "Who are you? Where are you taking us?"

"We're going to my father's house."

"Why?"

"It's a surprise."

The woman's childlike giggle made the hair behind Noor's neck stand.

The drive wasn't long. The van stopped in front of a large iron gate. When the security guard approached, Cat Mask shot him. She leaped from the vehicle, opened the gate, hopped behind the wheel, then passed through. The van screeched to a halt in front of a building. She grabbed a rifle from behind her seat. "I'll be back."

Aliza slid her handcuffs along the railing and inched closer to the window. "It looks like a bunkhouse." Gunshots broke the silence. "She's killing whoever is in there." Her voice shook with rage.

Hema whimpered.

Cat Mask returned, a bounce in her step. Spatters of blood covered her costume. She tucked the shotgun below her seat. "Tally ho and onward we go." The van wound around a steep hill, then stopped in front of a massive stone house. After securing their hands with a thick rope, Cat Mask ordered them to exit the van.

Double doors swung open. Two men descended the stairs.

The killer held her gun at Noor's temple. "Please let my father know I've arrived with guests."

"Who the hell are y—"

She shot both men.

Hema screamed. Aliza cursed. Noor closed her eyes and prayed she wouldn't be sick. How many people had this woman killed?

Cat Mask dragged Noor inside. "Hurry. I'm impatient to see my father."

"What's happening?" Hema wailed, stumbling behind them.

They passed through a foyer, headed toward paneled doors. As the group reached them, they swung open.

"What is all the commotion?" Farid Richter's gaze raked over them. "What is this?"

The woman skipped into a spacious study, dragging Noor behind her. "Surprise, Daddy. It's me." She yanked off her mask.

Noor gasped.

Richter narrowed his eyes. "Mercedes? What are you doing?"

Mercedes, Mina's no longer shy assistant, tore off her wig. A waterfall of chestnut hair fell to her shoulders. "I came to see you."

A woman rose from the couch. "Who are these people?"

Mercedes tilted her head. The corner of her mouth lifted. "Your lady friend's people kidnapped Noor in Frankfurt. She wanted it to look like you did it."

"What nonsense," the woman snapped.

Mercedes aimed her pistol at the woman. "She sent her niece after McKnight in the caves."

Richter's brows rose. "How do you know this?"

"I saw them."

Richter glanced at the woman with auburn hair. "Is it true, Magdalena?"

"You wanted the artwork. I sent my niece to secure it once McKnight discovered its location." She glared at Mercedes. "Why would you take this woman's word over mine?"

"Because I don't lie." Mercedes shot Magdalena Romanov in the heart.

Richer stepped back. Hema screamed. Aliza struggled with the ropes binding her hands.

Mercedes shoved Aliza toward the fireplace. "The three of you will sit on those chairs and behave, while I talk to Daddy."

Hema sobbed. Noor nudged her toward the chairs. There wasn't much she could do with her hands tied. A part of her brain registered the fact that neither Richter nor Mercedes cared about the bleeding Magdalena.

"You don't need her, Daddy."

Richter's brows furrowed. "Why do you call me that?"

A corner of Mercedes's lip lifted. It looked more like a snarl than a smile. "Remember Anna, the German girl you kept in Dresden? You knocked her up. She told me you didn't want or acknowledge me, and for years I believed her." She bobbed her head in affirmation. "When I grew older, she let her clients fuck me for a good price. I was dutiful, then realized I deserved better. I killed her and moved to America. To prove I'm worthy, I went to school, graduated with honors, then got a job with Mina von Mayer. Guess how Petrov found out about the Abromowskis?"

Richter's eyes gleamed. "You were Petrov's informant?"

She laughed and skipped toward him. "I'm your daughter, after all. I sent you the information on the Abromowski deal, then killed Johannsson. He was going behind your back for"—she glanced at the three women on the couch—"the other deal."

"I see."

"No one would believe Herr Richter would murder someone and leave the body at his own party, which is why I placed it there. Genius, wasn't it?"

"You killed Ingrid the receptionist!" Noor cried. "She was an innocent girl."

Mercedes shrugged. "I used her to give a packet to McKnight. She put two and two together. She had to die."

Richter's icy gaze landed on her. "Why did you bring Ms. Rahman here?"

She beamed at him. "I know you want to destroy the evidence of your father's collaboration with the Nazis. I'm holding her hostage until McKnight brings it to us."

Richter's voice hardened. "Now Gabriel McKnight and Ms. Rahman will know the truth."

Mercedes waved a hand. "I planned to kill them, anyway. They're a means to an end."

"She's Cyrus Rohan's niece. He's a valuable colleague."

"No one will trace it back to you."

Richter rubbed his chin, seemingly considering her plan.

They needed a distraction. Noor raised her chin. "Your father killed Mina von Mayer's daughter and raised his granddaughter. He gave Zita everything, not you. He doesn't like you."

Mercedes nostrils flared, and her grip on the gun tightened.

Richter shifted toward his desk. "That's not true, Mercedes. Your mother never told me about you. I didn't know you existed."

"See." Mercedes gripped Noor's hair. "Blood is blood. I'll kill the Zita brat."

A knock sounded. Erik Drussel entered. He didn't blink at the sight of the three women on the couch, nor did he acknowledge Mercedes. "Sorry for the interruption, sir. Have you seen the news?"

Richter frowned. "No, why?"

"The FDA is pulling Kroner's breakthrough drug from the market."

Richter reached for a remote. The flatscreen in front of his desk came to life.

"The FDA claims former Kroner CEO, Darren Johannsson, falsified lab results to hide lethal side effects for their latest drug, Titan. There are currently three class action lawsuits against Kroner. The company's stock has dropped significantly since the announcement."

Richter's face turned red. "How is this possible? We checked everything. If Kroner doesn't rebut the allegations, the company will go down. We'll lose—" He clenched his teeth.

Mercedes scratched her head with the gun. "Did you invest a lot in it, Daddy?"

Both men ignored her.

Erik shuffled his feet. "There's more."

Richter's head swung around. "More?"

"Check the other channels." Drussel shoved his hands in his pockets.

Richter switched the channel. Photos of Richter's father with Hitler and the Nazi Chief ideologue, Alfred Rosenberg, filled the screen.

"Hans Richter supported the Nazis during the war and helped hide art the Nazis looted in several secret locations. A valid source revealed Hans Richter gave his son, Farid Richter, a map to the locations of the looted artwork before he died.

"Authorities have searched two of Richter Holding's warehouses in Munich. Several missing artifacts were stored at both locations, confirming rumors Farid Richter has been selling the art in the black market. International crimes units and the German police are searching for Richter. Meanwhile, several organizations have already issued public statements promising to sever ties immediately with Richter Holdings."

The camera switched to a newscaster interviewing David Abromowski, who shook his head.

"Our organization will not conduct business with anyone involved with genocide. We do not partner with businesses that don't respect human rights."

Drussel raised his head. "Abromowski left a message. The deal's off."

Noor was certain this was Mina and Uncle Cyrus's doing. She smiled. "Mina von Mayer has been a step ahead of you the entire time."

"I'm going to kill you!" Mercedes cried.

"Silence!" Fury blazed in Richter's eyes. He gripped the remote so tight it cracked.

Mercedes went to kneel beside him, gun in hand. "We can get ahead of this, Daddy. I'll burn down the house. Magdalena and these three can burn with it. Authorities will think an anti-Nazi group attacked your home. We'll hide out for a bit and plan a response, one that shows you were framed." She scratched her head with the gun. "We can blame the Johannssons for framing you."

Richter's nostrils flared. He shared a look with Erik.

Drussel's nod was imperceptible.

"Erik, this is my daughter Mercedes."

Erik inclined his head toward her. Mercedes smirked.

Richter shifted. "Call the hanger and have them prepare the jet. My daughter and I will leave tonight."

"Very well."

Mercedes clasped the gun between both of her hands. "Really?"

"Yes, really. We'll leave in an hour."

"You're wasting your time," Noor cried. "He'll leave you behind. He only cares about himself."

Richter glared at her. "Looks like we won't need Mister McKnight after all. You may kill Ms. Rahman and the others."

Mercedes giggled. "Okay."

"First, come here, my child."

Mercedes skipped up to Richter, who punched her in the face as soon as she neared him.

As Mercedes crumpled, Aliza jumped up and kicked Drussel. Her boot cut a gash in Drussel's thigh. Drussel snarled and reached for his weapon. Aliza kicked him in the knee. He stumbled.

Richter stepped away from Mercedes. She latched onto his leg and pulled him down.

Aliza body-slammed Drussel. He toppled backward, his head striking the fireplace.

Mercedes shot Richter in the foot. His bellow echoed through the room.

Tugging awkwardly at Drussel's holster, Aliza tried to pull out his gun.

Infuriated, Mercedes shoved Richter aside then shot Drussel in the head. She fired at Aliza but missed by an inch. "Stay where you are, or I'll kill Noor."

Aliza froze.

"Back to your seat!"

Panting, Aliza complied.

Mercedes yanked a cord from the curtain, then tied Aliza's feet to the chair. "Move and I'll shoot." She then tied a pale Richter's hands and feet to a chair with another cord. "Naughty, naughty Daddy. You lied to me." She threw her head back and made a sound that was a cross between laughter and roar. Blood dripped from her nose. Her hair hung in tangles, covering half of her face. She ran to the side of the fireplace to retrieve a pot of kerosene. "I didn't want to resort to this, but it's the only way." She studied Richter. "Do you believe in reincarnation?" She didn't wait for him to answer. "It's a means to start over. If we die together, we'll be reborn in another life. You'll love me then."

"Crazy bitch!" The veins in Richter's neck stood out. "You shot me."

Mercedes poured kerosene around the room, through the hallway, then into the foyer. She returned to his office and flung aside the empty canister. "Everything I did was for you, Daddy. Can't you see? This is the only way to start over. Stop worrying. I'll take care of everything. I'm very efficient."

While Richter cursed and struggled against his ties, Mercedes hummed and danced.

"Do you like to dance, Daddy? My whore of a mother made me do it for clients. I had this routine that guaranteed a good tip. I'll show it to you." She undulated her hips and raised her hands to the ceiling while slowly undressing herself.

"Mercedes, he doesn't care for you. Let me help you," Noor cried.

Mercedes ignored her and peeled off her shirt.

SAM EASED OUT of the van's luggage compartment. Mom thought he was sleeping, but he'd been watching Noor's room and saw the woman with the gun take Noor and Aliza away. He'd followed them. Hopefully, Mom wouldn't find out he'd left their room.

After everyone left the van, he climbed out. A mansion like Bruce Wayne's stood in front of him. What would Jason Vann do? Sam ran to the wraparound porch to peek in the windows. The wind bit at his skin and goosebumps ran down his arms.

There was a larger terrace on the other side of the house. Lights shone from one of the rooms. He peeked through the glass and spied an empty office. Sam pushed open the window, then climbed inside. A pocketknife sat on the desk. He took it before sneaking into the hall. Where was Noor?

He tiptoed to another room where the lights were on. The door was ajar. Inside, the crazy lady fought with a man who shouted curses Mom didn't like. Aliza fought with another guy. Noor sat tied to a chair.

She saw him, and she shook her head, telling him without words to leave.

He couldn't. He had to be brave, like Jason Vann and Gabriel.

Sam sneaked behind a sofa as the crazy lady tied Aliza to a chair. Crazy lady started singing and pouring liquid everywhere. If he moved a bit more, he could throw the knife on Aliza's lap from behind the sofa. He waited until the crazy lady spun away, then threw the knife in Aliza's lap.

She covered it with her hands.

Smoke rose from the middle of the room. A man shouted. The other man lay on the floor. The crazy lady kept dancing.

He ran back to the office.

A phone sat on the desk. Good thing he'd memorized Gabriel's number. Heart hammering, he dialed. Gabriel didn't answer. He left a voice message. "We're at a house on top of the hill. It has golden bars around the windows. There are people hurt everywhere. Hurry, she's burning it down!" Sam ran back to the van to find something to free Noor.

Someone grabbed him.

CHAPTER FORTY-NINE

Shiruyeh imprisoned his father. One night when no one was watching, he stabbed Khosrow to death....

—Nezami, *Khosrow and Shirin*

SEMPER OPERA HOUSE, DRESDEN, GERMANY

MINA STEPPED THROUGH the elaborate stone front of the Semperoper, appreciating its elegance. The opera house had endured a fire, two world wars, and a flood. It had been damaged and rebuilt, regaining its grace and beauty after each disaster.

Her granddaughter followed her and Cyrus into their theatre box. Mina's heart constricted. Zita wore the silver gown she'd bought for her and looked like an angel.

"Should we be here? Isn't it dangerous? Are Gabriel and Noor safe?" Zita whispered.

Mina exchanged a look with Cyrus then patted Zita's hand. "I know it's hard because you don't know us well. Please trust us. Everything will be all right."

Zita gulped. "Okay."

Mina smiled. "Do you know the tragedy of Khosrow and Shirin?"

"Um, no. I don't."

Cyrus sighed. "Your grandmother is obsessed with this story. I can't understand why. I prefer happy endings."

Mina's heart lifted. This felt so normal. She leaned closer to Zita. "What I like most about Khosrow and Shirin is their love for each other. Regardless of the obstacles thrown their way, they remained devoted to one other."

The lights in the theatre dimmed, and the hum of conversation died. Despite her outward calm, a shiver crawled up her spine. An important part of the plan was for her and Cyrus to be distant from everything that would take place in the next hour. Everything she and Cyrus had worked for had led to this moment.

The curtains parted, and music poured into the theatre. One by one, the actors mounted the stage, then the magic began. She tried not to fidget. During an intermission, she introduced Zita and Cyrus to stunned reporters. They bombarded her with questions and took pictures. She offered vague answers and stayed close to her family. By the third curtain, Zita, had relaxed, her entire focus on the tragedy.

The last act arrived. Music soared and reverberated in the theatre, striking at every nerve in her body. Red and orange lights created a bloody horizon. On stage, Shiruyeh, Khosrow's son from his marriage to Maryam, stormed the palace.

GABRIEL'S PHONE BEEPED as he exited the tunnels. "Billy sent a copy of the surveillance video."

Michael, Brandon, and Rafael crowded around him while he played it.

"Son of a bitch!" He broke into a run.

Michael kept up with him. "You recognize her?"

He nodded and ran faster. At the hotel, he headed to the back parking lot and almost slammed into Detective Robin.

"McKnight!" Robin said. "I have a lead on who took Noor."

"I know who the killer is." He shoved his phone into Robin's hands. "Play the video."

"Where are you going?" Robin cried.

"To get Noor."

Robin followed them to the parking lot.

Gabriel clicked buttons on two different fobs until a duo of cars blinked their lights. He threw a pair of keys to Michael, then jumped into the other vehicle. "Follow me."

Rafael and Detective Robin climbed into the car with him. Brandon rode with Michael.

"Please God, let them be okay. Let her be alive!"

He didn't know he prayed aloud until Rafael placed a hand on his shoulder. "We'll get them back."

"She took Hema." Robin stared at Gabriel's phone. "The bitch took Hema."

Gabriel's phone beeped.

"You have a message," Robin said.

"Play it."

Robin put the phone on speaker. Sam's voice broke the silence. *"Hurry, she's burning the house down!"*

Gabriel accelerated. He'd memorized the location and soon reached the property, driving past the gate and up the winding road, not sparing a glance at the bodies lying on the ground. His stomach lurched when they arrived at the large stone structure.

Columns of smoke billowed from the second-floor windows. Flames blazed from every ground floor opening. "I'm going inside."

A man limped toward them—the one with a snake tattoo who took Petrov—followed by Morris.

Tattoo yelled, "There's a side entrance for servants! You can get in through there!"

"Find the kid," Gabriel ordered Rafael and Brandon before he and the others followed Tattoo into the house.

Fire scaled up the walls and staircase like a feral beast. Tattoo used a fire extinguisher to make a path.

Gabriel kicked open the door to the living room. "Noor!" He hoped she could hear him.

Tattoo created another path. Gabriel sprinted after him, Morris and Michael on his heels. Heat and smoke made it hard to breathe.

Someone shouted. He held his breath and surged forward. Terror clawed at him, and flames licked at his skin.

MINA CLASPED HER hands while the music reached a crescendo. Shiruyeh imprisoned his father in the castle. Shirin accompanied Khosrow into the dungeons. She stayed with him, consoling him with stories of love and changing fates. Each night, she watched over him, while a raving Shiruyeh plotted his father's death. One night, exhaustion took over, and Shirin fell asleep. Shiruyeh couldn't wait to have Shirin—to marry her. He sneaked into the dungeon and stabbed his father, killing him.

GABRIEL TOOK IN the bizarre scene.

A naked Mercedes undulated her hips, twirled, then aimed her gun at Noor's temple. "Time for you to die!"

The sharp knife of fear twisted his in gut. Acrid smoke and sweltering heat compromised his vision. He aimed his gun, then squeezed the trigger. The explosion was lost in the fire's fury.

Mercedes screamed. The gun toppled out of her hand.

"Step away from them, Mercedes."

For as long as he lived, Gabriel would never forget the way Noor looked at him, like he was her world. Tears streamed down her cheeks when he freed her from the ties. He pulled her to his side, keeping his gun aimed at Mercedes.

Michael reached for Aliza. Detective Robin helped a wobbly Hema.

"I don't care about them." A trickle of blood ran down Mercedes's nose. Her eyes gleamed with manic anticipation. "Daddy and I are going to burn."

"Morris, thank goodness," Richter cried. "Help me get out of here."

Gabriel stepped forward, but Morris held out his hand to stop him. He motioned to Tattoo. "Go with Asher. I've got this."

"Uncle Morrie, the fire!" Noor cried.

"I'll get out. Now go!" Morris never took his eyes off Richter.

Gabriel wrapped his arm around Noor and followed Tattoo—Asher—from the room.

"The fire's out of control." Asher pointed at the foyer. "Follow me." He led them to a smaller staircase. They ran up to the second floor, then into a bedroom. "You'll have to climb down. I'll get Morris." He ran from the room.

"Get the sheets." Gabriel slid open a terrace window.

Detective Robin and Michael yanked sheets off the beds in the bedrooms, then tied them into two ropes.

He knotted one around the foot of a solid mahogany bed. "Use this rope to climb down. Robin and Mike will tie their sheet around your waist, and we'll help lower you."

"I-I can't." Trembling, Hema backed away.

Robin murmured something to her. Hema shook her head, but he coaxed her to the terrace, then tied the makeshift rope around her waist. Talking to her, he gently nudged her out the window. Gabriel and Michael kept her steady while she climbed down. Rafael grabbed her before she hit the lawn.

"You're up, beautiful." Gabriel wrapped the sheet around Noor's waist.

She looked up at him. "Don't let go."

He leaned his forehead against hers. "Never again."

Michael helped him lower her, then Aliza took her turn. He kissed her before she went.

Robin didn't need support. He climbed down with one rope.

"We're up," Gabriel said.

"What about Morris?"

"He'll make it." He tied the second rope to the foot of the bed, then he and Michael climbed down.

Brandon came around the house, panting. "The kid ran inside. I couldn't go after him."

Shit! Gabriel gripped the sheets and climbed back up into the inferno. Fire consumed everything, a ravenous beast feasting. "Sam!" Coughing, he checked the kitchen, study, then living room. The hair on his arm singed. He headed toward the stairs. "Sam!"

A door slammed. He tracked the sound to a closet. The kid sat huddled inside.

"Gabriel!" The worship in Sam's eyes tugged at his heart.

He scooped up the boy, then made it back to the bedroom. "Hold on to me." He crouched for Sam to climb up his back, then gripped the rope. "No matter what happens, don't let go."

"Okay."

They hit the ground as the windows above exploded.

Gabriel shielded Sam with his body. Something sharp sliced his arm.

MORRIS FOLLOWED MERCEDES to the outer terrace. She'd dragged Richter's chair to the edge of the cliff. He stepped into the yard.

"Morris!" Richter cried. "Where are you going? Please help!"

Laughing, Mercedes twirled while tears streamed down her eyes. "We're dying, Daddy!" She tilted his chair toward the drop off.

"No!" Sweat poured down Richter's face. Blood seeped from his wrists and ankles where he strained against the ties binding him. "Morris, why won't you help me?"

"You killed Sarah, Mina's daughter."

"What does that have to do with anything? She was Mina's brat. I've never hurt Cyrus or you."

Morris glared at Richter. "Cyrus was Sarah's father."

Richter's eyes widened. "I didn't know. I—"

Mercedes pushed the chair over the cliff.

"No!" Richter's cry echoed into the night.

"We'll be together, Daddy." Mercedes spread her arms and leaped after him.

IN THE THEATRE, the crowd held its breath, while a grieving Shirin lay Khosrow to rest in a ceremony befitting a king. Shirin tricked Shiruyeh into thinking she would marry him in exchange for his permission to bid her husband farewell. Alone in Khosrow's tomb, she stabbed herself to join him in death.

The music rose, dipped, and fell.

Cyrus's phone beeped as the theatre broke into applause. He checked the message and closed his eyes.

Mina's heart stuttered. Had something gone wrong? Was anyone hurt? Did Richter get away?

The crowd stood. Applause thundered. Unable to wait, she rose on trembling limbs and reached for Cyrus. Her pulse pounded in her ears as her hand found his.

He lifted his head, and his smile said it all.

A deep wave of emotion erupted from the pit of her stomach and crested in her chest, drowning her in a tsunami of color. Joy and satisfaction flooded through her. Her eyes filled with tears. She gripped Cyrus's hand.

Zita turned away from the stage and furrowed her brows. "Is everything all right?"

Keeping her hand firm in Cyrus's, she threw her arm around her granddaughter. "Yes. Everything is as it should be."

CHAPTER FIFTY

Khosrow's funeral befitted that of a king.
—Nezami, *Khosrow and Shirin*

G ABRIEL GRITTED HIS teeth, while the paramedic patched up his arm. The local fire department had doused the flames and given the authorities access to the home to remove the bodies. Police officers scoured the property.

Rafael had his arm around Sam's shoulders. Like Aliza and Hema, Noor huddled with a blanket at the back of another ambulance.

When Gabriel met her gaze, she smiled. His heart thumped. He'd almost lost her. He thanked the paramedic, then rose to join Noor.

A car drove up the road. Detective Bruker of INTERPOL climbed out with Detective Hood. Bruker scanned the chaos, then joined Morris, who was texting someone.

Hood grinned. "You've had an interesting night."

Gabriel snorted. "That's one word for it."

She sobered. "You all right?"

"Yeah." He glanced at Bruker.

"She's clean. Bruker had incriminating evidence on Drussel and hoped to get him to rat on Richter. I believe she was collaborating with someone else." Her gaze jumped to Morris. When she spotted Detective Robin, who had his arm around Hema, her eyes twinkled. "Well, well. I need to check on my partner's new friend."

Pocketing his phone, Morris approached. "You did well."

"Thanks. I had help." Gabriel studied Noor's uncle. "Your friend with the tattoo took Petrov. What's he going to do with him?"

"I didn't ask." Morris glanced at the ambulance. "I'll check on Noor. Get some rest. We'll connect tomorrow."

"Aren't you coming back with us?"

"I have a ride." Morris waved for Brandon to join them, then pulled a thumb drive from his pocket. "Make it clear a confidential source gave this to you. It contains evidence of Richter's family history and his own crimes." When Brandon reached for the drive, Morris pulled it out of his reach. "This can't be connected to us. Tell your editor your source insists on remaining anonymous."

"Will do." Brandon took the flash drive. "Thank you."

Morris climbed into a black sedan, then drove off.

Brandon pointed to Gabriel's bandage. "How bad is it?"

"I'll live." He studied the man who had become a friend. "Richter and Drussel are dead."

"I know."

He pulled his sleeve over the bandage. "I told you revenge wouldn't make you feel better."

Brandon raked a hand through his hair. "You did, but Anna—" He sighed. "She deserved justice."

Gabriel rose. "Take it from someone who's been there. Grief doesn't fade. Face it, accept it, then learn to live with it."

Brandon's jaw tightened. "What happens when you learn to live with it?"

He glanced at Noor. "You create room for light to enter your life, and it will." Gabriel clasped Brandon's shoulder, then went to give the cops his statement.

Local authorities released everyone after interviewing them. Brandon brought the van around. Sam climbed onto it, dragging

Rafael with him. Gabriel and Michael stood aside, waiting for the others to board.

Michael tilted his head at his bandage. "Did the paramedics fix your booboos?"

"Yep, I'm all set."

"Good." Michael kicked a pebble and looked away.

"What's wrong?"

"We almost lost Noor and Aliza, Gabe. I don't know what—"

"We didn't. And we sure as hell won't let them out of sight again. But something else is bothering you."

"Let's say I have an opportunity to work with a powerful group whose influence brings change. I'm talking real impact—with global implications." Michael blew out a breath. "Thing is, people with that much power will engage in unethical or immoral actions for the greater good."

"You don't want to do anything unethical even if it's for the greater good, right?"

"Right."

"Fix the world without doing anything unethical." Gabriel slapped Michael on the shoulder. "You're Jason freaking Vann."

Chuckling, Michael climbed up onto the bus.

Gabriel followed. The seating arrangements didn't surprise him. Hood sat alone, texting. Rafael and Sam rode shotgun, chatting with Brandon. Robin sat beside Hema, who rested her head on his shoulder. Michael pulled Aliza into his arms and kissed the bruises on her face. Noor sat in the back seat.

He joined her, then pulled her into his arms. "How are you feeling?"

She snuggled into him. "Better than I have the past two weeks."

He tilted her chin up and met her gaze. "I'm sorry, sweetheart."

Her brows furrowed. "How could you know Mercedes was the killer?"

His lips brushed hers. "That's not what I meant. I never meant to hurt you or take your choices from you. I thought you cared about Rafael and believed you would be happier with him. Your happiness was why I stepped back. He's a better man than I am. He doesn't have death on his conscience."

Her eyes softened. "Rafael has his own scars." She stroked his cheek. "I don't know a man better than you. You have my heart. I love you."

"I don't know what I've done to deserve you, but I want you to know I'll always love you and will never make you regret your choice. And yes, you chose."

Her smile dazzled.

He pulled her closer. Stroking her hair, he inhaled her unique taste, that mix of summer flowers and light.

"Are you two gonna make sex?" Sam leaned over the seat. "It's what grown-ups do when they kiss a lot. Does that mean you'll have a baby? 'Cause babies come from sex."

Noor groaned and hid her face in Gabriel's shoulder.

"I know about sex," Sam continued. "Jason Vann makes sex all the time. It's why Mom whites out parts of the story." He glanced at Gabriel. "How come he makes sex when he doesn't want kids?"

"There are ways to make sex without having babies," Michael drawled from his seat.

"Michael!" Aliza chided.

"He's right," Rafael added.

"Really?" Sam wrinkled his nose. "I bet it's gross."

"Shouldn't you be in the front with Rafael?" Michael asked, unable to keep the amusement out of his voice.

"I came to give Gabriel the good news." Sam's eyes gleamed with excitement. "I talked to Mom. She cried because I was safe, so I guess she isn't mad I followed Noor. Anyway, we're buying a house in Georgetown. It's close to yours." He bounced up and down. "I can come visit you all the time."

The bus fell silent.

Sam glared at everyone "What? It's not like I'm trouble."

Michael threw his head back and roared with laughter.

~

BRANDON'S STORY BROKE the next day. It took up three full pages. Every news station around the world quoted it. He began with Hans Richter's collaboration with the Rosenberg Task Force and included a copy of a letter from Karl von Mayer to Hans Richter. In it, Karl had tried to persuade Richter to turn himself in for war crimes, otherwise he'd go to German authorities with the truth. It also had a page from Hans Richter's personal journal proving Richter had hired two men to murder, then frame, von Mayer for war crimes. The article exposed Farid Richter's crimes and corrupt businesses.

Brandon received invitations from major news stations for interviews.

German authorities found and identified the remains of Farid Richter and his unacknowledged daughter at the bottom of the cliff behind Richter's home in Bavaria. They ruled their deaths as suicides.

The German government proclaimed Karl von Mayer a hero. Several international entities partnered with them to catalog the artwork found in the cave by Neuschwanstein. Returning the treasures to their rightful owners would take years due to bureaucratic red tape.

Mina von Mayer and Cyrus Rohan's marriage was another topic in the papers. Mina released one press release claiming she couldn't hold Farid Richter responsible for his father's crimes and was relieved her father's name was cleared. She planned to move on with her life. Two days later, business news reported Mina von Mayer and her husband, Cyrus Rohan, had closed a major deal with Alum Pharmaceuticals. The company was going to produce a revolutionary drug for trauma and stress.

A smaller article reported the death of Yuri Petrov, a Russian capitalist whose body was found on a boat on the Danube River. Authorities were still investigating his death.

Gabriel and friends had returned to the hotel and stayed two more days to answer questions for local authorities. The hotel held a memorial for Arthur Trells. Gabriel and Noor attended, then they spent the rest of the day with Michael, Aliza, and their friends.

CHAPTER FIFTY-ONE

Shirin is my destined love.

—Nezami, *Khosrow and Shirin*

MINA PLACED FLOWERS by the graves of Sarah and her parents. *Sarah, my heart, Mama and Papa, Cyrus and I made it right.*

Cyrus kept his arm around her and Zita.

Her wonderful, kind Cyrus. He'd stood beside her despite everything. He'd given her Sarah and now Zita—beautiful and brave like her mother.

For so long, Mina believed love wasn't enough. She'd loved her parents and couldn't protect them. She'd loved Sarah and failed to protect her. She'd been wrong. Love was more than enough. Love had helped her endure when her strength waned. When she'd lost her way, love had drawn her back to herself and her family.

She recalled the day her mother foretold her future. Mina placed her hand on her mother's tombstone. *You were right, Mama. I became successful, I defeated the Richters, I found the love of my life, and I have a family to love.*

She glanced back. They were all there, waiting outside the cemetery—Morris and Noor's aunt Roshi, Gabriel and Noor, Michael and Aliza, Harvey, Brandon, Rafael, the sweet brave boy and his mother, and the three religious men Cyrus had befriended. Her heart soared. It was time to put the past to rest and live her life. She took Cyrus's and Zita's hands, and together they left the cemetery.

GABRIEL WOULD ALWAYS remember that evening as magical. The celebration dinner at Chateau Gutsch could only be described as dazzling. Cyrus had booked a lounge overlooking the river, with a view of the city lights and riverfront restaurants. The hotel staff had covered every surface of the dining room with flowers and candles. Friends and family mingled, joy evident in their faces.

Zita studied a server carrying a small pan with smoking seeds. "What did you say this was?"

"Esphand," Aunt Roshi explained. "It's a staple in every Persian home."

Zita glanced at her grandmother. "What is it good for?"

Mina's eyes twinkled. "It keeps evil away."

The server approached. Zita narrowed her eyes.

Mina laughed. "He'll just circle the pan over your head."

Cyrus motioned to the head server. Soon, music filled the room.

Rafael guided Marci, Sam, and Zita to the dance floor and showed them how to cha-cha. Michael had his arm draped around Aliza, while they discussed sports with Roshi and Morris. Mina leaned her head on Cyrus's shoulder, watching the dancing couples, whom Abarron applauded. Father Pierre and Brandon were in deep discussion.

Gabriel pulled Noor to her feet and, in the guise of dancing, swept her out to the terrace. When the song ended, he drew her farther away from the guests. The October wind teased and caressed.

She leaned against the balustrade. "Isn't it a glorious view?"

She looked like a siren from the novels he used to read as a child, all tumbling hair and enticing curves. He'd almost lost her. "Yes, it is." He pulled her close. "I have a question. I've wanted to ask for a while now."

"Oh?" She turned her face up to him. "What is it?"

He'd kept the box with him for weeks, unsure if it were too early. He realized it wasn't. "I love you, Noor, and I want to spend every day of my life with you. I want forever and all the happily ever after stuff with you. Will you marry me? Will you make a future with me?"

Noor gaped as he flipped the box open. Inside sat a gold band with a square emerald flanked by two diamonds on each side.

"It reminded me of you."

Tears filled her eyes. She met his gaze. "Yes!"

A deep wave of warmth moved through his body and into his heart. He slid the ring onto her finger.

She threw herself into his arms. "I love you!"

He kissed her, and his heart stuttered as it always did when she was in his arms.

Cheers erupted. The entire party stood by the windows.

"I saw you take out the box and told everyone," Sam announced.

They were pulled into hugs and embraces, while everyone congratulated them.

"It's about time," Abarron muttered when they sat down to dinner. "Are you going to be like your brother and take forever to choose a wedding date?"

Roshi, a new bride, beamed at Aliza. "What kind of wedding are you planning?"

Before Aliza could answer, Mina, Noor, Marci, and Roshi offered ideas.

Abarron scowled at Michael. "It's time you chose a date."

Michael leaned back in his chair. "Aliza and I will get married when Gabe and Noor decide to marry." He raised his glass at Gabriel. "We came into the world together. Might as well get married together." He leaned down and kissed Aliza. "Does that work for you, babe?"

"Hm, a double wedding." Aliza smiled. "It does."

"A double wedding!" Roshi clasped her hands together. "Oh,

we'll have to plan it." Roshi and Mina gave suggestions about venue. Noor and Aliza joined in.

Abarron stumped his cane into the ground. "Let's pick a date first."

The conversation died, and all eyes turned to him.

Gabriel wracked his brain until inspiration struck. "How about May twenty-first?"

Marci furrowed her brows. "Is that when you and Noor met?"

"No," Noor answered.

Roshi wiggled her brows. "Is it something special between the two of you?"

Noor shook her head. "No."

"Then, what's important about it?" Morris asked.

Sam beamed. "It's Jason Vann's birthday."

EPILOGUE

B RANDON FINISHED HIS interview with *Good Morning America,* then stepped off the stage. The world was still in shock over Farid Richter's criminal activities. His phone beeped. He grinned at the message—Rafael's congratulations for signing a book deal. He thanked the studio crew, then headed off set.

A solemn boy of twelve waited for him.

"Are you ready?"

The kid nodded.

Together, they walked up the sidewalk, stopping to buy flowers from a stand.

"That was a good interview," Tommy said. "Anna would have liked it."

"I'm glad you approve."

The boy cleared his throat. "Can I ask you something?"

"Sure." Brandon held back a smile. The kid was struggling with something and didn't know how to get it out.

"My sister—I mean, Anna—said you weren't the type to fall in love, so she pretended she didn't love you, but she did." He shoved his hands in his pockets. "Why did you become my guardian if you didn't love her?"

Brandon pulled the kid to a stop, then bent so they were eye-to-eye. "First of all, I cared for Anna. Second, I lost my parents when I was your age and hated being a burden to relatives who didn't want or have time for me. I asked to be your guardian because I wanted you to live with me. Get it?"

Tommy kicked at a stone on the pavement. "You were rich. I don't have any money."

"Good thing I do." He ruffled the boy's hair. "We're family, and family shares."

The boy's mouth lifted. "We can share adventures, like Batman and Robin."

Brandon laughed. "Let's focus on your school first. What do you want to do for Christmas break? We can stay here in New York, or we can go to Spain."

The boy's eyes widened. "Spain?"

Brandon nodded. "My friend Rafael has hotels in Spain and around the world. He invited us for Christmas."

Tommy grinned. "Cool."

They arrived at the graveyard. By unspoken agreement, the conversation died.

Tommy placed the flowers by his sister's grave. "We're fine, Anna. Brandon's taking me to Spain for the holidays."

MARBELLA SPAIN

RAFAEL PLACED THE small plaque beside his great grandmother's mantilla comb. He'd set up a small exhibit at the top floor of his signature hotel. The comb was the centerpiece, sitting on a white marble pillar bathed in warm light where its jewels shone and its creator's craftmanship could be appreciated.

"Thank you for finding it, my boy." Eduardo beamed and wiped a tear from his eye. "I wish you'd brought home a bride too. What about Noor Rahman? You spoke highly of her when we talked."

Rafael smiled. "Her heart belongs to another man. Sorry to disappoint, but no brides for now."

"You never have and never will disappoint me." He fiddled with his tie. "I'll see you tomorrow."

"Oh? You're not staying for dinner?"

"I am meeting someone." He glanced at the doorway, and his dark eyes twinkled. "You'll have company, anyway. Nothing gets in the way of young people like an old man." He chuckled and left through the back exit.

Rafael glanced at the entrance. Christina peered through the glass. She'd changed her hair color to a deep auburn, and her dress, a magnificent swirl of charcoal silk, showcased her very feminine attributes. She lifted a bottle of wine and his favorite take-out in invitation.

He unlocked the exhibit door.

"I thought you might want company," Christina purred, gliding inside.

"You thought right."

She patted her hair. "Do you like it?"

"Very much."

She leaned closer. "I'm auburn everywhere. Would you like to see?"

He grinned. He'd settle down some day, just not today. "Oh, yes." He leaned down to meet her upturned lips.

PROVENCE, FRANCE

FAN BAU CARRIED her champagne to the cellar she'd converted into a vault. The Rembrandt painting sat on a stand in the center. She sank onto the sofa and gazed at the painting.

Alex poked his head in. "Why are you gloating alone in the basement?"

Fan laughed and poured her brother champagne. "It's a vault, you beast, and yes, I'm gloating." She sighed. "It's good to have it back where it belongs."

Alex clinked his glass against hers. "I'll be out of pocket for a few weeks."

"Oh? Who is she?"

"She's fun. You should try it." He sobered. "One heartbreak doesn't mean you'll never be happy, Fan."

"I know."

"Do you?" Alex raised his brows. "Sometimes I think work is all you care about."

She leaned her head on his shoulder. "You're wrong, young one. Stop worrying about me and go play."

Alex kissed her cheek. "Very well, ancient one. See you in two weeks."

She waited for her brother to leave, then locked the vault. Slowly, she climbed back up the staircase into her bedroom, where a certain gentleman waited for her.

He pulled aside the covers. "You're back."

She smiled. "I am."

~

COLUMBIA UNIVERSITY, NEW YORK CITY

ZITA HUDDLED INTO her coat and crossed the street. The lively bustle of New York, its holiday decorations, and the throng of people rushing about lifted her mood. It was as if the city was making up for the bleak years she'd spent with Richter. In the short time she'd been with her grandparents, they'd shown her unconditional love, and she'd grown to love them back. After vacationing with her family in Lucerne and Spain, they asked what she wanted to do. She told them she wanted to study law in America.

When she received a letter from Columbia University, they cheered and supported her. She'd mentally prepared to be alone during the school year. After all, her grandparents had businesses to run. Then, her grandfather had asked her if she preferred to live alone. She admitted she didn't, as she'd been alone most of her life and didn't relish more of it.

They'd bought a house—a three-story wonder that took up half the street. They even had a private apartment with a separate entrance designed for her on the upper floor.

"In case your friends come over," her grandmother had said.

So, she'd settled in looking forward to college. The experience hadn't met her expectations. She enjoyed the classes and learning but couldn't relate to the other students.

"We've got class with Professor Dreamy." Lauren, a perky blond, giggled. "He's so hot."

"Are you referring to our Law and Poli Sci professor?" Zita asked.

"Yes. Doctor Bahari is a visiting professor from Georgetown University." Tasha, another student, sighed.

Zita feigned interest in their discussion. Had she made a mistake? Would it be better to take online courses? Or should she drop out and get a job? Would she ever relate to people her age? Had Richter broken her for good?

The professor entered, and the classroom fell silent. She had to give Lauren credit—he was incredibly handsome, more like a model than an academic. He soon enthralled the class with an introduction to law and its evolving role in society throughout history.

Intrigued, she wanted to ask him a few questions before deciding to drop out of school. She checked the campus map and made her way to his office. The door stood ajar. She knocked.

"Come in." His smooth baritone voice sounded distracted.

She hesitated, fearing he was busy, then decided to enter.

Someone was already meeting with him. The man shuffled back to give her better access.

Professor Bahari furrowed his brows. "Yes?"

She glanced uncertainly at the man with a limp. "I can come back later."

The professor smiled. "No, no. How can I help you?"

"My name is Zita Rohan. I'm in your Law and Political Science class."

He nodded then waved at the man by the bookshelf. "This is Victor. He's my teaching assistant. He'll lecture some of the classes."

Victor waved.

Professor Bahari steepled his hands together. "What can I do for you, Ms. Rohan?"

Zita cleared her throat. "I'm interested in law, but I'm not sure school is the right path for me. I'm thinking about dropping out, and I was hoping talking to you would help me figure things out."

"Oh?" He leaned forward. A pair of moss green eyes stared into her soul. "Why do you want to study law?"

"I—" The eyes were familiar. She gulped. "I want to make a difference in the world."

"Good for you." Specs of gold mingled with the green and brown of his irises.

Zita gripped the handles of the chair. Dear God, it was Sheila. She was certain of it. She knew those eyes, that twinkle. Sheila was a man, not a woman. How had he faked that voice? There had to be some sort of technology for that.

"Do you think you'll make a difference in the world without a degree?" Dr. Bahari asked. "We just had this discussion with another student, didn't we, Victor?" He turned his head toward Victor, who watched them with his arms crossed over his chest. The stance was familiar.

"Yes, we did," Victor confirmed.

Snakey? Was that Snakey? Victor had the same body type, the same facial features. Snakey had grown out his hair, and maybe those blue eyes were contacts, but it was him. She of all people knew how easy it was to change one's appearance.

Her grandfather had told her Sheila disguised herself to keep her clients safe. Now Zita was the only person aside from Victor who knew her real identity.

Sheila, or Dr. Bahari, leaned forward. "Can you make your mark without a degree?"

Zita raised her chin. "Absolutely. However, having a degree would make it easier."

Those moss green eyes gleamed. "Good. I'll see you in class tomorrow."

She rose slowly and left his office, deep in thought. What was it her grandfather had said? *"You must understand and appreciate the world if you want to make it a better place."* Sheila and Snakey had found a way to live a normal life while making their mark. They seemed to enjoy it too. It gave her hope.

Zita smiled. Maybe school wasn't such a bad idea. She checked her watch and picked up her pace. Tonight was a pizza-and-movie night with her grandparents.

MANHATTAN, NEW YORK

MINA ENTERED THE conference room with Cyrus. The faces in the room were familiar. She wanted to thank them for their support. This, however, was a formal Board meeting. There'd be no socializing until business was over.

Adisa handed a crystal bowl with folded papers to every member of the room. Everyone unfurled their notes.

"I'm speaker today." Morris reached for the antique gavel. "We've lost our president and some Board members. Therefore, our first call of order is to vote for a new president, who will then approve nominees. When called upon, you will call out the name of the individual you're voting for. I'll tally the votes, then announce the new president." He turned to Cyrus. "Mister Rohan?"

"Mina Rohan." Cyrus's voice rang clear.

Mina blinked. She had planned to vote for Cyrus, and not because he was her husband. She believed Cyrus would not abuse the position.

Adisa voted next. "Mina Rohan."

Round they went until the entire group, including Morris, voted for her.

Morris nodded. "Mina Rohan is our next president." Everyone cheered.

Cyrus, her rock, her everything, raised her hand to his lips.

Mina cleared her throat. "Before I welcome new Board members, I want to set two central rules of conduct. First, we will not engage in unlawful or unethical business. Former members did, and the consequences were dire. Second, I believe in nonproliferation. Too much power leads to corruption. There will be a limit to the amount of power each of us acquires. This is for the wellbeing of the Board and the world." She glanced at the members. "Those who agree please raise your hands."

It was unanimous.

Pleased, she beamed at faces she knew were allies. "First, we'll welcome Mark Oliveira. Mister Oliveira will take over Yuri Petrov's region and Latin America."

The members tapped their hands on the conference table in greeting. "Next is Ayesha Patel. Ms. Patel will replace Magdalena Romano."

They cheered Ayesha.

Mina nodded at the Lees. "You have invited two members to our meeting today. Will you explain your intention to the Board?"

Buck Lee nodded. "Kim and I plan to retire in eighteen months. My two children, Fan Bau and Alex Bau, will take our places. I have been grooming them for this role their entire lives."

Mischievous as they were, the twins' hearts were in the right place. Mina smiled. "Who will vouch for them?"

Cyrus raised his hand. "I will."

Mina nodded. "Ms. Bau, Mister Bau, you are welcome."

Fan and Alex bowed slightly.

"The next territory to fill belonged to Farid Richter." She paused. "While each of us have acquired his businesses, there remains one last territory. In the past, we've partnered with the wrong government agents and regretted it. Today I've invited a guest who is an official of the US government. I believe he's the ethical partner the Board needs."

LOTTE NEW YORK PALACE, MANHATTAN, NEW YORK

MICHAEL PACED OUTSIDE the conference room. His mentor and former TCU director, Arthur McMillan, had texted him the location. He was going to meet the Board, a myth known by few in his world. Satisfaction thrummed in his veins, while a shiver ran up his spine. Board or not, he was going to drop a bombshell and hoped to God it wouldn't backfire on him.

His mobile pinged. *Come in,* the text read. Michael straightened his shoulders and entered.

Part of him expected people in robes and masks like the old Illuminati. He held back his smile when he spotted Cyrus, Mina, and Morris. No surprise there. He suspected they were on the Board. Adisa Mombasa was no surprise either. Ah, Mark Oliveira had gained a seat at the table. The cartels would have to watch their backs. Tech CEO Ayesha Patel was among them. He supposed it made sense. The world ran on technology.

He almost laughed when he spotted the Bau twins. So, Buck Lee was Daddy dear. Wasn't that an interesting tidbit? Gabriel didn't know he'd rubbed elbows with the Baus in Morocco. It had been interesting. Last in line was his mentor, McMillion, who peered at him over the rim of his glasses.

Mina's expression held none of the amusement he'd seen at family events. "Mister McKnight, you must pledge complete confidentiality before we can proceed."

Michael raised his chin. "I will only proceed on one condition."

"Oh?" Mina furrowed her brows.

McMillan sighed. Buck Lee glared. Adisa's eyes narrowed. Cyrus leaned back in his chair, a hint of a smile hovering at his lips. People didn't set conditions for the Board. He could disappear, and no one would know why.

Michael resisted the urge to shuffle his feet. "I won't do anything unethical or immoral. That's a line I refuse to cross. Everything else is up for debate. If the Board accepts my condition, I'm your man. If not, I'll leave, and no one will ever know I've been here."

Mina's lips twitched. "As the President, I speak for all. We accept your condition."

Michael's body relaxed. *Jason freaking Vann!*

"Please raise your right hand and speak the pledge."

Michael raised his hand to give his oath.

PARIS, FRANCE

GABRIEL CARRIED A tray of wine with cheese and crackers upstairs. He loved the luxurious two-story duplex in the heart of Paris. It was where Noor had spent her childhood. He took the spiral staircase to the bedroom. Outside, Paris livened up as the lights to the Eiffel Tower flickered on. Holidays in Paris were magical, with decorations and an atmosphere of cheer embracing the city.

Noor sat on a plush armchair, huddled in a blanket. "I turned on the fireplace."

He set the tray on a coffee table, then yanked off her cover.

"Hey."

"I'll warm you." He picked her up, enjoying the feel of her glorious naked body, then settled into the chair with her and pulled the blanket around them.

Her body pressed closer to his. "Did Mina and Uncle Cyrus give Brandon proof of Richter's criminal past?"

He ran his hand down her hair. "Technically, Morris did. Zita took the proof from Richter's personal safe and gave it to Mina."

She leaned into him. "They've invited our families to New York for Christmas. Mina's planning a big holiday bash."

"Sounds like fun. Zita will enjoy it."

Noor reached for a glass of wine. "Life is good, Mister McKnight."

"I agree. With you in my arms, life's about perfect."

Her brows furrowed. "About perfect? What's missing?"

Ah, his Noor was a sharp one. He kissed the hollow between her neck and shoulder. "It would be perfect if you were my wife."

Her eyes softened. "We're getting married in May."

He sipped the wine she offered and smiled. "We could get married here."

She blinked. "We can't do that. It would break your mother's heart. Aunt Roshi and Grand-Mère would kill me. Besides, Aliza is coordinating everything with Grand-Mère, and—"

He kissed her. "No one would know. We would still do the wedding thing back in the states in May."

Her eyes twinkled. "You are a devious one, Mister McKnight."

"I want something special for the two of us. Something that's ours alone. We can get married here. Honeymoon in Paris, then go back home and do it all over again in spring."

She bit her lip. "You're sure they won't find out?"

He grinned. "I won't tell anyone."

She blushed. "Okay, let's do it."

"Really?"

"Yes, really."

A warm buzz hit him from head to toe, and it had nothing to do with the wine. He wanted to roll around and purr like a happy kitten. He buried his hands in her hair and took her mouth in a deep kiss.

She returned it with fervor, then pulled back, eyes wide. "You planned this, didn't you? You're seducing me to marry you here in Paris."

"Guilty." He grinned.

She set the wine aside. "What about the embassy? We'll be lucky if they can accommodate us."

Gabriel's eyes twinkled. "I already booked it."

She burst into laughter. "Am I that obvious?"

"No. I was that hopeful." He sobered. "I promise you won't regret marrying me."

"And I promise you won't regret marrying me." She kissed him.

Gabriel picked her up, dropped her on the bed, then blanketed her body with his.

"What are you doing?" She giggled when he kissed a trail from her ribs up to her neck.

"Practicing for our wedding night." His mouth covered hers. "I love the sound of your laughter."

OUTSIDE, STEPHEN JOHANNSSON stared at the apartment window and stubbed out his cigarette. Gabriel McKnight knew something. Darren knew less than Gabriel, and he'd been murdered.

There was too much at stake. The Board was protective of Gabriel and Noor. He would watch them both closely. When the time was right, he'd make his move.

God help Gabriel McKnight when he did.

THE END

ACKNOWLEDGMENTS

THANK YOU TO Staci Troilo, the best editor and friend a writer could ask for! Thank you also to the Roan & Weatherford Publishing team for your belief in me!

A big thanks to Dara, my partner in crime for as long as I can remember. I got the lucky draw when you became my brother! Many thanks to Saul, light of my life, you inspire me every day. And last but certainly not least thank you to my husband, Dr. Saeed Shadfar for pouring over Nezami's poetry with me. Your unwavering support is appreciated and the book I want to dedicate to you is special and coming!

POONEH SADEGHI is an Iranian-American executive who spent most of her life traveling to and living in foreign countries. A fan of the mystery and thriller genres, she combines her global experience with her Persian background to write compelling stories. Pooneh lives in Oklahoma with her family and two dogs.